THE FORGOTTEN BOOKSHOP IN PARIS

Daisy Wood worked as an editor in children's publishing before she started writing her own books. She has a degree in English Literature and an MA in Creative Writing from City University, London, and is the author of several works of historical fiction for children. This is her second published novel for adults. She divides her time between London and Dorset, and when not lurking in the London Library, can often be found chasing a rescue Pointer through various parks with a Basset Hound in tow.

By the same author:

The Clockmaker's Wife

The
Forgotten
Bookshop
in
Paris

DAISY WOOD

avon.

Published by AVON
A division of HarperCollins*Publishers* Ltd
1 London Bridge Street
London SE1 9GF

www.harpercollins.co.uk

HarperCollins*Publishers*
1st Floor, Watermarque Building, Ringsend Road
Dublin 4, Ireland

A Paperback Original 2022
1
First published in Great Britain by HarperCollins*Publishers* 2022

A catalogue copy of this book is available from the British Library.

ISBN (PB): 978-0-00-852524-8
ISBN (TPB): 978-0-00-853887-3

Typeset in Bembo by Palimpsest Book Production Limited, Falkirk, Stirlingshire

Printed and Bound in the UK using
100% Renewable Electricity at CPI Group (UK) Ltd

For Patrick and Nick

And in memory of over eleven thousand Jewish children arrested in France between 1942 and 1944, and deported to Auschwitz concentration camp in Poland, where they were murdered

Author's note

The story that follows is a work of fiction. To date, no one has discovered evidence of a bookshop in Paris with a secret chamber for hiding fugitives, although we do know of an underground newspaper that was printed in the basement of a bookshop. Nevertheless, I've tried to make the historical background of the book as accurate as possible. German troops marched into Paris on 14 June 1940 and occupied the city until 15 August 1944. France was divided in two: northern France was an occupied zone under German control and southern France was managed by a new French government based in Vichy, carrying out the Nazis' orders. During those four long years, Parisians were humiliated, regulated and starved. Food was exported from France to Germany, and supply lines within the country were in German hands. One of the earliest and most influential underground resistance groups started in the Musée de l'Homme, whose director, Paul Rivet, was an anthropologist fiercely opposed to the Nazi idea of Aryan superiority. Agnès Humbert was an art historian and member of the group, and her memoir *Résistance* describes the courage and resilience of those fighting for freedom.

I found a couple of other books particularly interesting: Hélène Berr's *Journal,* describing the occupation from the point of view of a Jewish student in Paris, and Ninetta Jucker's *Curfew in Paris* (now sadly out of print). Ninetta was an Englishwoman married to an Italian, who managed to escape the deportation to Besançon mentioned in this novel and stayed in the city throughout the occupation. I've also taken the liberty of writing about a person who actually existed: Abbé Franz Stock, the 'Archangel of the Prisons'. He was a German Catholic priest, responsible for looking after prisoners in Nazi jails such as Fort Mont-Valérien, La Santé and Cherche-Midi. He witnessed around two thousand executions and, at huge risk to himself, brought food, books and messages to his prisoners.

The plight of Jewish children in France during the war is heart-rending. Hundreds of Jewish orphans whose parents had been murdered or imprisoned were already in children's homes at the start of the war and they were soon joined by many more. The Jewish scouting movement, various charities, local groups and individuals worked tirelessly to keep these children hidden or smuggle them out of the country to safety in Switzerland. Approximately seven thousand Jewish children in France were saved, yet over eleven thousand were deported to Auschwitz between 1940 and 1942. Most were gassed on arrival. The fact that French police were in charge of rounding them up remains a matter of national shame.

It's important to remember the past, no matter how painful the process might be. I wrote much of this novel as the war in Ukraine was unfolding, and the theme of resistance versus submission seemed especially relevant. The devastation suffered by that country shows the cost of resisting invasion, but people across the world have been touched and inspired by the outstanding bravery of its people. It seems extraordinary that the same old stories of destruction and loss are playing out, over eighty years later — yet humanity and kindness are also in evidence, and an unquenchable human spirit that binds us together in times of greatest need.

Prologue

As soon as Jacques sets eyes on the empty shop, dusty and unloved, he can see what it might become. The letting agent is saying something about location and potential customer numbers but he's too busy imagining the future to listen. They're standing in a wood-panelled hexagonal foyer, which is where he will keep his till, and perhaps some racks of elegant stationery. To the right lies an airy room with tall picture windows facing onto the street; this will be his main showroom, large enough for shelves around the walls and a display case in the centre filled with first editions, when he can afford them. He might add a couple of stools for browsers to sit and read, and there'll be lamps dotted here and there, too, and soft music playing. To the left of the foyer, a few steps lead down to a cosier room with a pot-bellied stove where he'll have a carousel for children's books and a pile of cushions on the floor, and maybe a display of cookery books, with the pages of one open at a particularly enticing recipe. His bookshop will be a treasure trove: warm and safe in the winter, when the rain lashes down; airy in the summer, when breezes will waft the smell of baking bread from the *boulangerie* across the square and through the open windows. The quiet, welcoming atmosphere will soothe his customers' troubled minds. He'll be a discreet presence at their elbow, ready to offer advice if required but content to let them browse for as long as they choose. Jacques wants to share the joy of discovering an author who speaks to one's soul, the thrill of losing oneself in a story more vivid and exciting than real life. He will call his shop *La Page Cachée* – The Hidden Page – because he knows the magic that is to be found within the covers of a book.

The shop used to sell ladies' hats and stockings, the agent is saying, but the widow who ran it has retired to Deauville. Her apartment in the same building, two floors above, is also available, should Jacques be interested.

'Yes,' he hears himself saying, before he's even asked about the rent. 'I'll take them both.' Because Fate has stepped in and offered him the dream he's been chasing since he started selling books, five years before: a shop of his own.

He's fallen in love with Mathilde by then, despite the fact they've only spoken once. She's a curator at the *Musée de l'Homme* on the other side of the Arc de Triomphe, although she looks more like a film star than an academic. She came into the shop where he used to work, looking for books about Egyptology, and they started a conversation that Jacques replayed in his mind for days afterwards. He wouldn't have dared approach her – she's far too glamorous – but it's easy to talk to her about books, and then about her work, and the various exhibitions being planned at the newly revamped museum. The aim is to gather everything that defines a human being, Mathilde tells him, to celebrate our differences as well as the common threads that unite us. She's even more lovely when she's animated, her brown eyes alight with enthusiasm and her gorgeous lips curving in a smile. Jacques agrees that such an aim is particularly important in these dangerous times, given what's happening in Germany.

Soon he's a regular visitor at the museum and he and Mathilde have become friends. They have lunch together regularly, eating baguettes in the Trocadero Gardens while talking about society in Samoa and coming-of-age rituals in various Indonesian tribes. He brings flowers for her desk, the latest book he thinks she'll enjoy, a new pair of gloves when she leaves one of hers on the Métro. At night, he dreams of sweeping her up in his arms and carrying her over the threshold of *La Page Cachée* although in reality he daren't even kiss her for fear of spoiling the friendship they have.

The shop is taking shape. His friend Henri, a carpenter, happens to be working in a grand townhouse on Boulevard Haussmann that's being turned into apartments, and Jacques is able to reclaim several lengths of magnificent oak shelving, which Henri installs in the larger room over several evenings and weekends, together with a sliding library ladder. There will be books from floor to ceiling, and Jacques will know exactly where any title is to be found. He uses up his savings and borrows more money from the bank, spends long hours poring over publishers' catalogues and orders stock from the wholesaler. Henri sands and varnishes the shop's floorboards and Jacques scours the flea markets for rugs and lamps. He moves into the apartment two floors above, with only a mattress on the floor and a few pots and pans. There's a back entrance to the shop on the ground floor of the building so days can go by before he steps outside. A stray tabby cat turns up each morning, miaowing to be fed; he names her Milou and gives her a basket near the stove.

The shop is almost ready to open. He wonders whether to tell Mathilde how he feels about her. She seems to like him; they've been to a couple of exhibitions together now, and to the cinema, and discussed Bushman cave art in South-west Africa over crêpes and Breton cider. They share the same sense of humour, the same worries over the rise of Fascism and persecution of the Jews. If she weren't so beautiful, it would be easier for him to share his feelings, but how could such an extraordinary woman be interested in a short-sighted, asthmatic bookseller with uncertain prospects? She must be tired of men chasing her. Yet somehow the shop gives him courage; at least he has something to offer. He hasn't even mentioned *La Page Cachée* so far, wanting to wait until everything is finished before he shares his secret passion, but if he doesn't talk to Mathilde soon, he'll burst.

One warm spring evening, when the cherry trees are coming into blossom, he meets her at the museum after work. As they stroll towards the Arc de Triomphe, he steels himself to tell her about his dreams for the future. She listens intently, aware of the significance of this moment, and the air between them crackles with invisible lightning. The sights and sounds of the city disappear and he's alone with the woman he wants by his side for the rest of his life. They approach the Place Dorée, its ornate lamppost shining through the dusk like a beacon. A lamp is burning in the window of *La Page Cachée*, and the newly-painted golden sign gleams above the door. He unlocks it, fumbling with the key in his nervousness, and invites Mathilde inside. The shop looks just as he imagined it would all those months before: an oasis of peace, packed with stories waiting to be heard.

She walks around each room in silence, noticing every detail, while Milou twines around her legs and Jacques holds his breath. Occasionally she picks a book from the shelves to see its cover or runs her fingers down an embossed leather spine. She is only the third person to have seen the shop in all its glory, after himself and Henri.

'It's wonderful,' she says at last, turning to him with a light in her eyes that lets him know the time has come to kiss her. He puts his hands around her slender waist and pulls her close, and her lips are as soft and delicious as he's imagined.

'I've loved you from the moment we met, my darling Mathilde,' he says, when he can speak again. 'It's all right, I don't expect you to feel the same but I had to tell you. You're all I can think about from morning till night. The world has become a different place because you're in it and when we're together, I'm different too. You make me feel as though I can do anything.

This shop' – he waves a hand around – 'it's because of you. It's all for you.'

She smiles at him and he beams back, relieved. At least now she knows, and she doesn't look too appalled. 'Oh, Jacques,' she says, gazing into his eyes. 'Surely you realise I'm in love with you, too?'

'Really?' he asks, incredulous.

'Really,' she replies, laughing. 'Why wouldn't I be? You're clever and kind, and I can talk to you about anything. You're as interested in what I think and who I am as what I look like. We're soulmates. I've never met anyone who understands me so completely.' She cups his cheek in her hand for a second. 'And those dimples are irresistible.'

They kiss again, and the world stops turning. Jacques has everything he's ever wanted – heaven, within his grasp – and only the tiniest seed of dread that his happiness is too extraordinary to last, that the gods who've been so unexpectedly smiling on him will change their minds.

Soon after that magical evening, he slips a bottle of Champagne into a haversack and his grandmother's engagement ring into his pocket, takes Mathilde's hand, and asks her to be his wife as they sit on the steps of Sacré Coeur with Paris laid out before them, shimmering in the summer heat. 'Yes,' she says, laughing and crying at the same time. 'Yes, please. That would make me very happy.'

They are married in the town hall one day in early September, with a simple church ceremony between services that Sunday. The bells are pealing as they walk out into the sunshine, to learn that Britain and France are at war with Germany. It is both the best and worst day of Jacques' life; the fear of losing Mathilde is as great as his love for her, which is infinite.

'I can't bear to think of us being separated,' he murmurs that night, running his fingers down the bony indentations of her spine. 'You're as vital as the air I breathe. How could I exist without you?'

She draws back to look at him. 'My heart will always be yours, even if we're not together. We may have to part but never doubt me, Jacques. I love you, body and soul, and I always shall.'

'Stop,' he says, covering her mouth with his hand. He isn't ready for such talk, not yet.

For the next few months, France holds its breath, waiting to see when and where Hitler will attack. Jacques is declared unfit for military service on account of his asthma, to his shameful relief, but Henri is drafted and sent away for training. The following spring, German troops advance through Belgium and Luxembourg; in May, they break through the French defences and sweep through the country to the coast. The Luftwaffe bomb Paris at the beginning of June, triggering a mass exodus from the city.

'Should we go, too?' Mathilde asks. 'We could stay with my cousin Pierre in Provence.'

'And leave Paris to the Germans?' Jacques replies. 'We can't abandon our home and run away. Besides, Maman's in no fit state to travel.' His mother has been suffering from some mysterious stomach trouble and is losing weight dramatically.

All around them, people flee with their belongings packed in cars and bicycles, handcarts and wheelbarrows, blocking the roads with lines of stationary vehicles. The refugees have nowhere to stay, not enough to eat, no destination in mind – only a frantic rush to head south before the Germans arrive. In the chaos, families become separated, the elderly and children die of exhaustion and dehydration or are killed in traffic accidents, people steal from each other and fight for shelter at night. They are bombed from the air and raked with machine-gun fire. Reading the newspaper reports, Jacques and Mathilde are relieved they've stayed where they are. Jacques' mother soon joins them in the apartment. The doctor confirms what they've suspected: she has stomach cancer and not long to live. She wouldn't survive a journey but anyway, Jacques won't leave *La Page Cachée* to be looted by the Nazis, and Mathilde is determined to keep working at the museum as long as she can.

By June, the French army has collapsed and the government abandons Paris. Marshall Pétain announces the city will not be defended and days later, Jacques and Mathilde walk to the Arc de Triomphe and stand watching hand-in-hand as the Germans arrive. They come on foot, on horseback, in tanks and lorries and limousines. The grey-green uniforms of the Boche are everywhere (although now it's an offence to use that term), street signs are printed in German and banners emblazoned with swastikas hang from balconies and public buildings. Oil and petrol tanks have been set on fire at the start of the invasion and a dense fog falls over the city, followed by a downpour of sooty rain that leaves the pavements dark and slippery. Jacques feels as though Paris is in mourning; the sky is weeping black tears. The streets are eerily quiet because all the birds have been killed by pollution, and people are too frightened to go out.

'Have you heard?' Mathilde asks one day, rushing back from work. 'Pétain's asked the Germans for an armistice! He's giving up without even attempting to fight. I'm ashamed to be French.'

It's a national disgrace, although no one dare say so in public. A strict blackout is imposed at night and a curfew's declared, shops are shut, buses no longer run; even the clocks are changed to German time. Only the sound of hobnailed boots tramping as one and marching songs disturb the silence. *Ein, zwei, drei. Halt!* The sight of soldiers goose-stepping down the Champs-Élysées makes Mathilde furious, whereas Jacques feels desperately sad, as though a hand in a black glove is squeezing his heart.

Yet at least the Germans are polite, says Madame Bourdain, the concierge in Jacques' apartment building. The soldiers are disciplined; there has been no looting, no mass rape or uncontrolled violence. They might smoke on the Métro and bathe naked in the Seine but they seem to enjoy being in Paris, and many of them are undeniably tall and good-looking. Over the coming days, a strange sort of normality is restored to the city. The Parisians who fled south start to trickle back, shame-faced, to resume life under the new regime. Henri reappears, too, having managed to escape through the forests of Alsace and make his own way home – unlike most of his comrades, who've been sent to prison camp in Germany. Pétain heads a puppet government from Vichy, in the free zone, carrying out the Nazis' orders.

In Paris, it would seem the Boche are mainly interested in shopping. The exchange rate is rigged in their favour so everything is a bargain, and they seem intent on emptying the shops. One rarely sees an officer without a parcel or three under his arm, and porters are kept busy at the railway station, loading trolleys piled high with goods onto trains bound for Germany. Petrol is scarce so private cars are no longer to be seen in the streets but removal vans are everywhere, transporting rugs, furniture, paintings, linen, clothes and jewellery from requisitioned apartments. Paris is bled dry: the Nazis gorge on butter from Normandy, sausage from Toulouse and wine from the Loire. Hitler says every soldier should visit the city once, and his troops are driven in coachloads around the Eiffel Tower, Notre Dame and the Sacré Coeur, where they take photographs and buy souvenirs from the street sellers. Jacques reopens his shop and discovers a profitable new line, selling postcards and guide books. Mathilde thinks he should refuse to serve the Germans but what good would that do? The Duvals have to survive somehow, and Maman's medical bills are expensive.

Jacques moves slowly through these endless days, numb with despair, but Mathilde is filled with a raging, restless energy. She and Jacques have begun to argue in whispers at night, so Maman won't hear. Life is hard: food is rationed and women have to queue for hours at the shops to buy what little there is. And then, one evening, Mathilde bursts into their bedroom with the old light back in her eyes. She's been tuning in to wireless broadcasts from England, where the British air force has been holding off the Luftwaffe, and come across a French general by the name of de Gaulle calling on his countrymen to rise up against the Nazis.

'You should hear him,' she says, throwing herself on the bed. 'Instead of letting Hitler take over, he's encouraging us to join together and fight back. At last, we have a leader worth something!'

And the seed of fear that has never left Jacques' stomach grows into a tangled vine of despair, strangling his heart and his lungs so he can hardly breathe. He's going to lose his precious, darling wife. She's brave and passionate, and that passion is dangerous.

'No,' he says, his voice sharp with fear. 'I won't listen to him and neither should you. If the Germans find out, they'll arrest you and then God knows what will happen. Get rid of that radio before the neighbours hear. Please, Mathilde. It's not worth the risk.'

He doesn't sleep well that night, and neither does she. At dawn, she gets up to make coffee and he follows her through to the kitchen.

'We must have hope,' she says, 'or life isn't worth living. I can't stand by while the Nazis do as they please. You understand, don't you?'

Jacques can't speak. It feels as though he's lost her already. He holds her tightly in his arms, resting his chin on the top of her head, and together they watch the sun rise over the rooftops of Paris – their beloved city, so familiar and yet so alien.

Chapter One

'Kevin? Kevin, honey, you'll never—'

Juliette's husband was on the phone, as usual. He held up a hand to shush her, saying briskly to whoever was listening on the other end, 'Sorry, I gotta go. Let's keep in touch.'

She sat on the hotel bed, still fizzing with excitement. 'You'll never guess what I've found!'

'A new pair of shoes?' He smiled indulgently. 'The pot of gold at the end of the rainbow? Surprise me.'

'The square! You know, the one I've been looking for since we arrived. The one you said I hadn't a hope in hell of tracking down.'

'Not necessarily. I merely pointed out there must be a hundred squares just like that in Paris and your chances of coming across the right one were slim.'

'But I did. Look!' She held out the picture on her phone. 'There's that amazing lamppost in the middle with

12

the trees around it, and the café with the striped awning, and the shop on the corner. I'm sure it's the one in the painting.' She scrolled to the photo of the watercolour that had hung on her grandmother's bedroom wall and showed it to him.

Kevin glanced at the screen. 'If you say so. That's great, you found it just in time.'

Juliette lay back on the bed, clutching her phone and staring up at the ceiling. 'I did. It's like Mémé wanted to show me a place she loved. I sat under the trees for a while, watching the old men play *boules*, and then I had a beer in the café, and I felt really close to her. As though, somehow, she was watching me.'

'Well, you never know.' Kevin ran a hand absent-mindedly through his thick grey hair, clearly thinking of something else. He'd been in a good mood all day because they were flying back to Philadelphia the next morning. This trip to Paris had been Juliette's idea and she had paid for it with money she'd inherited from her mother, which were two reasons for Kevin to have taken against the vacation from the start. He'd only agreed to come because Juliette said she would otherwise go on her own, which his friends at the country club would have thought odd. Several times over the past ten days, she'd wished she *had* come alone. But now she had found her square and a connection to the French grandmother she could hardly remember. Mémé: the little old lady with white hair who always dressed in black, who had insisted on the importance of eating proper food on a beautifully laid table with a linen cloth, who had read her the stories of Babar the elephant in the original French and made sure Juliette and her brother had dual French and American nationality, just like their mother. Mémé had even stayed in France for a month when she was eight months pregnant to make sure her daughter, Suzanne, would be born there. Kevin resented the fact Juliette could join a shorter line at the airport and was waiting for him on the other side of passport control, but she had loved feeling properly French as she stood among her fellow countrymen and women.

That feeling soon disappeared, however. When she spoke French in restaurants or shops – which she still could, fluently, having been a high-school teacher in the subject – she was usually answered in English. She and Kevin were just another couple of tourists, taking a *bateau mouche* down the Seine, wandering around the Louvre, going up the Eiffel Tower, shopping in flea markets and the Galeries Lafayette. OK, so she had downloaded various guides from the internet and found a secret bar, hidden away in a hotel in Montmartre, but they were still themselves, sitting on the red velvet seats looking so thoroughly, unmistakeably American. Of course that was nothing to be ashamed of. And what else had she expected, after all?

'OK if I take a shower now or do you need the bathroom?' he asked, interrupting her thoughts.

'Go ahead. But Kevin, I've had an idea.' She smoothed the velvet counterpane, trying to choose the right words. 'That café in the square is so cute, I was wondering whether. . .'

'Whether what?' He pulled off his sweater and tossed it on the chair.

Hell, she might as well come out with it. 'Whether we could eat there tonight? I know we have a reservation already but we've had so many incredible meals in fancy restaurants. This is the kind of place where the locals go. Why don't we give it a try?'

He ticked off the reasons on his fingers. 'Number one, the food is probably awful. Number two, they won't speak English and the service will be terrible. And number three, we have a table at Chez Zelda this evening, which anyone else would die for. John and Nancy ate there when they were in Paris and said it was the highlight of their trip. John made me swear to try their crêpes Suzette.'

Juliette sighed. 'Sure. It was just a thought.'

'You won't regret it, I promise.' Kevin unbuckled his belt, sucking in his stomach when he saw her watching. He'd been making more of an effort to keep fit recently, pounding away on the exercise bike most evenings, and she was glad to have a husband who was still in shape. His clothes tended to be a little on the stuffy side but recently he'd been trying out a different style, including a leather jacket she still wasn't sure about. 'Dad's having a mid-life crisis,' their son had said. 'It'll be a tattoo next.'

Juliette had laughed, but fondly. She and Kevin been together for twenty-five years and the sex was still good. He had his foibles, but didn't they all? He had been her first boyfriend; she had married him when she was twenty-two and couldn't imagine being with anyone else.

He stepped out of his boxers and headed for the shower, buttocks wobbling, humming a jaunty tune. Juliette couldn't blame him for feeling happy. He was a creature of habit, adrift in foreign waters and longing for

15

home. She wasn't ready to go back, though. Whatever she'd been hoping to find in Paris still eluded her as she reached for it, like a wisp of smoke dissolving into the air. She looked at the pictures on her phone again: the watercolour painting that had hung on the wall in Mémé's bedroom, and the real-life square she'd stumbled across that afternoon. They might have been one and the same, but what did that mean? Her grandmother might have kept the painting simply because it had reminded her of France. She was sorry not to be eating in the café that evening but even if the food had been great, she'd have been so tense, worrying whether Kevin liked it, that she probably wouldn't have enjoyed the meal anyway.

Water thundered from the power shower in their en-suite bathroom. Kevin had insisted on staying in a modern hotel with decent facilities, as opposed to the quirky little place she'd found in Montmartre. He was probably right: the rooms would have been tiny and the plumbing erratic, and he'd have been in a worse mood than ever. At that moment, his cell phone rang. She reached for it; Kevin worked in commercial real estate and some big deal was hanging in the balance. 'Jacksons', said the caller display, the attorneys with whom he was negotiating. If the call was urgent, she'd have to drag him out of the shower.

As soon as she'd pressed the green button, a woman started speaking. 'Kev, sweetheart, I forgot to say we'll have to make it later on Tuesday. Say, seven? Stacey has a dental appointment after school. Kevin, are you there?'

Juliette disconnected the call. She sat for a moment with the phone in her hands before replacing it on her husband's bedside table. The words made no sense. If this woman hadn't repeated Kevin's name, Juliette would have assumed she'd dialled the wrong number. She'd recognised the voice on the other end of the line: it belonged to Mary-Jane Macintyre, who had moved into a house opposite theirs across the street a few years before. Why was she listed as 'Jacksons' in his caller ID? Juliette picked up the phone and tried to unlock it, but the PIN had been changed. For a moment, she felt like an actress in some second-rate TV soap opera. Kevin hated being called Kev, and he thought Mary-Jane was tiresome. Her husband was away in the military and she was always pestering Kevin to help around the house with odd jobs she could have managed perfectly well on her own.

'If that's Mary-Jane, say I'm not home,' he'd told Juliette once when the doorbell had rung.

'I think she has a crush on you,' she'd replied, and they'd laughed.

She took a tiny bottle of brandy from the mini bar and drank it down in one, still standing. Of course her husband wasn't having an affair with their neighbour, that would be ludicrous. Yet just supposing, for argument's sake, he was fooling around; it would make sense of a few things she'd noticed during the vacation and would have wondered about, had she not been so distracted by Paris. The calls he'd received early in the morning, for example, when it would have been the middle of the night in Philly. 'The attorneys have been pulling an all-nighter,' he'd said. And the fact he been unusually secretive with his phone, keeping it close at hand and walking away whenever he answered a call. He had let his guard drop that evening because they were nearly home; his suitcase was already packed and standing by the door. The shower was still running and after that, he would trim his nose hairs, brush his teeth and gargle with mouth wash. She had time.

Without being consciously aware of what she was doing, she crouched down beside his case and flipped open the locks. Quickly she rifled through the layers of neatly folded clothes: chinos, monogrammed polo shirts, casual and more dressy jackets. Her fingers met a rustle of tissue paper between two cashmere sweaters and she drew out a slim package tied with gauzy ribbon. Inside were a pair of oyster satin camiknickers and a matching padded bra. She couldn't have squeezed into either of them, not if she dieted for a year. 'You're a real woman,' Kevin liked to say, cupping her breasts in his hands. Mary-Jane was flat-chested, dark and skinny, with perfectly arched eyebrows. If she were a dog, she'd be a whippet. And what am I? Juliette wondered. A plump yellow lab, tail wagging and eager to please. She wrapped up the underwear as best she could, tied the ribbon in a clumsy bow and slipped the parcel back into the suitcase.

'This place is awesome, isn't it?' Kevin held out a fork loaded with what looked like wallpaper paste. 'Try some of my snail mousseline.'

'Actually, I'm OK, thanks. My—' Juliette couldn't remember what she was supposed to have been eating: something with textures, whatever they were. 'My appetiser is quite filling.'

'And to think you wanted to spend our last night in Paris in some hick café!' He swirled red wine around the enormous glass and sniffed appreciatively before swallowing. As soon as he'd put it down, a waiter glided forward to pick up their bottle and pour some more.

'*Merci,*' he said, smiling at Juliette to show he was making an effort. She smiled back automatically, pushing forward her glass to be filled. Alcohol was helping but she needed to keep her wits about her; better slow down after a couple of glasses. She looked around. The restaurant was minimalist, with a concrete floor, hard white chairs and a futuristic light canopy hanging from the ceiling like a glowing honeycomb. They were twelve storeys up, with the city glittering beneath them and an incredible view of the Eiffel Tower, lit up like a vast metal Christmas tree. She shivered. It felt as though they were sitting in an aircraft hangar, waiting to be blasted into space. As far as she could tell, there were no French people eating here: the tables around them were filled with other foreign tourists, taking pictures of their food to post on social media. Just like Kevin.

'You look gorgeous,' he told her from behind his phone when their main course had been delivered. She recoiled as the flash went off, but no doubt he could crop the photo to edit her out. 'John and Nancy are going to be so thrilled we came here.' He picked up a knife and fork and stared anxiously at the tiny structure in the middle of his plate. 'The chef is an artist, don't you think?'

'For sure.' At least her fish wouldn't take long to eat. It was enclosed in a nest of tough, bitter leaves that she decided were just for decoration, but who knew? Beads of jellied pine sap were dotted around the edge of the plate; she had tried one and discovered it tasted of toilet cleaner – or rather, how she imagined toilet cleaner to taste. Smearing one across the china with her knife, she found the tiny corpse of an ant. On any other evening, would she have complained? Probably not; Kevin would have taken any criticism personally. Investigating a few more green blobs, she discovered there were ants in all of them and raised her napkin to her mouth, stifling an urge to laugh.

'You know, now you've stopped teaching and your mom's passed away, maybe you should spread your wings a little.' Kevin leaned back in his chair. 'Go visit your brother in San Francisco.'

'Maybe,' she said. 'But that'll only take a few days. I need to figure out what to do with the rest of my life.'

'Relax a little, why not? You've worked so hard all these years, bringing up the kids and teaching. You deserve some time off. Take up a hobby. Golf, for example.' He frowned. 'Actually, maybe not golf. I don't think you'd enjoy it.' The country club was his domain.

He was right: she had worked hard. The twins had been born a year after they were married and she'd started teaching five years after that, when the kids were in kindergarten. Kevin had wanted her to stay at home but money was tight and she valued her independence, loved the chance to immerse herself in other cultures and languages. She taught Spanish, mainly, but French was closer to her heart. 'Mémé would be so proud of you,' her mother used to say. Juliette made the dishes at home that her mother had taught her, which she had learned in turn from her mother. Not this kind of fancy cuisine but peasant food, full of flavour: beef or lamb marinated in red wine and simmered for hours, potatoes dauphinoise baked in cream and garlic, tarte tatin with caramelised apples.

Kevin loved her cooking but deep down, she knew he regarded her Frenchness as an affectation. She'd been wanting to go to France for years but he'd never been keen. He wouldn't even watch French films with her; he said the subtitles gave him a headache. Apart from a semester in Poitiers when she was at college, she'd only visited the country once before. When she was five, she and her brother, their mother, and Mémé had spent ten days in Provence. She could hardly remember any of it, only a couple of random images: a meal under the pine trees at a table with a checked red cloth; a walk between rows of vines that had towered above her, stretching away to the horizon.

Now the waiter was bringing their dessert menu. Kevin waved it away. 'We'll have the crêpes Suzette,' he said. 'I hear that's a speciality of the house.'

'I'm so sorry, Monsieur,' the waiter murmured discreetly, 'but we do not serve this dish.'

'Yes, you do.' A flush was rising up his neck. 'My friends ate here recently and they specifically told us to try it.'

'But there is a new chef 'ere since last year, and 'e does not cook crêpes at all.' The waiter slid the dessert menu back across the table. 'The lychee foam with meringue shards and caramelised milk, that is 'is signature dish.'

Kevin opened his mouth but Juliette interrupted. 'Sounds delicious. I'll have that.' She was about to add that she could make him crêpes Suzette at home any day of the week when she remembered that everything had changed. She smiled at the waiter. 'And I'd like a coffee, please.'

Kevin raised his eyebrows. 'Are you sure? You'll be up half the night and we're flying tomorrow, remember.'

'Quite sure.'

He looked at her warily. All of a sudden, she felt exhausted and slightly nauseous. What did Mary-Jane see in him? His lips were stained purple from the wine, his jowls blotchy and pendulous. The smell of his aftershave revolted her. He was smartly dressed, all right, but he could be so pompous and self-righteous, determined to have the last word no matter what. Mary-Jane was only in her thirties; surely she could have found someone a little more exciting. Kevin was conveniently close at hand, Juliette supposed, which had to be the main advantage. She wondered whether the pair of them had ever had sex in her marital bed, but the image was so distasteful that she shook her head to dismiss it.

'What's the matter?' he asked.

'Oh, nothing.' She composed her face into neutral lines. 'Sad the trip's nearly over, that's all.'

'It's been awesome, hasn't it? But still, I'm kinda glad to be going home.'

Yes, she thought, I bet you are. 'By the way,' she added, 'I had a text from Lindsay. She and Peter are coming our way on Tuesday, so I thought I'd invite them for supper. Is that OK with you?'

He straightened his tie. 'Sorry, honey. I have a conference call Tuesday evening that'll probably go on until late.'

'Oh, never mind,' she said. 'We can see them some other time.'

Would there be another time? She doubted it.

Chapter Two

March 2022

Juliette lay beside Kevin in the pitch dark, her thoughts going around in circles.

'I've got your back,' that was his favourite expression.

'Sure, Dad, whatever,' Emily would reply, shrugging her shoulders. Their daughter had always been self-sufficient, from the moment she could walk. She would pack her own bag for kindergarten and make her own snack, and now she was a marine biologist at the age of twenty-three, working on a research project in Antarctica. She was the most independent person Juliette had ever known, and just a little intimidating.

'I've got your back, son,' Kevin said more frequently. 'If you get any trouble at school, you come and tell me about it, OK?' And Ben would give that sweet smile, pushing the hair out of his eyes. He never got any trouble, anywhere, because everybody loved him. You couldn't help it: he was kind and gentle without being a pushover, and he had a wicked sense of humour. She missed Ben. He'd been studying architecture for the past five years and was taking a break, working at a ski resort to fund six months' travelling in Europe. Kevin thought he was wasting his time but Juliette disagreed. Ben was young and single; what better time to see the world?

Kevin was a good father, she couldn't deny it, and the kids adored him (especially Emily), but he certainly didn't have Juliette's back now. Maybe he never had. She listened to the rumble and whistle of his breathing, the soundtrack to her nights for all these years. He had gone to sleep without checking his phone, she was pretty sure, but in the morning he would realise that Mary-Jane had called and that her call had been answered by someone else. Would Juliette challenge him or let him squirm? There wasn't much time left in which to decide.

She dozed a little, on and off, and then she got up around dawn and dressed quietly, feeling for her clothes. Her suitcase was packed and their flight wasn't until mid-day, so she had time. Writing a note on the hotel pad to say she'd gone for a walk, she took her phone and her purse and slipped out of the room, closing the door softly behind her. As she headed for the Métro, a few shops and cafés were already opening their doors and the traffic was building. She breathed in the chilly spring air, enjoying even the exotic gasoline fumes, and stopped at a *boulangerie* to buy a warm croissant, which she ate in greedy, tearing mouthfuls from the bag. There weren't many other passengers in her carriage: mainly construction workers and a couple of bleary-eyed kids who looked like they'd been up all night. Leaving the train at Ternes Station, she crossed the wide avenue and plunged into the back streets.

For some reason, she'd been convinced the square in Mémé's painting was located in Montmartre; she must have heard her grandmother mention the area at some point. Yet she'd combed the narrow streets the day before without success, seeing so many picturesque views but none of them the one she was looking for. And then, walking back towards the Arc de Triomphe, she'd glimpsed a food market in one of the side streets and headed down to explore. The tables under their striped awnings were a feast for the eyes as well as the stomach: silver fish arranged in gleaming shoals, whorls of green beans, pyramids of glossy peppers, tomatoes and aubergines, plus every kind of charcuterie, butter, cream and cheese one could imagine. She wanted to load a basket to the brim and spend the week cooking. Eventually, buying a crisp sugared palmier from a table of *pâtisserie*, she had fallen into conversation with the stall-holder, who turned out to be friendly and delighted to speak French. On an impulse, Juliette had explained her quest and taken out her phone to show the woman Mémé's watercolour.

'*Mais oui!* I know the square,' she'd exclaimed. 'It's not far from here, just a few streets away. Maybe ten minutes' walk?'

It was fate; Juliette had been meant to find the place. Now she retraced her steps, pulled by some instinct she couldn't identify. If she could only sit in that café for a while, her mind empty, then she would know what to do. For a moment, she wondered whether she'd been dreaming the day before – but there was her square, Place Dorée, with the ornate five-branched lamppost on a stone plinth in the centre. She walked around it and headed for the café. The place was nothing special: inside was a zinc-topped bar with a glass display case for pastries, black-and-white tiles on the floor, a menu chalked on the blackboard. She sat at one of the red basket-weave chairs outside and ordered a cappuccino from the waiter. A young woman in an oversized tweed jacket, skinny trousers and high heels sauntered across the square, the breeze ruffling her long straight hair; two little girls followed behind, holding hands, equally chic in satin bomber jackets and matching backpacks. An old man wearing a beret sat on a bench, smoking a cigarette in the slanting sunshine. Through the open doorway, she watched a couple of men knocking back espressos at the bar, while a tabby cat wove its way between the table legs. She'd found a glimpse of the real Paris, far away from the tourist hotspots, just before she was due to leave. How could she sit beside her cheating husband on a plane for the next eleven hours? The prospect was unendurable.

'If you can't think what to do,' her brother Andrew had once told her, 'at least decide what you *don't* want to do.'

Since when had he got so wise, she'd wondered at the time. Andrew deciding what he didn't want to do had left him drifting around the west coast, working in beach bars and surfing till he was well into his thirties. All the same, it seemed like weirdly good advice just then. She paid for the coffee and left, her mind made up.

'What do you mean, you're not coming back?' Kevin stared at her. She'd found him waiting over a coffee in the hotel lobby when she returned, with their luggage already loaded on a bellboy's trolley.

'I've decided to stay in Paris for a while.' She sounded calmer than she felt.

He laughed. 'Are you kidding? Our taxi's arriving in fifteen minutes. You can't suddenly spring this on me. And how long is "a while", anyway?'

'I don't know. A couple of months, maybe? Till the summer. Or maybe fall.'

'Don't be ridiculous.' He was losing patience. 'Where will you stay? And what are you planning on doing?'

'I'll find an Airbnb somewhere,' she said. 'And I'm going to take things easy, like you told me to. Enjoy being in France and spend some time figuring out what's next.'

'What's next?' His face was turner redder by the second. 'I'll tell you what's next. We have the Johnsons and the Reids for dinner this Saturday, and brunch at my mom's on Sunday, and that's just the weekend. The kitchen renovation's starting next month and there's the country club gala dinner in a fortnight, and—'

'And don't forget you're seeing Mary-Jane Macintyre on Tuesday evening,' Juliette couldn't resist adding. 'She called last night to say you'll have to make it later, because Stacey has a dental appointment after school.'

Kevin's mouth dropped open and his eyes widened. 'Oh, sure,' he said, collecting himself, 'I promised to fix her dishwasher. Didn't I tell you?'

'During your conference call? Well, you are good at multi-tasking these days.'

'Actually, my conference call is—' he began, but she cut him off.

'I know the two of you are having an affair. She's listed as "Jacksons" in your caller ID and you've been talking to her all week. Please don't carry on lying, it's so undignified.'

'You've got it all wrong,' he spluttered. 'I swear, the woman won't leave me alone. She's like some crazy stalker.'

'Kevin, I found the underwear you bought her. Don't you think I've been taken for a fool for long enough?'

Something in her voice must have got through to him. He dropped his gaze and fell silent, twisting a sachet of sweetener in his fingers. 'I'm sorry,' he said eventually, all the bluster gone. 'It didn't mean anything. She threw herself at me and I was flattered, I guess. And I felt sorry for her, with her husband away in Iraq. She was lonely and one thing led to another. . .' His voice trailed away.

Iraq had been Tony Macintyre's first tour of duty, Juliette remembered; after that, he'd been posted to Afghanistan. So the affair must have been going on for at least eighteen months. They'd met up so often with the neighbourhood crowd during that time: the Fourth of July fireworks, when she couldn't find Kevin for an hour, although he swore he'd been just a few feet away in the dark; those endless pot-luck dinners that she'd had to drag him away from, certain they were outstaying their welcome; even, she recalled sickeningly, the party for their twenty-fifth wedding anniversary, when he'd walked Mary-Jane home across the street and stayed to adjust the porch light. Was Juliette the last person on the Main Line to realise what had been going on?

'I'm almost glad you found out,' Kevin was saying. 'I've hated lying to you, Jules, honestly. I just couldn't think how to end it. Mary-Jane's not like you; she's needy and I was scared about what she might do if I left her. But as soon as we're home, I'll tell her it's all over, that I've made a terrible mistake and need to put things right with my family. Can you forgive me?'

Juliette looked at him. Drops of sweat beaded his forehead and his skin had turned a clammy grey, blotched with red. Perhaps he was having a heart attack. That would be interesting. 'I don't know,' she said.

'I'll do anything. Go to couples counselling, stay home every evening, take you away somewhere – you name it. Just give me another chance.'

'Here's what I want you to do,' she told him. 'Pick up your suitcase and get on that plane. Apart from that, I really don't care.'

He put both hands on the table and leaned back without speaking, looking at her. 'You know, Mary-Jane wasn't the only one feeling lonely,' he said eventually. 'You were away so often when your mom was ill, and I missed you. Maybe forgiveness is too much to expect but could you at least try to understand?'

My God, he had even said it to her then. 'I got your back, honey. Take as much time as you need to look after your mom, and don't worry about anything at home.'

She got to her feet. 'Goodbye, Kevin. I settled our bill last night so you only have to pay for extras from this morning. I'll tell you my plans as soon as I know what they are.'

He stood up too, pushing the table away with a scrape.

'What about the kids? And our friends? What am I going to say to everybody?'

'I'll text the kids,' she replied. 'You can tell anyone who asks that I'm staying on in France for a while. That's all they need to know.'

'You can't do this to me!' He'd raised his voice and Juliette became aware that people were staring: the receptionist, a well-dressed businessman peering over his copy of *The New York Times*, a maid passing through the lobby with a vacuum cleaner. 'You're upset and not thinking straight,' he added more quietly. 'We need to talk things through in private.'

'No, we don't. I've said all I need to.'

He narrowed his eyes, then sat down again abruptly. 'OK, if that's what you want. Let's see how long you stick it out before you realise what you're throwing away and come running home with your tail between your legs. You won't last a week on your own, let alone months. But I'm warning you: don't expect to find me waiting. I have other options, you know.'

She looked down at him. 'Goodbye, Kevin.'

He wouldn't meet her eye. She turned to take her suitcase and carry-on tote from the trolley, holding herself very straight as she headed towards the revolving door: twenty paces that took forever. She half-expected him to run after her, grab her arm and start yelling, but he'd never liked to make a scene in public. One strong push at the gleaming brass rail and she was out of the air-conditioned lobby and into the fresh air, the sun warm on her back. A taxi was pulling up at the hotel entrance; she walked quickly past it, suppressing the urge to run, her suitcase bumping at her heels and her heart racing with the enormity of what she had just done. She felt so light, if she'd let go of her luggage she would have floated up into the air.

'Before you realise what you're throwing away.' Those words ran through Juliette's head on a loop as she sat at the dressing table in her single room, eating a soggy tuna baguette and trying not to catch sight of herself in the mirror. She had chosen L'Hotel Corot because it was conveniently near to the Métro station and didn't look too expensive, and Corot was one of her favourite painters, but it was a depressing place: all dark corners, dusty plastic flowers and shabby furnishings. Still, her room was reasonably clean and a place to store her suitcase while she looked for somewhere more uplifting. She'd bought a bottle of wine from the supermarket and had had to brave the receptionist – a bored girl with a nose ring and a permanent scowl – for a corkscrew. Drinking tepid white wine from a toothmug on her own: what would Kevin have said? She imagined him somewhere over the Atlantic, ordering double whiskeys from the flight attendant and telling the stranger sitting in her seat that his wife had left him. No, he'd more likely keep the news tight to his chest, rehearsing the story he'd tell their friends until he believed it himself.

What was she throwing away? A comfortable life, for one thing. Being part of a couple was easy in so many ways. There was always someone with whom to share the worries of parenthood, to look for at a party when you were tired of talking to strangers, to spread suntan lotion over your back and tell you when there was spinach caught in your teeth. She and Kevin had a big house with a Peloton bike in the garage and a pool in the back yard, and plenty of friends to invite over for a barbecue. OK, so she had worked until her mother got sick and she'd taken early retirement to care for her, but that had been by choice rather than necessity. And now she was turning her back on all these blessings, along with a twenty-five-year marriage. Their friend Joy had had a fling with the builder who'd converted their garage into a gym, and Stan had forgiven her. They said their relationship was stronger than ever now, and that Joy's indiscretion had been 'a wake-up call'. Was Juliette being unreasonable, not agreeing to counselling? Ben and Emily would be devastated if their parents split up; she ought to make an effort for their sake.

'I'm staying on in France for a little while,' she'd texted the kids. 'Dad's flying home for work. It's been such a great trip! Talk soon!'

Her own parents had split up when she was seven and her brother nine, and she'd been determined never to inflict on her children the stress she had felt listening to the adults argue and then trying to comfort her mother through the dark times. Kevin was right, in a way: she had to take some responsibility for the state of their marriage. She had swallowed her resentment because taking a stand required energy and resolve, and she had been so tired all the time when the twins were small. She had let him think he could get away with anything.

She poured herself another mug of wine, kicked off her shoes and lay down on the musty candlewick bedspread. At least she didn't have to tell her mother what had happened. Suzanne had never liked Kevin; she'd tried to hide her antipathy but Juliette could tell she thought he was brash. Her mother had died a year ago and now she was losing her husband. She was alone in a city full of strangers, drifting without purpose. All the same, she was thankful not to have gone home with Kevin; at least she didn't have to face the inevitable gossip and pitying glances. For a moment, she thought about calling her best friend, Lindsay, but she wanted to sit with her feelings a little longer before she shared them. She was in shock, for sure, but alongside the hurt, a tiny seed of excitement had begun to grow. For so many years, every step she'd taken had been dictated by some-body else's needs: Kevin, the twins, her mother. Now she was beholden to nobody. She had an income of her own, thanks to the money Suzanne had left her, and she was footloose in Paris. At last, she had some time to herself and the chance to find out how she wanted to live.

Chapter Three

September 1940

The two men waited outside in the street, holding open the restaurant door for a couple who were leaving before stepping over the threshold. The cut of their long black trenchcoats and something in the sharpness of their gaze identified them instantly as members of the Gestapo. Jacques felt Mathilde stiffen beside him.

'*Mon Dieu*,' she muttered. 'Can one not get away from them anywhere?'

The men stepped into the room, hung their hats and coats on a rack near the door and pulled out chairs at the next table, glancing around the room as they did so. One was dark and the other fair, his short blond hair gleaming in the lamplight. The temperature of the room dropped by several degrees and an uneasy hush descended.

'Such a funny thing happened to me at the museum today,' Mathilde said in a bright, artificial voice, laying her hand over Jacques' on the table. 'You remember that young student I was telling you about?' And she began to recount an anecdote he'd heard the day before. 'Ignore them,' that's what she was telling him. 'Pretend they don't exist.'

Gradually the swirl of chatter resumed, glasses clinked and knives scraped on plates once more. Nobody looked at the Germans, although everyone was intensely aware of them as they sat stiffly in their seats, exchanging the odd comment in low voices. Jacques stole a surreptitious glance at their table and was dismayed to find he recognised one of the men, the darker of the pair, in his late thirties, wearing a double-breasted suit with a bowtie. He had a lean, handsome face with an aquiline nose and an ironic smile playing over his lips as he glanced around the room. He might have been a visiting professor, about to stand up and deliver a lecture. Jacques dropped his eyes and took a gulp of the cheap, thin wine, which caught at his throat and made him wince.

The patterns and rhythms of the room were shifting. Chairs had been moved and backs were turned so that the strangers' table now stood marooned in space. The waiters took complicated detours to avoid it, their eyes fixed on some distant point so they wouldn't have to answer the Germans' summons or even acknowledge their clicking fingers. The more urgent these gestures became, the louder everyone talked. The colour was blooming in Mathilde's cheeks as her voice rose above the din, tinged with hysteria. Jacques' sense of unease deepened; this was not going to end well. People were calling across tables, proposing toasts, clapping strangers on the back. A plump matron in black velvet pushed back her chair and sang a chorus from *'C'est mon gigolo'*, which earned guffaws and a round of applause. Neither of the foreigners were smiling now.

'We should leave,' Jacques whispered to Mathilde. She shook her head, a glint in her eye.

And then a harsh voice cut through the hubbub. *'Garçon!'*

The blond German had risen to his feet: a stocky, broad-shouldered young man with dangerous eyes. The room fell instantly silent, as though a switch had been flicked.

'Garçon!' he repeated. 'Boy', although the waiter was in his forties. 'Champagne, and quick about it.'

He looked around as though taking a note of each face, then turned his gaze back to the waiter who nodded, impassive, and laid down the cloth with which he'd been wiping a tray. There was no more clamour after that; a subdued, disgruntled murmur took its place.

'Here. You finish the wine.' Jacques slid the carafe towards his wife. 'I'm too full for dessert.' A lie which wouldn't fool her for a second.

A champagne cork popped behind them, followed by a fizz as the waiter poured out glasses at the next table. They carried on staring at each other, determined not to react.

Jacques took hold of his wife's hand and raised it to his lips. 'Happy anniversary, *chérie*. Remember this time last year?'

'Of course.' She made an effort to smile. 'How could I forget? It was so nearly perfect, until Herr Hitler ruined our plans.'

A snatch of guttural conversation made him turn, distracted, and he found himself catching the eye of the dark-haired German, who inclined his head.

'We meet again, Monsieur Duval.' Half-rising from his seat, he extended his hand.

Jacques steeled himself to shake it, his palm damp with sweat. He couldn't remember having heard the man's name, let alone his rank, but maybe that was just as well. From the look on Mathilde's face, she would have killed him if he'd used it.

'Kriminalassistent Werner Schmidt, at your service,' the man said. He continued in fluent French, as though acknowledging Jacques' unease and doing his best to help. 'Are you a regular here? We were told the food is excellent but the service leaves something to be desired.'

Mathilde stood up. 'Jacques, time we were going.'

'And this lovely young lady is your wife?' Herr Schmidt looked her up and down. 'Why, you lucky fellow. But I've seen you before, Madame Duval. Now where could it have been?' He tapped a finger to his lips. 'Of course! It was at the museum, wasn't it? You were at a meeting with the director when we arrived.'

'I don't recall,' Mathilde said, avoiding his gaze.

'I never forget a face, especially not one as pretty as yours,' Schmidt went on. 'What a coincidence that I should have met both you and your husband. Please, pull up a couple of chairs and join us in a glass of Champagne. We might even persuade that charming waiter to bring another bottle.'

'I'm afraid we must be going.' Mathilde put her arm through Jacques' and pushed him towards the door.

'Another time, then,' the German called after them, with his infuriating smile. 'I feel certain there will be another time, don't you?'

★   ★   ★

Without speaking, Jacques and Mathilde headed towards the steep, winding steps that led up to the basilisk of Sacré Coeur. They would often go to Montmartre after dinner to look out over Paris from the top of the hill, the great white monument behind them, dazzling against the night sky. Lights would be coming on all over the city, and there was nothing more romantic than the golden gleam shed by cast-iron lamps spilling down the narrow alleyways.

That evening, Paris lay dark and silent in the blackout and they had to find their way by moonlight since the streetlamps were shrouded. The steps were deserted. The curfew wouldn't begin for another hour but even so, no one wanted to risk being arrested because their papers weren't in order, or they'd committed some minor offence without even knowing.

'So how did you meet that man?' Mathilde asked, stopping under a lamp so they could both catch their breath. 'You know he's a member of the Gestapo?'

Jacques nodded. 'He came into the shop a couple of weeks ago, to check I wasn't stocking the wrong books.' Anything considered degenerate or anti-German, or that had been written by a Jew or a communist, was strictly *verboten*. Like every other bookseller in Paris, Jacques had been given a copy of the Otto list, specifying exactly which works were no longer to be read.

Mathilde gave an impatient sigh. 'So the Nazis want to control our thoughts, as well as everything we say or do. And did you get rid of the books they don't agree with?'

'What choice did I have?' Those men could close down his business as easily as they clicked their fingers for Champagne. 'Besides, Schmidt was only following orders. I could tell he was embarrassed. He's obviously a cultured fellow. Speaks English, French and Italian.' He leaned against the lamppost, breathing shallowly; the climb was hard on his lungs. 'That's why they gave him the job, I suppose. I almost felt sorry for him.'

'Oh, Jacques.' Mathilde sighed again, but less angrily this time. 'Not everyone is as sweet-natured as you. Being nice to a man like that won't keep you safe, it'll just make him despise you even more.'

'I don't think he despises me,' Jacques said mildly. 'We had an interesting conversation. He's building up a library back in Berlin and wants to add to his collection.'

She snorted. 'I bet he does. Of course the Boche despise us, and I don't blame them. Giving in without a fight, standing by while they march into our city – it makes me ashamed to be French.' She thrust her hands into her coat pockets. 'You're a peacemaker, Jacques, and I love you for that. You want to smooth things over and you can't bear hurting anyone's feelings. But those days are over, don't you see? The more you give these people, the more they'll take, and they'll laugh at you in the process. You have to harden your heart.' She started to climb the steps; slowly, so that he could follow more easily.

Jacques sighed. '*Soupe au lait*,' that's how his mother described Mathilde: milk frothing to the boil. He caught up with her and put his arm through hers. They walked slowly on in silence, until they had reached the broad terrace at the foot of Sacré Coeur. The vast cathedral glimmered in the dark behind them, a ghostly shadow of itself.

'You didn't tell me the Gestapo had come to the museum,' he said, sitting on a pile of sandbags. 'What did they want?'

She shrugged, sitting beside him. 'Who knows? They stick their noses everywhere. I expect we'll be closed down before long – the Nazis hate everything the museum stands for. All my work's being handed over to volunteers: rich, bored wives from Vichy who think Pétain is marvellous and France is on the dawn of a new age.'

Jacques put his arm around her shoulder and pulled her close. 'Be careful, my darling.'

She laid her head on his chest and sighed. 'I can't bear to live like this. When I see our gendarmes saluting the Nazis, it makes me want to spit.'

He stroked her thick, soft hair. 'Then you must look the other way. Better times will come, I'm sure.'

'Not unless we fight for them.' She hesitated. 'Jacques, some of my colleagues have been meeting to share ideas and information about what's really happening, instead of all this German propaganda we keep hearing. I'd like to join them but I wanted to talk to you about it first. I won't go behind your back.'

'It's so dangerous, though! How long do you think it'll take for the Gestapo to find out what they're up to? They'll be arrested and tortured, if not shot – the Nazis don't play around.' He took her by the shoulders and gave her a little shake. 'Mathilde, be reasonable.'

'I can't,' she said. 'It feels like part of my soul is being trampled on, day by day, and soon there'll be nothing left.'

'But how can I let you put yourself in harm's way?' he asked. 'You're my wife; it's my duty to protect you.'

'It's also your duty to defend the honour of our country, and mine, too. Please, if you love me, let me do what I think is right.'

'It's because I love you that I have to keep you safe,' he protested. 'It's not worth the risk, *chérie*. You and I are just two ordinary people. How can we resist the Germans when our government's carrying out their orders and our army's surrendered?'

She looked at him sadly. 'We have to try. A life without freedom is no life at all.'

Again, that terrible lurch of fear in the pit of his stomach. 'A life without *you* would be no life at all,' he wanted to say, but instead he kissed her, losing himself in the sweetness of her embrace, holding her so tightly that she laughed, and struggled to break free.

Jacques brooded for days over what Mathilde had said, the knot of anxiety in his stomach growing tighter. He was working late in the shop one evening when the doorbell jangled; he looked up with the usual alarm in case Schmidt might have come back to pay him another visit, but it was only his friend Henri, a week's wages weighing down his pocket.

'It's Friday. Time for a drink, *mon ami*. Come, have a pastis with me and forget your troubles.'

The two men had met at school, over twenty years before, and stayed friends ever since. They could hardly have been more different. Henri was short and stocky, a natural sportsman and extrovert who couldn't see the point of reading a book or visiting an art gallery. He'd protected Jacques from the playground bullies, while

Jacques had written his essays and corrected his spelling. Henri was part of a large family and his chaotic, noisy house had become a second home for Jacques while the boys were growing up. He had been a witness at their wedding and adored Mathilde, whom he was constantly trying to persuade to run away with him. Henri always had a girl on his arm, although rarely the same one for longer than a month or so.

Jacques turned the sign on the shop door to 'Closed' and locked up. He and Henri stood for a moment on the pavement outside, looking at the café on the corner of the square that had been their local until the Germans had taken over. '*Soldatenkaffee*' read a sign plastered across the window. Without a word, they turned the other way, heading away from the seventeenth *arrondissement* towards the seedier streets of Montmartre. A few Germans were wandering about but in ones or twos, rather than a patrol.

'I can't stay long,' Jacques told Henri as they entered a crowded bar on the rue des Dames. 'My mother isn't well and Mathilde's at a meeting tonight.'

Yet how welcome it was to breathe in the warm, smoky air, hear the gusts of laughter and feel the alcohol tingling through his body. For a moment, he could close his eyes and dream he was back in Paris as it used to be. Now there were as many women as men in the bar, which still surprised him, and those men were mostly elderly. So many of his contemporaries had been drafted into the army and ended up dead or sent to prison camps in Germany.

'So how's your lovely wife?' Henri asked. 'Coping with the mother-in-law?'

'Just about. Life isn't easy for anyone these days.' Jacques drank some more, although his head was swimming already and his stomach growled. 'What about you?'

Henri glanced around. 'Well, you know I was working at that big house in the Marais? The Boche came by last week and cleared it out. Carpets, pictures, furniture, china – all loaded into vans and driven away.'

'What about the people who lived there?' Jacques asked.

Henri shrugged. 'Who knows? They left the day before and no one's seen them since. But listen to this: the Nazis had an inventory, more or less. They knew exactly what was in that house, from the paintings on the walls down to the wine in the cellar.' He shook his head. 'I reckon they've had spies in the city for months. We've been taken for fools, my friend. The Boche have swept the rug from under our feet and sent it off to Germany, along with everything else. Have you noticed the number of removal vans in Paris these days? Those companies are doing good business, that's for sure.'

Jacques raised a warning finger to his lips. He added some more water to the pastis to eke it out, swirling the cloudy yellow liquid around the glass. Henri lit a cigarette and they sat for a while in silence, each busy with their own thoughts.

'I've a favour to ask,' Jacques said eventually. 'Would you be able to do some work for me? Remember that leftover wood in my cellar? I need some more shelves.'

'For all those guidebooks?' Henri smiled. 'Of course. I can fit you in the week after next.'

'Actually, this is urgent. Would you be able to work

over the weekend?' Henri raised his eyebrows. 'I'll help you,' Jacques added, 'and Mathilde might cook supper if we're lucky.'

Henri looked at him for a few seconds, considering. 'All right,' he said eventually. 'I suppose you wouldn't ask if it weren't important.'

'Thank you,' Jacques said. 'I'll explain later.'

He wouldn't though, not entirely. He trusted Henri more than anyone – except Mathilde, of course – but there were some secrets it was wiser not to share. Despite what he'd told his wife, a crate of the forbidden books was still sitting in his storeroom. He couldn't bring himself to send the copies back to some vast warehouse, to be pulped or burned or simply left to moulder away. Books were his livelihood, his passion, his *raison d'être*; how could he allow them to be destroyed? He had already accepted so much humiliation from the Nazis but this was a step too far. And yet the presence of those books was one of the worries keeping him awake at night. The world was becoming more dangerous by the day and *La Page Cachée* was no longer his sanctuary; he needed to make it safer without delay. Never had the name of his shop seemed more appropriate.

'So this is what you and Henri have been up to all weekend?' Mathilde ran her hand over the expanse of polished wood. 'Very nice. But do you really need any more shelves?'

Jacques glanced over his shoulder to check the shop's shutters were closed, then slid aside a wooden panel at the back of the middle shelf, put his hand through the narrow gap and unhooked a hidden catch. The whole centre section of the bookcase swung smoothly outwards, revealing a small, bare room beyond.

Mathilde gasped. '*Mon Dieu!* That's so clever.'

The storeroom at the far righthand corner of the shop was about six feet wide and twice as long. It had previously been accessed by a door, which Henri had now concealed behind a run of shelves. No one would guess this new entrance existed; to all intents and purposes, the storeroom had vanished. Henri hadn't asked why he was being asked to create this secret chamber and Jacques hadn't volunteered any information. All his friend had said was, 'You're not the only one in Paris wanting a hidey-hole.'

Jacques pulled the shelving door shut and latched it into place, then lit a candle in a wine bottle on the floor. 'Safer not to switch on the light. People will see it from outside.' He gestured to a window high up on the wall. This was the only flaw in his plan: someone walking down the street and turning the corner into his shop might notice that this window wasn't visible from inside, and wonder where it opened. Yet it would take a careful observer – or a suspicious one – to spot such a small detail.

'But what is this space for?' Mathilde asked, looking around. Seeing the crate, she picked up one of the books that lay on top and leafed through it. 'Ah, now I understand.'

If he was being honest, Jacques would have to admit he wasn't merely thinking about the books, although their existence had been weighing on his mind. He needed a safe place, somewhere he himself could shut the door and disappear.

Putting his arms around Mathilde, he held her close. 'Maybe we should stay here and let the world go on its merry way without us.'

She kissed him lightly. 'If only. How long do you think it would take your mother to realise we'd gone?'

'We could bring some cushions down, make the place comfortable.' He sat, pulling her down beside him. How lovely she looked in the candlelight, and how much he'd been missing her; they hardly had any time alone these days.

'So this is your plan?' Mathilde said, laughing. 'Well, you are a dark horse.'

'You've got to admit,' he said, unbuttoning her blouse, 'having my mother on the other side of the bedroom wall isn't ideal.'

'Not to mention the concierge always banging on our door, and the neighbours listening to every sound we make.' Mathilde pulled his shirt loose from his trousers.

'Let's not talk about them anymore.' Jacques' lips were on hers, his hands around her waist, and soon they'd forgotten all about other people, and their empty stomachs, and the fact there was only potato pie for supper.

Afterwards, Jacques watched Mathilde as she pulled on her clothes, shivering; it was too cold to stay undressed for long. Her hipbones jutted out at sharp angles and her ribs were clearly visible. He remembered how extraordinary she had looked on their wedding day, in a low-cut blue frock with a wreath of white roses pinned in her hair, her curves as smooth and soft as a luscious peach. He had vowed to protect and cherish her, and it seemed to him now that he had failed. He sensed she was deeply unhappy and that her desire not to hurt or defy him was contributing to that unhappiness. His wife was a force of nature; she had to be active, engaged, rushing forward like a river in full spate, and he couldn't change that.

'I understand how you feel,' he said, rubbing her frozen hands between his. 'Go to these meetings with your colleagues if you want to, I won't stand in your way.'

'Do you really mean that?' Her face lit up and she hugged him. 'Thank you, *chéri*. I'll be careful, I promise.'

Later, though, he would remember that moment and wonder whether he had made a terrible mistake.

Chapter Four

December 1940

Summer turned to autumn and winter came early in a blast of freezing air. Mathilde often stayed late at the museum; Jacques didn't ask why. Business at *La Page Cachée* was steady, although many customers seemed to want a place to come and be quiet for a while, as much as to buy a book. Herr Schmidt took to dropping into the bookshop at odd times, which was unsettling. He hadn't apparently noticed the new shelving, which was a relief, but his motives were unclear. He would walk along the shelves with his hands behind his back, humming under his breath while looking at the book spines as though he was inspecting troops on parade. He would choose one or two titles, then make awkward small talk at the till about random topics: the year he had spent studying in Paris when he was young, the ways in which the city had changed, how much he admired French culture. Jacques hated these one-sided conversations, in which

Schmidt held forth and expected him to agree. The German stood too close for comfort; Jacques could smell the cigarette smoke on his breath, see the nick on his cheek where he'd cut himself shaving. He was trapped, unable to get away until Schmidt released him or another customer needed help.

One morning, Jacques received a letter from his former employer, Monsieur Isaacson, asking if he could come to his home for drinks early the next Sunday evening. It would be best not to mention the visit to anyone, for reasons Isaacson would explain, and if there were Germans hanging around the building at the time, it would be wiser to postpone the meeting.

Jacques wrote back to say he'd be delighted to accept. Isaacson was generous and cultivated, as well as being an astute businessman to whom he owed a great deal.

The street was empty when he arrived but, even so, he couldn't help glancing over his shoulder as he rang the bell. A volley of furious barking from inside disturbed the peace, so his arrival was hardly unannounced; the maid who came to answer the door had put it on a chain and looked terrified until he smiled and took off his hat.

'I'm sorry about all this secrecy,' Monsieur Isaacson said, when they were sitting over glasses of *slivovitz* in his study. He stroked the plump, shaggy terrier who'd followed them into the room and was now sitting on his master's lap, looking suspiciously at Jacques. 'Sadly, Alphonse doesn't understand the need for quiet.'

Jacques was shocked by his old employer's appearance. Usually so immaculate, Isaacson looked haggard and was in need of a shave; there were stains down his tie and he wore carpet slippers instead of his customary polished shoes.

'They say people like us should leave the country, but where would we go?' he asked. 'This is my home. I fought for France in the last war, with the medals to prove it, and my daughter is studying music at the Conservatoire. Our life is here. We cannot pack our bags, just like that. My wife is not in the best of health and it would kill her.'

'Of course,' Jacques agreed.

'Anyway, there's no point complaining. I'll come straight to the point,' Isaacson went on. 'My shop has been closed, my bank account frozen, and I'm unable to trade any longer. I've managed to transfer the cream of my collection to a secure depot, and I wondered how you'd feel about selling the books for me? There are some valuable gems among them and your business would benefit. We could split the proceeds, half and half. What do you say?'

Jacques took a sip of the fiery liquid. He felt uncomfortable, being appealed to for help by the man he regarded as his mentor, and Isaacson's demeanour worried him as much as his appearance. All his usual confidence was gone; he seemed to have aged ten years in the last two. 'It's an interesting idea, but one that needs some thought,' he said carefully. 'There are risks involved for us both.'

'Nothing is without risk these days.' Isaacson set Alphonse down on the floor and topped up Jacques' glass. 'You're the only person to whom I could put such a proposal, Jacques. I trust you implicitly. I'd give you the keys to my depot and you could pick and choose among the books as you wanted, take as much time to shift them as you needed.'

'And where is this depot?'

'Very central. Faubourg Saint Martin, in the middle of the tenth *arrondissement*. You'd be able to come and go whenever suited you.'

'I hadn't thought of diversifying into antiquarian books so soon.'

'Maybe not, but an offer like this is too good to miss,' Isaacson replied. 'It'll get your business off to a flying start, and my terms are generous.'

'They are indeed.'

'Come on, what do you say?' The little dog barked, as though he was also waiting for Jacques' response.

Jacques might never have become a bookseller if this man hadn't taught him so much about the trade and encouraged his ambitions. He wanted to help but he hated being rushed into a decision and there was a lot to consider. 'How would I transfer the funds to you?' he asked, playing for time.

'It would have to be cash,' Isaacson said hurriedly. 'My daughter could come to your shop once a month to collect the money, if that's convenient? We can't risk being seen together.'

If the Nazis found out Jacques was conducting business on behalf of a Jew, they'd close him down. He'd been so reluctant to let Mathilde put herself in danger and now here he was, contemplating a venture that was equally hazardous. And it didn't seem right to take money from a desperate man. On the other hand, how else would Isaacson survive?

'You're like a son to me,' his old friend said. 'I've always dreamed of the two of us becoming partners. We could set up together after the war. I'll make you rich, my boy.'

He tried to smile and Jacques' heart ached. Of course, he would help. Mathilde was right: the time for crossing one's fingers and hoping everything would work out in the end had passed. He knew what she would do in this situation. 'All right,' he said. 'Let's give it a try for a couple of months and see how we get on.'

'Marvellous!' Isaacson struggled to his feet to shake Jacques' hand, while Alphonse mounted his master's leg enthusiastically. 'You won't regret this, I promise.'

The next time Herr Schmidt sauntered into *La Page Cachée*, Jacques was ready for him. 'Just the man,' he said, to Schmidt's evident surprise. 'I've acquired several fine volumes I know you'll appreciate.'

A new display case stood in the centre of the larger room, as Jacques had always intended, filled with forty or fifty first editions and rare titles that were hard to find. Schmidt had told him he was interested in Charles Dickens, and Isaacson had mentioned a first edition of *The Memoirs of Joseph Grimaldi*, edited by Dickens and illustrated by George Cruikshank. Jacques unlocked the case with great ceremony and drew the book out.

'You can tell it's a first edition,' he told Schmidt, as Isaacson had told him, 'because the illustration on page 238 – here we are – appears without a border. See?'

'Oh, yes. That's very fine. May I?' Schmidt took the book reverently, an acquisitive gleam in his eye. 'I'm glad to see you're diversifying, Monsieur Duval.'

In the end, he bought the Dickens, two titles by Ernest Hemingway and a slim volume of Goethe's poetry for daily reading – not a first edition but in excellent condition. 'I shan't haggle over the price,' he said, when the time came to pay. 'I'm an honourable man, you know. If I see something I want, I'm prepared to pay for it.'

Schmidt was getting a bargain, given the current exchange rate, but at least Monsieur Isaacson would have some money coming in. Jacques started a separate account for what he termed 'antiquarian books', deciding for the sake of fairness to keep only a quarter of the receipts for himself. Isaacson needed the money more than they did. All the same, Mathilde would appreciate the extra money for their household budget, since the eggs she queued to buy for his mother's sake were expensive.

Madame Duval was hardly eating. One evening she developed a fever and a dangerously high temperature, tossing and turning in her sweat-soaked sheets, despite the apartment being so cold you could see your breath on the air. They took turns sitting by her bed and sponging her face until the doctor finally appeared, somewhere around dawn.

'But I don't want this man,' Maman cried, half delirious. 'Who is he? Where's Dr Weisz? He'll make me better.'

'Dr Weisz has gone away,' they told her repeatedly. 'Don't you remember?'

'Gone away where?'

'To the country,' Mathilde replied. There was no point

telling her that Polish-born, Jewish Dr Weisz had been interned at Drancy prison camp.

The new doctor, brusque and unsympathetic, declared Madame Duval had picked up an infection and might not be strong enough to survive it; the next twenty-four hours would be critical. He gave her an injection and wrote out a prescription for more pills they could barely afford, then left with a cursory nod.

'It's hardly worth going back to bed,' Mathilde said, with a yawn. 'I might as well start queuing at the baker's.'

Jacques watched her as she scooped her thick curls deftly into a knot, gazing at the graceful line of her neck, smooth and white as cream against the faded crimson kimono she wore as a dressing gown. There was a determined set to her mouth these days and a haunted, wary look in her eyes.

'We'll have coffee when you get back,' he promised. 'And take my mother's fur coat. We can't have you falling ill as well.'

She smiled and kissed him, and then she was gone. He laid his head on his arms at the kitchen table and must have fallen asleep, because some time later, he was woken by Mathilde bursting back into the apartment and gabbling at him.

'Slow down!' He rubbed his bleary eyes. 'I've got no idea what you're trying to say.'

'The police are rounding up foreign women,' she said, the words spilling out in a rush. 'I saw them just now on my way to the shops. The women are British, that's what the gendarme told me, and they're taking them all to be interviewed at the town hall.'

'And what has that got to do with us?' he asked.

'Because of Madame Scott-Jones, of course!' Mathilde pulled him up from the chair. 'We must warn her, tell her to hide somewhere. You'll have to come with me – she'll listen to you.'

Blearily, Jacques tried to focus. Madame Scott-Jones was an English spinster in her forties who lived in the apartment opposite theirs and had become a friend as well as a neighbour. She'd worked as a governess for several years, most recently for an American family who'd gone back to New York, leaving her behind, and was one of his best customers. If Jacques came across a particularly fine first edition, he would put it aside so she could have the first look. 'You'll ruin me, Monsieur Duval,' she would say, with her toothy smile. In fact, he was in greater danger of ruining himself since he only charged her as much as he'd paid the dealer. She loved French poetry, particularly the works of Baudelaire, Rimbaud and Verlaine, and he had once come across her in an empty corner of the Parc Monceau, reciting a dramatic speech by Racine. She wore sensible cardigans, thick stockings and lace-up shoes, no matter what the season, but a passionate heart clearly beat beneath the layers of wool.

He followed his wife across the corridor. Madame Scott-Jones came to the door in a pair of striped men's pyjamas under her habitual cardigan, her wiry grey hair sticking out in all directions. It took her a while to understand what Mathilde was trying to say.

'But why would they want to question me?' she asked, bewildered. 'What am I supposed to have done? I never go out after the curfew, and I'm reporting to the police station every day.'

'They don't need a reason,' Mathilde told her. 'Please, Madame, you must hurry – they're only a few streets away. Pack a bag with some essentials and . . . and hide in our apartment till the police van has gone.'

'But what will I do then? The British embassy is closed, and there must be police everywhere.' Madame Scott-Jones ran a hand through her hair, leaving it more dishevelled than ever. 'How stupid I am! I should have left Paris weeks ago.'

'Stay with us for a few days until the fuss dies down. Then, when everyone's forgotten you exist, you can slip back across the hall.' Mathilde looked at her husband. 'That's all right, isn't it, Jacques?'

'Of course,' he replied, after the briefest of pauses. What else could he say?

'I couldn't possibly impose on you,' Madame Scott-Jones replied. 'No, I must think of another solution. Perhaps I could go to the American Embassy and ask for their protection? The ambassador was very helpful to the Goldsteins.'

'But you would have to show your passport at the checkpoints,' said Mathilde. 'And besides, there are so many German soldiers about, you probably wouldn't make it to the end of the street.' Madame Scott-Jones could scarcely look more British were she to wrap herself in a Union Jack.

'If they find me in your home, they'll arrest you too,' she said. 'I can't ask you to put yourselves in danger.'

'Then we'll have to make sure you're not found.' Mathilde gave her an encouraging pat on the back.

'And you're not asking; we're offering. Now go, *chère* Madame, and gather your valuables quickly. We shall wait for you here.'

At last she left, wringing her hands in a flurry of indecision.

'Are you sure about this?' Jacques asked his wife when they were alone. 'What are we going to do with an Englishwoman who's wanted by the police? We have enough on our plate as it is looking after Maman.'

'She can help us with your mother. We'll put a mattress down for her in Maman's room and maybe we'll finally get some sleep, too.' She took his hand. 'This English lady is our friend. Remember those horrible mince pies she makes for us at Christmas? And the socks she knitted for you last winter? We can't stand by and watch while she's carted off God knows where.'

'But what if we're making things worse? She might get into real trouble for hiding from the police when she could have gone to the town hall and had everything sorted out in a few hours.'

Mathilde snorted. 'Come on! You can't seriously think they're going to have a quick chat and let her go?'

Jacques sighed, tucking his hands under his armpits for warmth; this apartment was even colder than theirs. He looked around the modest *salon*, sparsely furnished with a couple of chairs, a table for one by the window, a writing desk and a bookcase stacked with much-loved volumes, their spines creased and faded. He didn't want to accept they were living in a world where a law-abiding middle-aged woman could be taken from her home simply because of her nationality. He preferred to believe the gendarmes – who were French, after all – would escort Madame Scott-Jones to the Mairie and ask her to fill out a few forms before letting her go home again. In his heart, however, he realised Mathilde was right. His world had changed forever, and it was time he accepted it.

Chapter Five

December 1940

Madame Scott-Jones reappeared with her belongings spilling out of a bulging carpet bag. They had only just managed to settle her into the apartment before several pairs of boots came marching up the stairs outside, followed by a tremendous hammering on a door somewhere and shouts of, 'This is the police! Open up!'

In the kitchen, Mathilde and Jacques exchanged apprehensive glances over their coffee cups. 'I'd better see what's going on,' Jacques said. 'You wait here.'

He opened their door a crack and peered out. Two uniformed gendarmes were standing outside Madame Scott-Jones' apartment, preparing to kick down the door. The concierge, Madame Bourdain, came toiling up the stairs behind them.

'I have a key,' she puffed. 'No need for all this commotion.'

They stood aside to let her unlock the door and walked in, calling from room to room.

'Why are they here?' Jacques asked Madame Bourdain. 'Is the Englishwoman in trouble?'

'Don't ask me,' she replied. 'Anything can happen these days. *Aie!*' She brought out a small ginger kitten from her apron pocket and held it aloft by the scruff of its neck. 'Don't want one of these, do you? Somebody left five of them in a sack on my doorstep last night.'

The kitten gave an outraged, reedy cry, twisting to dig its tiny claws into her fingers. Shaking her head, she dropped it back in her pocket.

'I'm sorry, I have enough trouble feeding Milou as it is,' Jacques said. He would have done Madame Bourdain a favour if he could; she was lazy and liked a gossip but she was amiable enough, and life ran more smoothly if they kept on the right side of her. She took in parcels, passed on messages and knew everything that had happened or was about to happen in the building and indeed, the whole neighbourhood. She was as wide as she was tall, with small currant eyes in her bun of a face, and hair worn in a plait around her head.

The gendarmes reappeared. 'The woman's not there. You can lock up again,' one of them told the concierge. He turned to Jacques. 'And who are you?'

'I live opposite.' He nodded across the corridor towards his open door, through which the aroma of coffee was drifting.

'Then I shall have to ask you some questions,' the policeman announced. 'And examine your apartment also.'

'Oh, come on,' his colleague said. 'Surely there isn't time?'

'You go down and guard the others. I shan't be long.' He produced an identity card and held it out to Jacques.

'My name is Dupont, as you can see, and that is my number. I must insist you allow me entry, Monsieur—?'

'Duval.' Jacques stepped aside. 'Come in, by all means, but my mother is sick and I'd appreciate it if you didn't disturb her.'

'It isn't right,' Madame Bourdain added, peering past him into their apartment, 'bothering decent people at this hour of the morning. How is your poor mother, Monsieur Duval?'

'As well as can be expected, thank you, Madame,' Jacques replied, following the gendarme through and closing the front door firmly behind him.

Taking off his cap and tucking it under his arm, Dupont walked into the kitchen.

'This gentleman is looking for the Englishwoman,' Jacques said hastily to Mathilde, who'd emerged from his mother's bedroom.

Dupont sniffed the air. 'Thought I could smell coffee,' he said, looking pointedly at the stove.

'You're not a policeman for nothing,' Mathilde remarked. 'May I offer you a cup, Monsieur? It won't take a second to heat up the pot.'

'Thank you. That would be most welcome.' Dupont pulled out a chair and sat at the table, gesturing for Jacques to join him. 'I've been up since dawn and it's going to be a long day, that's for sure. Why didn't the foolish creatures leave Paris when they had the chance? It would have saved us all a great deal of trouble.'

'Has Madame Scott-Jones committed some sort of crime?' Mathilde asked, turning around from the stove. 'She seems such a harmless creature.'

'Oh, it's merely a formality,' the gendarme replied. 'We need to check her details, that sort of thing.'

'You seem very anxious to find her.' She pushed a steaming cup across the table and fetched a bottle from the dresser. 'Here, have a splash of brandy in your coffee.' She poured a generous slug into his cup. 'It's such a cold morning and you're working so hard.'

The gendarme took a sip and closed his eyes. '*Sacré bleu*, that's good.'

'I believe the English lady reports to the police station every day,' Mathilde went on. 'You must have her details already, surely.'

Dupont glanced at her sharply. 'And what business is that of yours? This woman needs to be accounted for and that's an end of it. Tell me, when did you last see her and where?'

'Forgive my wife,' Jacques interrupted. 'She's fond of our neighbour and worried about her, that's all. We haven't seen the lady since the day before yesterday. She was feeling unwell and said she might go to the American hospital at Neuilly. You'll probably find her there.'

The gendarme tutted with exasperation. 'We haven't got time to go rushing halfway across the city. Oh, well.' He drained his cup. 'Thank you, Madame Duval. And now I must search your apartment, if you'll permit the intrusion.'

Mathilde gave a nervous laugh. 'Is that really necessary?'

'I'm afraid so.' Dupont replaced his cap. 'Questions will be asked and I must be seen to do my duty.'

He walked officiously around the kitchen, peering into a few cupboards and checking the larder thoroughly, in case a stray Englishwoman happened to be crouching between the shelves. Jacques and Mathilde followed, watching as he tweaked aside the towels in their tiny bathroom and examined the pills in their medicine cabinet, rifled through the clothes in their wardrobe and crouched down to search under the bed. Jacques held his breath but luckily Monsieur Dupont didn't bother to lift the mattress, which would have revealed Mathilde's wireless. There were no likely hiding places for Madame Scott-Jones in the sitting room, so he merely checked behind the shutters and tipped up the armchairs with the toe of his boot.

'So that's that. Now I suppose you'd better be on your way,' Mathilde said, chivvying him down the hall.

Dupont ignored her. He was standing outside the last remaining door. 'And this, I presume, is your mother's room? Don't worry, I'll be discreet. She'll hardly know I'm there.'

And before they could protest, he'd opened it and stepped inside.

Jacques started forward. 'This is quite unnecessary! Please, my mother must not—'

The gendarme held up his hand for silence, gazing around. The figure in the bed lay still, her breathing harsh but regular. The curtains were not quite drawn and in the dim light that filtered through the gap, all that could be seen of the old lady was the outline of her head on the pillow. On the chair beside her bed sat a tapestry bag, containing a pair of knitting needles stuck into a ball of grey wool. Jacques held his breath, heart thumping. All three of them stared at this bag, which suddenly seemed bigger than anything else in the room and horribly significant.

'Ah, my knitting!' Mathilde exclaimed, a little too late. 'I've been looking for it everywhere.'

Monsieur Dupont paid her no attention. He advanced purposefully, making straight for the bed and the shadowy figure asleep in it. He was a few paces away when she stirred, lifted her head and let out a surprisingly loud scream.

'*Mère de Dieu!* What's happening?'

Jacques sprang forward. 'It's all right, Maman. This man is a policeman, he won't hurt you.'

'But what is he doing in my bedroom?' His mother sank back on her pillow, drawing the sheet up to her throat with trembling, mottled hands. The fever seemed to have broken and she sounded coherent, if exhausted. She was undeniably ill, and old, and French.

'Apologies, Madame.' Monsieur Dupont retreated. 'I'll leave you in peace.'

'I should hope so,' Mathilde said, ushering him out and closing the door firmly behind them. Jacques stayed to pour his mother a glass of water and make sure she was comfortable. The room smelt fusty so he opened the window to let in some air, then dropped to his hands and knees and lifted the counterpane to meet the frightened eyes of Madame Scott-Jones, who was lying on her back underneath the bed. He put a finger to his lips before straightening up.

'What a strange day this is,' his mother murmured. 'A rather odd woman came to visit me and now she seems to have disappeared. Perhaps I was only dreaming.'

'Hush, Maman.' Jacques kissed her papery cheek. 'I'll explain later, when the policeman has gone.'

By the time he emerged, Mathilde had ushered the gendarme outside onto the landing. 'Thank you for your cooperation, Monsieur Duval,' he said, touching the peak of his cap. 'And for the coffee, Madame. If you see your neighbour, you must report her to the police immediately.'

When the sound of his footsteps had receded down the stairwell, Mathilde shut the door and turned to Jacques, letting out a shaky breath. 'That was close. Where's she hiding?'

'Under the bed.' Jacques held out his arms and Mathilde fell into them. He could feel her heart thumping against his chest.

'I can't believe our police are doing the Nazis' dirty work for them,' she said eventually. 'We'll have to keep the Englishwoman here, Jacques – God knows what will happen to her otherwise.'

'Of course,' he replied. Yet he felt in need of some brandy himself. Madame Scott-Jones was in serious trouble and now she was their responsibility. How long could they keep her safely hidden? And what would happen to them, were she to be found?

Madame Bourdain waylaid Jacques on the landing as he made his way downstairs. She was carrying a basket, which squeaked and rustled.

'Ah, Monsieur Duval. What an unpleasant business! I had to let the police in, they were most insistent. But where do you think the Englishwoman could be? I was talking to her yesterday and she didn't mention anything about going away.'

'I have no idea,' he replied, avoiding her beady black eyes. 'Still, perhaps it's just as well she wasn't home.'

'Perhaps someone tipped her off about what was happening.' Madame Bourdain pushed down the head of an adventurous kitten. 'I haven't seen her leave the building, though. It's my guess she's holed up somewhere. In one of the empty apartments, perhaps?'

'Who knows? Now if you'll excuse me, Madame, I must open up the shop.' He pushed past her, sensing her gaze on his back as he descended. The woman was no fool; she probably knew exactly where Madame Scott-Jones was to be found.

He let himself into the shop by the back entrance, locking it behind him. The quiet atmosphere of *La Page Cachée* usually calmed him, but not this morning. Nowhere was safe. Schmidt could appear at any moment, with his sly insinuations and leading questions, and what if the Gestapo were to search his apartment? They would be more thorough than a lazy gendarme going through the formalities. A hammering on the front door made him look up in alarm, but it was only one of his more eccentric customers, clamouring to be let in.

Guillaume Bruyère was a minor celebrity, the author of a novel that had been a *succès fou* ten years before. He hadn't had anything published since, and looked increasingly tortured every time Jacques saw him. The bags under his haunted eyes grew puffier, his hair wilder, his expression more desperate.

'Thank goodness you're open,' he said. 'I'm looking for *Beware of Pity*. You know the title? By Stefan Zweig.'

'Of course, but that book is on the banned list,' Jacques replied. 'You won't find it anywhere in Paris.'

Monsieur Bruyère groaned theatrically, fists clenched at his temples. 'I lent my copy to a friend and he's run off with it. What am I to do? I'm nearing the end of my novel, you see, and I must study Zweig's narrative technique and structure before I can finish.' He grabbed Jacques' sleeve. 'You don't have one I can borrow? Name your price.'

Jacques shook his head, although some hesitation must have showed on his face. Bruyère took him by the wrist. 'Can you help? I tell you, money's no object.'

'I might be able to get hold of a copy, but I'm not promising anything.' Jacques disengaged his arm. 'Could you come back on Monday?'

'Yes!' Bruyère kissed Jacques soundly on both cheeks. 'My good man, you have saved my life. I shall dedicate the book to you.'

'And don't tell anyone, understand?'

'Not a soul. *A demain, mon ami!*' Bruyère rushed out of the shop, setting the bell jangling furiously.

The rest of the morning was quiet, thankfully. He was about to close for lunch when the bell above the door jangled again and a friend strode in. Estelle was a statuesque, brilliant redhead who wrote poetry and short stories by day and supported herself by dancing in the Folies Bergère at night. Although she was primarily Mathilde's friend, Jacques liked her too.

Estelle had a flamboyant sense of style: she favoured long velvet cloaks and sweeping skirts worn with high-necked blouses, riding jackets and lace-up boots. That morning she was looking more elegantly restrained in a military-style coat trimmed with gold braid and a fur hat and muff.

'I've had to track you down,' she said, tossing back her vivid hair. 'I haven't heard from Mathilde for weeks and she wasn't at the museum this morning. Does she still work there?'

'She was probably out at a gallery,' Jacques replied uneasily. He and his wife had come to a tacit agreement that, for safety's sake, she wouldn't tell him anything he didn't need to know about her daily routine.

'Just so long as I haven't offended her somehow,' Estelle said.

'How long have you been friends? She'd tell you soon enough if you had.'

Estelle smiled. 'You're right. Well, I'd like to invite you both to the show on Saturday.' She laid a couple of tickets on the counter. 'I've got a solo number at last and it would be nice to see some friendly faces in the audience. We could have supper afterwards, my treat.'

'That sounds wonderful,' Jacques said. 'Are you sure, though? It costs a small fortune to eat out these days.'

'Don't worry about that.' She gazed around the shop. 'How lovely you've made this place – one could almost forget the madness outside. Is that a new display case? Business must be good.'

Jacques unlocked it for her so she could browse. Estelle spoke good English and he had a leather-bound edition of *Sonnets from the Portuguese,* Elizabeth Barrett Browning's love poems, that he knew she'd appreciate even if she couldn't afford it.

'Oh, Jacques,' she said, gazing up from the pages misty-eyed, 'this is what I needed to read. Thank you. I'll take it.' She also bought a copy of Rimbaud's *Le Bateau Ivre,* the long poem he wrote at the age of seventeen, and a book about Rodin's sculpture.

'So you're doing well, too?' he asked, wrapping the books in brown paper. There was a well-fed sheen about Estelle that made him think she had to be buying food from the black market.

'I can't complain. See you on Saturday.' She flashed him a dazzling smile and tucked the books away in her muff, letting in a blast of cold air as she left the shop.

'Do you think we can leave your mother on her own?' Mathilde asked that evening, when Jacques told her about Estelle's invitation.

'But Madame SJ will be here to look after her,' he said. 'We might as well make the most of her being here.'

The Englishwoman had urged them to call her simply SJ, but he couldn't bring himself to do so, not to her face. She and Maman were getting acquainted; the old lady had taken surprisingly readily to the idea of having a companion and referred to SJ grandly as 'my nurse'. They'd all agreed she should spend most of her time in the old lady's bedroom, with intervals in Mathilde and Jacques' room when the strain of such forced proximity became too much for anyone.

Mathilde was massaging a few drops of olive oil into her chapped hands. 'It feels wrong to go out enjoying ourselves when everything's so awful. Have you heard? They've condemned Jacques Bonsergent to death.'

'I know, it's awful.' Jacques shook his head. 'The poor man.'

Bonsergent was an innocent bystander who'd witnessed a minor altercation between some Parisians and German soldiers, and somehow ended up arrested.

'He wasn't even involved in the fight,' Mathilde went on, rubbing her skin in slow circles. 'Well, it was hardly a fight – somebody else shook his fist at a German soldier, that's all, and Bonsergent's the one who ends up in prison! He was only walking past.'

'It's not too late. Maybe he'll tell them who was responsible and they'll let him off.'

'He'll never do that.' Mathilde's eyes were flashing sparks. 'He's taking the blame on purpose, showing everyone these Nazis are bastards enough to shoot a man in cold blood for no reason. He's a hero!'

Jacques took his wife's slippery fingers. 'You're right. But that doesn't alter the fact that you haven't seen one of your closest friends for ages and she's treating us to dinner.'

'She's treating us?' Mathilde raised her eyebrows. 'How did she look?'

'Smart,' Jacques replied, after a few seconds' thought. 'She was wearing a fur hat and carrying a muff.'

'Hmm,' said Mathilde. 'I wonder what she's up to.'

★ ★ ★

By Saturday, the lure of a night on the town had become irresistible. Madame SJ was doing her best to keep out of the way but she was another body in their small apartment, and the constant clacking of her knitting needles set their teeth on edge.

'You're right,' Mathilde told Jacques, applying her lipstick. 'An evening out will do us good.' She'd piled her hair on top of her head and was wearing a silk frock that the local dressmaker had copied from a design by Schiaparelli. 'How do I look?'

'Wonderful,' Jacques said, pulling her down on the bed. 'Let's stay home instead.'

'And miss Estelle in the spotlight?' Mathilde protested, laughing.

Yet when they walked into the music hall, Jacques wished they'd made an excuse not to come. The auditorium was a sea of grey-green: row upon row of Germans in uniform, whistling and catcalling loudly enough to drown the pianist.

Mathilde turned to him, appalled. 'We can't stay.'

'But the show's about to start.' Jacques took her arm. 'Come on. We'll just have to grin and bear it.'

Luckily their seats were at the end of the row. Mathilde sat next to the aisle and he was able to shield her from their immediate neighbours. She sat, rigid with loathing, as the red velvet curtains parted, the orchestra sprang into life and the long line of dancers was revealed. The audience stamped their feet in appreciation and Jacques squeezed Mathilde's hand. Only two hours to go . . .

Afterwards, they made their way to the dressing room Estelle shared with the other dancers. Through the open door, they saw half-naked girls sitting about among discarded costumes and champagne bottles, chatting, smoking and drinking from toothmugs. A gust of warm air, scented with flowers and face powder, spilled into the corridor.

'I'll wait here,' Jacques told Mathilde, as Estelle caught sight of them from her seat at a long line of mirrors and turned to wave.

The two women joined him ten minutes later. Her face now bare of the heavy stage make-up, Estelle had a bouquet of red roses in one arm and Mathilde on the other.

'So, did you enjoy yourself?' Estelle asked, passing Mathilde her flowers so she could link arms with Jacques and sweep them both along with her, out through the stage door and into the street.

'Absolutely,' he replied. 'Such a wonderful spectacle. And you were extraordinary.'

Estelle was part of the chorus but she'd also danced a solo turn in a long gown made of peacock feathers, which she swept about, displaying her marvellous legs to their best advantage. A few puffs of thistledown were still caught in her red hair. 'La Renarde' – the Vixen, that was her stage name.

'Matti?' She turned to Mathilde.

'It was marvellous,' Mathilde said carefully.

Estelle stopped, disengaging her arm. 'What's the matter? Didn't you enjoy the show?'

'The show was fine,' Mathilde replied. 'It was the audience I couldn't stand. How can you bear to dance for that mob every night?'

Estelle laughed. 'Come on, under that uniform they're only men, same as all the rest.'

'They're not, though, are they?' Mathilde said. 'They're the conquering heroes, drunk with power. You're nothing to them – they think Frenchwomen are sluts.'

'How do you know?' Estelle asked. 'Have you even spoken to a German? Anyway, they can think what they like. I'm earning good money and giving them a good time. If they choose to spend their wages on Champagne and flowers, who am I to complain?'

'Speaking of flowers.' Mathilde passed her back the roses. She picked up the card that fell from them and glanced at it. 'Who's Otto?'

'Nobody in particular,' Estelle said, although she blushed.

'Now listen, you two,' Jacques interrupted, taking each of their hands and pressing them together, 'time to change the subject. We don't often get an evening out, so let's enjoy it.'

'I'm sorry,' Mathilde said, giving Estelle a brief, fierce hug. 'Sitting among the Boche has made me a little tense, that's all. We won't talk about it anymore.'

'That's the spirit.' Estelle kissed her cheek. 'Come, I've found a wonderful bistro in the rue Bleue and they'll have Champagne waiting for us on ice. *Mange, bois et sois heureux!'*

And for the next few hours, they did manage to eat, drink and be happy. The restaurant was secluded and luckily free of Germans, and they spoke mainly about the past: the party at which the two women had met, talked all night and wandered home along the riverbank at dawn, still talking; the time they had met Picasso in the Café Deux Magots and he had sketched Estelle on the back of a napkin; the various unsuitable men with whom she'd had disastrous affairs. They ate pâté flavoured with wild thyme, *daube de boeuf* – which might have been horsemeat but was delicious anyway – and green beans with almonds. Jacques wanted the evening to last forever, but eventually the waiters were putting chairs up on tables and they would have to hurry to get home before the curfew.

'Thank you for coming.' Estelle put her hands on Mathilde's shoulders as they stood by the door.

'Thank you for inviting us,' Mathilde replied. 'And I'm sorry if I spoke out of turn. I'm worried about you, that's all. You may end up paying a high price for Champagne and flowers.'

'You're wrong to think all Germans are the same,' Estelle said, flushing. 'Lots of them are only following orders because they don't have any alternative, and some believe Hitler's gone too far. There are decent, honourable men among them.'

Mathilde gazed at her. 'My God, I know that look. You're in love with one, aren't you? Estelle, this is madness! Can't you see how it will end?'

Estelle's eyes flashed. 'No, because I can't look into the future and neither can you. It's all right for you, with a lovely husband at home, but the rest of us have to take our pleasures where we can find them. Who knows what will happen tomorrow? I'm happier than I've ever been and just because the man I love is German, I'm not going to give him up. You haven't even met him. How do you know what he's like?'

Mathilde's jaw tightened. She opened her mouth to speak, then shut it again and turned away without a word.

'Goodbye, Estelle,' Jacques said. 'I'm sorry.'

Sorry for what, though?

He and Mathilde walked home in silence. It was a cloudless night and a full moon lit the empty streets. There were strays everywhere, dogs and cats abandoned in the rush to leave Paris who'd turned feral and survived by scavenging through piles of rubbish. Somewhere in the distance, they could hear the stamp of hobnailed boots and harsh, guttural voices raised in a marching song.

'I don't know how much longer I can carry on living in this city,' Mathilde said at last, disengaging her arm from his. 'Tonight was awful.'

She'd stopped in front of a lurid yellow poster on an advertising hoarding, announcing the imminent execution of Jacques Bonsergent and warning that anyone else who insulted or threatened the German Reich would suffer the same fate. Before Jacques could stop her, she had stepped forward, grasped a corner of the paper and ripped off a wide strip.

'What are you doing?' Horrified, he grabbed her arm.

She shook him off, scrabbling at the poster until half the hated message had been torn away. Then, taking out her lipstick, she scrawled, '*Vive de Gaulle!*' in blood-red letters over the white surface left behind.

'Enough!' Jacques pulled her away, dragging her down the street as fast as he could without breaking into a run. The heavy footsteps were getting louder and soon the patrol would be upon them, though he couldn't tell from which direction it was coming. They had to get as far away from the scene of the crime as they could – but now they had reached a side turning and the Germans were there. Five men in tight formation, one at the front with two pairs behind.

'*Halt!*' said the leader, holding up his hand. 'Papers?'

Jacques stepped in front of his wife, breathing fast. He reached for his identity card, hands shaking, and held it out without meeting the soldier's eyes. The man scrutinised the card by torchlight, nodded, and gave it back.

'Madame?'

Mathilde looked back at the German without blinking, as though she had been turned to stone. Jacques took her handbag from her arm, found her pass and handed it over, raising his shoulders apologetically as if to say, 'Women, eh? What can you do?' His heart was beating so loudly, he thought everyone must hear.

The soldier stared at Mathilde, who consented at last to drop her eyes. He handed her card back to Jacques, barked some command at his men and shouldered his rifle before preparing to move off.

Jacques grasped his wife's arm and steered her along the street, staggering like a drunk. His legs seemed to have turned to jelly. When they were a safe distance away, he stopped to point wordlessly down at her coat. A long ribbon of yellow paper was trailing from the pocket.

Chapter Six

March 2022

The Place Dorée became Juliette's fixed point, the centre of her universe. She would walk to the café each morning, casting off the gloom of the hotel, and take the same table in a secluded spot near the back of the room for her daily cappuccino and croissant. She was making friends with the cat – whose name, she learned by eaves-dropping, was Cocotte – and beginning to recognise the regular customers. The same three men would arrive one by one and stand at the counter, chatting over their espressos. The tallest looked like an intellectual, with a beard and glasses; he wore open-necked shirts and beau-tifully cut jackets. The middle one was scruffy, in jeans or cargo pants and usually a Breton sweater with the sleeves pushed up. Completing the trio was a short, plump guy with a smarter work dress code. Beard and Glasses, Breton and the Suit, she called them to herself, and would observe them surreptitiously, trying to work out what made them so quintessentially French: the cut of their clothes, their Gallic shrugs, the mobility of their faces, or maybe just her imagination? The Breton usually seemed to be in a bad mood, throwing his hands around as he described some outrage or another, one foot up on the rail around the counter. Yet he was the nucleus of the group – the other two came alive when he appeared – and he was the one she always found herself watching.

Apart from these three, an elderly couple usually appeared some time around ten, and sometimes a beautiful girl would drop by and sit at a table near the door with a pot of tea, her thick, chestnut hair tumbling in waves down her back. The three musketeers, as she thought of them, would glance at her occasionally with an unabashed interest that managed to be appreciative rather than creepy. They might catch each other looking and exchange a wistful smile or shake of the head. They ignored Juliette for the most part, although once the Breton nodded at her when he arrived at the same time she did. The men would leave after twenty minutes or so, while she would stay for a couple of hours, planning her day, reading a book or searching the internet for an apartment to rent. The waiter would call, *'L'habitude?'* soon after she sat down, and bring over her coffee and croissant. He wasn't particularly friendly but he wasn't actively hostile, which she counted as a win. Fortified, she would then set off to explore Paris, one *arrondissement* at a time.

She was drawn to quieter places rather than the main tourist attractions: a tiny crêperie in the backstreets of Montmartre, a shaded corner beside the fountain in the

Luxembourg Gardens, a pew near the back of the Sainte-Chapelle church where she sat for hours, bathed in coloured light from the huge stained-glass windows. I'm learning to be alone, she thought, and most of the time that wasn't too frightening. Maybe that was why she hung on at L'Hotel Corot: to test herself. She didn't want to keep moving either, and many of the apartments she looked at on the internet were only available for a few days or the odd week here and there. The weather was fine – cold but sunny – so she stayed out for as long as she could, eating lunch in a café because that wasn't as sad as supper by herself. Sometimes she'd go to the cinema in the evening, but more often she'd curl up in her room with a book, a baguette and some cheese or ham from the market. The receptionist still hadn't smiled but one morning she told Juliette in an offhand voice that a room with a better outlook had become available, which she could have for the same price, if she wanted. So now she had a small balcony and a view of people with busier lives than hers streaming towards the Métro station each morning and coming up again for air in the evening. The room had the same brown nylon carpet underfoot, unfortunately, frosted with grey like a sprinkling of cigarette ash. She tried never to stand on it barefoot.

After she'd been at the hotel for a week or so, Kevin texted: a short message to say he had told everyone she was staying in France to research her family history and would be back soon. Also the cat had lost weight while they'd been away and was off her food. Juliette felt a pang then: Mittens had wandered through their back door nineteen years before and refused to leave. Yet she knew Kevin would take care of their family pet; he wasn't a monster. She thanked him for letting her know and asked him to keep in touch. Were he and Mary-Jane rolling around on her bed even now? She couldn't decide whether she cared. When she was feeling brave, she texted Lindsay to tell her briefly what had happened and re-assure her she was OK. Lindsay called back immediately and they had a long conversation that was only occa-sionally tearful. 'I'll come over right away if you need me,' Lindsay said, but she was awaiting the birth of her first grandchild and Juliette couldn't expect her to miss that. Anyway, she was managing perfectly well on her own – most of the time.

One evening her brother called, wondering whether she was free for dinner in a couple of days' time; he had to visit New York and thought he would 'swing by' Philly on the way home.

'So what's going on?' he asked, when she told him she was still in Paris and Kevin had gone home alone.

'Long story,' she replied.

They'd never really talked about personal things and it was hard to start now on the telephone. Andrew had lived a very different life from hers and somehow they were always out of sync. When their parents were getting divorced, they were too young to articulate their feelings, and Andrew had turned into the classic sullen teenager, locked away in his bedroom. While Juliette was bringing up her children, he founded a software company and started making serious money – according to Kevin, who was most put out by this unexpected turn of events. When Andrew married Patsy, a terrifying divorce attorney with whom Juliette had less than nothing in common, she and her brother grew more distant still. Even when the marriage broke up a few years later (on terms that were highly favourable to Patsy, obviously), Andrew was too far away in every sense for the two of them to recover lost ground. Even when their mom had died, it had been hard for them to communicate. Andrew was far away in San Francisco and Juliette had been so exhausted by the end of Suzanne's illness, she'd had no emotional energy left for him.

'But you're OK?' he asked now, and she had to swallow a lump in her throat before telling him, sure, she was fine. And then in the café the next morning, her equilibrium was rocked again when the waiter told her they would be closing the next day.

'*Non! Pourquoi?*' she cried, too loudly, and sensed people turning to stare.

'For renovations. Only for a week or so,' he reassured her, looking appalled.

Juliette recovered and said of course she understood, but she had to blink away tears and concentrate very hard on her coffee. It took only the smallest nudge to throw her off balance. She got up to leave as soon as she'd finished breakfast and found herself reaching for the door at the same time as the Suit.

'What shall we do these next days?' he asked, smiling at her as held open the door.

'*Oui, c'est dommage,*' she replied stiffly.

'*Ah, vous parlez français!*' He beamed, falling into step beside her and continuing the conversation in French. 'Madame, do not worry. There is a charming café just a couple of streets away. The view is not so nice but the croissants are excellent. May I show you?'

Oh God, she was going to cry again. 'Thank you.' She dug her fingernails into her palms. 'That would be very kind.'

'My name is Arnaud.' He reached out his hand. 'Arnaud Chauvigny.'

'Juliette Fox,' she replied, taking it. The shock of his warm skin made her realise this was the first time in ten days that she'd touched another human being. Arnaud had a round, good-natured face with clear blue eyes and curly brown hair, flecked with grey.

'Forgive me,' he went on, 'I don't wish to intrude. My wife is always telling me I should mind my own business but I'm naturally curious about people. You speak excellent French, Juliette.' 'For an American', was the unspoken phrase hanging in the air.

'That's because my grandmother was born and brought up in Paris.' Juliette began telling him the story of the painting she had inherited and the discovery of 'her' square, hardly pausing for breath until they'd reached the replacement café. Arnaud invited her for another coffee so she could see whether she felt at home there, and suddenly the day seemed a lot brighter.

'You three seem very good friends,' she said at last, aware she'd been talking almost exclusively about herself. Too much time alone was not good for anyone's social skills.

'Oh, we've known each other since we were students. Now Baptiste, with the beard, is a research scientist and Nico is in property.' He looked at his watch. 'And I work for a bank, where I should be heading right now.'

'Thank you, Arnaud.' Juliette got to her feet, suddenly awkward. 'It's been so lovely to talk to you.'

'And we shall talk again, I'm sure.' He smiled before turning away.

I must get a grip, she thought, and not frighten the poor man. She felt instinctively that Arnaud wasn't hitting on her; he was just a kind person who must have sensed she was lonely. Perhaps she radiated desperation rather than the air of mystery she'd been hoping for. She glanced around. This other café was fine, although it faced on to a nondescript street rather than her beautiful square. Still, it would do for a while. She had a week to find a sense of purpose and, with a bit of luck, somewhere less depressing to live. When she'd told Arnaud she was staying at the Hotel Corot, he'd pulled an extremely doubtful face.

Juliette was careful to keep her distance from Arnaud over the next few days so he wouldn't worry she might be a stalker. She didn't visit the replacement café every morning and neither, it turned out, did the three musketeers. She and Arnaud waved at each other a couple of times in passing before her solitary day began, but it felt good to know there was someone she could turn to for advice or help in an emergency.

One night, coming back from an early-evening showing at the cinema, she heard her name being called as she crossed the cobbled Place des Ternes and turned to see Arnaud waving at her. He was sitting with two other people on the terrace of a café overlooking the square.

'Come and have a drink with us,' he said as she

approached, pulling out a chair. 'This is my wife, Thérèse, and you already know my friend Nico.'

Thérèse and Arnaud could have been brother and sister, they looked so alike: both with the same curly hair and open, friendly faces. And there was the Breton, wearing a leather jacket instead of the usual striped sweater. She shook hands with them both, suddenly shy. All this human contact was hard to cope with after living in her lonely bubble.

'And what are you doing in Paris?' Thérèse asked once Juliette was installed at the table.

'Well, I came here with my husband on holiday,' she began, 'and now he's gone back to the States and I'm staying on here for a while to—' What could she say? To avoid him? 'To research my family history,' she went on. Kevin's pretext would do for the time being.

'Your family history in Paris?' Nico had quizzical eyes and a downward turn to his mouth. He was looking at her intently, which made her feel awkward and shy, and the most basic French phrases seemed to have suddenly deserted her.

'Yes, my grandmother was French, and brought up here,' she managed to say, more or less.

'Which is why Juliette speaks the language so well,' Arnaud put in. Nico raised his eyebrows, and Juliette decided she hated him.

'Did she live in this area?' Thérèse asked. 'Do you have an address?'

'Not exactly,' she replied. 'But she had a painting of the square with the lamppost hanging on her bedroom wall, so I'm thinking it must have meant something to her.'

'Or she might have visited Paris from anywhere in the whole of France and bought this pretty picture as a souvenir,' Nico commented.

'I guess,' Juliette replied, 'but it's worth a shot.'

'And then what?' he asked. 'You think you'll find some magical connection with her by drinking your coffee in Place Dorée every morning?'

'Nico! Be nice,' Thérèse warned. 'He's in a bad mood because his girlfriend has stood him up,' she added to Juliette.

'Well, I don't understand this obsession with the past,' Nico declared, leaning back in his chair. 'Say you uncover a few random facts about your grandmother – you can never really understand what she thought or how she lived. You can't use her life to add meaning to yours.'

'I'm not trying to.' Juliette regarded him steadily over her glass. 'But you can't blame me for being curious. My grandmother left France at the end of the war to live with my grandfather in America. I know nothing about her and my mother died recently, so there's no one left to ask.'

'Yes, it's all very well for you, Nico,' Thérèse put in. 'You can speak to your grandmother any time you like.'

'Is she still alive?' Juliette asked, incredulous. Nico looked her age, if a little older. His dark wavy hair was greying at the temples and there were crows' feet around his eyes. He was lean and good-looking, though, in a weather-beaten, ship's captain kind of way; she had to give him that.

'She's ninety-seven,' he said crossly.

Touché, Juliette thought, glad to have rattled him. She knew exactly what he was thinking when he looked at her: here's another tourist, reducing French life to a series of photos on Instagram that she hopes will impress her friends.

'Well, I'd better be getting back to the hotel.' She drained her glass.

'Stay for supper with us,' Arnaud pressed her.

'Yes, you can take Delphine's place,' Thérèse added. 'Nico's girlfriend's having a work crisis, apparently.'

Nico looked so horrified, Juliette almost laughed. 'Thanks,' she said, smiling sweetly. 'I'd love to.'

They'd probably had a row, if Nico was as grumpy as this all the time. Juliette spent most of the meal talking to Thérèse, who was just as curious about people as her husband, if not more so. She was a high-school science teacher and asked a ton of questions about the US educational system that pushed Juliette's tired brain to its limits. Nico occasionally glanced at her as she struggled to answer. She didn't care, though. Here she was in Paris, eating the most delicious roast chicken and *pomme purée*, otherwise known as mashed potato, with two out of three congenial French people, and she didn't have to worry about Kevin: whether he was bored, or arguing with someone, or cross with her for talking too much. A passer-by would have thought she was happy.

'Would you like ketchup with that?' Nico asked.

Thérèse slapped his hand. 'What is wrong with you this evening?'

Juliette shrugged. 'That's a cheap shot – it doesn't bother me.'

'Oh, look! Here's Delphine after all,' Thérèse exclaimed, as a tall, rangy brunette with her hair in a messy bun strode up to their table. Delphine kissed Nico and then the others, once on each cheek, unwinding a scarf from around her neck.

'You made it!' Arnaud looked around for a spare chair.

Juliette got clumsily to her feet. 'Here, have my seat. I should be going anyway.'

Delphine looked at her coolly as they were introduced. She was in her late thirties or thereabouts, and the epitome of Parisian chic in tight leather trousers and a silk shirt.

'Don't rush off.' Thérèse pulled Juliette back down. 'We've only just finished. Stay for dessert or coffee, at least.'

'Yes, don't leave on my account.' Delphine seized a chair from another table and jammed it in between Nico and Juliette, who almost ended up in Thérèse's lap.

Nico poured his girlfriend a glass of wine. 'Rough day?'

'Awful.' Delphine waved an elegant hand, laden with silver rings. 'Don't ask me about it. I'm at the end of my tether.'

'Well, it's Friday night,' Arnaud said. 'Time to forget about the office and—'

'I honestly think my boss is losing the plot.' Delphine turned to nod at the waiter. 'I spend so much time clearing up after her, I'm neglecting my own work. Did you have the chicken, as usual? Was it good?'

'But we're about to order coffee,' Nico protested. 'Chicken will take forever to arrive. Why don't you take dessert with us, or some cheese?'

'Because I haven't eaten all day and I hate cheese, as you very well know,' she replied icily. 'I didn't realise you were in such a hurry.'

He frowned and shook his head, and an awkward silence fell over the table.

'By the way,' Juliette said brightly, 'I need to find somewhere to stay for a few weeks or months. Preferably with a kitchen, so I can cook for myself. I don't suppose you guys know anyone with an apartment to let?'

'Couldn't Juliette use your grandmother's place?' Thérèse asked Nico. 'Well, it's yours now, isn't it?'

'Zizi's apartment?' He frowned more ferociously than ever. 'But it will take weeks to clear out all the junk, and then the place would have to be cleaned and decorated, and I simply haven't time at the moment.'

'What a shame.' Thérèse looked at him with her head on one side. 'It's in such a great location, looking out over the square. Seems a waste to leave it lying empty.'

'But it's not empty.' Nico drummed his fingers on the table top. 'I told you, it's full to bursting with all the rubbish Zizi's collected over the years. You can hardly get through the door.'

Juliette's heart had begun to race. 'I don't mind that. Perhaps I could help you tidy up?'

'I'm too busy to think about it now,' he said irritably. 'I'm sorry, the apartment needs a lot of work. Everything's old-fashioned and falling apart, and there isn't even an internet connection. You wouldn't like it.'

How do you know what I'd like? Juliette thought. Also, Nico never looked particularly busy in the café with his friends.

'You ought to have somebody living there, though,' Delphine said. 'What if squatters move in?' She nodded at Juliette. 'Why don't you let her have a look around?'

'Delphine's right,' Thérèse added. 'The place is probably a fire risk, too.'

Nico threw up his hands. 'All right, all right. I can see I won't get any peace until I agree. How about tomorrow afternoon? Say, five o'clock?'

He took a pen from his jacket pocket and wrote the address on the back of a beer mat, sliding it across the table. 'But don't blame me for wasting your time.'

'Thank you.' Juliette pocketed the mat and smiled as politely as she was able. Delphine stared at her across the table, one arm draped around Nico's neck, and took a drag on her vape pen. You don't need to worry about me, Juliette could have told her; I'm no threat.

'You see? I wasn't exaggerating.' Nico stood back so Juliette could look down the hall. It was lined on both sides with cardboard boxes and piles of newspapers stacked up to the ceiling, some of them wedged at precarious angles, and the narrowest of paths in between.

'Well, maybe it's not ready to be listed on Airbnb just yet,' she said.

He led the way down the corridor to a small kitchen on the left, dominated by a large butler sink and an old-fashioned cooker. Every surface, including the floor, was piled with rusty saucepans, frying pans, casserole dishes, biscuit tins, whisks, trays, bowls, sieves, knives and crockery – enough *batterie de cuisine* to prepare a banquet. More pans hung from a circular iron rack suspended from the high ceiling, and the sink was full of them too. What she could see of the room was clean, though, and smelt of disinfectant rather than rotting food.

'There's no dishwasher and the fridge is tiny,' Nico pointed out. He was speaking in fluent English, perhaps because they were alone, which was actually quite a relief. 'Not what you're used to, I'm sure. You'll want a fridge as big as a tank that makes ice cubes and tells you when to buy more milk.'

'Because I'm American? Well, naturally.' She was determined not to rise to the bait. 'But it's possible to manage with just a sink. And once you've cleared out all the pots and pans, this room could look great.' Beneath the clutter, it had such a homely, vintage feel, with a glazed larder door in one corner and flowered curtains across the cupboards.

'You think so?' Nico looked around, shaking his head. 'It'll take weeks to sort through everything.'

'Not weeks. Days, maybe, but you'd be surprised what little time it takes to make a difference. And where's your grandmother living now?'

Nico moved a colander and a stack of plastic cups from a chair and sat down. 'In a residential home not far from here. I bought the apartment from her so she could move into care but I haven't the time to go through all her belongings at the moment. I can't face the thought of it, to be honest.'

'I understand. Trust me, though – it's better to do it now, while she's alive.'

Clearing out her mother's house had been one of the saddest things Juliette had ever done. Every item she picked up had its own trail of memories. She could picture Suzanne drinking coffee from this chipped mug, whipping eggs in that cracked bowl, lacing up those muddy walking boots before a hike. No one else would want these things but she couldn't bear to throw them in the garbage as though they meant nothing.

Nico glanced at her. 'You said your mother had died not long ago. I'm sorry.'

'Thank you. She kept a lot of junk but your grandmother beats her, hands down.'

'Wait till you see the bedroom.' He led the way to a door across the hall and pushed it open.

'Oh, my goodness.' Juliette gazed around. There must have been hundreds, if not thousands, of dolls – ranged along every shelf and windowsill and piled on the bed and the floor. Most were stacked in transparent plastic cases and wore French national costume: lacy Breton headdresses, Provençal print aprons, straw hats and tiny buckets hanging from yokes across their shoulders. There were some contemporary dolls, too: Barbie and Cindy, Elvis, even the Spice Girls, lying in a heap with their lurid hair tangled together like victims of a massacre in Toyland.

'Does your grandmother miss all her possessions?' Juliette asked.

'She says she can't be bothered with them anymore.' Nico pulled one doll's legs out straight and sat her down on the windowsill. 'Shall we finish here or do you want to see the *salon*?'

He seemed in a better mood than the night before, Juliette reflected, following him down the hall. Maybe he'd made up with Delphine. She still didn't like him: he was attractive but he knew it, his assumptions about her were irritating and he was probably lazy rather than sensitive. Kevin was a hard worker, at least. She pinched herself. Kevin was a liar and a cheat, and she wasn't about to let him off the hook.

'How come you speak such good English?' she asked, making awkward small talk.

'I spent some time in the States,' he replied briefly, which explained the trace of an American accent she'd detected.

'Really? Whereabouts?'

But he was opening the living-room door and ignored her question. 'Here we are.'

'What a lovely room!' Juliette made her way through stacks of cardboard boxes to the window and pulled the tall wooden shutters fully open. Beyond a narrow balcony with wrought-iron railings lay her square, Place Dorée, and she was looking down on the ornate five-branched lamppost, set among the trees. She could glimpse the striped café awning through their branches, hear snatches of conversation and laughter from the outdoor tables where people were already gathering for early-evening drinks.

'I've started clearing up in here,' Nico said with a sigh. 'It's taken me all day to get this far.'

The chaos was a little more organised: cardboard boxes had been stacked around the walls leaving a space in the middle and there was actually room to sit down on the chaise longue. Stuffing was falling out of the torn uphol-stery, but she could cover that with a throw.

She turned around in a slow circle, drinking everything in. Although she'd sooner have nothing to do with Nico, she could put up with him for the sake of his apartment. 'I don't care about the mess,' she said. 'Will you let me tidy the place up? I'll put aside anything that might be valuable and show you everything we might throw out. Think of a reasonable rent and I'll pay you a month in advance.'

'Are you serious?' He gave her a suspicious glance. 'Why do you want to live here?'

'Because it feels like a home.' Not her home yet but it could be, for a while. She gazed up at the high ceiling, the shutters, the faded pictures on the wall, then down at the glimpse of wide oak floorboards. She could imagine sitting at a table by the open window, sipping coffee while she watched life going on in the square; coming back from the market with a laden basket and spending hours cooking complicated dishes; lighting that potbellied stove and reading all evening – all night, if she felt like it. Being kind to herself; licking her wounds.

Chapter Seven

March 2022

Juliette didn't regret her decision to stay in Paris but every day was a challenge; it took some effort to speak French all the time, to negotiate her way around the shops and unfamiliar currency, to be alone without feeling lonely. I must throw myself into Parisian life, she told herself firmly, and talk to people. One day she visited the American Library near the Eiffel Tower and hung about in the aisles, thinking she might find suitable victims there. It was peaceful, soaking up the library hush, and she was running out of things to read so, on a whim, she took out a year's subscription. The librarian looked motherly and there was a programme of regular talks, which would while away a few hours. In fact, an author whose name she vaguely recognised happened to be talking about her latest book early that same evening, and there would be wine. Juliette had bought a ticket immediately.

The author was a young woman with a mournful face who had written a 'searing exploration of contemporary relationships', in which a betrayed wife had murdered her husband and then stalked his mistress, breaking into her house and living in the attic for several months before descending in the middle of the night and taking her hostage. The two women had ended up falling in love, which struck Juliette as unlikely. She couldn't help sniggering, wondering what Mary-Jane Macintyre would say if she climbed down from her loft one evening, and caught the eye of the woman sitting next to her, who smiled too.

'Have you read the book?' her neighbour asked, when the talk had come to an end and they were falling on the wine with some relief.

Juliette shook her head. 'It doesn't sound my cup of tea.'

'Nor mine. But we like to keep up-to-date with modern writing, and listen to these talks to improve our English.' She was a tall, striking woman, with silvery hair cropped short and bright red lipstick, wearing a plaid jacket and a short black skirt that should have looked ridiculous on someone her age but somehow didn't. 'This is my husband, Claude, and I am Ilse.'

'Your English is pretty good already,' Juliette said, although she was thinking, 'Yes, yes! Talk to me! I have weeks' worth of conversations ready to go.'

She tried to strike a line between friendliness and hysterical devotion; they seemed such an interesting couple and she didn't want to frighten them. Claude was French and Ilse, German; he was a retired academic, older than his wife, while she was a psychotherapist. Best of all, they lived in the Batignolles district, not far from where Juliette was staying.

'There is a farmer's market on Saturday morning,' Ilse said, after they'd been chatting for half an hour or so. 'Would you like to come shopping with me, if you're free?'

'Sure,' Juliette replied casually. 'Don't think I'm doing anything.'

She hadn't moved into Nico's apartment straight away; she couldn't even see the bed, let alone lie on it. Instead, she stayed at the hotel for the time being, walking to the Place Dorée every day to begin the task of sorting, cleaning and throwing away. Nico had given her a spare key so she could come and go as she pleased. He was ridiculously casual; she could have squatted there and turned the place into a marijuana farm. However, he had at least managed to arrange a rubbish collection for all the old newspapers and random junk beyond repair.

'You must pile everything in the street with this code,' he told her by text. 'The lorry should come on Friday, mid-morning. I'll drop by first thing to help.'

Once all the junk had been cleared, Juliette could begin piling Zizi's belongings into categories so they could decide what should be done with them. She still felt uncomfortable around Nico. There was no denying he was an attractive man and now she didn't think of herself as married anymore, she couldn't seem to act naturally around him.

'I'd like to meet your grandmother,' she said, as they traipsed up and down the stairs that Friday, laden with boxes and refuse sacks. 'I ought to find out whether there's anything in particular she wants to keep.'

'She seems to have forgotten all her possessions,' he said. 'But you can talk to her if you like.' He picked up a box. '*Merde*, this is heavy. What have you put in here?'

'Bricks,' she said. 'Just to annoy you.'

He didn't laugh. Suit yourself, she thought, stretching her aching back. She wasn't going to let his moods affect her. Perhaps he didn't want her poking around in his family's business after all, or maybe he'd had another row with Delphine. Or he might be having second thoughts about giving her free rein in his grandmother's apartment; it was quite a leap of faith. They carried on working in silence, managing to ignore each other most of the time. At one point, though, they both reached for the same box. She glanced up to see the sun shining full in Nico's face and a long-forgotten sensation ran through her body: desire. Apart from his personality, he was the most attractive man she'd met in years. He had gorgeous hazel eyes and olive skin, and she couldn't help looking at the curve of his mouth and his improbably perfect teeth. The smile died on her lips. My God, she'd better not make a fool of herself. What was the matter with her?

'That one's all yours,' she said, turning away.

At last, all the old newspapers and magazines, the threadbare rugs and bags of other unidentifiable rubbish had been stacked on the sidewalk outside the empty shop on the ground floor of their building, directly beneath the apartment. Juliette had noticed the place in passing but had never paid it much attention. She peered through the tall, dusty windows but couldn't see much, only a pile of post on the floor and walls covered in peeling circus posters.

'What used to be here?' she asked Nico.

He shrugged. 'Most recently a shop selling candles and strange hippy clothes. No one's been able to make a success of the place.'

'What a shame. These windows are beautiful.' She gazed up at the sign above the door, trying to decipher any words under the flaking paint.

'Well, thanks for your help.' Nico rolled down his shirt sleeves. 'I've told the concierge the lorry should be arriving soon, but maybe you could keep an eye out too? Although who knows whether it will come on time – or at all.'

Juliette was learning that any kind of transaction in Paris required huge amounts of patience and paperwork; even returning a faulty kettle to the store had taken hours, and her plan to open a French bank account seemed like an impossible dream.

'Sure. And thanks for organising everything.' She had to admit Nico had also done all the heavy lifting, and he'd arranged the boxes efficiently in order of size. Whenever she and Kevin embarked on some job together, it usually ended in an argument. 'And, about your grand-mother,' she added. 'I'm free on Saturday afternoon or all day Sunday, if that would suit?'

'I'm not sure,' he said, frowning at his phone, which had begun to ring. 'I'll have to text you.'

The lorry eventually arrived around three that afternoon, and the bags and boxes were loaded and taken away within half an hour. It was only rubbish, after all, yet Juliette was worried by the responsibility she'd taken on as she watched the lorry disappear. What if she'd thrown away something that meant the world to Zizi?

She'd been sorting and tidying in the apartment for a couple more hours when a ring on the doorbell made her jump. 'Yes? I mean, *oui*?' she said into the intercom.

It was Thérèse, Arnaud's wife, come to see what progress she was making. 'I thought this apartment would be perfect for you,' she said, looking around once Juliette had buzzed her in, 'but I didn't realise it was in such a state. You're doing Nico a huge favour, making the place fit to live in. I hope he's going to reflect that in the rent.'

'I don't know, I think he's beginning to wish he'd never let me get involved,' Juliette said. 'He seems fairly grumpy.'

'Don't mind him.' Thérèse flapped her hand. 'He can be gruff sometimes but he's kind-hearted underneath.'

Really? 'He doesn't seem to like Americans much,' Juliette confided. 'Or perhaps it's just me. Listen, can you stay for a drink? I've laid in a few supplies.'

'Don't ever let Nico know I told you this,' Thérèse said, when they were settled with a glass of wine, 'but he was in love with a girl from California who broke his heart. He doesn't have great taste in women, I'm afraid.'

They exchanged knowing smiles, and Juliette realised with a pang how much she'd been missing the kind of gossipy, light-hearted conversations she used to have with Lindsay.

'I can't work him out,' she said. 'We're virtual strangers but he's trusting me with all his grandmother's possessions, as well as her apartment.'

'He's like that,' Thérèse said. 'Impulsive. And I think Delphine's taking up all his attention at the moment.

He's renovating her apartment, did he tell you? That's how they met. He's just finished wallpapering the whole place but she's changed her mind about the pattern and making him start again. He's probably glad you're dealing with Zizi's place so he doesn't have to think about it.'

'Arnaud said Nico was in property. What does that mean, exactly?'

'He's refurbished a couple of apartments and rented them out. So if there's any problem with your plumbing or heating, he should be able to fix it.' Thérèse glanced around the room. 'When are you planning on moving in?'

'When I've got rid of dolls.' Juliette picked up her wine glass. 'Come and see. I warn you, though, they're scary.'

'Oh my goodness, so many!' Thérèse stared at the collection, open-mouthed. 'What are you going to do with them?'

'Well, Nico says his grandmother doesn't want to keep anything, but I ought to ask her if she has one or two favourites. Then maybe I'll try to find a dealer. I've had a look on Ebay and vintage dolls are fetching good prices.'

'Do you know about the flea market at St-Ouens?' Thérèse asked. 'It's not far from here – we must go some time. I have a friend with a stall there who might be interested in selling Zizi's things, or know someone who would take them.' She shivered. 'Let's get out of here. Feels like these girls are listening to every word we say.'

'I've come up with this little fantasy,' Juliette said as they made their way back to the kitchen. 'My grandmother was around the same age as Nico's – she was seventy-one when she died, twenty-seven years ago – so what if she

101

and Zizi knew each other when they were young? Apparently Zizi lived in this square all her life.'

'Well, I suppose it's possible.' Thérèse sounded doubtful. 'But all you have to go on is your grandmother's painting, yes?'

'I know, it's a long shot.' Juliette sighed. 'I'm convinced that picture's significant, though. It was the only thing my grandmother kept to remind her of France, and it was always hung in her bedroom.' She hesitated. 'I'll ask my husband to send it to me once I'm settled.'

She and Kevin had texted a few times: business-like messages about cancelling the kitchen renovation, missing paperwork, the plumber's phone number, and that sort of thing. She didn't know whether he would make the effort to send her Mémé's painting, but it was worth a try.

Thérèse looked at her kindly. 'So is this a permanent separation? Forgive me, you don't have to answer that question.'

'I'm not sure.' Juliette topped up their glasses to give herself time to think. 'For the moment, this just seems like the right place for me to be – this city, this square, this apartment. It probably sounds crazy but I feel like I've been led here for a reason.'

'Not crazy at all.' Thérèse clinked glasses. 'If nothing else, I'm glad we've met. And you must definitely talk to Zizi, I think you'll find her fascinating.'

Nico called around early the next morning, bringing Delphine with him. She was wearing a cashmere coat and a pair of sky-high heels, while the sight of Nico in a suit and open-necked shirt was enough to stir up all sorts of unwelcome feelings. Juliette felt at a distinct disadvantage in rubber gloves and her hair tied back with a scarf.

'You have been working hard,' Delphine said, glancing around the apartment. 'Well done.'

'My grandmother's happy to see you at four tomorrow afternoon,' Nico said. 'We're off to Deauville for the weekend so I can't be there, I'm afraid, but she doesn't bite. I'll text you the address.'

'Thanks so much. I'd love to talk to her,' Juliette said. 'I've found something she might like to see.' She took off her gloves and passed him the worn, leather-bound album she'd discovered the night before, pushed under the chaise-longue. 'It's full of photos from the 1930s and 40s.'

'I haven't seen this for years.' Nico leafed through a couple of pages.

'It's private, though.' Delphine was leaning against the doorframe, her hands in her pockets. 'You might have asked permission before looking at somebody else's family photographs.'

Juliette felt herself blushing. 'I'm sorry, I should have thought. I don't know any of those people, you see, so I thought it would be all right.'

Delphine ignored her apology. '*Chéri*, we have to go,' she told Nico. 'We're late already.'

'Another time, perhaps.' Nico closed the album and gave it back to Juliette.

'Sure. But just one other thing,' she said, ignoring Delphine's glare. 'What shall I call your grandmother?'

'Zizi,' he called over his shoulder. 'Everyone does!'

They could have waited five minutes before rushing off, surely. Juliette had wanted to ask Nico about the photo that had leapt out at her: a shot of the store below, but freshly painted and with the windows filled with books. The sign above the door read '*La Page Cachée*', and a glorious man was sitting on the step, stroking a tabby cat that could have been Cocotte. He had thick, dark hair falling over a pair of horn-rimmed glasses, sculpted cheekbones and the most wonderful smile; you couldn't look at him without feeling happy. Juliette had stared at the picture for ages, and then she'd found the photo of Mémé's painting on her phone. She located the bookstore easily, now she knew where to look for it, and she could decipher the faint squiggles of paint that had suggested the sign. A bookstore! How perfect.

Grabbing her coat, she ran downstairs to take another look through the shop windows before heading to Batignolles to meet Ilse. Browsing in the local bookstore had been her weekend treat when she was young; Suzanne had taken her first and then she went alone with her pocket money and later, earnings from a paper round. All this time alone in Paris had rekindled her love of books. Reading on a tablet just wasn't the same; she had to hold a physical copy, smell the pages, look at the cover, flick back to a passage she wanted to remember or hadn't understood. Bookstores and libraries were her spiritual home, so quiet and calm and full of knowledge – and now here was the ghost of a bookstore on her doorstep.

Ilse was waiting for her outside the Métro station in wide-legged linen pants and a leather jacket. Everyone in Paris looked so chic; Juliette would have to make more of an effort herself. She was tired of wearing the same clothes day after day, and the vacation wardrobe she'd chosen so carefully back home now felt middle-aged and frumpy.

Still, Ilse seemed pleased to see her, even in jeans and a sweater. 'And how is everything going?' she asked, kissing Juliette on both cheeks. 'Settling in?'

There was so much to talk about, they decided to have coffee before exploring the market. They found a pavement café near the entrance to the market and took a couple of seats outside to chat and watch the passers-by. Juliette told Ilse all about the apartment, including the dolls, and the plans she had for painting everything white if Nico would let her. 'He doesn't seem to mind what I do, amazingly enough.'

'You're lucky,' Ilse said. 'Apartments in Paris are hard to find, and this one sounds a gem. Especially with a landlord who'll let you decorate.'

'You'll have to come and see it sometime soon. I'd appreciate your advice.'

Ilse smiled. 'I was hoping you'd say that. I love nosing around other people's homes.'

'So tell me about yourself,' Juliette said, leaning back in the sunshine. 'How long have you lived in Paris? And how did you meet Claude?'

'I came to study here from Germany forty years ago and never went back,' Ilse replied. 'Claude was my lecturer and I fell in love with him at first sight. A *coup de foudre*, as they say. I knew he wouldn't have anything to do with me while I was his student but we kept in touch after

I graduated and eventually, he couldn't resist me any longer. I knew what I wanted.'

'Did you?' Juliette sighed. 'Wish I could say the same.'

'Want to talk about it?'

'Oh, I don't want to bore you. My husband and I are having a few problems, that's all, and it's not been long since my mother died. I'm taking some time to sort my head out.' She laughed. 'Listen to me. That's the kind of thing my kids come out with, and I'm forty-seven.'

'Forty-seven is nothing.' Ilse looked at Juliette with her head on one side. 'You have plenty of time to try all sorts of things. Imagine yourself in a year's time. Where are you and what are you doing? Don't think too hard, just tell me the first thing that comes into your head.'

Juliette closed her eyes. 'I'm here, in Paris, living in my apartment in the Place Dorée and running a book-store,' she heard herself say.

'There you are, then.' Ilse was smiling again. 'That wasn't so difficult, was it?'

Chapter Eight

December 1940

'Jacques, I have something to tell you.' Mathilde tipped the carrots she'd been chopping into a pan of water on the stove and turned to face him.

'What is it?' he asked, alarmed by her expression.

'I've lost my job, I'm afraid.' She came to sit opposite him at the table. 'Most of us have been sacked, apart from a couple of toadies to take orders from Vichy. We've been told not to come back in the new year.'

Jacques felt a surge of relief. 'Don't worry.' He patted her hand. 'We'll manage. Things might be tight for a while but maybe it'll be good for you to have a break from the museum.'

'But I love working there,' she said, 'or rather, I used to. You know how much it meant to me. What am I going to do now? I can't stay at home all day with those two.' She nodded towards Maman's bedroom. 'It'll drive me mad.'

'Perhaps you could help me,' he suggested. 'It'd be lovely to have the company and you could take over our art section. The rare books are doing well, too.'

He'd already made a couple of trips to Isaacson's storage facility in the middle of the city, one of a number of rooms in a furniture warehouse, where almost a thousand valuable books were stored in locked cases. A caretaker who was sitting in an office by the front door asked him to sign in and out of the log book but, apart from that, nobody paid him much attention.

A pale, dark-haired girl of fifteen or so had come to *La Page Cachée* the previous week and said, 'My aunt is looking for a copy of *Les Fleurs du Mal*.' To which he'd replied, 'You're in luck. I have one left,' and slipped an envelope of cash into one of the shop's paper bags for her.

He'd wondered whether to tell Mathilde where all this fine stock had come from, but decided in the end it would be safer for her not to know. He wouldn't lie to her if she asked, but she never did, although he saw her looking at the display case curiously when it first appeared. They'd made a tacit agreement to trust each other.

'Serving in your shop means I'd have to be polite to the Boche, though, and I'm not sure I could manage that,' Mathilde said. 'Your pet German's always hanging around. Something about him makes my flesh creep. What's he after?'

'Books, for one thing. He's building up a private collection and he'll pay good money to add to it.'

'But the Nazis are looting libraries all over the place,' Mathilde said. 'You'd think he'd just take what he wanted.'

'He's keen to present himself as an honourable man,' Jacques told her. 'He seems to want my good opinion, for some reason. And I think he's lonely. It can't be easy, knowing everyone hates you.'

'With good reason.' She shuddered. 'Just keep him away from our apartment, that's all.'

That was another worry. 'What on earth are we going to do with the Englishwoman?' Jacques asked. SJ had been with them for a week and the strain was beginning to tell. 'I'm worried the concierge is going to spot her any minute.'

'Oh, Madame Bourdain's all right,' Mathilde said carelessly.

'Is she, though? I've been thinking, she told me she had to let those gendarmes into the building the other day, but she could have told them Madame SJ didn't live here anymore and sent them away. I don't trust her.'

'It's being taken care of,' Mathilde told him. 'I met up with Béatrice a few days ago.'

Jacques felt a shiver of disquiet. Béatrice Lemoine was a colleague of Mathilde's at the museum, an art lecturer who wrote for several radical magazines. She was a striking woman: tall and languid, with pale skin and cropped, white-blonde hair, who dressed in men's clothes and lived with her lover somewhere across the river on the Left Bank. Mathilde said Béatrice only got away with wearing trousers because people thought she was an unusually beautiful man.

Mathilde lowered her voice, even though they were alone. 'We're getting false papers drawn up so SJ can leave the occupied zone and go south. From Marseilles, she should be able to get a boat to Gibraltar and from there back to England.'

'And do you think she'd make it through the country?' he asked.

'Béatrice is looking for a *passeuse* to take her,' Mathilde replied, 'but we have to pick the right person and it's hard to know who to trust.'

His unease deepened. 'By the way,' she added, 'I found out what happened to those British women who were escorted to the Mairie.'

A chill ran down Jacques' spine. 'And?'

'They were kept all day without food – thousands of them, some pregnant, some elderly, some carrying babies in their arms – then driven to the Gare de l'Est and put on a train to Besançon. That's over four hundred kilometres away. They're being held there in military barracks, apparently.'

'For how long?'

Mathilde shrugged. 'For the rest of the war, I suppose, the poor creatures. There are three lavatories for the whole camp and the troops who'd been living there left it in a shocking state. So thank goodness SJ's safe with us. She mustn't risk going back to her apartment, that's for sure. It's just as well she eats like a sparrow.' And with that she got up to carry on cooking their meagre supper.

They made love silently that night, ignoring both Maman and the Englishwoman next door. Jacques held Mathilde in his arms afterwards, filled with tenderness. She hardly ever complained, despite having to cook and care for his mother, who could be difficult, and queue for hours outside shops in the freezing cold.

'I'm sorry about your job,' he whispered. 'I know how much it meant to you.'

She sighed. 'Oh, well. There are plenty of people worse off than me. But we've been doing important work, Jacques, and who's going to continue it?'

'I've been thinking,' he said, after a pause. 'Now you're no longer at the museum, maybe it's time you went to stay with Pierre and Renée.'

Mathilde's cousin in the south had invited them to come whenever they wanted. Jacques had his doubts about Pierre: a wiry, intense young man with an argumentative streak, prone to outbursts about everything from the state of the roads to corruption in the Catholic church. He'd been a member of the communist party before it was banned at the start of the war, and was still politically engaged. The only consolation was that Pierre's wife, Renée, was so patient and long-suffering as to be virtually a saint. She could be relied upon to calm him down. It would be warmer in Provence, with more food and fewer Nazis. If – when – Jacques' mother died, they had considered moving there, should life become intolerable in Paris.

Mathilde lifted her head from his chest. 'And leave you to cope with Maman and *l'Anglaise* by yourself?'

'I could talk to Béatrice about SJ,' he said. 'You don't have to be the one she deals with. And Sylvie's always offering to sit with Maman.'

'You know why that is.' There was a smile in Mathilde's voice. 'She'll spend more time mooning over you than looking after your mother.'

Sylvie was the sixteen-year-old daughter of their upstairs neighbour who blushed whenever she saw

Jacques and was constantly inventing excuses to drop by the apartment or his shop.

'You must think of yourself for once,' he said. 'I hate to see you looking so tired and anxious. You could rest in Avignon, get some colour in your cheeks, and I'll join you when . . . when I can.'

'We'll see,' she replied. 'Let's get the Englishwoman off our hands and then we can think about the future. I'm meeting Béatrice tomorrow to see if there's been any progress.'

She turned over and fell asleep almost immediately, but Jacques lay awake for hours, worrying about the future.

'I'm not hungry.' Madame Duval pushed a spoonful of beans around her plate. 'This dish tastes strange. Is it meant to be cassoulet?'

Ah, cassoulet! Jacques could smell the gravy now, rich with pork rind and goose fat, taste the chunks of garlic sausage, meltingly tender confit duck legs and creamy haricot beans soaking up all the wonderful flavour. He looked down at the bowl of gruel in front of him, a few cubes of carrot floating disconsolately among the beans in a watery vegetable stock, flavoured with a ham bone that had been boiled several times before.

'Try to drink some of the broth,' he told his mother. 'You must keep your strength up.' She seemed to be shrinking by the day, and he even found himself missing her acerbic comments now she no longer had the energy to make them.

His mother sighed and laid down her spoon. 'I'm going back to bed. Where's Mathilde?'

'She's meeting a friend from work.' He was beginning to worry; Mathilde should have been home hours ago.

He helped his mother to her room, where SJ was waiting. The Englishwoman took her meals there, not wanting to risk being seen in the kitchen. She wasn't much trouble really, yet she was somehow always in the way, and her constant apologising was becoming a trial.

'Delicious soup,' she said, giving him her empty bowl. 'I'm so lucky, being waited on hand and foot! Now shall I read to you, Madame Duval?'

On Jacques' recommendation they had just started *My Mother's House,* by Colette, which was proving a great success. He would sometimes wake in the small hours to the murmur of SJ's voice on the other side of the wall and let her lull him back to sleep. When they were done with Colette, he thought a little Montaigne might be in order, to encourage a philosophical state of mind, or maybe some Chekhov short stories.

He washed the supper dishes and dried them, then sat by the stove with a book of his own: *Le Grand Meaulnes*, which he had once thought the most perfect novel ever written. But reading was no longer a comfort; he couldn't lose himself in a book these days. He glanced at the clock for the hundredth time. What could have happened? Mathilde had been due to see Béatrice at four, and now it was getting on for ten. He didn't know where they'd arranged to meet, or even where Béatrice lived, so there'd be no point going out to find her. Sighing, he went downstairs to fetch his account book from the shop and go through some overdue invoices in the warm.

'Ah, Monsieur Duval.' Madame Bourdain waylaid him on the stairs. Damn the woman, she could smell him coming. 'Is Madame still not home? She'd better get in before the curfew or there'll be trouble. Don't worry, they've probably just closed the Métro. Travelling is a nightmare these days.'

'I'm sure she'll be back soon,' he replied, through gritted teeth.

'Any sign of the English lady?' the concierge asked. 'I've taken in a parcel for her.'

'Better hang on to it,' he called, hurrying past. 'You never know, she might turn up one day.'

He'd been back upstairs for half an hour or so, making a futile attempt to concentrate on his ledger, when someone knocked on the front door.

Herr Schmidt was standing on the step, with Madame Bourdain hovering behind.

'Forgive me for troubling you at home, Monsieur Duval,' he said. 'May I come in?'

'I do hope nothing's wrong,' the concierge called, craning to look down the hall inside the apartment.

'Of course.' Jacques stood back for Schmidt to enter, realising too late that he should have knocked a warning on his mother's bedroom door. He shut the front door as quickly as possible, saying, 'Good night, Madame,' to the concierge.

Schmidt walked down the hall. 'Do you have company?' he asked, stopping outside Maman's room. 'I heard a voice.'

'My mother is ill,' Jacques replied, as calmly as he could manage. 'She's very devout and prays aloud.'

Schmidt looked at him, then smiled. 'My mother is ailing and her mind wanders, too. You have my sympathy.'

'Come into the kitchen,' Jacques said. 'It's the warmest spot in our apartment.'

He followed Schmidt into the room, his heart hammering. What would he see? Three plates draining on the rack, three glasses in the sink, his accounts ledger open on the floor.

'How pleasant to sit in someone's home. My hotel is luxurious, yet it has no charm.' Schmidt took off his cap and sat down at the table, crossing one booted leg over the other. He took off his gloves and rubbed his hands. 'The air is still bracing, though. I hope your mother is warmly wrapped.'

'May I offer you a drink?' Jacques fetched the brandy and a couple of glasses from the dresser, splitting the last precious inches of alcohol between them.

'*Santé!*' Schmidt raised the glass with his usual ironic, amused expression. 'I see your wife is not at home.'

Jacques swallowed. 'She went out shopping earlier and seems to have been delayed. I'm sure she'll be back soon.'

Schmidt lit a cigarette, offering the packet to Jacques, who shook his head. 'In fact, I've come to bring you news of her,' he said, blowing out a long plume of smoke. 'She's been detained, I'm afraid.'

'Detained?' Jacques jumped up. 'Where? And for what reason?'

'Sit down, my friend. She's in police custody and you won't be able to see her. I wanted to set your mind at rest, that's all.'

'That's very good of you.' Jacques let out his breath. 'But do you know why she's been arrested?'

'Not arrested so far,' Schmidt replied. 'However, it's a relatively minor matter and she'll probably be released in due course, as long as she behaves herself. She was found with one of those anti-German leaflets in her basket. You know the sort of thing, filled with the lies some women are silly enough to believe.'

'Oh, dear,' Jacques said. 'I had no idea she looked at anything like that.'

'I believe you.' Schmidt looked at him gravely. 'I think you have enough sense to stay out of trouble, unlike your wife. But a word of warning: some of my colleagues may pay you a visit, now that she has come to their attention.' He glanced at the accounts book. 'You might want to put your paperwork in order. You and I have a sound business relationship, and I should like it to continue.'

'Of course. I quite understand.'

'Good fellow.' Schmidt reached for his hat. 'I shall put in a good word for her, should the opportunity arise.'

'Thank you,' Jacques said. 'I'm most grateful.'

He showed the German out, then stood for a moment with his back against the door, his head spinning. He'd kept no written record of his transactions with Isaacson and didn't imagine the Gestapo would go through his accounts in any detail, but he'd have to move the Englishwoman out of their apartment without delay. Only once she was hidden somewhere else could he begin to think about Mathilde.

★   ★   ★

116

It was another night without much sleep. The next morning, Jacques was checking a recent order of books when he was startled to find Béatrice standing in front of him, wearing a double-breasted overcoat and a tweed cap.

The shop was empty so they could speak freely. 'I didn't hear the bell,' Jacques said. 'Do you know Mathilde's been detained? A policeman came to tell me last night. Apparently she was found with some incriminating leaflet.'

'Yes, and thank goodness that was all,' Béatrice said in her gravelly voice. 'I was about to give her this forged identity card.' She brought out an envelope from her breast pocket. 'The Englishwoman might as well have it now. Where is she?'

'In a safe place, for the time being. I'll pass the papers on.' He still wasn't entirely sure whether to trust this strange woman. 'We need to move her quickly, though. The Gestapo might be coming here any minute.'

'It's not as easy as all that,' Béatrice replied. 'We're having trouble finding someone to take her.'

Jacques rubbed his forehead. 'Do you have any news of Mathilde? Do you know how she is? The policeman who came to see me said they probably wouldn't hold her for long.'

Béatrice shrugged. 'Who knows? They can do what they like.'

Thank you for that, Jacques thought, with a flash of irritation.

'Someone has seen your wife and she's in good spirits,' Béatrice went on. 'We shall have to communicate with you while she's away. Is your shop being watched?'

'Not that I know of,' he replied. 'Although as I told you, the Gestapo—'

'Yes, you said.' Béatrice waved her hand. 'Then I'll be careful. By the way,' she added, 'we refer to each other by code names. Mathilde is Colette and I'm George Sand. You'd better pick a writer if you're going to play a part in this.'

Jacques thought for a moment. 'Alain Fournier, then.'

'Good. And the Englishwoman can be Emily Brontë.' Béatrice turned to leave. 'I'll send you a message as soon as I can.'

'Please hurry,' Jacques called after her. 'I'm not at all comfortable with this situation.'

He was distracted for the rest of the morning, giving the wrong change to a woman buying a diary for the coming year and duplicating an order of exercise books. At lunchtime, he locked the door, pulled down the blind and turned the sign to 'Closed'. Then he removed a couple of books from the new run of shelving, knocked three times on the wood behind and swung open the concealed door.

Madame SJ was sitting on the mattress he'd brought down the night before, her back against the wall and a bundle of wool in her lap. 'Morning, Jacques,' she whispered, giving him a toothy grin. 'Everything all right?'

'So far, so good.' He crouched down beside her. 'Did you get any sleep?'

'Oh yes, plenty. I listened to the BBC very quietly, as you told me. It was absolutely marvellous! The sound of home. And I'm learning how to knit without a sound. Don't you fret about me.'

'Well, your new identity has arrived.' He gave her the envelope.

'How exciting!' She took it out of the envelope with trembling fingers. 'Clementine Thonat, very glamorous. And the card looks most authentic.'

'And your code name is Emily Brontë,' Jacques told her. 'Béatrice came up with it. I suppose that's how we'll refer to you in messages.'

'This is like something out of a spy novel,' she said, with a nervous laugh. 'But how appropriate. I know *Wuthering Heights* almost by heart.'

'The whole thing seems extraordinary.' Jacques looked around the room. Along with the mattress and wireless, he'd provided a basin and jug of water, plus some soap and a towel, and a tray with a plate, glass and knife for the baguette and half sausage from their rations. At night, a candle stuck in a wine bottle could be lit with matches when strictly necessary. Conditions were hardly luxurious; the tiny window had to be open for some ventilation and the place was freezing cold. He told SJ she could borrow Maman's coat, but she wouldn't hear of it.

'I'm causing you enough trouble as it is. What a nuisance I am! Who's looking after your mother now?'

'Our neighbour's daughter, Sylvie, is sitting with her,' he said. 'It won't be for much longer, Madame. We're just looking for someone to accompany you.'

'Don't worry about that,' she said. 'I shall be fine on my own.' Yet her eyes told a different story and her fingernails, he noticed, had been bitten to the quick.

'It will be safer for you to go with a guide.' He squeezed her arm. 'I'll see you tonight. Don't give up.'

She glanced at a lidded bucket in the corner that served as a chamber pot, blushing furiously.

'Shall I empty that?' he asked, getting to his feet.

'I'm so sorry about all this,' she said, avoiding his gaze. 'How can I ever repay you and your wife for your kindness?'

'You would do the same for us, I'm sure.'

He summoned up the most convincing smile possible under the circumstances. He was fond of Madame SJ and glad they'd saved her from the camp at Besançon, but he hadn't counted on having to keep her for so long, and now without Mathilde's support. The risks they'd taken so far seemed manageable but he seemed to have been bounced into a game with much higher stakes. The penalty for hiding an enemy of the Reich was death.

Chapter Nine

That afternoon, a regular customer appeared in *La Page Cachée*. 'My aunt is looking for a copy of *Les Fleurs du Mal*,' said the dark-haired girl on the other side of the counter.

'You're in luck, we have one copy left.'

Jacques reached under the counter for the cash box in which he kept Isaacson's money. He and Miryam, Isaacson's daughter, had met several times by now but they still repeated the agreed phrases; one day someone else might come in her place and it was wise to keep up the habit. He slipped the bulging envelope of cash into a bag and handed it over. Word had spread and the rare books market was booming: he had several regular German customers and one or two Parisian collectors whom he telephoned whenever he brought over a new consignment of stock from the warehouse.

'How is your father?' he asked Miryam, since the shop was empty.

She glanced over her shoulder. 'Not well. My mother has been having trouble with her nerves and everyone is suffering. We're trying to get visas for America but it seems we may have left it too late. The more books you can sell, the better.'

'I'll do my best,' he replied. 'I don't want to arouse suspicion, though. My customers are greedy but they'll start asking questions if I bring in too much stock at once.'

She nodded. 'The money is a lifeline. Thank you.'

'For me, too.' Yet Jacques was only taking a minimum in commission, just enough to cover the costs of his journeys to and from the warehouse. Sometimes the collectors bought modern books or stationery too, he reasoned, and Isaacson needed the money more than he did. Herr Schmidt might have guessed these fine books had once belonged to a Jew but assumed Jacques had stolen them or bought them at a knockdown price, so he felt safe enough.

Just as Miryam was leaving, Guillaume Bruyère appeared. His presence made Jacques uneasy, although neither of them ever referred to the banned book, *Beware of Pity,* that he had sold the writer. Bruyère spent some time browsing the shelves before selecting a copy of the epic poem *Beowulf,* and a volume of heroic legends.

'So have you finished your novel, Monsieur?' Jacques asked, giving the man his change. Bruyère looked better than he had for months; almost normal, in fact. His clothes were reasonably clean and his hair had been brushed.

'Oh, I've abandoned that old ragbag,' Bruyère replied. 'Couldn't make it work. No, I've embarked on a new project. I can't say much about it, only that my hero is a young German soldier in Paris and it's the best thing I've ever written. You'll hear about it in due course, Monsieur Duval, of that I'm sure.' He smiled with satisfaction. 'I shall let you know the publication date.'

But Jacques was no longer listening. A man and a woman had just walked through the door. The man was Kriminalassistent Schmidt, and the woman was Mathilde. Jacques took hold of the counter to steady himself.

'Monsieur Duval.' Schmidt lifted his hat. 'I have brought you a special delivery.'

'So I see.' Jacques was about to embrace his wife when he remembered he ought to be cross with her. 'And what have you got to say for yourself?' he asked Mathilde. 'I couldn't believe it when Herr Schmidt told me why you'd been detained.'

She was about to give him a dusty answer, he could tell from her expression, before she stopped herself. 'I'm sorry, *chéri*, it was a moment of madness. I won't be so foolish again.'

Schmidt smiled. 'You'll need a conversation, I'm sure. But we must also talk, the three of us.' He looked around. 'Is there somewhere private?'

'Come upstairs,' Jacques said hastily. 'I'll take an early break for lunch.'

He saw Bruyère out, locked the front door and led Schmidt through the back way up to their apartment, smiling at Mathilde behind the German's back. She looked fine, as far as he could tell; a little pale and tired, but that might have been down to a lack of make-up. Always elegant, she hated to be seen without powder and lipstick.

123

'How is Maman?' she asked quietly, once they were inside. 'I've been so worried.'

'Not good,' he replied. 'We may have to call the doctor again, though I'm not sure how much he can do.'

'You talk to Herr Schmidt first,' Mathilde said, knocking on the door to Madame Duval's bedroom. 'I'll see you in a minute.'

The two men went through to the kitchen. 'Would you like a coffee?' Jacques asked, filling the kettle.

'No, thank you,' Schmidt replied, throwing his hat on the table but keeping his coat on. 'What a very modern couple you are. Madame Duval has a job, or she used to, and you are at home in the kitchen.' He pulled out a chair and lit a cigarette, crossing his legs. 'And have any of my colleagues paid you a visit?'

'Not so far. Thank you for bringing my wife home, Herr Schmidt. I'm most grateful.'

'She needs to be careful. This sort of low-level aggravation can lead to more serious offences and I won't be able to help her a second time. She has some dubious acquaintances – that museum was a haven for hotheads and radicals. Perhaps it's just as well she no longer works there.'

They heard a cough from the doorway, where Mathilde was standing with her arms folded.

'Ah, Madame, there you are.' Schmidt's eyes were cold. 'Shall I put our proposal to your husband?'

'Please do,' she said, inclining her head.

'Very well.' He turned to Jacques. 'Your wife tells me she has relatives in Provence. In our opinion, she should go there without delay. I have arranged an *Ausweis* for

124

her to leave the occupied zone and travel south.' He reached into his breast pocket and took out a folded card, stamped with an eagle holding a swastika in its talons. 'This is valid for one day. There's a train that will take you to Tournon at six tomorrow morning. Make sure to arrive in good time, at least two hours before it's due to leave.'

'So soon?' Jacques was startled.

'Get her out of the city,' Schmidt told him. 'There's no place here for troublemakers.' He stubbed out the cigarette and picked up his hat. 'And now I shall leave you in peace. No doubt you'll have plenty to discuss.'

Jacques showed him to the door, then rushed back to Mathilde. 'Thank God you're home,' he said, taking her in his arms. 'Are you all right? How did they treat you?'

'Not too badly,' she said, hugging him back. 'It was only a leaflet, for heaven's sake! They might have got nasty but your friend poked his head around the door and the next thing I knew, they'd come up with the idea of letting me go if I agreed to leave Paris.'

They sat together in the *salon*. 'Why is this man getting involved, Jacques?' she asked. 'What's his game? Do you think he wants you all to himself?'

He shuddered. 'I hope not. Listen, he hasn't ordered you to go. You don't have to.'

'That's true, but I've been thinking things over and leaving might be for the best. I shall end up in trouble if I stay here, we both know that. And now I can take Madame SJ with me – she can make it down to Marseilles along the river. It's perfect timing! Where have you put her? Down in the storeroom?'

Jacques nodded, his head whirling. 'Her code name is Emily Brontë, by the way.'

'I'll say she's my aunt from Alsace, to explain her accent,' Mathilde went on. 'I'm completely legitimate, thanks to our friendly Nazi. But it means leaving you here to care for Maman by yourself.'

They looked at each other for a moment without speaking. Jacques was first to break the silence. 'Sylvie will help me. She's been wonderful while you were away. And I can come south to join you, when – when I'm free.'

It would mean leaving the shop but he could start again in the south; he'd sweep the streets if he had to. Mathilde meant more to him than anything else. They were hoping to start a family when the war was over, and he could imagine no greater joy than seeing her with a brood of children. Four or five, if possible, with dark, curly hair and mobile, passionate faces like hers.

'I shall miss you terribly but it won't be forever,' she replied, squeezing his hands. 'And now I must send a telegram to Pierre and start packing.'

The rest of the day passed in a blur. Jacques was becalmed, watching his wife in a daze while she sorted clothes and gave him instructions about cooking and shopping. 'You'll have to pay Sylvie for her time,' she said. 'We don't want to take advantage of the poor girl.'

He opened up the shop that afternoon, glad of some distraction, and in the evening Mathilde cooked *confit* duck from a jar she'd been saving for a special occasion, which no one had the appetite to eat.

'I don't understand why you have to go,' Madame

Duval said, laying her knife and fork together. 'When will you be back?'

'Soon, I'm sure,' Mathilde promised. 'In the spring, or perhaps the summer.'

She was biting her lip in an effort not to cry, and there were tears in Maman's eyes, too. Madame Duval had been jealous of Jacques' new wife at first – he was an only child whose father had been killed in the last war when Jacques was four, so it had been just the two of them for years – but Mathilde had gradually won her over.

'Come, let me settle you into bed,' she said, taking the old lady's arm. 'You must look after yourself while I'm away, you hear?'

'Nag, nag, nag,' Maman grumbled. 'We shall be glad of the rest, won't we, Jacques?'

When Mathilde emerged from his mother's bedroom, her eyes were red and swollen. 'Come here,' he said, taking her in his arms and rubbing her back. 'You're right, it's for the best. Everything will be all right, I promise.'

'I'd better clear up and then try to get some sleep.' She broke away from him to blow her nose. 'We'll have to be at the station by four to be sure of getting that train.'

Jacques looked at the clock. 'There's another couple of hours till the curfew. Put on your coat and let's go for a walk.'

They made their way by torchlight through the deserted streets towards Montmartre, avoiding the inevitable patrols as best they could. At one point, they heard gunfire in the distance, and Jacques hugged Mathilde closer. There was little point climbing the steps to Sacré Coeur for the view but they took them anyway, matching their paces. At least they could feel free, standing on the terrace in pitch darkness with the wind in their faces and their hearts too full for words.

'We'd better go, I suppose,' Mathilde said at last. 'No point getting picked up now.' She switched on the torch.

'Wait,' Jacques said. 'I have to ask, what if you move for some reason, or I have to leave Paris, and we can't keep in contact with each other? How will I know where to find you?' It was his worst fear: that she might disappear without trace and he'd spend the rest of his life searching for her, not knowing what had happened.

'Let's make a pact,' she said. 'If the worse comes to the worst and we lose touch, we'll try to meet here – each year, if we possibly can, at a particular date and time.'

'Yes, let's do that. On our wedding anniversary, say, at six in the evening?' He searched her face, looking for reassurance. 'Six o'clock, 3 September. I'll be waiting for you.'

'And if either of us can't make it, we'll try to send a message somehow.'

They hurried home then, slipped into their icy bed and made love for the last time.

'We'll be together by spring, I'm sure,' Jacques said afterwards, stroking Mathilde's back. 'Imagine summer in Provence, with the sun beating down on lavender fields and a bottle of rosé chilling in the stream. We'll swim in the sea and eat peaches soaked in brandy, and none of these damn Germans will bother us.'

★ ★ ★

He lay awake for much of the night and he could tell from Mathilde's restlessness that she couldn't sleep either. It was almost a relief when she gave up the pretence and slipped out of bed to dress by candlelight. He watched her deft movements as she moved quietly around the room, bracing himself for the moment they'd have to part. At last she came to sit beside him on the bed.

'Are you sure I can't come with you and SJ to the station?' he asked, reaching for his glasses.

'Positive. We'll be safer on our own.' She took his hand, smoothing his skin with her thumb. 'Jacques, would you do something for me? I've been feeling guilty for parting on such bad terms with Estelle. Would you keep an eye on her for me, and tell her I'm sorry? She's my dearest friend and I haven't even been able to say goodbye.'

'Of course.' He kissed her hand. 'I'll drop by whenever I can.'

'Thank you.' She took a deep breath. 'We've run out of time but you know how much you mean to me, don't you? I was lost until I found you, standing there with a book in your hand and smiling at me as though we'd known each other for years. We recognised each other straight away, didn't we? I fell in love with you before you'd even said a word. You were my fixed point from that moment on, the centre of my world, and you always will be.'

Jacques swallowed the lump in his throat and tried to speak, but she stopped him with a kiss. 'Everything I am is down to you. Your spirit gives me the courage to hope and dream and fight for what's right. One day our children will grow up in a free country, we have to believe that, and they will be able to act and think as they please.

129

Don't be afraid, *chéri*. Death is coming for all of us, sooner or later. It's how we live that matters.' She gave a shaky laugh. 'Well, that's enough of a speech. Madame SJ will be waiting for me downstairs.'

'Don't leave,' he wanted to tell her. 'Stay in Paris, we'll work things out somehow.' Yet she was counting on him to be brave too, and he couldn't let her down. They kissed briefly, clumsily, and then she was gone.

The dark, lonely days passed. Handwritten letters between the zones were banned but Jacques sent Mathilde one of the pre-printed cards with blanks left to complete, saying he was 'well' (he could have chosen 'very well', which seemed overly effusive, or 'fairly well', which might have alarmed her), and received one from her in return, saying she had received this exciting missive and was also well. The weather in Paris became colder still; blocks of ice floated in the Seine and fuel was hard to find. Snow fell and children slid on tea trays down the hills in Montmartre. On 23 December, Jacques Bonsergent was executed by firing squad. *La Page Cachée* stood virtually empty. The few customers who came made their purchases hurriedly and left the shop without chatting. It was hard to tell what anyone was thinking and any comment could be dangerous.

'An unfortunate business,' Schmidt said, arriving to buy Christmas presents for his friends and family. 'Most regrettable. I see you've had a new consignment of stock, Monsieur Duval.'

'Including some books that I haven't had time to put out for sale.' Jacques reached under the counter for a wooden crate. 'As a valued customer, would you like first look, Herr Schmidt?'

He'd slipped into the role of obsequious shopkeeper, slightly dim but willing to help, and Schmidt seemed to take him at face value. He only once asked after Mathilde, whose safe arrival Jacques reported, yet he took a keen interest in any other customers who happened to be in the shop. It was a great relief to Jacques that Madame SJ was no longer languishing in the storeroom – the banned books were incriminating enough, but at least they couldn't make any noise.

He went to church early on Christmas morning. Overnight, flowers had been pinned to the posters announcing Bonsergent's death, both real and artificial: hellebores and winter-flowering jasmine, paper pansies and silk roses, with tiny French and British flags among them. Parisians everywhere were mourning this ordinary, extraordinary man who would not bow his head to the Nazis. Jacques was overcome with emotion at the sight of these shrines, anger sharpening his grief.

'These are hard times,' Madame Bourdain said, leaning on her broom to watch him pass. 'Have you heard any more from your wife, Monsieur Duval? I'm sure she'll write again soon.' For all that was worth.

To distract himself, Jacques spent hours reading out loud to his mother. He remembered lying wide-eyed in the half dark as a child while she read him the stories of Hansel and Gretel, Rapunzel, Little Red Riding Hood and so many others. Sometimes she would make up tales of her own about a boy called Jean, who set sail across the ocean to find his fortune. Jacques liked those adventures best of all, imagining himself as the brave lad who leapt aboard a pirate ship with a knife clenched between his teeth, or fought off a sea serpent with his bare hands.

Colette was his mother's favourite author. When he read from *My Mother's House*, he could see her picturing herself as the earthy peasant woman who drew water from the well, milked goats, collected eggs from the chickens and sawed logs. In reality, his mother had never done anything so strenuous, having a hearty dislike of the great outdoors and manual labour. The countryside was full of dangers: cows that might trample a person to death or rivers one might fall into and drown; even wasps with their savage stings were a force to be reckoned with. Yet she listened with a faraway gaze as Sido collected honey from her hives and butchered animal carcasses.

Jacques let his mother have her fantasy. She might have been over-protective but he'd never doubted for a moment that she loved him, with an intensity that often felt like a burden too heavy for him to carry alone. He was glad they'd been able to spend some time together, that he'd been able to repay a fraction of the debt he owed her. She was hardly eating now and spent most of her time in bed.

The new year arrived with little fanfare. Jacques paid Sylvie to sit with his mother and queue for their shopping, or mind the shop while he ran errands and collected Madame Duval's medication. He sensed her slipping away, although she seemed content.

The snow gradually melted and one day there were buds on the branches of trees in the Parc Monceau, and the green spears of bulbs pushing through the earth. Jacques closed all the windows in his apartment and listened to Radio Londres from the BBC. The Germans did their best to jam the airwaves with hoots and whistles but he could generally catch the gist by fiddling with the dials. Britain was still being bombed by the Luftwaffe but the RAF were shooting down their planes by the dozen and Hitler hadn't invaded the country yet. Rally around the V for victory sign, urged the French-language radio broadcasts, and Churchill was photographed sticking up two fingers. Chalked or painted Vs began appearing on walls all over Paris and Jacques' spirits lifted when he saw them: proof that other people were secretly tuning in to the forbidden programmes. The Nazis tried to make the symbol their own, putting up a huge V on the Palais Bourbon with a banner proclaiming *'Deutschland Siegt An Allen Fronten'* underneath, but no one was fooled. Germany wasn't winning on all fronts, not when Britain stood firm.

One afternoon in March, Sylvie came to fetch him, saying his mother's condition had changed and they should call the doctor. She was frightened, he could tell. He telephoned the doctor from the shop, then closed up and took the stairs two at a time. Maman was breathing in a way he hadn't heard before: harsh, rasping breaths with such long gaps in between that he was afraid she wouldn't take another.

'I'm here,' he said, smoothing the hair away from her forehead. He turned to Sylvie, hovering in the doorway. 'Thank you but we'll be fine. You can go now.'

His mother grabbed his hand and seemed about to

speak but no sound emerged. He began to pray out loud, the familiar words drifting back to him from childhood.

'*Notre Père, qui es aux cieux, que ton nom soit sanctifié.*'

Our Father, who art in heaven, hallowed be thy name.

Neither he nor his mother were regular churchgoers, but the sound of his voice was calming and gave them both a focus. Her grip on his fingers relaxed a little and she lifted her eyes to the ceiling, as though she were looking for someone.

'*Mon Père, je m'abandonne à toi, fais de moi ce qu'il te plaira. Je suis prêt à tout, j'accepte tout.*'

Father, I surrender myself to you, do with me what you will. I am ready for anything, I accept everything.

Somebody knocked on the front door and he hurried to answer it. Instead of the doctor, however, two men in civilian clothes stood there. They looked unremarkable, with bland, indifferent faces; one wore spectacles and the other did not. Both produced identity cards which they held out before him.

'Monsieur Duval? German police,' said the bespectacled man, who seemed to be the more senior. 'We need to ask you a few questions.'

'Not now, I'm afraid,' he said calmly. 'My mother is seriously ill.'

'Yes, now. This is an urgent matter. We cannot wait at your convenience.'

They forced their way in, one man taking hold of Jacques and frogmarching him down the hall while the other closed the door behind them.

'Is this really necessary?' Jacques protested. 'What am I supposed to have done?'

He received no reply. The bespectacled detective took him through to the *salon* and sat him down while the other man disappeared, presumably to search the apartment. From time to time, Jacques could hear the rustling of paper and the thump of furniture being moved as he was being questioned. His heart was thumping and he felt alternately hot and cold. Had the Gestapo found out about his arrangement with Isaacson? Had Bruyère blabbed about buying that wretched book? Had Béatrice betrayed them? The policeman seemed particularly interested in Mathilde, and Jacques was seized by a new fear that his wife was in trouble.

'Tell us about Pierre Bouchon,' the policeman said. He had receding sandy hair arranged in strands across his freckled scalp, and a soft, lisping voice. 'He is your wife's cousin, I believe?'

'I've only met him a handful of times,' Jacques replied. 'He's a car mechanic, runs a garage.'

'And he's a communist. Does Madame Duval share his views?'

'He's not a communist anymore, and besides, my wife isn't political. She never went to any rallies or meetings, not even before they were banned.' He strained to listen to any sound that might be coming from Maman's room. 'Please, will you let me go back to my mother? I have nothing to tell you and I've done nothing wrong. You can ask Werner Schmidt, he's been coming to my shop for months now. He'll vouch for me.'

Yet on and on the questions went. Had he ever been a member of the communist party? Did he associate with communists, Jews or homosexuals? Had he ever stocked books by Jewish authors? Was he a Catholic?

'None of these things,' he replied, over and over again. 'I run a bookshop, and that's all.'

The second policeman reappeared. His colleague glanced at him, raising his eyebrows, and he shook his head briefly.

'Then we had better take a look at this famous shop,' the senior detective said. 'Up you get, Monsieur.' He hauled Jacques out of the chair and bundled him towards the door.

'Please, my mother shouldn't be alone,' he implored. 'Will you at least let me ask someone to come and sit with her?'

The men ignored him, marching Jacques downstairs to the shop's back entrance. They were clearly familiar with the layout of the building; maybe Schmidt had briefed them. Jacques unlocked the door, sweating despite the cold.

'As you can see, just an ordinary bookshop,' he said, keeping his voice steady. An ordinary bookshop with an extraordinary storeroom, containing a crate of forbidden books and a mattress for stowaways.

He watched as the two men prowled from room to room. They swept books to the floor, overturned chairs and upended the cash register, sending coins spilling over the floor. The junior detective stopped directly in front of the shelves concealing the hidden storeroom entrance and rattled a swordstick along the top of them. Madame SJ would have been terrified.

The bespectacled man approached his display case, peering at the books inside.

Jacques stepped forward. 'I can unlock that, should you

wish. These are my first editions, in which Herr Schmidt is particularly interested.'

The policeman gave him a sardonic smile. 'Don't bother.' He spoke a few words of German to his colleague, then turned to Jacques. 'Thank you for your time, Monsieur Duval. Unlock the front door for us, would you?'

Jacques let the two men out, then ran through the mess that had been made of his shop and upstairs to their apartment. His mother's room was silent. The only sound he could hear was the wheezing of his own lungs as he made his way over to the bed. Maman lay still, her eyes wide open but seeing nothing. Gently he pressed them shut, then sank to his knees and wept. He had failed his mother when she needed him most. She had died alone and he would never forgive himself for that – or the Germans, either.

Chapter Ten

March 1941

The doctor arrived early the next morning, in time to certify Madame Duval's death. Jacques sat beside his mother's body, keeping her company until the undertaker came. He smoothed a lock of hair away from her waxen forehead, consoling himself with the thought she was free from pain at last. The fingers that had plucked so fretfully at her sheets were still, her eyes closed for eternity. She had shrunk from life rather than embracing it, but no one could blame her for that: her husband had been killed and she had tried to keep her only child safe in a dangerous world, teaching him to do as he was told and never step out of line.

Now she was dead and Mathilde didn't even know. The two most important women in his life were gone; he was hollowed out by loss. Mathilde should have been there beside him so they could comfort each other, as he had consoled her when her own parents had died within six months of each other. She had borne that loss so bravely and now they'd be apart when she received the printed card he'd have to send, with its bald statement of Maman's passing. The shock of her death had driven everything else from his mind, but suddenly the policeman's questions from the night before came back to him with ominous clarity. Had something happened to Mathilde? And why the interest in her cousin, Pierre?

When his mother's body had been collected, he sat for a while in her room, inhaling from his atomiser until his breathing eased. Then, rousing himself, he went downstairs to start putting the shop back to rights. Heartache gave way to resentment as he returned his books to their rightful place on the shelves, smoothing the pages as best he could. Nowhere was safe; the Gestapo could swoop in at any moment and there wasn't a single thing he could do about it. Someone was knocking on the shop door but he ignored them.

'We're closed,' he called as the knocking continued, yet even then it didn't stop.

Sighing, he got to his feet and picked his way through upended books to the door. Wrenching it open, he found a woman standing there, with a headscarf pulled low over her face, carrying a child on her hip.

'Renée?' He peered closer, unable to believe his eyes. 'What are you doing here?'

Her face was grey with fatigue, her eyes huge and frightened. She swayed for a moment and he reached forward to take the child out of her arms. 'Here, let me help you.' What was their son's name? Louis, that was it.

'Thank you,' she said in a low voice as he ushered her inside, locking the door quickly behind her.

'I had a visit from the Gestapo last night,' he said, to explain the mess, but she hardly seemed to notice. The little boy stared at him gravely and he smiled in a manner he hoped was reassuring. 'Shall we go upstairs?' he asked, but Renée shook her head.

'We need to talk first,' she said. 'I have bad news.'

His heart thumping, Jacques led the way through to the lower room, which at least was out of sight. He settled Louis on one of the floor cushions by the stove and lit the kindling, having a feeling comfort would be needed on this cold spring morning. As the fire crackled into life, the boy's eyelids drooped and he fell asleep almost immediately, resting his cheek on a grubby stuffed bunny with one ear missing. He was wearing shorts, and his skinny legs were blue with cold.

Jacques turned to Renée. 'Has something happened? The police were asking me questions about Pierre.'

She leant against the bookshelves, closing her eyes for a moment. He found a chair and helped her into it, kneeling beside her.

'Pierre's dead,' she said, her voice flat. 'He was sabotaging a railway line and the police shot him on the spot. Mathilde's been arrested but I don't know whether she was part of the plan, or what they have against her.'

'Oh, Renée,' he murmured. 'I'm so sorry.' The words were inadequate but what else could he do except say them?

She buried her face in her hands. 'I still can't believe it, even though I've seen his body. The police took me in for questioning but they left us unguarded for a minute and I managed to slip away. I grabbed Louis and we took the overnight train to Paris. We hid in the lavatory for most of the journey.'

'And Mathilde's still being held?' Jacques asked. 'Do you know where she is?'

'I'm not sure if she's still at the police station. They might have transferred her to a prison by now.' Renée bit her lip, looking at him anxiously. 'I'm sorry, Jacques. You probably think we should have kept her out of all this.'

'Of course not,' he said, putting an arm around her shoulder. 'Once my wife gets an idea in her head, there's no stopping her. I know that better than anyone.'

Renée gave a wan smile. 'She and Pierre are cut from the same cloth; I'm so proud of them both. Pierre gave his life so our children could grow up in a free world. I miss him desperately but he didn't die for nothing.' She blinked away her tears and added, 'Mathilde saved me, you know. She could have tried to escape too but she stayed behind, barricading the door so I had time get away.'

Jacques' heart swelled. He was longing to bombard Renée with questions about his wife but that would have to wait. 'You must be exhausted. Have you eaten anything?'

'I'm not hungry.' Renée took a folded sheet of paper from her handbag. 'Mathilde managed to write a note for you and slipped it to me. She'd told me to come here should anything happen to Pierre, but I don't want to put you in danger. The police will be searching for me everywhere by now.'

Dearest Jacques, Mathilde had written, *try not to worry about me. I'm in good spirits and will get through this. I know you'll look after Renée. Go to George Sand's house — the address is in the usual place — and ask her to help. In the meantime, Emily Brontë's old room might come in handy? Books are important to save but so are people. Everyone has a story to tell and what a great one ours will be when all this is over. Stay strong! All my love, forever M x*

'I have false papers but they won't stand up to much scrutiny,' Renée told him. 'We had to get away as soon as possible, but now what? I have no idea what to do.' She glanced at her sleeping son, her eyes filling with tears. 'Louis doesn't even know his father's dead — I can't bring myself to tell him.'

'Don't worry,' Jacques said, with more confidence than he felt. 'My apartment isn't safe but I have a hiding place where you and Louis can stay for a few days, and I'll contact people who will help you get to safety.'

'Thank you.' She squeezed his hand.

'Stay here for the moment while I make your room ready,' Jacques said, although it was hardly a suite at the Ritz. 'The shop door's locked so nobody should bother you. If anyone knocks, just ignore them and keep out of sight.'

He hurried upstairs to fetch blankets and an eiderdown from his mother's bed, and scratch together some food for his guests. The sight of Louis lying asleep on a cushion, so innocent and vulnerable, had touched him deeply. A sudden knock at the door made his heart jump in his chest, and he was even more alarmed to see Schmidt standing there when he opened it.

'I called at your shop but it appears to be closed,' the policeman said, walking into the apartment without waiting for an invitation.

'My mother passed away last night,' Jacques said, his fear for Renée and Louis giving way to anger. 'Your colleagues have no sense of occasion. They questioned me for some time while my mother was dying before turning my apartment and my premises upside down. As you can imagine, I have a certain amount of tidying up to do.'

'My condolences.' Schmidt took off his hat. 'And did they mention why they were paying you a visit?'

Jacques shook his head.

'I don't wish to add to your troubles,' Schmidt went on, watching him closely, 'but I have more bad news to impart. Your wife's cousin was killed by the police yesterday, and she has been arrested.'

'No! That's impossible.' Jacques took a step back, feigning shock. 'Mathilde arrested? What for?'

'Pierre Bouchon was sabotaging a railway line and she was picked up nearby. Acting as a lookout, most probably.'

'I don't believe it,' Jacques said. 'Mathilde would have nothing to do with a stunt like that.'

'Perhaps you don't know your wife quite as well as you think. She seems to have gone from bad to worse.' Schmidt glanced at the quilt and blankets, bundled up in the hall. 'Setting up camp somewhere, Monsieur Duval?'

'I'm taking my mother's bedlinen to the laundry,' Jacques replied. 'Is it really true, though, what you say? Where's Mathilde being held?'

'I don't know and besides, it's immaterial. You won't

be allowed to see her.' Schmidt put his hat back on. 'Well, I've told you what I came to say so I won't take up any more of your time. No doubt we shall find out more details in due course. A word of advice, though: I'd tread carefully from now on. My colleagues wanted to bring you in to the Avenue Foch for questioning but I've managed to persuade them, I think, that you aren't involved in your wife's activities.'

'Thank you,' Jacques said, as some response seemed required. 'That's very good of you.'

'I've become fond of your little shop,' Schmidt went on. 'I shouldn't like to see it closed down. We've had some interesting conversations and you know my literary tastes by now. My interest in Goethe, for example. I'm sure you'll carry on looking out for volumes I'd appreciate.'

'Of course.' Something was clearly expected of Jacques but he couldn't work out what.

'Good. We can be useful to each other. I've brought news of your wife and offered you some protection and in return, you are helping to build my library.'

'Indeed.' Jacques caught on at last. 'In fact, I have an early nineteenth-century almanac edited by Goethe, which may be of interest. Allow me to present it to you as a token of my gratitude.'

'Splendid.' Schmidt shook his hand with a smile. 'Thank you. And if any of your wife's former colleagues make contact, will you tell me straight away?' As Jacques nodded, Schmidt added casually, 'Do you happen to know a woman by the name of Béatrice Lemoine?'

'Vaguely,' Jacques replied. 'She's been to the shop once or twice.'

'Well, if she ever comes again, would you keep her here and call me at once on this number?' Schmidt gave him a card. 'Thank you, Jacques. I'm glad we understand each other.'

Jacques inclined his head. He should probably have called the man Werner in return, but he couldn't bring himself to go that far.

Madame Bourdain was hovering outside on the landing when Jacques emerged from his apartment ten minutes later. 'So your poor mother has died, God rest her soul.' She eyed the bedclothes. 'Clearing out already?'

'Just off to the laundry.' He made as if to push past the concierge, but she stood her ground. 'Monsieur Duval, I'll take her shoes off your hands if you like. Decent footwear's so hard to find these days and I should like to have some reminder of the dear lady. She and I were close, you know.'

'Really? I didn't realise.' Jacques had never seen his mother exchange more than a frosty greeting with the concierge, whom she considered several rungs below her, socially speaking.

'Oh, yes.' Madame Bourdain stuck to her guns. 'We had many conversations about the sorry state of the world. When she was still up and about, of course.'

'I'll have a look for some shoes,' Jacques promised, seeing that otherwise he would never been released.

'Thank you.' Madame Bourdain stood aside to let him pass. 'And let's hope you'll be left in peace for a while. It never rains but it pours, eh? There'll be no more visits from the police, I hope.'

'So do I,' Jacques called, hurrying down the stairs and through the back door into his shop. Louis was still asleep and didn't stir as his mother scooped him up.

'It's a fairly basic space,' Jacques explained, unlatching the secret door, 'but at least you should be secure.' He made up the mattress with sheets and gave Renée a blanket to wrap around her son before she laid him gently down and tucked the toy rabbit beside him. They gazed at the child and then smiled sadly at each other.

'And here's a little food.' Jacques laid half a baguette, a few slices of sausage and an apple on the crate. 'I'll bring you some more this evening.'

'We'll be fine,' Renée told him, 'and are so grateful for everything you're doing.'

'I have to go out now,' Jacques said, 'but I'll see you later. Oh, and here are a couple of books.' He'd brought *Histoire de Pierre Lapin* by Beatrix Potter for Renée to read to Louis and Hemingway's *Le Soleil Se Lève Aussi* for her.

'Perfect,' she said, smiling. 'What more could we want?'

Jacques took his bicycle from the hall and set off in search of Béatrice. He'd found her address in the book Mathilde kept in the bureau drawer; she lived in a street on the other side of the river, near the Luxembourg Gardens. The name beside the bell for Béatrice's apartment had been scratched out and when he rang it, a man's voice answered. Nonplussed, Jacques told him he was looking for George Sand, and was told to wait. After several minutes, he heard footsteps approaching on the other side of the door, which was opened by a man in his fifties who stared at him suspiciously.

'Who are you?' he asked.

'Alain Fournier,' Jacques replied tentatively. The stranger still looked doubtful so he added, 'I'm married to Colette.' The man nodded and told him George Sand had moved to an apartment near the Gare d'Austerlitz, a little further east.

Half an hour later, Jacques was standing on a different doorstep, ringing another bell and again announcing himself as Alain Fournier, to a woman this time. After a few minutes, she flung open a window a few storeys above to look him over before throwing down a key and telling him to come up to the third floor. She was waiting in an open doorway as he approached: a petite, plump girl with freckled cheeks and a mass of brown curls, bundled up in a coat and scarf.

'Come through,' she said, without introducing herself.

At first, he wondered whether he'd walked into a trap: the woman who rose to greet him had long dark hair and glasses, and wore an outfit that might have come from Madame Scott-Jones' wardrobe: a tweed skirt and woollen twinset. Béatrice's voice was unmistakeable, however.

'How did you find me?' she asked.

'I went to your old address and gave our code names,' he replied. 'Mathilde wrote and told me to come. Have you heard? She's been arrested.'

Béatrice sat down with a thump. 'How do you know? Tell me everything.'

Jacques glanced at the brown-haired young woman who'd followed him into the room. 'It's all right,' Béatrice said, taking out a packet of cigarettes. 'You can talk in front of Camille.'

So he recounted the story Renée had told him while Béatrice listened, smoking, her brow furrowed in concentration. 'The Paris police know what's happened,' he finished. 'And they're interested in you, too. My contact in the Gestapo asked me to tell him at once if you come to my shop.'

She turned her pale eyes on him. 'That police officer who arranged Mathilde's pass, you mean? Does he still visit you?'

'Yes, he's a bibliophile.' Jacques hesitated. 'I'm selling some books for . . . a friend, who's in a difficult situation. Schmidt and his friends buy them and I pass on the money. The man's presence makes me uncomfortable but he has his uses.'

Camille sat beside Béatrice on the sofa and reached for her hand. Béatrice squeezed it briefly, then let go. 'We'll have to find out where they're holding Mathilde,' she said. 'There might be a way of getting her out before—' She stopped abruptly. 'In the meantime, I'll see what we can do about the widow and child.'

'They can stay with me for as long as they have to,' Jacques said. 'I think the storeroom's fairly secure.'

'We'll be as quick as we can,' Béatrice replied. 'Mathilde's strong but she might not hold out forever.'

Despair fell upon Jacques like a dead weight. He'd been so relieved Mathilde was alive that he hadn't stopped to consider what might be happening to her now – or maybe the idea of torture was simply too awful to contemplate. And Pierre had been killed. Was the sacrifice worth it? Mathilde had told Jacques he inspired her to resist, though he couldn't imagine how. Now he wished with all his shameful heart that he'd inspired her to stay at home instead.

'She might not have known what Pierre was up to,' he said, clutching at straws. 'The police might simply question her and let her go.'

Béatrice looked at him with her usual cynical expression. 'We'll have to find another place to meet,' she said. 'How about the Tuileries Gardens? That's midway for each of us. I'll see you by the Round Pond at one this Friday so we can exchange news. And don't come here again. If you need to contact me urgently, leave a note at the *tabac* on the corner. Camille's name, incidentally, is Anaïs Nin.' She stubbed out the cigarette and uncoiled her long legs, distracted, clearly thinking ahead. 'Goodbye, then, and good luck. Hold your nerve.'

When Jacques visited the storeroom that evening, he found Renée holding the basin in her lap, looking sicker than ever in the candlelight while Louis sat on the floor beside her, playing with his rabbit.

'Are you ill?' he asked. 'Shall I call a doctor?' Although he had no idea how to find one who could be trusted.

She shook her head, swallowing. 'Don't worry,' she said, a few moments later. 'I'm expecting another baby, that's all. It'll pass.'

'Oh, Renée.' Jacques poured her a glass of water. What should have been joyful news was now so poignant and sad. 'Are you angry?' he asked, before he could think about it.

'Not with Pierre.' She took a sip. 'With the Nazis, yes,

but not him. There have to be people brave enough to make a stand, people like Pierre and Mathilde. And you.'

'I'm not doing much,' Jacques said.

'Of course you are. Mathilde knew you'd help us without question. And look at this room – you must have helped other people, too. We'll win in the end, Jacques.' She drank some more water and sighed, stretching out her legs on the floor. 'Mathilde knew she'd end up landing you in trouble if she stayed in Paris. It was hard for her to leave, though. She talked about you all the time.'

'How was she?' he asked eagerly.

Renée smiled. 'On good form. We loved having her with us. She's a bundle of energy, that's for sure. On top of working in a vineyard nearby, she took over the cooking so I could rest and put Louis to bed for me every night.' Her son looked up at the mention of his name. 'Tante Mathilde's fun, isn't she?' Renée ruffled his hair. 'Although she let you stay up far too late, reading stories,' she added, which made the boy smile for the first time since they'd arrived.

'Shall I read to you now, Louis?' Jacques asked, taking up the picture book. 'And look, I've found some of the tin soldiers I used to play with when I was a boy.' He brought out a handful from his pocket and laid them on the mattress.

Settling the little boy on his lap as Mathilde must have done so many times, Jacques felt her presence in the shadowy room so strongly that he could almost smell the blend of lavender and *Je Reviens* that was her signature scent. She was always with him, but sometimes more tangibly than others.

150

'She always knew immediately what to do,' he said to Renée, breaking off from the story. 'Knows what to do, I mean. It takes me a little while to catch up.'

'And that's in your character. Thinking things over isn't a crime.' Renée put her arm through his and closed her eyes, leaning back against the wall. The candle flame guttered in a draught from the window and somewhere in the distance, they could hear the faint tramp of marching feet and Germans singing. Louis tensed.

'Now Peter's safe home in bed,' Jacques said, closing the book, 'and maybe we should tuck you up, too. Sleep tight. Maman's right here and I'll see you in the morning.'

Poor kid, he thought, swinging the door shut; he'd have to grow up without a father, just as Jacques had done. The road ahead would not be easy.

Chapter Eleven

March 2022

Zizi's residential home was a short ride away on the Métro. Juliette arrived ten minutes early and was shown into a lounge to wait until Nico's grandmother arrived. It was a pleasant room, with potted palms dotted here and there, a piano in the corner and chairs grouped invitingly around small tables, but air freshener couldn't mask the smell of disinfectant, medication and maybe something worse. An elderly couple sat by the window, holding hands, and two women played cards, twittering to each other in fluting voices. Juliette felt her eyes beginning to close. She'd slept badly the night before; a couple had arrived in the room next door at one in the morning and proceeded to have enthusiastic sex for longer than she'd thought humanly possible. Pulling herself together, she sat up as a stooped, elderly woman was escorted towards her on the arm of a care assistant. Zizi had white hair cut in a sharp bob that ended at her jawline and the same tawny eyes as her grandson, although hers were rheumy and buried in wrinkles. She wore black patent court shoes and a shirt dress with a leopard-print scarf, and her make-up was immaculate. Juliette readjusted her expectations.

'Thank you so much for meeting me, Madame,' she said in her best French, offering a box of macarons she'd bought at the market.

Zizi inclined her head graciously and the assistant said, 'How lovely', and that she would bring them a pot of tea. She took the box and hurried away, and Juliette was left to start the conversation. She wished more than ever that Nico had briefed her before the visit. How did his grandmother feel about having to leave her apartment? Would any mention of it upset her? Had she realised she was never going back?

'This is a nice place,' she began, desperately looking around the room. 'How are you settling in?'

'Yes, I like it well enough.' Zizi looked around, too, as though seeing the room for the first time. 'The staff do their best and if you fall over, they pick you up straight away. You don't have to wait, not even for a minute!'

'Oh, good.' Not leaving someone to lie on the floor seemed a minimum standard of care, but Juliette was glad Zizi was pleased. Taking a deep breath, she went on, 'I don't know whether Nico told you, but I'd like to rent your old apartment in the Place Dorée. I'll take very good care of it, and all your belongings, of course.'

'I don't care about them,' the old lady said, tucking one elegant foot behind the other. 'I used to have so many things and now I have nothing at all. Still, at least there's nothing to worry about. I sit in my tidy room and read books or watch the television, and think about my life. I seem to have become a different person.' She fixed Juliette intently. 'Do you think that means I'm ready to die?'

'Goodness, I have no idea.'

Zizi fixed her with a steely glare. 'You don't need to look so worried. I'm ninety-seven, it's only to be expected.'

'I suppose so.' Juliette sat up straighter; Zizi was as fierce as her grandson. 'As a matter of fact, my grand-mother was born and brought up in Paris. She would have been around the same age as you but she died years ago.'

'She was lucky,' Zizi observed.

'Well, possibly.' Seventy-one had seemed ancient to Juliette at the time, although now she realised it was no age at all. 'Anyway, I feel as though the Place Dorée was important to her, that maybe she might even have lived there. Her maiden name was Marie Garnier. I don't suppose you knew anyone by that name?'

'Marie Garnier,' Zizi repeated, and shook her head. 'No, I don't think so. That would be an extraordinary coincidence, would it not?'

'Stranger things have happened,' Juliette countered. 'You might have been at school together, for example.'

'But it was so long ago.' Zizi crossed her legs at the ankle. 'My best friend was Clothilde Berger, a clever girl but enormously plain. I wonder if any of my classmates are still alive? Probably not.'

They were interrupted by the care assistant bearing a tea tray with the macarons laid out on a plate – about half the original number, Juliette noticed. Zizi didn't seem to be enormously impressed with her so far, so she brought out her trump card: the photograph album. 'I found this in your apartment,' she said, 'and thought you might like to have it here.'

'Well, well, well.' Zizi ran her hands over the scuffed leather but seemed reluctant to open the album, much to Juliette's frustration. After what Delphine had said, she daren't admit to having looked through it already.

'My father took many of these pictures,' Zizi said, turning the pages at last. 'He was a keen photographer.'

Early shots of countryside and beaches with distant figures, too small to be distinguishable, soon gave way to more ambitious city scenes. Two girls in cloche hats and long coats walked down a rainy street under an umbrella; sunshine slanted through a café window to fall on a man smoking a cigar; skinny boys in underpants jumped like frogs from a quay into the water. Juliette watched until Zizi came to the picture she'd been waiting for her to find.

'Who's that, I wonder?' she asked, pointing to the man sitting on the step.

'The first love of my life,' Zizi replied simply, gazing at the photograph.

'Your husband?'

The old lady sighed. 'No. He was older than me, with a wife already. I couldn't have him so I married his best friend. That was later, though.' She looked at Juliette with softer eyes. 'I was fifteen when the war started and twenty-one by the end, so you could say I came of age under the Nazis. The experience must have shaped me, though

155

I'm not sure how.' She turned the page gently, as if laying her beloved to rest.

Juliette remembered a photograph she had seen later in the album of a café – it might even have been 'her' café in the Place Dorée – with a German sign above the door and tables full of uniformed soldiers in long black boots. Mémé had lived in Paris through those tumultuous years; Juliette should have asked her about them when she had the chance. Yet she'd been a teenager when her grandmother had come to live with them, too absorbed in her own dramas to have time for anyone else's.

'How did you feel when the Germans took over?' she asked Zizi now.

'Not so bad at first. It was exciting, even, seeing all these young men parading about. They were very keen on health and fitness. We French had been defeated so we slunk about in shame but the Germans, well, they were full of themselves, and they had plenty of money. Some of my friends went out with them but I never did.' She wrinkled her nose. 'We were humiliated. All those signs everywhere in that ugly Gothic script we couldn't understand, it was like living in a foreign country. The British suffered terribly but at least they stuck together. The Nazis made us turn against each other, you see; that was the worst thing. People would spy on their neighbours and betray them just to win favour with the Boche. You couldn't trust anyone.' She closed the album. 'Thank you for bringing my pictures. I'll have a proper look at them later.'

They seemed to be getting along better so Juliette dared to ask, 'Did the man you loved work in the bookstore?'

'It was his business,' Zizi replied. 'I used to help him sometimes.'

'So what happened to him? And the store?'

The old lady gave Juliette a suspicious look. 'I don't want to talk about that.' She began struggling to her feet. 'I'm tired. This conversation has gone on long enough.'

Juliette hurried to help. 'Of course. Forgive me for intruding. I only asked because – well, it might sound a ridiculous idea but I'm thinking of taking over the lease.'

'I beg your pardon?' Zizi disengaged her hand from Juliette's arm.

'I want to bring a bookstore back to the Place Dorée. *La Page Cachée*, just as it was,' Juliette said proudly. 'Well, not exactly as it was, obviously, because I'll be selling English-language books, mainly, but—'

'That's a bad idea,' Zizi told her. 'Nothing good will come of digging up the past.'

'But this is the future, too,' Juliette said. 'The store looks so sad, standing there empty.'

'That's because it has a sad history,' Zizi snapped. 'You have no idea what went on there, and no right to trample over my memories in your ugly shoes.'

'I'm so sorry, Madame.' Juliette edged behind the chair, hiding her sneakers. 'I didn't mean to upset you.'

'I'm not upset,' the old lady replied, clutching the album to her chest. 'But I'm warning you, leave that place alone.'

'Time for a rest, Madame Bertillon?' The care assistant came forward, smiling inanely. 'Let's take you back to your room.'

'I'm sorry,' Juliette repeated, twisting her fingers together. 'I only thought—'

'You young ones can't imagine what we went through,' Zizi went on, 'and why people acted the way they did. I won't have all that raked up again, do you understand?'

'Of course.'

Juliette couldn't begin to work out what had just happened. She'd already made an appointment to look around the store and wouldn't have dreamed of pulling out, but Zizi had made her think. Was she being insensitive, dragging a piece of history into the twenty-first century? What if everyone in the neighbourhood felt the same?

'It was awful,' she told Ilse the next day, as they waited by the shop door for the real-estate agent to arrive. 'The old lady really doesn't want me to touch it.'

'But you can't let that put you off,' Ilse replied. 'It's not as though you're planning on selling tacky souvenirs or sex toys.'

Juliette sighed. 'Maybe there is some sort of curse on the place and everyone knows about it except me. Do you think I'm crazy, trying to start a business here?'

'For the hundredth time, no!' Ilse replied. 'Obviously you'll have to go about things in a professional way, but there are people out there who advise entrepreneurs. And I'll call my friend Elisabeth to see if you can help in her bookshop for a few weeks, get some experience.' She took Juliette by the shoulders. 'Look, I can see why you're nervous but you've come up with a great idea and if you don't give it a try, you'll always wonder what might have happened. And what else are you going to do? Fly back to America and tell your husband you can't manage without him?'

At that moment a young man in a shiny suit and pointed shoes arrived, not at all apologetic for being late. He unlocked the door, pushed it open against a mountain of post and invited them inside. Juliette walked through the echoing rooms, breathing in the musty, undisturbed air. The store was small, basically two rooms connected by a chamber in the middle with a tiny cloakroom at the back. The walls were covered in hardboard and torn posters, and she had no idea what lay behind: decaying brickwork and rising damp, most probably. Yet, somehow, she felt at home here, like a soft-skinned crab scuttling into an empty shell.

'So, what do you think?' Ilse had come to join her.

She'd decided already. 'You're right, I can't let Zizi stop me from taking over the lease. I have to, Ilse. This place has been waiting for me.'

Juliette could keep her plans for the store a secret from Nico's grandmother for the time being, but she decided to tell Nico before he found out from anyone else. She knew he wouldn't think much of the idea and he didn't let her down when he turned up to fix the shower in Zizi's apartment before Juliette moved in the following week.

'You, taking over an empty shop that no one's been able to make a success of?' He looked at her sceptically. 'Have you any idea how difficult it is to run a business in France? And do you know the first thing about bookselling?'

'A little. I've been reading up on it online,' she said, ignoring his supercilious tone. 'And a friend of a friend runs a bookstore on the Left Bank so I'm going to work there for a while to learn the ropes. Also, Arnaud's going to help me apply for a bank loan.'

'Is he, indeed?' Nico whistled. 'He kept that quiet. Well, good luck. So you'll be staying here for the long term, then?'

'Looks like it.'

Nico took an envelope from his jacket pocket and gave it to her. 'I've drawn up a tenancy agreement for three months starting from next Monday, the beginning of April. After that, we can see whether the arrangement still works for both of us.'

'Of course.' She could be business-like too. 'And I've made an inventory of everything that's left in the apartment. I haven't got a printer so I'll email it and you can check to make sure I haven't missed anything.'

'Thank you,' he said grudgingly. 'Who'd have thought those dolls would fetch such a good price?'

Thérèse's friend with the market stall had taken them all as a job lot, plus most of the kitchen equipment that Juliette had cleaned and polished. She'd told him to send the money directly to Nico.

'Sure you can manage without a dishwasher?' he asked, looking around the kitchen.

'I can wash a few plates in the sink. There's only me to clear up after.' The rent he was charging was very reasonable, and she could exist without a few mod cons for a while. She loved handling the pretty china, faded from years of use, and ironing the monogrammed linen sheets that might have been part of Zizi's trousseau. At least the washing machine was efficient; Nico told her he'd replaced it the year before. He was an attentive grandson, she had to admit.

'You probably don't like all this old-fashioned furniture,' he went on, nodding towards the oak dresser.

'No, it's great,' Juliette assured him. 'Shabby chic without even trying.'

'If you say so.' He looked around the kitchen, then walked through to the bedroom for a last tour of inspection.

'I would like to decorate the apartment, though, with your permission,' she asked, following on behind. 'Nothing dramatic, just painting the walls white and maybe taking up the bedroom carpet and sanding the floor. Let me show you.' A corner of the carpet had come loose and the same wide floorboards as those in the *salon* could be seen underneath.

'I'm not sure,' Nico said, frowning as he tucked the carpet back in place. 'I'm too busy to help, as I said, and what if you fall off a ladder and sue me?'

'I have health insurance,' Juliette replied, 'and I know what I'm doing, honestly.' She'd painted and wallpapered the apartment in Philadelphia where she and Kevin had lived for four chaotic, happy years before the twins had grown so big that their home was bursting at the seams.

'I'll sign a letter saying I'm doing everything at my own risk, if you like,' she added. 'Not all Americans love a lawsuit.'

'I'll think about it.' He looked around the room. 'But you'll need a decent bed. You can't sleep in that old thing.' A narrow single bed with a vinyl headboard stood forlornly under the window.

'It's perfectly comfortable,' Juliette said quickly. 'Honestly, I don't mind.'

'No, this won't do at all. You must have a double bed for your Parisian adventure.' He grinned, and she felt her insides melting into a pool of golden syrup. Dear God, was he flirting with her?

'And now I must fix the shower. If you're making coffee, I'd love a cup.' He picked up his tool bag and headed for the bathroom with a look of grim determination.

She should have called a plumber, Juliette decided, filling the stove-top espresso maker with coffee grounds. Nico's assumption she was an idiot did nothing for her confidence, which was shaky enough already.

'There you are.' She put a cup beside him on the sink. 'By the way, I enjoyed meeting your grandmother, but she wasn't keen on me taking over the store either. She seemed to think there was a curse on the place. Have you heard any rumours?'

'Can't say that I have.' He grunted with exertion, wielding a spanner, and Juliette found herself looking at his muscly forearms, lightly covered with dark hair. *'Merde!'* he cried suddenly, and Juliette leapt back as a jet of freezing water shot out from the pipe and sprayed her in the face. She staggered against the wall with her arms held up to protect herself.

'Turn that wheel under the sink!' he shouted above the torrent, and she scrambled between his legs to reach it.

'It won't move!' she called back, trying her hardest to move the damn thing, and he swore some more before pushing her out of the way to take over. They were both saturated by now and the bathroom floor was inches deep in water. At last he must have succeeded because the pipe suddenly stopped gushing and she no longer felt as though she were standing under a waterfall. The room seemed suddenly very quiet.

Nico was looking at her so sheepishly that she couldn't help smiling; soon she was laughing and he began to laugh too, running a hand through his sodden hair, making it stand up in dark spikes. What must she look like? Juliette flipped rats' tails out of her eyes as she sat there on the floor, laughing so hard that tears ran down her already wet cheeks and her stomach hurt. At last she tried to struggle to her feet. He reached out a hand to help her up and she found herself standing very close to him, close enough to smell the wet cotton plastered against his skin and a faint trace of aftershave. A bead of water ran down his cheek and dropped into the hollow between his neck and his collarbone. She glanced down and saw her own T-shirt clinging to her body, and he noticed it too, and a current passed between them that was so strong, she felt the air crackle. The smile died on her lips.

After a few seconds' silence, he passed her a towel. 'Sorry. I must have hit the wrong pipe.'

'Thanks,' she said, backing out of a room that seemed suddenly too small for two. 'I'll leave you to it.'

An hour or so later, he emerged to say the shower was running properly and she could inspect it if she wanted.

'I'll take your word for it,' she said, hardly daring to look at him. 'Thanks.'

'Short of replumbing the whole apartment, that's the

best I can do,' he went on. 'It's not what you're used to, I'm sure, but this is an old building.'

'It's fine. Thank you,' she repeated. Thank goodness, just then her phone rang. 'I'd better take this,' she said, glancing at the screen. 'Goodbye. And thanks again.'

She walked into the *salon*, her heart still thumping. What had just happened?

'Mom? It's me,' said her daughter, Emily, sounding very far away. 'I'm calling from the base and the line's not great so we'll have to be quick.'

'How's everything going, honey?' Juliette tried to sound normal, clutching the phone to her ear. 'It's wonderful to hear from you.'

'I'm good,' Emily said impatiently, 'but Dad just emailed to say you're going to be spending the summer in France on your own. What's going on? He didn't sound too happy about it.'

Juliette sank into a chair. 'He didn't explain why?'

'He just said you wanted some time by yourself. I don't get it, Mom. Dad's lost without you, he can't even boil an egg. Have you guys had an argument?'

Juliette had texted Kevin the day before, telling him she'd found an apartment and would be staying in Paris for at least another few months. He'd called her immediately to say how unreasonable she was being, and how difficult it was for him to field questions about her from their friends and neighbours. In the end, she'd agreed to send everyone an email saying she was discovering so much about her family history that she was taking more time to explore but would be back in the fall, if not before. She'd break the news about her plans for the bookstore when they were nearer reality.

'What about the kids, though?' she'd asked, and Kevin had said he wanted to talk to them first. She'd assumed he'd find some way of justifying his actions; it hadn't occurred to her he wouldn't mention the affair at all.

'By the way,' he'd added, 'I had to have Mittens put to sleep last week. The vet said it was the kindest thing.'

'And you didn't think to discuss it with me first?' Juliette had asked.

'You've given up on all of us and that includes the cat,' he'd replied. 'Face it, you have no rights in this family anymore.'

'You're being pretty selfish,' Emily was telling her now. 'How much time do you need? Are you not even going to come back for Dad's birthday in July?'

Juliette took a deep breath. 'I'm sorry if this comes as a shock,' she began, 'but you ought to know the truth. Your father's been having an affair for the past couple of years. Emily? Are you there?'

After a few seconds' stunned silence, she heard her daughter laugh. 'No! Dad? Are you kidding?'

'I'm afraid not. I know this must be hard to accept – I couldn't believe it myself, but he's admitted it.'

Another pause, and then Emily asked, 'Who with?'

'One of the neighbours.' The admission was so banal, Juliette felt ashamed on Kevin's behalf.

'Not that woman across the street? Mary something?'

'Mary-Jane,' she replied. 'Yes, that's the one.'

'Oh my God,' Emily said slowly.

'I'm sorry to tell you over the phone. Are you OK, honey? Do you have someone on the ship you can talk to?' Emily was a daddy's girl: she and Kevin had always been close and Juliette hated to think of her dealing with this news alone, so far from home.

'I'm fine,' Emily said, clamming up already. 'Mom, I have to go.'

'OK. I'll email you, and call again any time if you can.' But the line had already gone dead.

Juliette sat for a moment with the phone in her hand.

'Is everything all right?' She looked up to find Nico standing in the doorway.

'Yes, absolutely,' she said, getting to her feet. 'Thank you for sorting out the shower, more or less, and for the agreement. I'll sign it and give it back to you as soon as I can.'

As he was leaving, he turned to her and said, 'Listen, I'm taking Zizi out to lunch on Thursday. Why don't you come too, if you're free?'

'I'm not sure,' she replied, at a loss for words. 'I have a lot to do, and your grandmother's not keen on me taking over the shop.'

'Don't worry about that. She'll come around and she likes talking about the old days.' He picked up his tool bag, adding, 'I need to make up for almost drowning you.'

'All right, then. Thanks.' Juliette tried to sound casual. 'That'd be great.'

Chapter Twelve

Lunch with Zizi was not to be, however: Nico texted the evening before to say something had come up and he'd have to cancel. Juliette was torn between aching disappointment and relief. She'd gone shopping in Le Marais with Ilse that day and bought a few clothes for the warmer weather: a couple of dresses and some wide-legged linen pants that she wouldn't have looked at twice without Ilse's encouragement.

'See? You're so chic,' Ilse said, putting her head around the changing-room door. 'And here's a jacket that will go with everything. Blue is definitely your colour. Hey! What's the matter?'

Juliette had been looking at herself in the mirror when she'd suddenly been consumed by such a profound wave of sadness that she'd allowed herself a brief sob, hoping she could pretend to have a cold.

'Oh, it's nothing,' she said, smiling through her tears.

'Just that my cat had to be put to sleep last week and I wasn't there. She was nineteen and didn't know who we were anymore, but still, I feel like I've let her down.'

'Of course.' Ilse patted her back and gave her a tissue. 'That must be hard.'

'I should pull myself together.' Juliette blew her nose.

'You're going through a lot,' Ilse said. 'And if you ever want to talk about anything in particular, I'd be more than happy to listen.'

Juliette took a shaky breath. 'Not yet. Maybe later, if that's OK?'

Her emotions fluctuated from day to day; sometimes even hour to hour. Paris in the springtime was heart-breakingly lovely: the cherry trees a sea of pink, the parks full of flowers and the café terraces filling up with interesting people. The thought of a new life here filled her with excitement alongside the nerves but she was lonely and grieving for much of the time. She didn't particularly miss Kevin, but she missed the familiarity of her old routines in the home they'd made together. The bulbs would be coming up in her garden and the plum trees frothing with blossom; she'd have been filling the house with vases of scented narcissi and feeding the roses, cycling to Pilates twice a week and going to book club once a month, chatting to her neighbours when she picked up the mail and buying groceries at the big box store.

Shopping in a Parisian supermarket was a different experience altogether. Everyone seemed to be in a hurry, particularly the people waiting in line behind her; she was constantly finding herself nudged forward and leaving an inch of space in front was an invitation for some little old lady with a wheeled cart to cut in, banging her on the ankles. The local shops were less intimidating and Thérèse had taken her around the neighbourhood one afternoon, pointing out which *boulangerie* baked the best bread, which *fromagerie* had the widest selection of cheese, and which *épicerie* the most freshly roasted coffee beans.

'Don't be afraid to ask for what you want,' Thérèse instructed. 'If you like your baguette well-cooked, you must say so. And don't forget to greet the person behind the counter, that's very important.'

Thérèse invited Juliette for supper that Friday, so she'd have a chance to wear her new clothes after all. She dithered for a while about what to bring, not knowing the etiquette, deciding in the end on a bottle of wine and some tulips from the flower shop where she was becoming a regular. Flowers made her hotel room slightly less dreary; only a few more days and she'd be out of there for good. She couldn't wait.

Thérèse and Arnaud lived on the first floor of a tall, elegant building with an elaborate façade and wrought-iron balconies facing the street. The interior was just as lovely.

'Oh, what a beautiful apartment,' Juliette said, gazing around as Thérèse took her coat. Tall windows and pale walls flooded the apartment with light, while the floor shone with polished, honey-coloured parquet in a herringbone design. 'Is this what's known as a Haussmann building?'

'That's right.' Arnaud poured her a glass of wine. 'Do you know much about Baron Haussmann?'

'Not a great deal,' she said. 'Tell me more.'

'So, Haussmann planned these wide boulevards in the mid-nineteenth century, after the revolution, to bring fresh air and sanitation to areas that had once been slums.'

'Enough,' Thérèse scolded. 'Juliette hasn't come for a lecture.'

'No, I'm interested,' she insisted, smiling. 'I love hearing about a country's history.'

'Well, he designed broad, airy roads with buildings in blocks to conserve heat and energy, and make plumbing easier.' Arnaud was warming to his theme. 'And lots of smaller apartments brought all sorts of people into the city, making it more diverse. Of course, the reason so many of these old buildings are still standing today is because we French surrendered to the Germans without a fight during the second world war – unlike the British, who had to suffer London being bombed to pieces. So, *voilà*: what we lost in self-respect, we gained in architecture.'

'And lives saved, I guess,' Juliette said.

'Yes, there is that,' Arnaud conceded. 'Is it better to die gloriously for the sake of freedom or live under enemy occupation? I'm not sure what I would choose.'

'He can go on like this for hours,' Thérèse said. 'Still, better to get it out of the way before the others arrive. Baptiste is coming with his partner Michel, and we've invited Nico and Delphine, too.'

Juliette's heart leapt and sank so quickly she felt giddy. 'Oh, great.'

'And now we really are going to change the subject,' Thérèse said. 'Tell us how your plans are going, Juliette.'

'Well, I've found a company who advise entrepreneurs here,' she began, 'and they're helping me write a business plan, but my head is exploding from all the rules and regulations. I do think there's a market for an English-language bookshop in this *quartier*, though.' She took a mouthful of wine, telling herself not to gabble. 'I'm thinking of calling it "The Forgotten Bookshop". What do you think?'

'Very poetic.' Arnaud raised his glass. 'We should be breaking out the Champagne.'

'I'd like people to feel as though they've found a place off the beaten track that the locals know about, rather than a tourist trap,' Juliette said. 'I want this shop to become part of the community, with maybe a book club, and poetry readings, and writers dropping by.' She couldn't suppress a thrill of excitement. This was actually happening; she was going to stay in Paris and run her own business, once she'd found a way through the red tape.

Baptiste – Mr Beard and Glasses – was next to arrive with Michel, a French-Canadian food writer. Michel had been truffle-hunting in the Dordogne the month before and brought a couple of the knobbly black tubers as a gift. They were passed from hand to hand and inhaled reverently before he and Thérèse went off to the kitchen to prepare them. Juliette asked Arnaud and Baptiste about the expat community in Paris, and they asked her about her French grandmother, and her plans for the bookshop. Nobody mentioned her absent husband.

'Nico and Delphine are always late,' Thérèse explained, coming back with a couple of laden plates. 'They won't mind if we start on the truffles without them.'

She and Michel had spread thin slices of French bread with egg mayonnaise, chicken-liver pâté and coarser pork

171

rilletttes, and shaved slivers of truffle on top. Michel had also brought a bottle of Gewürztraminer, which he said they had to try with the chicken-liver pâté, so fresh glasses had to be brought and the conversation ground to a halt while the combination was sampled.

'Heaven,' Michel declared, his eyes closed. Juliette had to agree, content to sit back and let the discussion in French and English about earthy base notes swirl around her. She had found her people.

The buzzer sounded again and Nico and Delphine appeared. Juliette's stomach lurched at the sight of Nico; she felt herself blush and hoped no one would notice. People were kissing each other on both cheeks so she offered him hers, basking for a second in the smell of his aftershave and the feel of his stubble against her skin. The night before, she'd dreamed that he'd taken her to Deauville and kissed her on the promenade. It was the sort of dream you didn't want to wake up from; she blushed more deeply, remembering. Delphine gave her a languid wave, to show that was as far as she was prepared to go. She was looking particularly ravishing in a black silk shift with her hair loose and Juliette felt a part of herself wither and die. A few weeks in Paris and she was acting like a hormonal teenager.

Some of the magic went out of the evening after that. Nico seemed to be on edge and Delphine didn't like truffles; she also stepped out on the balcony for a cigarette almost as soon as they'd arrived. Everyone was part of a couple except Juliette, and she had better get used to it because this was going to be her life for the foreseeable future. She took her place at the table between Arnaud and Nico, disturbing the symmetry of the seating plan.

'Goodness, I still haven't signed our rental agreement,' she said to Nico, putting on a false, bright voice. 'I've been so busy, I completely forgot.'

'Don't worry, I trust you. If you'd wanted to trash the apartment, you could have done so by now.' He smiled and her stomach lurched again.

'And yet you're not usually so casual,' Delphine said from across the table, accepting a plate of *boeuf bourgignon* from Thérèse. 'Are you getting soft in your old age, *chéri*?'

'But Juliette has worked so hard, clearing out the place,' he replied. 'And you should be grateful, too, *chérie*, because she's given me time to concentrate on your kitchen.'

'How is it coming along?' Thérèse asked, passing Juliette her plate.

'Slowly,' Delphine replied. 'The cupboards are taking forever to arrive from Italy, and the sink, which we ordered months ago, only came yesterday and it's cracked, so the marble worktops can't be fitted. But that's immaterial because they appear to have been cut to the wrong size. The whole thing is a nightmare, frankly. I'm beginning to wish I'd never started.'

Thérèse smiled brightly. 'Well, I'm sure it will be spectacular when it's finished.'

Juliette racked her brains for something to say. 'And did you have a lovely time in Deauville?' she asked.

Delphine considered her for a moment, flicking back her beautiful hair. 'Yes,' she said eventually. 'We did.'

Luckily Baptiste was able to engage Delphine in conversation about a play she'd seen, for which he and

Michel had tickets, so Juliette was able to talk to Arnaud about loans for start-up businesses, and an accountant whom he'd recommended. It was a delicious meal and she was so grateful to the Chauvignys for befriending her. Parisians had a reputation for being standoffish but they had proved the exact opposite.

'You'll have to come for dinner at my place once I'm settled.' She couldn't resist helping herself to a slice of Brie from the cheese board, despite having eaten enough to burst.

'When are you moving in?' Arnaud asked.

'On Monday, all being well,' she replied. 'It'll be wonderful to have a proper home at last.'

'And Zizi's not in mourning for her dolls?' Thérèse asked Nico.

He shrugged. 'She seems almost glad to be rid of them.'

'Yes, we took her out to lunch on Wednesday and she was in a very good mood.' Delphine smiled at Juliette. 'I hope you enjoy living in her old apartment. It's a sweet little place. Nothing like the Haussmannian style, of course, but I'm sure it will suit you very well.'

'I think so.' Juliette met her gaze. 'It has such a homely feel and it's perfectly located. The rooms will look quite different once I've painted them and sanded the floor.'

'What?' Delphine glanced sharply at Nico. 'Do you know about this?'

'Of course,' he replied. 'Juliette asked permission and I said yes.'

'That sounds lovely.' Thérèse began collecting the plates. 'And now for dessert. Apple tart, anyone?'

'I couldn't manage another thing,' Delphine said. 'Just

coffee for me, please. And I might have another cigarette first. Nico, will you join me?'

'Don't mind her,' Thérèse whispered when they'd gone, patting Juliette's hand.

'I won't,' she replied, helping to clear the table. Yet as she was taking dishes through to the kitchen, she overheard a snatch of conversation through the open balcony door that made her blood run cold.

'Can't you see what she's up to?' Delphine was hissing at Nico. 'She'll claim she's increased the value of that apartment and claim a stake in it. Don't let her touch a thing!'

'She's harmless,' Nico replied wearily. 'Honestly, she just wants somewhere to stay while she tries to get this business up and running. It'll probably fail and she'll go back to America and that will be that.'

Juliette felt as though she'd been punched in the stomach. She put the plates on the counter top and said to Thérèse, 'It's been such a wonderful evening but I have a migraine coming on. Would you mind if I just slipped away?'

'Of course not,' Thérèse said. 'You look a little pale. Shall I come back with you?'

'No, I'll be fine. Just too much red wine.' Juliette kissed her on both cheeks. 'Sorry to be so feeble, and please say goodbye to the others for me.'

She walked back to the hotel, tears stinging her eyes. Harmless! Really? She couldn't bear to look at Nico again. She would have to have some dealings with him because he was her landlord, but their relationship would be on a strictly professional basis from now on.

★ ★ ★

After a restless night, she slept late and found to her dismay that the last person she wanted to see had reached the café before her. Nico was standing at the bar. He walked over as soon as he saw her and said, looking somewhere above her head, 'I'm glad to have caught you. Listen, I'm afraid my plans have changed.'

'How do you mean?' she asked stiffly. 'What plans?'

'About the apartment.' He gave an impatient sigh, as though she shouldn't have asked. 'Well, I've decided to sell it.'

'Seriously? When?'

'As soon as possible.' He glanced out of the window, down at his feet, behind the bar – anywhere rather than directly at her. 'It'll be going on the market next week, so I'm sorry but obviously you can't move in on Monday.'

'Does this have anything to do with me wanting to decorate?' she asked. 'I don't have to, I'll rent the apartment just as it is.'

He had the grace to look embarrassed. 'No, it's not that. I need funds for other projects, you see, in a lump sum, and being a landlord takes up too much time.'

'But you were prepared to let the apartment lie empty for months,' Juliette said, her anger rising. 'You didn't seem to need the money so urgently then. You've let me clear it and clean it for you, and now you're going to throw me out on the street?'

'Not technically,' he replied, 'since you're not actually living there yet. Presumably you can carry on staying at the hotel until you find somewhere else for the long term.'

'You can't do this to me.' Juliette's voice cracked. 'I

love that apartment and I need an address here. You know how hard it is to find a rental property in Paris.'

'I'm sorry, my mind's made up.' He stepped back. 'Thank you for everything you've done. I'm happy to pay for the time you've spent cleaning. Say, fifteen euros an hour? Just let me know. And if you could return the key to me by Monday, I'd be grateful. You can leave it for me behind the bar.'

Juliette let him walk away. 'You complete and utter asshole,' she said to the empty air.

Nico hadn't been too trusting; she had, and he had played her like a fiddle.

Chapter Thirteen

April 1941

Renée and Louis stayed in Jacques' storeroom for ten days. He kept *La Page Cachée* closed for a week, with a message on the door announcing a family bereavement, and spent the time organising his mother's funeral, sorting out her belongings, and trying to lay his hands on as much food and clothing for his guests as possible. The priest at Henri's church had apparently helped several fugitives already; Jacques approached him after Mass one morning and came away with some warm trousers and a jumper for Louis from a box of clothes in the vestry.

Madame Duval's funeral was a quiet affair, attended by only a few friends and neighbours. Madame Bourdain sat in a pew near the front, wearing a pair of Jacques' mother's shoes and dabbing her eyes with a handkerchief. He accepted all the muted condolences and assured anyone who asked that Mathilde was enjoying life in Provence.

Sylvie gave him a bunch of tulips after the service. 'We're so sorry,' she said. 'Your poor mother, may she rest in peace.'

'Thank you.' He was deeply touched. 'And thank you for all your help with Maman. I couldn't have managed without you, these past weeks.'

She was blushing now. Such a sweet girl, and so young; he would have to be careful not to encourage her.

That Friday, he cycled to the Tuilieries Gardens to meet Béatrice. She was late and he wondered whether she would even appear but eventually he saw her distinctive figure in the distance, wearing a camel coat and a beret over the black wig.

She fell into step beside him. 'We've had news of Mathilde.'

He searched her inscrutable face for clues. 'What is it? Tell me!'

'We think she might have been taken to Mont-Valérien. We don't know how long they'll keep her – depends what she was carrying when they picked her up. She wasn't armed, though.'

'Armed? Of course not,' Jacques said. Béatrice raised her eyebrows at that with her usual ironic expression. 'I'll go there and try to see her,' he went on. The prison stood in the suburb of Suresne on the western outskirts of Paris, the far side of the Bois de Boulogne; he could take a train there tomorrow.

'Are you mad?' Béatrice exclaimed. 'You haven't a hope of getting in. But there's a Catholic priest who cares for the prisoners in several jails around here and he's on our side, even though he's German. He should be able to visit her and tell us how she is. We're trying to reach him now. As soon as I hear anything, I'll let you know.'

'Thank you.' Jacques dug his fingernails into his palms. 'I can't bear to think of her in a place like that. They must have some evidence against her, surely? Or they'd have let her go already.'

'Who knows?' Béatrice shrugged. 'Don't give up hope, she may still be released.'

They walked on, their feet crunching over the gravel. A spring breeze lifted their hair and set a thousand diamonds glinting on the surface of the water.

'How are your guests?' Béatrice asked.

'Managing,' he replied. 'Renée is pregnant but she seems to be coping. I'm worried about the boy, though. He has bad dreams and I'm afraid someone will hear him crying in the night.'

'I'm making arrangements. We're aiming to come for them by the middle of next week.'

'Thank you,' Jacques said. 'The sooner the better.'

'By the way,' she added, 'I'm not being followed at the moment but I have been recently. If I ever come towards you with my hands in my pockets, like this,' and she demonstrated, 'don't acknowledge me. Just walk past.'

He nodded. 'Until next time, then,' she said. 'I'll be in touch.' And with that, she melted away.

'If only you could go outside,' Jacques told Renée that evening. 'Some fresh air would make you feel so much better. It's just the matter of getting you there – I don't trust our concierge and she's always hanging around. I'm sure she thinks I'm up to something.'

'We're fine,' Renée said, though the shadows under her eyes were darker than ever. 'We'd sooner stay here than take any risks.'

'It won't be for much longer,' he promised. 'Just a few more days.'

Swinging the door shut after each visit made him feel like their jailer, and Louis' miserable little face haunted his days and nights.

Jacques opened *La Page Cachée* for business the following Monday and in one sense he was glad to feel his guests so close at hand behind the shelves, but in another, he felt so anxious whenever a customer appeared that he could hardly concentrate. It was a huge relief when curly-haired Camille came into the shop and slipped him a note saying the two volumes for dispatch would be collected that evening at eight o'clock, by the lamppost in the square.

Renée hugged him when he passed on the news at lunchtime. 'That's all I know,' he said. 'I have no idea where you're going next.'

'It'll be an adventure, won't it, Louis?' She picked up the boy and held him to the window so he could get a breath of air.

'Will Papa be meeting us?' he asked, twisting a strand of her hair between his fingers.

'Not this time,' Renée said, her voice breaking. She swallowed. 'Papa has had to go far away and we won't be seeing him for a while. But I know he'll be watching over us to make sure we're safe.'

★　★　★

That evening, Jacques brought down a coat and hat of his mother's for Renée to wear on the journey. He passed Madame Bourdain, climbing up the stairs with a mop as he was hurrying down. She eyed him suspiciously. 'Working late again, Monsieur Duval? You'll wear yourself out.'

'Stocktaking, Madame,' he replied, shifting the coat to his other arm. 'It takes my mind off things.'

Renée and Louis were waiting in the storeroom. Jacques had found the small messenger bag his mother had given him when he was Louis' age. 'This is for you,' he said, putting in *Histoire de Pierre Lapin* and a few of the tin soldiers. 'Be a good boy, won't you?' It was the wrong thing to say: Louis was worryingly, unnaturally good.

'How can we ever thank you?' Renée threw her arms around him.

'No thanks necessary,' he said, hugging her back. 'Look after yourselves, all three of you.'

He led them out of the back door and through the apartment building, checking first to make sure that Madame Bourdain was safely out of sight and no one else was around. A couple were sitting on a bench by the lamppost, wrapped in a tight embrace. As Jacques approached, they separated. The man tipped his hat to Renée and took Louis' hand, while the dark-haired woman nodded at Jacques. It was Béatrice. Renée turned for a second, blowing Jacques a kiss, and then she was swallowed up in the night. It was over. Jacques let out his breath, feeling curiously deflated.

'Come with me,' Béatrice said in a low voice. 'I have something to tell you.' When they had gone around the corner she went on, 'We've been in touch with the priest at Mont-Valérien. He'll be visiting the prison on Saturday, so he'll try to see Mathilde then. If you want to write her a letter, he'll take it in.'

'That would be wonderful. Thank you!' Unable to contain himself, Jacques seized her by the shoulders and kissed her on both cheeks.

She allowed herself a brief smile. 'You must meet him at the café by the eastern entrance at ten in the morning. Say you'd like him to pray for your aunt, who died in Montpellier last week. He should reply, "Blessed are the meek, for they shall inherit the earth." Then you can give him a bible with your letter inside. Got that?'

Jacques nodded. It would mean closing his shop on the busiest day of the week, but that was a small price to pay. He spent the rest of that evening, and the evenings to come, composing a letter that would give Mathilde some idea of his feelings without adding to her distress. He was free now, that was the irony. If she hadn't been arrested, he could have closed the shop and come to join her in Provence; they might even have crossed the Pyrenees themselves and escaped through Spain to Gibraltar, run away from the war and started the new life they'd dreamed of. Why had she let Pierre lead her into such danger? In the end, he merely wrote that Maman had died peacefully in her bed, that he missed Mathilde with all his heart and lived for the day when he'd see her again, which would surely soon come, and that she mustn't give up hope. His longing for her was a physical ache in his chest that lasted from morning till night. Sometimes she would appear in his dreams but waking without her was such agony, this brief joy seemed hardly worth it.

Finally, Saturday arrived and he set off for Suresne, feverish with anticipation. Despite what Béatrice had said, he might be able to slip into the prison somehow. The thought of being so close to Mathilde but not able to see her was deeply frustrating. German guards boarded the train twice along the route, checking each passenger's papers at gunpoint. There was a brief commotion the second time, when a young woman was bundled on to the platform and hauled away, her feet dragging along the ground. The train lurched slowly on, past the Bois de Boulogne. Jacques remembered a day he and Mathilde had spent in the woods shortly after they were married, when the war still seemed far away. They had hired a boat and rowed across the lake to an island where they had eaten lunch: a baguette stuffed with cheese and ham, washed down with a *pichet* of red wine. The weather was still glorious and Mathilde had worn a blue summer dress with a straw hat. She had found a patch of wild strawberries and he had tasted their sweetness on her lips. If he closed his eyes, he could will himself back to that time when they had been so utterly in tune with one another, so certain nothing could come between them. Now she had forged ahead and he was struggling to catch up. He had wanted to protect her and instead, he had driven her away.

The fortress at Mont-Valérien was enough to put the fear of God into anyone. Surrounded by a brick wall around the perimeter, the grey stone of the prison itself was just visible above the leafless trees. Jacques couldn't bear to look at it. He sat in the café with his back to the window, ordered a cup of insipid barley coffee and waited for the priest to arrive. Yet it was worse, sensing the building behind him and not having a clear view of the café entrance. He swivelled his chair around in time to see a slim man in a black soutane with receding, reddish-brown hair push open the door. Clutching the bible, he rose to his feet.

'Father, would you pray for my aunt who died last week?' he asked.

The priest smiled. He had kind, tired eyes. 'Of course, my son,' he replied, his German accent unmistakeable. 'And where did she pass away?'

For a moment, Jacques couldn't think. Béatrice had mentioned a place, but where was it? Somewhere in the south. Marseilles? Toulouse? 'Montpellier,' he blurted, remembering at last.

'Blessed are the meek, for they shall inherit the earth,' the priest said, taking the bible from him. 'I shall be back in a couple of hours or so. Sorry not to be more precise.'

Jacques watched him stride towards the arched prison gateway, the cassock flapping around his ankles. The guard checked his papers and stood aside to let him pass. One lone man walking into the valley of death, armed only with a bible. Jacques wondered whether he still believed in God. He ordered another cup of coffee and took out the book he'd brought along with the bible – another Jules Verne – but he couldn't concentrate. The idea he'd had of somehow slipping into the prison unnoticed was ridiculous, he realised now he was actually here; he had as much chance of travelling to the centre of the earth with Otto and Axel. He'd imagined jumping aboard a lorryload of workmen being driven through the prison gates, or maybe stowing away in a laundry van, but the streets in this remote suburb were deserted. Apart from the priest, nobody came and went; the fortress was self-contained. And even if he managed to get inside, he had no idea where the female prisoners were being held, let alone the exact location of the woman he was desperate to see.

Unable to sit still any longer, he paid for his coffees and set off for a walk to pass the time. A narrow path ran around the perimeter wall so he took it, threading through the bushes and under trees that were bursting into bright green leaf. Occasionally he caught a glimpse of the prison looming above but for the most part, he might have been in the country. The sun was warm on his back and a tang of wild garlic scented the air. He stooped to pick a bunch, burying his nose in the delicate white flowers, and imagined Mathilde standing beside him. He tried to conjure up the smell of her hair, the feel of her skin, but she was slipping away from him, day by day. He stood, becalmed, his mind empty. Somewhere in the canopy above, the liquid song of a blackbird spilled into the sky, and he saw a rabbit watching him further along the path, its nose twitching.

And then suddenly the world exploded. A volley of shots rang out, six or seven of them, close together. The rabbit disappeared with a flash of its white tail and a flurry of birds rose up into the sky. Jacques turned and ran too, scattering stems of wild garlic as he went, desperate to get away from that awful sound. A root snaking across the path caught his foot and he flew headlong, landing with a thump that winded him. After a few seconds he struggled to his knees, his hands pressing into the damp, springy earth. Mathilde sat on her heels in front of him in the blue dress he loved, her eyes mischievous.

'What are you doing?' she asked, smiling at him with that familiar blend of exasperation and affection.

'What are *you* doing?' he replied. 'Can't you hear? They're shooting people. How can you—'

But she had vanished. He struggled slowly to his feet, brushing off his muddy trousers. Another volley of shots split the air and this time he stayed where he was, listening to the sound of someone's last moments: killed for the crime of defacing a poster or damaging a railway track or helping a so-called enemy of the Reich. Somewhere inside the prison, Mathilde was probably listening, too.

'How can you run these risks?' he'd wanted to ask her. 'Don't you care about me at all? You must know I can't live without you.'

The firing stopped and he walked slowly on.

'A life without freedom is no life at all,' Mathilde had said. Had she stayed in Paris, he could imagine her growing more miserable by the day. It was because he loved her that he'd let her go. How brave she was, and how honest! He'd been afraid to face reality, hiding away in his shop and only acting when she encouraged him to. The one step he'd taken on his own was to hide the books the Nazis had ordered him to return. Finally, he allowed himself to hate them for what they were doing

187

to his country, for their careless, casual cruelty, their arrogance, their ignorance and greed. Mathilde had been right all along. Of course they had to fight back, no matter how high the cost.

Back at the café, the minutes dragged by, turning into hours, and still there was no sign of the priest. He tried to read, bought a newspaper from a *tabac* down the street, ordered a bowl of soup, which was all he could afford and which he could barely swallow. At last, the priest arrived. Jacques rose to greet him, his heart in his mouth.

'Walk with me,' the abbé said, motioning Jacques to follow. They left the café and took one of the side streets. 'I'm sorry to have been so long,' he continued. 'It's been a difficult morning.'

'I heard the shots,' Jacques said.

The priest glanced at him. 'You know that women aren't put to death here? It's only men who have to face the firing squad.'

'I didn't, thank you,' Jacques said, and then, unable to wait any longer, 'But have you seen my wife? Did you give her my letter?'

'I haven't, I'm afraid. Although that might be a good thing.'

'What do you mean? Why not?' Jacques asked.

'Because she isn't in the prison. I've seen details of all the recent arrivals and her name isn't on it. I talked to a woman there who knew Mathilde in the south and was interrogated with her at the same police station. She only saw her briefly, and when the prisoners were transferred to Mont-Valérien, Mathilde wasn't among them.'

'But that means the Nazis might have killed her!' Jacques cried.

'Yet her name hasn't appeared on the lists of those executed. And this woman overheard the guards talking – she speaks German, though she was careful not to let on – and they were discussing someone who'd escaped from custody that morning. She thinks that person must have been Mathilde.'

'Oh, thank God.'

'Indeed.' The priest gave him a wry smile.

Jacques collected himself. 'Sorry, Father. I don't mean to be disrespectful.'

But was the news such a relief, after all? Pierre was dead and Renée had fled Avignon to find Jacques in Paris; Mathilde might be stranded alone somewhere, terrified and not knowing where to turn.

The priest clapped him on the back. 'These are difficult times. It isn't easy, being the one left behind to wonder and worry.'

Jacques looked into his calm face. 'How do you find the strength to keep coming here?'

'I have faith, which helps. And for me, there's no alternative; these people have nobody else. I can't do much but at least I can stay with them until the end. And now here is my car.' The priest stopped beside a dusty Renault. 'Ah, I almost forgot.' He gave back Jacques' bible. 'You might try reading this from time to time. The words may provide some comfort.'

'Thank you so much.' Jacques shook his hand. 'I'm very grateful.'

'And stay busy.' The abbé opened the car door.

'Action will stop you brooding. See what needs to be done and do it.'

'I will,' Jacques promised. He felt as though he had come back to life, a new vigour running through his veins. Sitting on the train on the way home, he tore his letter to Mathilde into pieces. Were he to write now, he would tell her that finally he understood what she'd been telling him from the start. It had taken him a while to catch up but he would honour her by following the example she had set, and when they met again – for he was certain they would – she would be proud of him. He closed his eyes and leant back against the seat, hearing her voice in his ear.

'Death is coming for all of us; it's how we live that matters.'

Chapter Fourteen

April 1941

Jacques was walking home from the Gare Saint-Lazare that afternoon when a passer-by caught his attention: a tall young man wearing a thin jacket and ill-fitting trousers that flapped a couple of inches above his feet, which were shod in heavy boots that were caked in mud. He was bearded, which was also unusual, and his fair hair was matted, his face dirty. Added to these peculiarities, he held a cigarette casually between his first two fingers, pointing outwards, when the usual way was to grip one's Gauloise firmly between finger and thumb with the burning end facing inward. Parisians walked with their eyes down but this man had his shoulders back and his head up, glancing about with an air of curiosity. And then, to cap it all, he looked the wrong way when crossing the road and stepped into the path of a motorbike, whose rider had to swerve to avoid him.

See what needs to be done and do it, Jacques heard the priest say. It was so simple, if one had the nerve.

'Ça va, mon ami?' he cried, seizing this stranger by the arm and propelling him down a side street, away from the sentry box manned by German soldiers up ahead.

As he'd suspected, the man didn't seem to understand a word of French, but he was content to be propelled along the street. Jacques tried to convey by smiles and gestures that he meant no harm, and the tramp smiled and nodded back to show he understood. Jacques led the way, taking detours to avoid any points where they might be stopped. And then, rounding a corner, they walked straight into a sea of grey-green uniforms. A prison van with its doors open had been parked across the street and troops were pouring into a nearby house, from which screams and shouts could be heard. Those who weren't taking part in the action were stopping and checking passers-by for their own entertainment.

His heart racing, Jacques reached into a pocket for his identity card. If the man beside him even had a card, it was bound to have been forged.

'Schnell! Quick!' rasped the German in front of them: a thin-faced, ratty youth with pockmarked skin.

The stranger made a show of patting his pockets, his movements becoming increasingly desperate. Beads of sweat stood out on his forehead and he looked positively deranged.

'Idiot!' Jacques shouted, cuffing him on the back. 'Hurry up and don't keep this good man waiting.' He turned to the soldier. 'This is my cousin from the country. He's a little, you know. . .' And he tapped the side of his head.

Catching on, the foreigner hung his head and shifted from foot to foot, mumbling incoherently.

'Stand up straight, you great oaf!' Jacques yelled, reaching up to clip him around the ear. 'I'm ashamed to be seen with you.'

The German was smiling now. He made some comment to a couple of the others, which had them all laughing, and soon Jacques and his companion had an audience for their performance. The more Jacques berated his new friend, the louder the Huns roared, until he began to worry they were attracting too much attention and put his arm through the stranger's to drag him away. Nobody tried to stop them, but it took all his self-control not to break into a run before they were out of sight.

They might have left the Boche behind but weren't out of trouble yet. This man was far too conspicuous for Jacques to risk taking him home in daylight; Madame Bourdain was bound to spot them and the stranger would be hard to explain away. He would have to leave him somewhere safe and come back for him after dark. The Parc Monceau would have been ideal but it was locked at sunset. Racking his brains, the only place Jacques could come up with was a derelict building not far from his apartment that had been hit by a stray bomb when the Germans had attacked the year before. Tramps sheltered there in the winter and courting couples used it in summer for privacy. He doubled back down a side road and took a circuitous route to find it in case they were being followed. Then, motioning to his companion to wait, he lurked about until the street was empty in both directions, scuffing his feet and checking an imaginary watch as though they were waiting to meet someone.

When the coast was clear, he seized the foreigner's arm and pulled him through the open doorway into a hall that was piled with rubble and open to the sky. The lefthand side of the building had been completely demolished; stumbling across a carpet of bricks to the right, he pushed open a door hanging off its hinges that led to a couple of interconnecting rooms. Anything of value had long since been stolen and half the strays in Paris were using the place as a lavatory, but at least his fugitive would be hidden. Now, at last, he could take a look at the man. He'd obviously been sleeping rough for a few days, to judge from the state of his clothes and hair, and he didn't smell too good either. He had a boyish, open face that was quick to smile, despite the danger they were in, piercing blue eyes and a dusting of freckles across his nose.

'David,' he said, shaking Jacques' hand. *'Merci. Anglais.'*

Which turned out to be the only French words he knew, and Jacques' English was rudimentary. Taking a card from his pocket with useful phrases translated from English into French, David managed to ask, 'Are the enemy nearby?' (which clearly they were, everywhere) and, 'Can you help me?' (which Jacques had already shown himself willing to do) and, more bewilderingly, 'Where are the nearest British troops?' Jacques shrugged and threw up his hands at this, which made David laugh, but they weren't getting very far.

'You must wait here,' Jacques said, pointing to a packing crate that had served as a seat for somebody, to judge from the empty beer bottles lying around it. He mimed sitting, and the hands of a clock moving around a dial. 'Understand? Don't move. I will come back for you after dark.' He put his hands together and pretended to sleep.

David nodded and shook his hand again. 'I'll be back,' Jacques promised. 'Just wait until nightfall.'

He hurried on home with a renewed sense of purpose. There were people everywhere who needed help, once you opened your eyes – and found the courage not to look away.

Dusk took forever to fall, but eventually it came. Jacques locked *La Page Cachée* and set off, heading first to call on the café where he knew Henri would be having a drink after work. He had to talk to somebody and if there were one person he'd trust with his life, it was his childhood friend. Henri was standing by the bar, reading a newspaper. He threw it down when Jacques appeared. 'Don't know why I waste my money,' he said. 'Nothing but German propaganda.'

Jacques took him outside and hurriedly explained his predicament. Henri whistled softly. 'Well, I'll do what I can. Are you sure about this, though?'

'Absolutely. Thank you, *mon ami*.' He shook Henri's hand. 'I knew I could count on you.'

Henri went back to the café and Jacques hurried along the quiet streets by torchlight, his heart racing, until he came to the patch of waste ground where the derelict building loomed, a forbidding shadow. Steeling himself, he paused for a moment on the threshold, listening for any tell-tale sounds. Pointing his torch at the ground, he stepped gingerly inside, stumbling occasionally as he headed to the right.

Slowly, he pushed the door open, bracing himself for a sudden attack. The room was silent. 'David?' he said softly, flashing his torch into each corner. The packing case was unoccupied, the place deserted. All he could hear was the scuttering of a rat or a mouse in some far corner.

'David!' he called again, more loudly this time. 'It's me, Jacques.'

Cursing under his breath, he made for the door at far end of the room, which led to a small scullery with a cracked sink in the corner. That, too, was empty, the back door locked and rusted immovably shut.

Abandoning caution, Jacques searched as much of the place as he could access, even shining his torch up into the ruined stairwell. Something brushed against his face in the hall and he staggered back in fear, but it was only a bat, its leathery wings outstretched as it flew past him into the night with an angry chitter. Nothing else stirred. David had disappeared.

Jacques peered ahead into the dark, cursing under his breath. What could have happened to the daft fellow? One of the German soldiers might have followed them to his hiding place, but surely they would both have been arrested if that had been the case. A patrol must have found him, or perhaps a down-and-out, looking for somewhere to sleep. Jacques felt like a blind man searching for a husk in a sack of sunflower seeds. He turned for home, choosing a different route that swung by the Arc de Triomphe, calling softly for David whenever he dared and shining his torch into every shadowy doorway. Spotting a café ahead, he was about to hurry past, hoping to be unnoticed, when the glimpse of a blond head as the door opened stopped him in his tracks. It couldn't be, surely? He put away the torch and went inside; fear, anger and relief battling it out in the pit of his stomach.

David was sitting in full view, drinking a glass of red wine and smoking in that ridiculous way. A girl sat opposite him: rather lovely, with long brown hair and beautiful bare arms. They were smiling at each other – to make up for the lack of anything to say, presumably. A trio of German soldiers were in full flow at the next table, shouts of laughter punctuating their noisy conversation. They looked at Jacques with mild curiosity as he approached David and his companion.

'Do I need to pay for your drinks?' he asked the girl in a low voice.

'The Germans have treated us,' she replied, her eyes sparkling with mischief. 'The barman sent me over as an escort in case of trouble.'

A waiter caught Jacques' eye and nodded.

'Thank you. I'll take over from here,' he said, getting to his feet and indicating David should do the same.

The Englishman made him wait while he drained his glass, then he waved to the soldiers and ambled out of the café. The girl came with them, attracting many appreciative glances as she passed. When they were outside, David pointed to her and raised his eyebrows, but Jacques shook his head, so David kissed her goodbye: a long, lingering embrace that Jacques eventually had to interrupt, first with a tactful cough, then with a tap on the shoulder, and finally a determined arm wrestle. On the other side of the window, the Germans whooped and whistled.

Jacques hurried David away, holding him firmly by the elbow and, when they were safely out of earshot, giving vent to his feelings with a long and pointless speech in French about the risk David was running, wandering off and fraternising with the Boche.

'Everyone in that café could tell you were English,' he muttered. 'God knows how the Germans failed to realise.' And now they would have to hurry to get home before the curfew.

Henri was waiting for them by the door of *La Page Cachée*. 'At last,' he said. 'I was about to give up on you.'

'Long story.' Jacques jerked his head in David's direction. 'This one decided to make friends with the Germans.' It was the sort of stunt Henri might have pulled; they should get on well together.

A silent shadow slipped out of the night: Milou, twining around their legs as Jacques led the way by torchlight through the shop to the storeroom's concealed entrance. Together, he and Henri unlatched the bookshelf door and swung it carefully open, while David's eyes widened in surprise. The three of them had just enough space to stand inside the room together without treading on the mattress. The bucket was back in place and Jacques had brought a razor along with soap and a towel. He lit a candle and stuck it in an empty wine bottle.

'So, over to you,' he told Henri. 'Ask him what he's playing at.'

Besides being his closest friend, Henri also happened to speak English. One of his many uncles had fallen in love with the nurse who'd looked after him during the last war and followed her back to London as soon as he was fit. Henri had often stayed with his cousins in England while growing up, and learned to speak the language as a child. Soon he and David were deep in conversation while Jacques leaned against the wall with his hands in his pockets. Occasionally he intervened with a question he couldn't keep to himself any longer, but the other two ignored him.

At last they shook hands and Henri turned to Jacques to share what he'd been told. David was a British pilot, shot down near the city over a week ago while on a reconnaissance flight. He'd made his way to the centre of Paris, hoping to find someone sympathetic to the Allied cause who would help him get back to England.

'He thinks you're going to save his life,' Henri said. 'I didn't tell the poor man he's deluded. What are you going to do with him now?'

'Talk to people I know,' Jacques replied. 'And keep him here till everything's arranged – as long as he behaves himself. Tell him not to go wandering off again, and no smoking in the daytime or he'll give us both away.'

Henri whistled. 'Good luck. Rather you than me.'

Béatrice stopped and stared at Jacques. 'Well, that was the last thing I expected you to say. You picked up a British airman, just like that?'

'I had to,' he replied. 'He was wandering about in the middle of Paris for all the world and his wife to see.'

They carried on walking around the pond. 'There's a network that can help him but it'll take a while to arrange false papers,' Béatrice said.

'He's given me a couple of photographs to use.' Jacques reached into his pocket for an envelope. 'And he has some money, about two hundred francs.'

'Good, that'll be useful.' Béatrice tucked the packet inside her coat. 'Sounds like he's being sensible.'

Jacques pulled a face. 'I wouldn't go that far. He doesn't seem to understand the danger he's in.'

'Is that Gestapo officer still visiting?' Béatrice asked.

Jacques nodded. 'He doesn't seem to suspect anything – yet. He says he'll pass on any information he hears about Mathilde but I think he's mainly trying to find out how much I know.' He lowered his voice, even though no one was nearby. 'Listen, though, what I also wanted to tell you was that Mathilde's not at Mont-Valérien. The priest heard a rumour she might have escaped from the police station before they could bring her up here.'

'Let's hope so,' Béatrice said. 'I'll ask around, see what I can find out. Well, goodbye for now. Leave me another message whenever you need to.'

'You and Mathilde were right,' Jacques said, 'I realise that now. I want to help in whatever way I can.'

'Good.' She allowed herself a brief smile. 'Welcome to the struggle, *mon ami*.'

Jacques felt Mathilde's presence close by over the next few days as he tried to keep his business running with a modicum of effort. He thought about her constantly, as though by holding her in his mind, he could keep her safe. And he was always aware of David, too, only a few feet away behind the shelves. Whenever a customer entered the shop, he tensed, dreading some noise from the storeroom would betray them both. The pilot was young and energetic, and couldn't stay confined in such a small space for long. When the shop was safely closed and shuttered in the evenings, Jacques would release David from his cell and together they would slip outside to walk around Paris under cover of darkness before the curfew fell. There was always a risk they might be stopped and asked for papers, but he felt the Englishman had to breathe fresh air and smoke a cigarette or two, and there was always the imbecile act to fall back on if necessary.

He'd lent David some French phrase books to pass the time and, back at *La Page Cachée*, they would hold whispered conversations long into the night, acting out any phrases that were hard to understand. The Englishman loved animals and had made a friend of Milou, who was often to be found snoozing on his lap. Gradually they got to know each other. Jacques showed David a picture of Mathilde, and David took a photograph from his wallet of a girl with curly blonde hair to whom he was going to propose when he made it home. If he made it home; there were many dangers to be faced before he reached Spain.

One morning, Miryam Isaacson made her usual visit. She was looking thinner and paler than ever. 'How are things?' Jacques asked.

'Getting worse,' she replied. 'We're still hoping we may be granted visas. My father is paying someone with influence at the American Embassy to help us.' She placed a newspaper on the counter and Jacques slid the envelope of cash inside. 'Thank you, Monsieur. If by any chance I'm prevented from coming next time, a friend may call instead.'

She hurried away, passing Herr Schmidt on the way out who held open the door, and turned to watch her pass. 'Who was that?' he asked Jacques, approaching the till.

'No one in particular. A customer, that's all,' he replied. 'Why do you ask?'

'Just curious. She has a distinctive face. Rather Jewish-looking, wouldn't you say?'

'I didn't notice,' Jacques said stiffly. Sometimes the role of obsequious shopkeeper was a little harder to play.

Schmidt glanced at him. 'And Béatrice Lemoine still hasn't been in touch?'

Jacques shook his head. 'I would have told you.'

'I certainly hope so.' Schmidt walked off to browse in the larger room.

Jacques followed him through. 'I've a new acquisition you might like to see. Dickens' *Christmas Carol*, illustrated by Arthur Rackham.' He unlocked the cabinet and took out the book. 'I was hoping you'd call by before anyone else spotted it. Would you like to sit downstairs by the stove and have a look?'

They were too close to David in the storeroom for comfort and to compound the danger, was that cigarette smoke he could smell, drifting underneath the door?

'I'm happy here, thank you.' Schmidt put on a pair of reading glasses and settled himself down on a stool.

Jacques daren't leave him alone so he rearranged some books in that corner of the room, humming under his breath in an attempt to hide any noise David might make. The smell of smoke grew stronger. Milou appeared, twining around his legs, although he was too distracted to pay her any attention.

'Well, what do you think?' he asked, when he could bear the tension no longer.

'It depends on the price, but I could be tempted.' Schmidt peered over his spectacles. 'I'm sure you'll give me a generous discount. What is your cat up to?'

Milou was scratching at the bottom of the secret doorway, miaowing. Jacques tried to shoo her away but she wouldn't be distracted.

'She can smell mice,' he said desperately. 'There's a nest of them somewhere under the floorboards and it's driving her mad.'

Schmidt closed the book and stood up. 'One can often hear mice by putting one's ear to the floor. Shall we try to locate them?'

'No, don't bother. It's too dusty and you'll make a mess of your clothes. Shoo, Milou!' Jacques nudged her away with his foot.

'She does seem agitated,' Schmidt remarked, strolling closer and gazing down at the cat. 'What is it, little one?' He bent to stroke Milou, whereupon at last, thank God, she ran away.

'Now let's go through to the other room and discuss terms,' Jacques said.

Schmidt wrinkled his nose. 'I smell cigarettes. Where could that be coming from?'

Jacques racked his brains. 'The cellar. I had a delivery just now and the driver was smoking down there.'

'You must be careful. A stub carelessly tossed away and your whole shop could go up in flames.' Schmidt stared at the shelves, stocked with nineteenth-century novels and obscure volumes of poetry that would attract little attention. He pulled out a handful of books and looked behind them. 'Very fine workmanship.'

'Thank you.' Jacques' voice came out in a yelp. He cleared his throat. 'These shelves were reclaimed from the library of a house nearby.'

Schmidt ran his fingers over the wooden panelling at the back, rapping in places with his knuckles. 'Beautiful dovetail joints,' he murmured, before replacing the books and turning to Jacques. 'I'll think about the Dickens and let you know.'

'Of course.' Jacques escorted him out. 'Do you have any news of my wife?' he asked, opening the door. 'I don't even know where she's being held.'

'I can't help you there,' Schmidt replied. 'No doubt you'll be informed in due course but if you take my advice, you'll let her go. Being associated with that woman will bring you nothing but trouble and I can only do so much to protect you. I hope you're not stupid enough to think of following her example.'

Jacques did his best to smile. 'You needn't worry on that score. I'm one for a quiet life.'

'Glad to hear it.' Schmidt tipped his hat. 'Good day to you, then.'

Chapter Fifteen

May 1941

It was two weeks before Béatrice's girlfriend Camille appeared at *La Page Cachée* with a note to say Jacques should prepare his consignment for collection at eight the next evening, in the usual spot. That night, he and David celebrated with a half-bottle of wine. Jacques would miss the Englishman in some ways but he was glad to hand the responsibility for keeping him safe to somebody else. And there would be other people taking David's place in the storeroom, he was sure. Lying in bed that night, he wondered whether Madame Scott-Jones had managed to reach England, and where Renée and Louis were at that very moment. He would probably never find out. He sat up and took a small notebook and pen from the drawer of his bedside table. It seemed suddenly important to keep a record of all the fugitives who had passed through that cramped room below. Everyone has a story, Mathilde had written, and it was his responsibility to tell theirs; he couldn't let these people disappear without a trace. He imagined Mathilde looking over his shoulder as he wrote, smiling with approval. She kept a diary and was always telling him he should do the same.

The Puppy

He's tall, with long limbs and large feet that are always tripping over things, fair hair and piercing blue eyes with a chip of ice at the core. He has a prominent Adam's apple and a mole on his right cheek. There is an air of innocence about him, despite the things he must have seen, and an enthusiasm for life which may be stronger because death flies next to him. He loves animals and has made a friend of the shop cat. Most of his friends have been killed. He's twenty-one, and not afraid of anything.

The following evening, Béatrice and a companion – a large, swarthy man with a beard – arrived as darkness fell. Jacques had been looking out for them from the safety of his unlit shop. He'd done his best to make David less conspicuous: the Englishman was now clean-shaven, his hair covered with a workman's cap and his dirty clothes swapped for some which fitted him better, thanks to Henri's priest. He and Jacques waited to make sure no one was following the pair outside, then slipped out together into the night.

'*Adieu,*' David whispered, clasping Jacques' hand for a moment, '*et merci*. For everything.' And with that, the bearded man ushered him away. Jacques felt a brief pang of sadness, followed by an overwhelming gush of relief.

Béatrice stayed behind. 'Will you show me where you've been keeping him?' she asked Jacques in a low voice.

'The shop door's open,' he whispered. 'I'll go first. Wait a few minutes and follow me through.' He was proud of what he and Henri had achieved and keen to show off the converted storeroom.

Béatrice spent some time examining the opening mechanism from both sides. 'And you're sure he doesn't suspect anything, this Nazi of yours? He only comes here as a customer?'

'I think so. He seems to trust me.'

'Good. That could be useful.' Béatrice stepped inside the cell, wrinkling her nose a little at the smell and disorder David had left behind. Considering he'd had so few possessions, he was remarkably untidy. Noticing the crate in the corner, she took off the tablecloth cover and picked up one of the books inside, glancing at Jacques without comment. 'This is better than some of the places I've seen,' she said eventually.

'I need to tidy up, but it's served its purpose,' Jacques replied modestly.

'We have an emergency,' Béatrice went on. 'One of our mountain guides has been wounded and his current lodging isn't secure. Can you keep him here for a few days? He might not make it but there are no other options and he's extremely valuable to us. He's saved the lives of dozens of Englishmen just like yours.'

'Of course,' Jacques said.

'Good.' She shook his hand. 'We'll bring our man round in an hour or so. Sorry for the short notice, but we need to move quickly.'

★ ★ ★

207

It was a couple of hours, in fact, before a taxi drew up outside the shop and two men emerged, supporting another between them. Jacques opened the shop door and beckoned the trio inside, scouring the darkness for any sign of life. The men moved awkwardly, communicating in grunts and whispers. They staggered, crablike, to the back of the shop and stopped for a moment to catch their breath while Jacques swung open the secret door. He had covered the mattress with a fresh sheet, emptied the soil bucket and mopped all the surfaces with disinfectant, so the room at least smelt clean.

The larger of the two bearers laid the injured man tenderly down on the mattress and stood back, breathing heavily. The other passed Jacques a haversack, which turned out to contain fresh bandages and a tin of antiseptic powder.

'Change his dressing every day,' he instructed. 'And give him boiled water to drink when you can. We'll be back in a week or so. A doctor may come in the meantime. He'll ask for a copy of the Larousse medical encyclopaedia, 1933 edition.'

Jacques nodded, dazed, and escorted them back through the shop and out into the night. Alone with his new guest, he lit another candle and approached the mattress for a better look. It was hard to tell the man's age: in his forties, perhaps. He seemed to be barely conscious, his breathing fast and shallow, his teeth chattering although his forehead was clammy and hot to the touch. Jacques unlaced the fellow's boots and took them off. He poured some water into the basin, washed his own hands then moistened a sponge and washed his patient's face, hands and chest. A grubby bandage had been tied around his upper right arm and shoulder, a rusty stain seeping through. Bracing himself, Jacques untied it and removed the dressing beneath as gently as he could. The man groaned, clenching his teeth. The wound in his upper chest looked angry and swollen around the puckered stitches.

'Easy now,' Jacques murmured, applying a fresh layer of powder and a new dressing, though he felt far from easy himself. What if this fellow were to die? What was he expected to do with the body, and who should he tell? He replaced the bandage with a clean one from Mathilde's medicine chest, making a right old hash of tying it, then laid a blanket over the new arrival. He was about half the height of David, which was just as well, stocky and broad-shouldered with a neck as thick as an ox.

'Good night, my friend,' Jacques whispered, blowing out the candles and switching on his torch to light the way. 'I'll be back in the morning.'

He couldn't sleep. After tossing and turning in the bed, which seemed far too large without Mathilde, he threw on an overcoat, collected a flask of boiled water and a couple of cushions and crept back downstairs by torch-light to keep vigil.

His visitor was restless, too. He'd thrown off the blanket and was drenched in sweat, muttering under his breath. 'Hush,' Jacques soothed, bringing the flask to his lips. The man seized Jacques' hand with burning, wiry fingers, spilling water down his chest as he gulped and spluttered.

'*Mon Père, je m'abandonne à toi, fais de moi ce qu'il te plaira. Je suis prêt à tout, j'accepte tout,*' Jacques murmured, remembering how prayer had soothed his mother, but the patient only swore and pushed him away with surprising force.

'Sorry. I'll just sit here for a while.'

Jacques settled his cushions against the wall, stretched out his legs and closed his eyes. They might have been the only two people awake in the whole of Paris, waiting to see what the morning would bring. His world had shrunk to this small cell that he was sharing with a stranger who might not survive the night. He had to stay, even though there was little he could do except sponge the man's face. It was important to bear witness.

Jacques made frequent trips down to his storeroom the next day. It was a Sunday, luckily, so he had no need to open the shop. 'Stocktaking,' he assured Madame Bourdain, who was mopping the stairs with infinite slowness. The guide was restless and occasionally he groaned, tossing his head from side to side on the pillow, but he seemed calmer than he had during the night. By evening, the fever had broken. Jacques had been to see Henri's priest after church and told him he was caring for an invalid; he had come away with two eggs and a bottle of milk, which he baked into a custard and fed his guest in tiny bites. The man tried to grab the spoon but his hand shook so much that he had to allow Jacques to take charge. He also submitted to being washed again and having his dressing changed, watching Jacques warily. The wound was already looking a little less angry.

He has a nose like a beak and hooded, far-seeing eyes. He doesn't want to talk and I know better than to ask questions. His hands are rough and covered in callouses, and his legs are battered. He will have a scar on his right shoulder. His movements are considered, economical; he doesn't waste actions or words. He's conserving his energy for the journeys that lie ahead and the people whose lives he will hold in his hands. All day long, he gazes at a small patch of daylight, dreaming of the time he will be free.

The next day, Jacques decided to open the shop, having warned his patient to keep quiet. An elderly man with a briefcase appeared at lunchtime and asked for a copy of the 1933 Larousse encyclopaedia; Jacques locked up and showed him through to the storeroom.

'Our man seems to be on the mend,' the doctor said, emerging fifteen minutes later. 'Well done. I've given him a tetanus shot and left some more antiseptic but what he really needs is rest.'

'And that's what he shall have,' Jacques replied.

He brought a couple of books on his next visit to the storeroom – adventure stories by Jules Verne – and although his patient eyed them suspiciously, he was soon halfway through the first novel and asked to take it with him when he left, a week later. He was collected one evening by the same burly, bearded fellow who'd dropped him off, and Jacques knew as little about him as when he'd first arrived; it was safer that way. He made sure to show the man a photograph of Mathilde, though, asking him to send word in the remote chance he should ever see or hear of her.

Jacques was meeting Béatrice each week in the Tuileries Gardens now, and she would tell him whether anyone needed shelter, when they'd be arriving, and what passwords he should memorise. Sometimes he would be asked to store equipment rather than human beings: mysteriously heavy boxes or crates, rolls of paper, machine parts. He might receive consignments in the middle of the night, or cycle to addresses in various parts of the city to collect them himself under the pretext of delivering books. In fact, he was legitimately busy on that score, since his regular customers were increasingly reluctant to come into *La Page Cachée* for fear of bumping into Germans.

Schmidt was a frequent visitor, sending Jacques' heart thumping if there was a resident *in situ* behind the shelves. He was tougher with the new arrivals than he'd been with David though, and they were generally better behaved. He took in another Allied pilot – a German Jew who'd moved to England before the war and was now fighting against Hitler – and then a sweet girl from the country who looked about sixteen. He was embarrassed to show her the mattress and chamber-pot bucket, but she didn't seem at all put out. She carried a bulky suitcase and he noticed a gun beside her pillow. Several others followed, fugitives of one kind or another who mostly stayed for a few nights before slipping away under cover of darkness, intent on their own business. An elegant Frenchwoman in her fifties told him her English husband had been killed in a bombing raid so she'd come back to France to work undercover against the Germans; a boy who didn't look old enough to shave arrived at three in the morning wearing a shirt stained with blood that wasn't his.

A few wanted to talk and Jacques was happy to listen, although he never initiated the conversation. He wrote about each of them in his notebook – his visitors' book, he'd taken to calling it – and showed them all a photograph of Mathilde before they left. Maybe she in her turn was being helped by a stranger in some distant place. In his worst moments, he knew she must be dead, because otherwise she would surely have got a message to him somehow. She must have known he'd be frantic with worry. Béatrice hadn't found anyone who'd seen or heard from Mathilde; she seemed to have vanished into thin air.

Tossing and turning one night, Jacques suddenly remembered that he still hadn't seen Estelle, as Mathilde had asked. He called at the stage door of the Folies Bergère the next day but the caretaker said she was no longer working there, so he swung by her apartment on the way home. Estelle lived in the attic of a pink-washed building with green shutters; it glowed like a beacon that evening in the setting sun. Jacques laboured up the steep, cobble-stoned hill towards it, wishing he'd called sooner. The front door was always open so he paused to catch his breath on the threshold before tackling the stairs. When he knocked on Estelle's door, there was no reply, although he could hear the sound of movement inside.

'Estelle? It's me, Jacques,' he called, putting his ear against the wood to listen. After a few more minutes of rustling, the footsteps became louder and he jumped back from the door seconds before Estelle opened it. She was wearing a long green kaftan with billowing sleeves and her feet were bare.

'I haven't seen you for so long,' he said. 'Is everything all right?'

'Yes, fine,' she replied quickly. 'Only I'm a little under the weather today.'

'May I come in?' he asked, since she didn't seem inclined to open the door any wider. 'I have a message from Mathilde.'

Estelle looked past him down the corridor before stepping back, wrapping the kaftan around her. Jacques followed her through to the *salon*, which was as untidy as he'd expected. A typewriter stood on the table by the window, which was covered in sheets of paper.

'Busy writing?' he asked, wondering for a moment whether Estelle's German lover was there. Her bedroom door was shut and she was clearly uncomfortable. He looked at her face more closely. She had put on weight but she seemed in good health; blooming, in fact. He wouldn't have thought she was ill.

'I'm typing up manuscripts for struggling authors,' she replied, with an artificial laugh. 'Plenty of those about these days. So how are you both? Here, sit down.' She cleared a pile of books and newspapers from the sofa.

'Mathilde has left Paris.' Jacques knew instinctively he couldn't tell Estelle the truth; not until he found out what she was hiding, and maybe not even then. 'She's staying with relatives in Provence.'

'Lucky her,' Estelle commented, looking out of the window.

'Why don't you sit down too.' Jacques patted the cushion next to him. 'Mathilde wanted to see you before she left but there wasn't time. She was sorry not to have said goodbye.'

Reluctantly, Estelle made her way to the sofa and perched as far away from him as she could manage. She gave him a sideways glance and said abruptly, 'I've got some news of my own. There's a reason why I haven't been to see you for a while. I'm going to have a baby. See?' She smoothed the fabric over the now unmistakeable swell of her stomach. 'Quite soon, in fact.'

'Oh, my goodness,' Jacques said stupidly. 'So you are.'

Estelle glanced at him. 'No doubt you disapprove.'

'I don't know.' He smiled. 'Despite all this horror, there's still something miraculous about a new life beginning.'

Estelle edged a little closer. 'I couldn't bear to face Mathilde, knowing what she thought of Otto. I've been missing her, though.'

'So have I,' Jacques said.

'When will she be back?' Estelle took a breath. 'I want to ask her to be the baby's godmother. Do you think she'll agree?'

'She'd be honoured, I'm sure. You're her dearest friend, she told me so before she left. She only spoke sharply that evening because she was worried for you.' Jacques squeezed Estelle's hands. 'It may be a while before we see her again but I'm here. How can I help? Are you all right for money?

'I'm managing. Otto gave me some but he's not too pleased about the situation and he won't leave his wife. He's sending me extra ration coupons, though.' She took a handkerchief out of her pocket and blew her nose. 'I've been so desperate to talk to Mathilde. Will you write and let her know?'

'I'll do my best,' Jacques promised. 'When's the baby due?'

'In about six weeks.' Estelle cradled her stomach. 'I suppose I'll have to give it up for adoption but I'm hoping Otto will change his mind once it's born. He has two girls already – what if I could give him a son? That's what all men want, isn't it?' She didn't wait for a reply. 'It's such a relief to have told you at last. Will you come and see me again?'

'Of course. I'm quite busy at the moment, with one thing and another, but I'll try to drop by whenever I can. Is there anything in particular you need?'

'Some company would be nice.' Estelle put on a brave smile. 'Thank you, darling Jacques. You're a good man and your wife is a lucky woman.'

Early one morning in the middle of May, Jacques bumped into his neighbours, the Feldmans, as he was setting off to buy bread. 'Out for the day?' he asked out of politeness, seeing Madame Feldman was wearing a jaunty hat.

'Official business. I have to verify my status at the police station, accompanied by a relative,' Monsieur Feldman replied importantly.

'That sounds alarming.' Jacques thought instantly of Madame Scott-Jones.

'Oh no, it's just a formality.' Feldman took a green postcard out of his jacket pocket and waved it at Jacques. 'See, all above board and well-organised. They have my name and address and date of birth, correctly listed. We've always done everything by the book.'

'And we're French citizens now,' Madame Feldman added.

The couple were Polish by birth, but they'd been living in France for years and their three children had been born in the country. Monsieur Feldman was an electrician and had done some work in *La Page Cachée*, so Jacques had got to know the family a little and liked them. They were hard-working and fiercely proud of their adoptive country, and their three daughters were adorable. Jacques was particularly fond of the youngest, who had a head of flaming red curls.

'I really think it would be wiser not to go,' he said. 'Why don't you lie low for a while and see how things play out?'

'But we have to,' Monsieur Feldman told him. 'You see here: it says the harshest penalties will be imposed on anyone who doesn't attend. Then we should really be in trouble.'

'What do you think is going to happen?' Madame Feldman asked.

'I'm not sure.' Jacques didn't want to worry them unnecessarily. Glancing around, he lowered his voice to add, 'I keep remembering what happened to the Englishwomen last winter.'

'But they were English, foreigners. Our case is completely different.' Monsieur Feldman took his wife's arm. 'Come along, my dear, or we'll be late.'

Jacques watched them go with some misgivings. There were more police about in the streets than usual, he noticed, joining the end of a queue snaking down the pavement outside the *boulangerie*. He was still waiting to enter the shop an hour later when Madame Feldman came hurrying back down the road by herself.

'Lots of other men turned up along with Anatol,' she said, 'and we wives have been sent away to fetch a suitcase of their things. No one will tell us where they're going or why.'

Jacques' unease turned to dread; he should have been more insistent. The women queuing around him murmured their unease between themselves but nobody wanted to catch his eye or talk out loud. 'Do you want me to come to the police station with you?' he called after Madame Feldman, but she was already out of earshot.

He passed a slow day in the shop, with only a box of underground newspapers languishing in the storeroom to keep him company, so he closed early and went to ask Madame Bourdain whether the concierge network had any news of the men who'd been summoned by postcard.

'They were all arrested,' she said, 'taken to Austerlitz station and shipped off God knows where.'

He turned to leave. 'I must tell Madame Feldman.'

'Save your breath, she already knows,' Madame Bourdain called after him, and indeed, nobody answered when Jacques rapped on the Feldmans' door upstairs, although he stood there for fifteen minutes.

Over three thousand foreign-born Jews had been rounded up and sent out of Paris to a camp further south, it emerged via whispers and reports in partisan newsletters over the next few days. German soldiers roamed the streets, openly looting abandoned apartments and searching for escapees. They'd been given licence to act as they pleased. Jacques saw a thug with a machine gun pistol-whip an old man who fell into the street, hitting his head against the kerb. The soldier nudged his body with the toe of his boot, his face indifferent.

'The Nazis will be coming for us next,' Miryam Isaacson told him. 'They won't stop at foreigners.' She was going into hiding, and asked Jacques if he'd deliver the family's money to a piano shop off the avenue des Ternes each month.

'The clean-up has begun,' announced Guillaume de Bruyère, sauntering into *La Page Cachée* one afternoon. 'We'll soon send all these grubby money-lenders packing. Now, how is my book selling? Would you like me to sign some more copies?'

The writer was back in fashion: his latest novel featuring an heroic son of the Reich, *It Happened in Paris,* had recently been published in both French and German and he'd embarked on a second career as a journalist, peddling the Vichy line.

'We have plenty of stock, thank you,' Jacques replied. 'I'm afraid sales of the title are a little slow.'

He was finding it increasingly difficult to hide his feelings and had come close to punching a man who'd spat at an elderly woman in the street and called her a filthy Jewish whore. Jews were fair game since the mass arrests; any playground bully could take a swipe at one. He still hadn't seen anything of Madame Feldman, though he regularly went upstairs to knock on her door.

One evening he heard someone moving around inside the apartment.

'Madame Feldman, are you all right?' he called. 'It's me, Jacques Duval. I only want to help.'

But when the door opened, Madame Bourdain was standing behind it. 'They've gone,' she said curtly. 'Stop making such a racket, you'll bring the police here.'

'So what are you doing?' he asked.

'Tidying up,' she replied, narrowing her eyes at him, 'making sure there's nothing for the Gestapo to steal. If that's any of your business.'

Jacques kept his own front door ajar so he could hear the concierge going back downstairs. When she emerged from the Feldmans' apartment half an hour later, she was carrying a suitcase. Evidently the Germans weren't the only ones raiding Jewish people's homes.

Chapter Sixteen

August 1941

Paris sweltered in the heat, with scarcely a breeze to stir the air. Close-packed apartment buildings basked in the sun all day and roasted their inhabitants gently at night. Madame Bourdain sat in her *loge* with her feet in a bucket of water and a damp towel over her forehead, and Milou drowsed on the doorstep of *La Page Cachée*. Jacques' storeroom had turned into an oven; any papers left uncovered became faded and scorched, and any people he sheltered left after a day or so. Despite the torpor, though, Parisians were jittery with nerves. The war was now moving in a different direction: Hitler had turned his attention away from Britain and invaded the Soviet Union in June.

'He must be mad,' Béatrice whispered to Jacques one night when she collected a crate he'd been keeping in the storeroom. 'Now Stalin and all the communists will turn against him and help us.'

An undercurrent of resentment against the German occupiers gathered force. In the middle of August, a group of young people streamed out of the Saint Denis Métro station, waving a French flag, singing the Marseillaise and shouting *'Vive la France!'* German troops and French police broke up the march, and six of the protestors were arrested.

Sylvie from upstairs was helping Jacques in the shop during her summer holidays. 'Have you heard?' she asked him as they unpacked a consignment of books a few days later. 'Two of those demonstrators have been sentenced to death. One of them's a Jew but the other was only a communist. Still, I suppose they're both as bad as each other, that lot.'

'Not so bad, really, just singing and waving a flag.' Jacques sat back on his heels, mopping his brow with a handkerchief. 'I'm afraid this will lead to more trouble.'

That trouble came more quickly than he'd anticipated. Two days after the protestors had been executed, a German midshipman was shot and killed at a Métro station by a young French communist.

'Now we're for it,' Henri told Jacques over a beer. 'Have you seen the posters? Anyone the Boche arrest from now on will be treated as a hostage, and you know what that means.' He drew a finger across his throat. 'Whenever the fancy takes them.'

'But that will just make people angrier and more determined,' Jacques said.

'Only if they're crazy.' Henri lowered his voice. 'I hope you're not still keeping anything illegal in that storeroom of yours. I can't believe I'm saying this to you, of all people, but be sensible, Jacques. It's not worth the risk.'

The random attacks on German soldiers increased and now police were everywhere in the city, checking identity cards and rounding up more Jews. The whole of the eleventh *arrondissement* was surrounded at dawn. Police went from house to house with lists of names, and over four thousand Jews were arrested in a single day and shipped off to prison camps. Jacques felt guilty for not having called before now to see how the Isaacsons were. Now he was no longer seeing Miryam, he had no news of them, and the next time he went to leave their money at the piano shop in the avenue des Ternes, he found it locked and shuttered. That Sunday, he pulled a hat low over his eyes and cycled to the Isaacsons' house. There was no reply when he rang their bell, and none of the barking from Alphonse he expected either. Stepping back, he noticed a notice written in large letters that had been pasted on one of the ground-floor windows.

'Here lived two Jews who have killed themselves. This course of action is highly recommended to others.'

Jacques leant against the wall, blank with shock. He couldn't bear to think of the desperation that had driven the Isaacsons to take their own lives, and the callousness of those words broke his heart. Did Miryam even know her parents were dead? Had she seen this notice? Launching himself at the window, he tried to rip it from the glass – thinking of Mathilde as he did so, on that winter night after their dinner with Estelle – scrabbling and tearing at the hated words. Monsieur Isaacson was a kind, clever man who had fought for France and loved his family, and the Nazis had robbed him of all he had, even his dignity. Jacques gave way to a sense of desolation that was close to despair. Everything and everyone he cared about were threatened by the evil sweeping through his country and he couldn't protect them, no matter how hard he tried. Sinking to his haunches, he buried his head in his hands.

Something cold, damp and whiskery pushed against his cheek. Startled, he found himself gazing into the shaggy brown face of the Isaacsons' dog – thinner but instantly recognisable. Alphonse sat there, looking at him expectantly with his head on one side.

'I'm sorry,' Jacques said, feeling in his pockets, 'I have nothing to give you.'

He staggered to his feet, shaking off Alphonse who was attempting to mount his leg. Despite himself, he laughed.

'Come on, then,' he said, picking up the dog and depositing him in his bicycle basket. 'Let's see what food we have at home. Milou won't be pleased, though.'

On the evening of 3 September, Jacques went to Sacré Coeur to sit on the steps of the terrace and look out over the city. He wasn't expecting Mathilde to appear – that would have been a miracle – but he wanted to feel close to her, to think of her at the time and place they'd agreed and know that she was thinking of him too – if she was still alive. I'm glad you don't have to see how terrible things are in Paris, *chérie*, he told her silently, but I miss you so much, it sometimes feels too heavy a burden to bear. He imagined her sitting beside him, her arm through his and her head resting against his chest. I went to see Estelle this afternoon, he went on. You're not going to believe this but she's had a baby, a little girl. You were right to be worried: Otto's not going to support her and if anyone finds out she's been sleeping with a German, she'll be in serious trouble. Her daughter's adorable, though. She's called Celeste and her middle name is Mathilde. Estelle was going to have her adopted but she's changed her mind. She asked me—

And here Jacques stopped. He couldn't tell Mathilde, even in his imagination, that Estelle had asked whether the two of them would be willing to bring up Celeste as their own child. 'I could keep her with me till Mathilde comes back to Paris,' she'd said, 'and then you can take over. What do you say? Please, Jacques. I can't think of two better parents.'

That might have been the moment to explain that his wife had been arrested and he currently had no idea where she was, or even whether she was still alive, but he couldn't trust Estelle not to share the news with Otto. She might not mean to but she was indiscreet and in a febrile state at the moment; he'd been alarmed by her pallor and distracted expression as she talked, almost hysterically at times.

'I'm sorry,' she'd apologised, twisting her fingers. 'I haven't had much sleep, that's all, and I'm so besotted by this little creature. She is the most beautiful baby in the world, though, isn't she?' And Jacques had agreed.

Well, that's enough for now, he told Mathilde, standing up and dusting off the seat of his trousers. The only other thing to add is the fact we now have a dog. I hope you won't mind. He's not much trouble, apart from the fact he wants to mount everything in sight, including poor old Milou. Happy anniversary, *chérie*. Maybe we'll be together next year.

He couldn't bring himself to look too far ahead; the future seemed murky, and fraught with danger.

He was to collect his next two fugitives from Père Lachaise cemetery the following day: the rendezvous had been arranged for eleven o'clock at the tomb of Oscar Wilde. Someone would approach him and say, '*The Sphinx* is my favourite poem of Wilde's,' to which he was to reply, 'I prefer *The Ballad of Reading Gaol*.'

'We must be especially careful,' Béatrice had warned him the night before when he'd met her by the lamppost in the square. 'There are police all over the city, and everyone will be looking for this pair. You won't have to keep them for long – we'll move them on after a couple of days. I'll tell you the arrangements on Friday, in the Tuileries Gardens. And remember, don't come near me if I have my hands in my pockets.'

Chaining up his bicycle outside the cemetery entrance, Jacques recalled another sunny morning, this time in spring, when he and his wife had cycled here to wander among the gravestones. She'd wanted to visit the tomb of Heloise and Abelard, the medieval lovers who'd had a child out of wedlock, married in secret and then been forced to part. Abelard had become a monk and Heloise a nun, and they had written to each other for years until they were finally reunited in death.

'You wouldn't forget me, would you, if we were separated?' Mathilde had asked, and he'd laughed, because the question was too ridiculous to answer.

It was perfect autumn weather, the trees ablaze with russet and gold, and leaves that had begun to fall swirling about on the breeze. He had arrived in good time so he took the long way round, gazing at vast family mausoleums and reading the dedications to devoted wives and husbands. A couple of nuns passed by, their hands clasped together and eyes downcast, and a woman pushed an old-fashioned perambulator along the path, its wheels squeaking over the cobblestones. Jacques glanced inside as he approached. It was a huge carriage for a tiny baby, and he wondered what she might have been hiding under the mattress. Everyone in Paris had their secrets now.

Eventually he reached Oscar Wilde's tomb. The plain, rectangular block of stone with its straight lines and winged figure staring ahead stood out among the ornate sepulchres and bronze busts. Jacques couldn't decide whether he found the monument ugly or admired its simplicity.

He remembered a line from Wilde's poem and murmured it aloud. 'Fawn at my feet, fantastic Sphinx! And sing me all your memories!'

There was nobody about. He walked five minutes in one direction, then five minutes in the other. A couple came towards him, arm in arm. The woman wore a fur coat, despite the sunshine, and wooden-soled shoes that clattered on the ground like castanets; the man was broad-shouldered and substantial. They might fit in Jacques' storeroom, but it would be a tight squeeze. The pair passed him by and headed for The Sphinx, where they stopped. The man stayed on the path, lighting a cigarette, while the woman approached the statue and stood before it with her head bowed. Jacques strolled towards her and stood nearby at a respectful distance. He must have waited for five minutes or so before he gave a discreet cough. Lifting her head, she stared at him, expectant yet nervous. He smiled to show her there was nothing to fear, she could go ahead and tell him *The Sphinx* was her favourite poem. She had to repeat the words; he couldn't say them for her.

Suddenly he was grabbed by the coat collar, lifted off his feet and whirled around.

'What's your game?' snarled the broad-shouldered man, cigarette clenched between his teeth.

'I'm so sorry,' Jacques stammered. 'I didn't mean any harm. This is an unfortunate misunderstanding.'

'Oh, yes? Looks clear enough to me what you're up to.' The man spat out his cigarette and drew back his fist.

'No!' They both turned to see the nuns running towards them, waving. 'Please stop,' the shorter one gasped. 'This is a peaceful resting place, it mustn't be defiled by violence.'

Approaching Jacques' assailant, she laid her hand on his arm and looked up at him with such innocent good-ness that he dropped his fist.

'Thank you,' she said. 'And may God bless you for respecting my wishes.'

He jabbed a finger in Jacques' chest. 'You're in luck, you pathetic creep. Take this as a warning and don't pull a trick like that again. Understand?'

'Of course.' Jacques straightened his collar. 'I really didn't—'

'Don't push it.' The woman in the fur coat had joined them by now. 'If it wasn't for the sister here, you'd be flat on the ground by now.' She tossed her head and off they stalked, full of righteous indignation.

Jacques thanked the young nun, trying to regain some dignity. 'This wasn't what you think.'

'I know.' She smiled again, a hint of mischief in her eyes this time. He stared at her and then her companion, the light dawning.

'I think *The Sphinx* is my favourite poem of Wilde's,' said his rescuer, gazing at the tomb.

Jacques let out his breath. 'And I prefer *The Ballad of Reading Gaol*. Shall we go? I'll wheel my bicycle and you can follow.'

He only dared glance round once or twice to check the two nuns were walking demurely behind him, expecting at any moment to hear shouts and running feet. A closer look at the taller of the pair had revealed a masculine face with the beginnings of a moustache. They were members of the Young Communist league, he discovered, once they were safely installed in his storeroom, and to make matters worse, the young man was also a Polish Jew. Communists were being hunted all over the city, blamed for the attacks on Germans.

'You must stay absolutely quiet,' he told the couple. 'I can keep my shop closed for another few days but there are people walking past in the street who might hear you.'

'Thank you. We'll be careful,' the girl said. She did most of the talking while her boyfriend stayed quiet, his dark eyes fixed on her. The names they gave were Antoine and Nicole, although Jacques called them Romeo and Juliet to himself.

'I'm afraid the conditions are primitive.' He glanced at the bucket in the corner. 'Maybe you could stay upstairs in my apartment while your friend sleeps here? I have a spare room.'

'We'd sooner be together,' she replied, and they smiled at each other.

That evening, Jacques knocked on the wooden panelling concealing the storeroom door and swung it open. Antoine was lying with his head in Nicole's lap, reading one of the books Jacques had left for them – Saint-Exupéry's *Le Petit Prince* – while she stroked his hair.

'Sorry to intrude,' he said, although they weren't at all embarrassed. He remembered those heady early days with Mathilde, when all he had wanted was to be with her and any time apart, no matter how short, was filled with the ache of longing. These two were so young; this cat-and-mouse existence might have seemed like a game to them, except they must have known prisoners of sixteen and seventeen were being shot every week.

'I've brought you some bread and a few carrots,' he said, taking out the supplies from his rucksack. 'I'm sorry there's so little. I'll try to find more tomorrow.'

'That's wonderful, thank you.' Antoine sat up, swinging his legs around.

'You won't have to stay here for long,' Jacques said. 'I'll be seeing my contact soon and she'll tell me the arrangements for moving you on.'

Yet they would be hunted wherever they went; nowhere was safe.

She's very young, no more than sixteen or so, with dark hair cut in a bob and an air of fierce determination. She has a scar over her left eyebrow and her fingernails are bitten down to the quick. The boy is a couple of years older, slower to speak but with an air of quiet authority. They are driven by passion: for each other, for the communist ideals that have brought them together, and for the fight for freedom. The idea of separation frightens them more than death.

La Page Cachée stayed closed for the next couple of days. Béatrice's warning had alarmed Jacques, and he needed to find food for his guests. Henri's priest gave him half a sausage and a packet of macaroni, but he had nothing to put on it, not even butter. How much longer could everyone survive like this? On Friday, he walked to the Tuileries Gardens to meet Béatrice and find out when and how the young couple were to be collected. The weather was turning and a cold wind made him wrap his jacket more tightly around himself. One of his shoes had a hole in the sole that he'd stuffed with newspaper, but that wouldn't last long in the rain.

He spotted her on the other side of the pond, wearing a brown wig this time and a swing jacket with a fur collar. She came towards him with her hands in her pockets. Her hands in her pockets. He stopped for a moment, remembering, and they passed each other without making eye contact. A man in a trench coat and fedora was walking some fifty paces behind her. Jacques was careful not to look at him, either. He made a circuit of the pond and followed them both at a distance along the wide path towards the Louvre.

Béatrice was hurrying now, taking longer strides with her trousers flapping. The man in the trench coat broke into a leisurely jog and now she was running, too, heading left down the avenue du Général Lemonnier, her jacket flying out behind her as she zigzagged between the trees. Jacques tore after them, although there was little he could do, narrowly avoiding a woman walking a poodle on a lead who shouted after him. He caught a glimpse of Béatrice's brown wig ahead as she sprinted towards the rue de Rivoli, gaining ground; with a bit of luck, she'd get away. Her pursuer stopped and raised his arm, and a shot rang out.

'No!' Jacques cried, but the wind tore away his voice and he was too far behind to reach Béatrice as she swayed for a moment before staggering on, clutching her arm. The next thing he saw was a black Citröen swinging around a corner and into the park, the passenger doors flying open before it had come to a halt. Two men burst out, raced towards Béatrice and grabbed her, one on each side. In the space of a couple of minutes, they had bundled her into the car, slammed the door and driven off, tyres screeching. The man who had fired the gun put it away, straightened his coat and strolled in the opposite direction. Nobody gave him a second glance.

Jacques turned for home, his heart racing and his head down. It had all happened so quickly, and he was numb with shock. He'd grown to like Béatrice over the months and thought he'd earned her respect in return, so much more valuable for being hard-won. Her laconic presence was reassuring; she made him feel brave, encouraged his first tentative steps to resist and was there to help when necessary. He couldn't help feeling that he'd let her down. Maybe if he'd stayed closer behind her, or run faster, or suggested they meet somewhere else? But then he'd have been arrested too. The implications of her capture began to sink in. She would most probably be tortured to reveal the names of her associates and there was no knowing what she might say; the Gestapo had the cruellest methods. Not everyone could hold out and there was no shame in that, but they were all in even greater danger now.

He hurried back to his apartment building, then through the back door into the shop, where he knocked on the panelling and swung open the concealed doorway. The young lovers were asleep, looking more childlike than ever. Hardening his heart, he shook them awake.

'We'll have to move you on,' he said, as they blinked and rubbed their eyes. 'The Germans have arrested my contact and I don't know how long she'll hold out.'

Yet where could they go? Béatrice and Camille had moved from their apartment near the Gare d'Austerlitz and he didn't know their new address. He might approach Henri or the priest who'd been giving him supplies and ask them to help, but how could he expect them to risk their lives when they'd done so much already? And then there was the matter of Béatrice herself. He ought to tell Camille what had happened, urgently, but he had no idea how to find her. She might come to the shop, of course, when she realised something was wrong, and that he and Béatrice had been due to meet.

His hands were shaking so he folded his arms and leaned against the wall. 'Do you have any friends in the city?' he asked the young couple, trying not to sound desperate.

'Not anymore. They're either in prison or in hiding.' Nicole's face was pale.

'It's all right, we'll make a plan,' he said. 'Perhaps—'

The words died on his lips as a shaft of light fell into the room, and the secret door, which he was sure he'd latched, swung slowly open. Sick with fear, he straightened, ready to – what? He had no idea.

The stumpy, square figure of Madame Bourdain appeared on the threshold. 'Well, this is quite the party,' she said. 'Who have we got here?'

Antoine scrambled to his feet, fists clenched, and Nicole reached up to lay a restraining hand on his arm.

'Two people in need of help,' Jacques said, his mouth dry.

Madame Bourdain tutted. 'With all of Paris looking for them, no doubt, and you rushing about leaving doors unlocked behind you. I've told you a hundred times, Monsieur Duval, I don't want trouble and you seem intent on causing it.'

Nobody spoke for a few seconds. 'So what are you going to do?' Jacques asked.

'Give you a piece of my mind,' Madame Bourdain replied. 'I know perfectly well what you're up to, have done for months – creeping about at all hours with your food and your slop bucket. You're not the only one playing this game and you'll give us all away if you carry on like this, especially with that German sniffing around.

I'll bet he can see through you as easily as a window pane.' She glared at Jacques with her usual hostility.

Us? he thought. So was Madame Bourdain working against the Nazis too? An image of her emerging from the Feldmans' apartment with a suitcase flashed into his mind; maybe she hadn't been looting the place for her own ends after all.

She inspected the two young people. 'How long are you planning on keeping this pair?'

'I need to find them somewhere else as soon as possible,' Jacques told her. 'They're not safe here anymore.'

'Marvellous. So that's why you're rushing around like a headless chicken. Well, then, I'd better visit my niece in the country tomorrow. There's a place nearby they can stay.' She nodded at the nuns' habits, hanging from a nail in the wall. 'A convent, would you believe. They should feel at home.'

Antoine reached for Nicole's hand and they both looked at Jacques. He knew what they were asking: could this woman be trusted or would she hand them over to the Germans? He shrugged. They had no other option.

'Do you have identity cards or is that too much to expect?' Madame Bourdain asked the pair, hands on her hips.

Antoine reached under the mattress, took out their papers and passed them over.

'Better than nothing, I suppose, but only just.' She handed the cards back to him. 'I'll meet you by the lamppost at seven tomorrow morning. And have a shave first, young man.'

That night, Jacques brought down a couple of cushions and slept – or tried to – on the floor outside the storeroom. There was nothing he could have done were the Gestapo to have discovered his hiding place but he wanted to be close at hand. If Antoine and Nicole were found, the Nazis would come for him next; he might as well get it over with.

Early the next morning, two nuns were waiting for Jacques in the storeroom. He embraced them both. 'Keep the book,' he said, handing *Le Petit Prince* to Antoine. 'And by the way, this is a picture of my wife, Mathilde Duval. If you see or hear of her on your travels, could you send me a message? Her code name is Colette.'

Antoine studied the photograph. 'But I know this woman,' he said, handing it back to Jacques. 'I have met her.'

'Are you sure?' Jacques could hardly believe the words he'd been longing to hear. 'Have another look.'

'Oh yes, that is her.' Antoine smiled. 'There are not many who look like this.'

'Where was she? And when did you see her?'

'She was working in a vineyard, somewhere south of Lyon. I saw her about a month ago, when the harvest was beginning.'

'Really?' That didn't sound like Mathilde. Although, wait – hadn't Renée mentioned something about a job in a vineyard? 'Whereabouts, exactly?'

Antoine shrugged. 'I'm not sure. We were walking for many days and I saw her only one night. I don't know the name of that place.'

Jacques wanted to shake the boy, to look inside his head and see a picture of his darling Mathilde there.

Relief surged through his body. She was alive! Not shut up inside some awful prison or police cell like poor Béatrice, waiting to be interrogated. He stared at the photograph, taken on their wedding day. Did she still love him as much as she had then? And if so, why hadn't she managed to send him a message?

Chapter Seventeen

April 2022

'So here we are.' Juliette threw out her arm with a flourish. 'What do you think?'

'Hmm.' Her brother inspected the shop from top to bottom, wrinkling his nose and pushing up his glasses in a gesture that took her straight back to their childhood. His sandy hair was almost completely grey now but she could still see the gangly twelve-year-old he used to be. 'Well, it needs a coat of paint, that's for sure.' He peered through the window. 'Have you been inside?'

'Of course.' She tried to suppress her irritation. 'It'll need fitting out with shelves and probably some electrical work but apart from that, it's perfect.'

Andrew looked around. 'And this location: it's kind of tucked away, isn't it?'

'Not really,' she said, bristling. 'We're close to the Métro station and I'll make sure there are plenty of signs. There's a big ex-pat community around here because of all the multi-national companies in La Défense, and lots of students and tourists heading for Montmartre. But don't you recognise this square? It's the one in Mémé's painting.'

'What painting?'

'The one that always hung in her bedroom.' Impatiently, Juliette found the picture on her phone and showed it to him. 'I'm sure this place meant something to her.'

'Hmm,' Andrew said again. 'But a bookshop, Jules? Are you sure? A bookshop in Paris?'

'Absolutely a bookshop in Paris. This is what it used to be, see?' She scrolled through her phone some more and showed him the photo of *La Page Cachée* in all its glory. 'You know what a bookworm I am. And we're both a quarter French, though you don't care to admit it. Don't you think Mémé would love to think of me living here?'

'I guess she would. I'm proud of you, sis.' Andrew put his arm through hers. 'And you know I don't have much imagination. Let's have some lunch and talk it all through.'

They walked towards the café, arm in arm. Juliette had been surprised when Andrew had texted to say he was going to visit her in Paris and surprised, too, by the rush of affection she'd felt, seeing him walk through the airport Arrivals gate. If she needed help, she realised, he would drop everything and come running.

As they approached the café, the door opened and out came the last person she wanted to see: Nico. Dammit, she'd given up her morning coffee here but she'd thought lunchtime would be safe. At least he had the grace to look embarrassed. Returning his greeting with a cold nod, she sailed through the door he was holding open with her head high.

Andrew raised his eyebrows. 'Who was that? He gave you quite the stare.'

'Oh, nobody in particular. I was going to rent his apartment but it fell through. He messed me around, that's all, but it's no big deal.' She smiled at Pascal, the waiter, and they took a table by the window.

'So you still don't have anywhere to live for the long term?' Andrew asked, opening the menu.

'Not yet, but I'm sure I'll find somewhere soon. And you have to admit, the apartment I'm looking after is beautiful.' Thérèse had come to Juliette's rescue; she'd been so appalled by Nico's behaviour that she'd asked around and managed to find someone in their building who was going away for three months and needed a house sitter.

They ordered their food and Pascal brought over a couple of beers and some bread.

'This is just a lot to take in,' Andrew said, tearing a slice of baguette. 'One minute you're going on a two-week vacation and the next I hear, you're planning a whole new life. Are you sure you're doing the right thing?'

'Not really,' Juliette replied. 'How sure can anyone be about anything? But I'm going to put everything into this and see how it works out. And Paris is where I want to be, I know that much.'

'Aren't you homesick, though? Don't you miss all your friends and family?'

'A little.' She chewed reflectively. 'But now the kids have both left home and Lindsay's moved to Florida, I've been feeling kind of lost. All my life, I've been making decisions based on what other people wanted. This adventure is just for me. Is that selfish? Maybe, but I don't want to wake up in thirty years' time and realise I've wasted my life. We only get one shot – might as well make the most of it.'

'But you and Kevin. . .' Andrew shook his head. 'You seemed like such a great couple, perfect for each other. Patsy and I were always fighting so nobody was surprised when we split up, but I thought you two would be together forever.'

Juliette smiled. 'Me too. I'm not sorry, though. I mean, of course I'm sad in lots of ways, but I've been coasting for years, putting up with a load of crap because it was easier than trying to change the situation. I needed a kick up the ass, and that's what Kevin gave me.'

'Does he know about the bookshop idea?' Andrew asked. 'You need to tell him, Jules. If you set up a business and it fails, he'll be liable too. You could lose your house.'

Juliette held up her hands. 'It's OK, I'm getting legal advice. There's some declaration I can make which means my assets won't be seized. I just want to wait until my plans are more definite and then I'll share them with Kevin, I promise.'

'I never took you for a businesswoman,' Andrew said. 'And in France? Isn't the bureaucracy a nightmare?'

'Things are becoming easier for entrepreneurs.' Juliette felt a glow of pride: she liked to think of herself that way. 'If you're running a micro enterprise, you can get up and running quite quickly.'

'But a bookshop isn't a micro enterprise,' Andrew said. 'Apart from fixing up the premises, you'll have to invest in stock and that's expensive. How are you going to raise the capital?'

'I have the money Mom left, and I'm applying for a bank loan. I think it should work out. At the moment, I'm trying to sort out an agreement with the shop's landlord. I'm subletting because the previous owners went out of business, you see, so it's a bit complicated.' She suppressed a shiver of disquiet. 'I'll need to pay a deposit up front but if the bank doesn't agree to give me a loan, he'll refund the whole amount.'

Andrew still didn't look convinced 'Listen, I'm putting together a business plan with a marketing strategy and cash flow projections,' she said, ticking off the list on her fingers. 'I've got a business adviser, an accountant, a lawyer, and a friend of a friend with a bookshop who's going to act as my consultant, and let me work on the shop floor for the next few weeks to gain experience. I'm serious about this.'

'I'll take your word for it,' Andrew said. 'Just one question: if you don't have a fixed address, how can you register your company or get a bank account?'

'I'm working on that.' Another shiver. She had signed and dated the rental agreement Nico had left, scribbled an illegible squiggle under his name and given a copy to the bank and the Chamber of Commerce. If any post arrived at the apartment, he would have to pass it on for her, and serve him right. He owed her.

Their steaks arrived in a puddle of garlic butter, along with a basket of golden *frites*, crispy and delicious.

'So I have another question,' Andrew said. 'When the food is this good, how come you've lost weight?'

Juliette laughed. 'I've taken up running, would you believe.' Most evenings, she made a couple of circuits of the Parc Monceau, pounding along the paths to forget the stresses of the day and make herself tired enough to sleep. She was glad to have left L'Hotel Corot and grateful to Thérèse for taking so much trouble to find her somewhere to stay, but the apartment was so minimal, she didn't feel comfortable. Everything was white: carpets, walls, kitchen cabinets, furniture, bedlinen. At night, she lay awake in the snowy bed, feeling like a lettuce leaf in a giant refrigerator.

'Well, you look great.' Andrew raised his glass. 'Here's to you and The Forgotten Bookshop. May she soon be remembered.'

Andrew stayed for a week. He found staying in other people's homes too personal so he wouldn't share Juliette's apartment or book an Airbnb; instead, he'd found a hotel nearby in Montmartre. Juliette was becoming increasingly taken up with the business administration course she'd started and her sessions in the bookshop, but they would meet every day for at least a couple of hours, either having dinner together or exploring some hidden area of the city Juliette had discovered. The afternoon before he was due to leave, she took him to the *Cité des Fleurs*, in the Batignolles district, close to Ilse and Claude's home. The 'city' was in fact a long, cobblestoned street, bordered on each side by the back gardens of elegant villas. It was a pedestrianised area, an oasis of calm amid the hustle of Paris.

'This place is awesome,' Andrew said, gazing around. 'How did you find it?'

'A friend showed me one day,' Juliette said. 'Apparently you have to follow the rules if you live here. Your fence can't be too high, the layout of your garden has to be approved, there can only be so many trees, you can't build an extension. . .'

'And no satellite dishes,' Andrew commented.

'Satellite dishes? *Quelle horreur!*'

They wandered on, stopping frequently for Andrew to take photographs. The lane was punctuated by tall, slender lampposts and bronze urns on pillars, amid the fresh green foliage of trees newly burst into leaf. Each view was more beautiful than the last.

'This is what I wanted to show you.' Juliette pointed to a plaque attached to an iron gate outside house number 25. In 1944, the house had been raided by the Gestapo because false papers were being produced there; one woman was shot on the spot and six others died after being deported.

'It's hard to imagine people with guns running down this street,' she said, while Andrew read the inscription. 'I bet it looked much the same in 1944. And Mémé lived through the whole thing, you know. She would have been fifteen when war broke out.'

'She never wanted to talk about the past,' Andrew said. 'I asked her about the war once, and she wouldn't tell me a thing.'

'What else do you remember about her?'

'I remember the tart she used to make after Christmas. What was it called? The *galette des rois*, that's right, for Epiphany, with the tiny figures hidden in the almond paste. I nearly broke my tooth one year but it was worth

244

it to be king. And the way she cooked chicken in a pot with leeks and carrots. So . . . I remember her food, basically.' He smiled. 'And those Edith Piaf records she used to play, waving her arms around. Oh, and once we watched the film *Casablanca* together and she cried over that scene in the café when they sing the Marseillaise. She was very patriotic.'

'Yet she left France to marry Grandad when she'd only known him a fortnight, and she hardly ever went back,' Juliette said. 'I don't recall her talking about her parents, or her brothers and sisters.'

'Well, I guess Mémé's a mystery we may never work out.'

'I'm going to start looking into our family history,' she told him, 'just as soon as I get the chance. That's the excuse Kevin's come up with to explain why I'm still here. Maybe I should turn it into a reality.'

'Honestly, I think you have enough on your plate without historical research.' Andrew looked at his watch. 'And perhaps we should think about making for home, if you're having people over for dinner tonight.'

'Oh, goodness, yes. There's a million things I need to do.'

She'd invited Thérèse, Arnaud, Ilse and Claude for dinner that evening to repay some of their hospitality – and maybe also to show off her French friends to Andrew. If things had been different, she might have invited Nico, but she wasn't going to waste her time even thinking about him. The shoulder of lamb was already slow roasting but she had the meringues to poach for *iles flottantes*, potatoes and green beans to prep, and flowers to buy.

'Something colourful,' she told Sophie, the assistant. 'The apartment I'm staying in is so white, I might as well be living in an igloo.' She'd better warn her guests to take off their shoes and pray no one spilt red wine on the carpet.

'And you are having people for supper?' Sophie asked, arranging red and yellow tulips in a dazzling Catherine wheel and tying them with raffia. 'That's nice.' She had long, straight hair, parted in the middle, and sad, blue-grey eyes.

'Do you want to come?' Juliette asked, on a whim. 'You might find the conversation a bit boring but at least it'll be practice for you.'

Sophie worked part-time in the flower shop while she studied for a degree in business and English, so she was keen to speak as much as she could. Juliette had chatted to her one afternoon, discovering that her parents lived miles away and that she was lonely in Paris.

'I'd love to!' Sophie brightened immediately. 'And it's all right, I don't mind talking to old people.'

'Great.' Juliette bit back a smile. 'I'll see you around seven thirty, then. Give me your number and I'll text you the address.' Sophie was around Emily's age and brought out all Juliette's maternal instincts; it would be good to feed her up a little.

She thought about Emily and Ben as she walked back to the apartment. Emily hadn't been in touch again so Juliette had emailed, trying to explain why she'd decided to stay in Paris. She didn't feel angry towards Kevin anymore but she didn't want to fight for their marriage, either. Ben had called one evening so she'd reassured him that she was coping on her own and that maybe both she and Kevin might be happier apart in the long run. She missed the kids, though, and talking over the phone was no substitute for a hug. When she was settled somewhere and Emily had come back from the Antarctic, she'd invite them to stay. She sighed as an image of Zizi's apartment flashed into her head; so perfect, for some other lucky person who wouldn't appreciate it half as much as she did.

'A toast to the chef!' Arnaud raised his glass. 'What a meal, Juliette. Anyone would think you had French blood in your veins.'

It had been a great evening, more successful than she'd dared hope. There had been no awkwardness; conversation had flowed from the beginning in both French and English, and everyone had got on. Thérèse and Arnaud had been students at the university where Claude had taught, and Ilse and Claude had lived in San Francisco for a while so they had plenty to talk about with Andrew. Juliette felt proud of her brother. He could be uncomfortably blunt but he had interesting opinions and knew how to listen as well as talk. Sophie had held her own, too. She'd wanted to hear about Juliette's plans for the bookshop and had asked whether she could use the proposal as a case study for her business course. She was wearing a dress that showed off her figure and looked completely different now she was animated and happy.

'I want to drink a toast to you all,' Juliette said, looking around the table at their faces in the candlelight. 'People say Parisians can be unfriendly, but you've been so kind and welcoming when I needed it most. I can't thank you enough. Here's to each and every one of you – and to my big brother, for leaving the Golden City for the first time in years.'

'And here's to Mémé, our French grandmother,' Andrew added. 'Wouldn't she be delighted to see us now?'

Juliette had been sitting next to Claude. When the hum of general chat had resumed, he said, 'So tell me about Mémé. What was she like?'

'I wish I knew,' Juliette replied. 'She died when I was a teenager and I didn't talk to her as much as I should have. She lived in Paris and left at the end of the war, in 1945. My grandfather was an American soldier who'd come to Europe after D-Day. He fell in love with her at first sight, apparently: a *coup de foudre*.'

'You should try to find out more now you're here,' Claude said. 'I've been looking into my own family history and the process is fascinating. May I tell you a little of my own story?'

'Please do. I should love to hear it.' Claude was charming, so clever and gracious. She could quite understand why Ilse had fallen for him.

'So, I was adopted as a baby,' he began. 'I was born in 1944 to an unmarried mother, which was bad enough in itself, but my father was German, which of course made everything ten times worse. *Enfants maudits*, they called us: cursed children who bore witness to their mothers' shame. My adoptive parents were loving and careful to protect me, but I asked them about my birth mother when I was older and they told me the truth.'

'Do you know anything about your father?' Juliette asked.

'Unfortunately not; he isn't named on my birth certificate. My mother never married but I managed to trace her brother's family. His children knew their aunt had fallen in love with a German who had been killed later in the war. At least she hadn't been raped, thank goodness.'

'And now you're married to a German woman,' Juliette said.

Claude smiled. 'The past has been laid to rest, or so I choose to think.'

It was late by then and soon everyone was getting up from the table. 'Oh, I nearly forgot,' Thérèse said, reaching into her pocket. 'Nico gave me this letter for you. Apparently it was delivered to Zizi's apartment.'

'Thanks,' Juliette said, accepting the envelope. 'I may have given a couple of people the address when I thought I was going to be living there.'

'Of course,' Thérèse said. 'He let you down at the last minute, and we all know who was behind that. But the good news is, he and Delphine have split up. One too many tantrums about the kitchen fitting, I suspect.'

'Well, good luck to them.' Juliette had no interest in Nico's romantic status and, turning the envelope over, she noticed who the letter was from. When she'd closed the door behind Sophie, the last to leave apart from Andrew, she tore it open.

'What's the matter?' Andrew asked, hearing her gasp of dismay.

'It's the bank,' she said, looking up in disbelief. 'They're not going to grant me a loan. What am I going to do?'

249

Chapter Eighteen

April 2022

'What a fool I've been.' Juliette held her head in her hands. 'I was so sure the bank would lend me the money, even though Arnaud said it wasn't a done deal.'

'You can always apply for a loan somewhere else,' Andrew told her.

'But I'm not sure there's time. If I don't sign the shop lease by the end of the month, I'll lose my deposit. I need to have the financing sorted before then.'

'Then maybe you should ask for your money back now and start again with different premises somewhere else?'

Juliette shook her head. 'I'm not ready to give up on The Forgotten Bookshop. It's where I'm meant to be, I know it.'

'In that case, I guess there's only one thing for it,' Andrew told her, collecting the dirty dishes. 'I'll invest in the business.'

'What do you mean?' She followed him through to the kitchen.

'Exactly what I say. You're under-capitalised, Jules. I'll put in a chunk of cash, you can get a top-up loan and we'll become partners.' He smiled. 'What could possibly go wrong?'

'You could lose all your money, for one thing,' she said. 'Or we could disagree about the business and end up never speaking to each other again.'

He started loading the dishwasher. 'OK, I promise only to interfere if things are going badly wrong. And if I lose the money, so be it. I can't think of a better way of using Mom's inheritance, can you? I just needed to find out how serious you were about this plan before I made a commitment.'

'You really mean it?' Juliette threw her arms around his neck. 'Oh, thank you, thank you! Are you sure?'

'Of course,' he said, shaking her off. 'If I'm honest, I've been expecting you to ask me for a loan from the minute you told me about the shop. This is in my interests too, you know. If you're settled and happy in Paris, I can come visit.' He straightened, pushing back his glasses. 'And bring my girlfriend.'

'What?' Juliette screeched, after a second's stunned silence. 'What girlfriend? How come you're only telling me about her now?'

'Because I knew you'd be interrogating me the whole time if I mentioned her earlier. This way, I only have to put up with it for a few hours.'

Juliette took his arm. 'Leave the dishes. There's half a

bottle of wine left – let's finish it while you tell me everything. And I mean everything, OK?'

Despite her best efforts, all she managed to find out was the mystery woman's name – Rachel – and her job – physiotherapist. 'A physio! That seems kind of unlikely somehow.' Andrew might have surfed when he was younger but he was no athlete now. 'Show me a photo so I know she exists.'

'Here you go.' Andrew passed over his phone and Juliette found herself looking at a dark-haired woman with a beaming smile.

'She looks great.'

'Yeah, she is.' Andrew smiled too, his eyes soft. 'In fact, she was the one who suggested I come over here. She thought you might need some moral support.'

'Oh God, I love her already,' Juliette said. 'Bring her to Paris as soon as you can, OK? It's the most romantic place in the world.'

There were lovers everywhere she went: wrapped in each other's arms on park benches, kissing on the banks of the Seine, feeding each other titbits on every café terrace. Talk about rubbing in the fact she was single. More than sex, she missed knowing she was special to somebody, the person they thought about last thing at night and first thing in the morning. Kevin had felt like that about her once, she was sure, but it was Mary-Jane Macintyre he'd been longing to go home to while in the City of Love with his wife.

Still, soon she would be too busy to think about romance, or the lack of it. There was so much to be done: brief her lawyer and accountant, draw up a revised business plan, register the company name, design a logo, think about a website, find a property surveyor – the list was endless. And all while she was working shifts at Elisabeth's bookshop. Hard graft would take her mind off everything else; she couldn't wait to get started.

Taking the Métro each morning made Juliette feel like a true Parisienne. At first, she was mainly conscious of getting in the way at Elisabeth's store, bothering the manager with unnecessary questions and forgetting how to ring through sales on the till or arrange refunds. By the end of the week, though, she was actually becoming useful. Her head hurt from the amount of new information she had to absorb, but she was learning so much: what to consider when choosing stock, how to shelve books and arrange effective displays and, most important of all, how to deal with customers. Soon she could tell when to offer advice and when to step back, who was open to suggestions for new authors and who would regard any such attempts with deep suspicion. She even spotted her first pickpocket. She was turning into a bookseller.

'Don't expect to make your fortune,' Elisabeth had warned her, 'but if you love books and you like people, you can have a great life.'

Elisabeth's shop was spacious, with a café at the front spilling on to the pavement. There wouldn't be room for coffee and cakes at The Forgotten Bookshop, but maybe Juliette could talk to Robert, who ran the Café Doré, and fix up some reciprocal discount arrangement. He might be interested in hosting literary suppers or launch parties – and of course, there would have to be an opening party for the bookshop itself. She'd try to think of a local celebrity who could bring a crowd to the Place Dorée. Every afternoon, she raced back from the shop and straight into meetings with her accountant or lawyer, or college seminars for her business administration course. In the evenings, she pored over publishers' catalogues and book reviews, emailed her website designer and made long lists of tasks that absolutely had to be done right away. Sophie was becoming invested in the bookshop, too. She'd helped Juliette draw up her new business plan and found a graphic art student to design the shop's logo: a half-open book with a key unlocking the cover.

Easter came and went, and Juliette might hardly have realised if not for Ilse and Claude's invitation to Sunday lunch with their family, including several grandchildren, and an Easter egg hunt around the garden. On the last working day of April, she texted Andrew to say she'd just signed the contract and The Forgotten Bookshop was theirs. After that, she sat down to compose an email to Kevin. It might have been braver to call but this news was quite something to spring on him and she wanted to choose her words carefully.

She got to talk to him anyway because he rang half an hour later.

'So you're staying in France for the long term?' he asked, his voice unexpectedly subdued.

'Looks like it,' she replied.

'Are you just trying to show me you can manage on your own? This crazy idea is bound to fail.' Now he was blustering. 'You're no businesswoman, Juliette – reading a few novels on vacation doesn't qualify you to run a bookstore. And don't expect me to bail you out when it all goes pear-shaped.'

She sensed the fear behind his words. He didn't want her to succeed; her role had been to admire his achievements. And she did, genuinely. Kevin was hard-working and successful; he'd been the main bread-winner for years and given her a comfortable life, which she'd no doubt taken for granted.

'I've signed an agreement to make sure our joint assets will be protected,' she said. 'But maybe we should think about getting a divorce, so we can both move on.'

He hung up without replying.

Although the lease on the shop wasn't due to start till the beginning of June, the landlord had given permission for Juliette to visit the premises with her contractors so they could make a preliminary survey, measure up and start work as soon as she got the keys. The sooner she could fit out The Forgotten Bookshop and open for business, the sooner she'd start making money – or at least, stop losing it. Upgrading the electrical circuits and arranging internet access was her first priority. Thérèse recommended an electrician called Jerome, whom Juliette eventually managed to track down and meet at the shop a couple of weeks later. He had long hair tied back in a ponytail and a permanently dazed expression, as though he'd just woken up from a long sleep, but Thérèse had assured her he knew what he was doing. Juliette was talking to him about where to place the till – either in the larger of the two rooms or the inter-connecting foyer – when Nico knocked at the door.

'Some post for you that was delivered to the apartment,' he said, handing over a sheaf of letters.

'Oh, thanks.' She took them, managing to drop a couple on the floor, which he picked up for her. 'I gave the bank that address when I thought I was going to be living there.'

'Sure. It's OK.' He pushed up the sleeves of his sweater and cleared his throat. 'May I come in for a moment? There's something I'd like to ask.'

'Actually, I'm quite busy with the electrician,' she said. 'Can it wait?'

'*Salut, Nico.*' Jerome waved from inside, his face brightening for a moment, and Nico waved back. She might have known they'd be friends.

'This won't take long,' Nico went on. 'I've been talking to my grandmother about the shop, you see, and I think you might be interested in what she had to say.'

Reluctantly, Juliette held open the door. 'All right, then. Come in.'

Knowing what Nico thought about her business venture, she didn't want him setting foot on the premises. The shop looked grimly unpromising, its floor covered in cracked lino and its walls plastered with faded circus posters featuring clowns with sinister grins. She'd been terrified of clowns when she was young and she didn't much like them now. Nico shook hands with Jerome and they started on some manly banter. He was carrying a tool bag, Juliette happened to notice, and his sleeves were rolled up. She tried not to notice his arms but looking at his face in the sunshine slanting through the window was just as dangerous. She loathed him.

'What was it you wanted to talk about?' she asked. 'Only we can't stay here for too long and Jerome has a lot to do.'

'Sure,' Nico said. 'Well, according to Zizi, my grandfather fitted out this shop before the war. Did I tell you he was a carpenter? Apparently the shelves came from the library of a house that was being demolished.'

'That sounds great,' Juliette told him, gesturing around the room, 'but, as you can see, they're not here anymore.'

'There's a chance they might be.' Nico put his bag on the floor and took out a screwdriver, hammer and drill. 'Would you let me have a look behind the panelling? I'll be very careful.'

'You'd better,' Juliette said. 'The landlord's only letting us in here as a favour. We're not meant to be tearing the place apart.' And I don't trust you with tools, she might have added.

'You can blame me,' Jerome put in, blinking. 'Say I needed to look at some wiring.'

Nico was already attacking one of the panels, which split down its length with an alarming crack.

'Really?' Juliette started forward.

'It's OK,' he said over his shoulder. 'I can patch it up if necessary. And just look at what's underneath.' He stood back to let Juliette see.

'Cool,' Jerome commented, walking away. 'I'll let you guys get on with it.'

Rows of wide oak shelving stretched away behind the hardboard. Juliette caught her breath, stroking the wood that had been polished over so many years by other people's hands. 'I can't believe it. Who would cover up workmanship like this?'

'Papi was a real craftsman. I've inherited some of his tools, though he died before he could teach me anything.' Nico took a breath. 'Would you let me get rid of this panelling and repair the shelves if they need it?'

'I'm not sure. Forgive me for saying this, but you haven't been exactly reliable so far. I'd sooner employ somebody I can trust.' What did he expect? That he could just waltz in here and she'd forget the way he treated her? 'Anyway, I'm surprised you'd bother,' she added. 'Aren't you waiting for the business to fail so I'll go back to America?'

'What?' Then she saw the light dawn in his eyes. 'Oh, I see.' He was blushing now. 'I'm sorry.'

She folded her arms. 'So you should be.'

'I misjudged you. At first, I thought you were playing at living in Paris so you could get a few photos for your Instagram feed.'

The arrogance of the man! 'You called me harmless,' she said, the heat rising in her cheeks. 'How dare you?'

He looked at her then as though he was seeing her for the first time. 'I'm sorry, that must have been an awful thing to hear.' He laid the hammer in his tool box and scratched his head. 'This is hard to explain, but I was trying to reassure Delphine. She's very possessive, you see. Other women are a threat to her, particularly those who. . .' He hesitated. 'Particularly those I. . .' He was blushing again, and Juliette's anger softened as a warm glow spread through her body like an invisible hug.

'Well, let's just say I wasn't telling her the truth,' Nico went on. 'From Delphine's point of view, you weren't harmless at all. Quite the opposite, in fact.'

Juliette couldn't help smiling and he grinned back. They understood each other; he didn't have to spell everything out.

'All right,' she said, extending her hand. 'I'll accept your offer and I appreciate it. Thanks. I'll be getting the keys in three weeks' time.'

'Great,' he said, as they shook on the deal. 'Jerome and I have worked together before so we can liaise with each other.'

They turned to look at the electrician, currently scribbling calculations in pencil on a crumpled scrap of paper. 'Thérèse recommended him.' Juliette lowered her voice. 'She says he's very good.'

'Of course. Everyone knows Jerome,' Nico assured her, a little too heartily. 'Well, I'll let you get on. I'm working upstairs so you'll know where to find me.'

'Making the apartment ready for sale, I suppose,' Juliette said. She wasn't a saint, after all.

A few days later, Ben texted to say that he was about to start his travels and could he stay with her for a while in Paris, arriving that weekend? Sure, she replied, it would be lovely to see him – which of course was true, only she was already so busy and stressed that she could hardly think straight. She would have to leave the snowy wastes of her apartment in a month or so, too, and she'd had no time to look for anywhere else. There was always L'Hotel Corot, which at least was cheap and convenient, but she needed to move forward, not back. She would lie awake at night, exhausted, her heart pounding at the thought of what could go wrong. No one would come to her shop, she would lose all the money her mother had left her, and Andrew's too, and end up a mad old bag lady with no family and no friends, roaming the streets of Paris in her slippers.

Things didn't look so bleak in the daytime but there was just so much to organise, so many pieces of the puzzle that had to fall into place at the correct time. She even had to attend a meeting held by the residents of the building to submit her renovation plans for their approval. Most of them seemed to think a bookshop would be a useful addition to the neighbourhood, luckily, and Nico was there as an apartment owner, able to confirm the interior would be sensitively restored. He asked her for a drink after the meeting, but Ben was arriving the next day and she still wasn't sure she could trust her feelings about Nico. He'd only recently split up with Delphine, after all, who wasn't the type to let him go without a fight.

Ben didn't want her to meet him at the airport and when he turned up at her apartment that Saturday afternoon, he wasn't alone.

'Kevin?' Juliette stared at her husband, loitering behind Ben in the hall. 'Seriously?'

'Thought I'd give you a surprise,' he said, bouncing on the balls of his feet like he always did when he was nervous. 'Well, are you going to let us in?'

'Sure.' She hugged Ben and let Kevin kiss her on the cheek. He had a small carry-on tote, which he wheeled into the apartment, bringing that metallic airport smell with him.

'Just be careful with your luggage,' she said, still dazed. 'Everything's white and I'm terrified of making a mark.'

260

'Should have kept my sunglasses on,' Ben said, looking around.

Juliette glanced at Kevin. 'It's OK,' he said quickly, 'I'm not expecting to stay here. I've booked a room in that hotel we found. It's not far.'

The hotel where she'd learned of his affair, a lifetime ago. She turned to Ben. 'Was the skiing good? Love the tan – you look great.'

'So do you,' he replied. 'You've turned into a Frenchwoman overnight.'

'Have you lost weight?' Kevin asked.

'I've taken up jogging, would you believe.' Juliette felt suddenly self-conscious. 'It's great for stress and life is fairly hectic these days.' They were making small talk like strangers at a cocktail party. 'Well, make yourselves comfortable. Do you want a drink or anything?'

'I might just head straight for the shower and take a nap afterwards,' Ben said diplomatically. 'Leave you guys to catch up.'

Juliette showed him to his room and brought him a towel. 'Why didn't you warn me?' she hissed when they were alone.

'Because Dad made me swear not to,' Ben whispered. 'I'm sorry, Mom, but he's desperate to see you. Won't you give him a chance? He's only staying a couple of nights.'

'Have you talked to Emily about what happened between us?' she asked.

'Yeah.' Ben rubbed his forehead. 'I can't believe he'd do something so dumb. I get it that you're angry, Mom, but I think he realises he's made a mistake.'

'Well, I'll leave you to it,' she said. 'Don't sleep too long or you'll never adjust.'

Kevin was sitting on the white sofa, his feet planted firmly on the carpet. She should have told him to take his shoes off. He looked better than he had the last time she'd seen him: back in control. She felt a knot of anxiety clenching her stomach. You don't owe him anything, she reminded herself.

'I've brought you something,' he said, holding out a padded bag. 'Careful, it's fragile.'

She opened it warily, pulling out a framed picture. 'Mémé's painting!' she exclaimed in delight. 'Thanks, Kevin. That's thoughtful of you.'

He beamed. 'Sorry it's a little beat up.'

A corner of the frame had come apart and the glass was loose. 'I can easily get it mended,' Juliette said. 'I'm going to hang it in the shop, by the till.'

'Sit down, Jules.' He patted the sofa cushion. 'We need to talk.'

She perched as far away from him as possible. 'So come on, then. Why are you here?'

He placed a hand on each knee, straightening his back. 'OK. Well, I've come to tell you in person that I don't want a divorce. I'm still your husband and that's how I'd like to stay.'

Juliette opened her mouth but he held up a hand. 'Don't say anything yet. Just tell me we can have dinner together tonight, the two of us. I've booked a table at that café in the square, the one you wanted to visit last time.' He looked at her with a contrite expression that seemed a little studied; perhaps he'd been practising in front of the mirror. 'I've been a jerk and I'm sorry. At least hear me out?'

Juliette sighed. 'All right, then.' She might as well get it over with.

Chapter Nineteen

May 2022

It felt so strange to be sitting opposite Kevin in the café, a place Juliette thought of as hers. He'd chosen it as a concession to her but she wished they could have gone somewhere else. How many dinners had they shared throughout their married life? This must have been the most awkward of all.

'So how are you doing?' she asked once they'd ordered their food. It was early so the café wasn't crowded, which was a relief.

'Fine,' he said, tearing into a slice of bread. 'The freezer's full of casseroles and Mrs Sweeney's been bringing over fried chicken on a regular basis, so I'm not going hungry.'

'That's good.' She could imagine the neighbourhood gossip; Kevin wouldn't be short of female attention.

He coughed and took a sip of water. 'Crumb in my throat. The Macintyres have moved away, incidentally. Rented out their house and gone to Alaska.'

She smiled. 'That's kind of drastic.'

Pascal was bringing the wine so they stopped talking until he'd poured it. Juliette glanced around. There was nobody else in the café she recognised, apart from one of the old men who played *petanque* in the square; she wanted to eat quickly and get rid of Kevin before anyone saw them together. They ordered *steak frites* with a salad and she hoped it would come soon.

'I made a mistake,' he said when Pascal had gone. 'People do. It's what's known as being human.'

'Of course,' she told him. 'I'm not angry anymore. I forgive you, it's fine.'

'Thank you.' He lifted his glass. 'So what shall we drink to?'

'New beginnings,' she said, raising hers.

'Perfect.' He clinked her glass. 'I was hoping you'd say that. I've learned my lesson, Jules. I haven't been paying you enough attention but all that's going to change. Maybe we can run this bookstore together? You could set it up and find a manager, and we could even rent an apartment in Paris for regular trips together. You don't have to come back with me now, that's not what I'm after, but at least tell me you'll think about it. All this' – he waved his hand to gesture around the café – 'it's very quaint and fine for a vacation but it's not real life. You belong in America with me and the kids; we don't work without you. This is our family, the one we made together, and you're at the heart of it.'

'But Ben's travelling and Emily's in Antarctica,' Juliette said. 'How is she, by the way? I haven't heard from her in a while.'

'She's good.' He drank some more wine. 'Worried about you, though. She wants you home almost as much as I do.'

He wouldn't be diverted. 'My home is here now,' Juliette said. 'I'm not on a vacation, I'm building a future for myself. Can't you see how exciting that is? We've had twenty-seven years as a couple and no one can take that away but face it, Kevin, that time is over.'

'I won't accept that,' he said, crestfallen but still stubborn. 'One day you're going to need my help and it might be sooner than you think.'

'You've been the major breadwinner all through our marriage and I know it hasn't been easy,' she told him. 'I've had a good life – a comfortable one – because of your support and I appreciate it, but now I have the chance to try something new. My grandmother died when she was seventy-one, and Mom wasn't that much older. The women in our family don't make old bones. Mom was so angry when she was ill; she thought she'd wasted her life and now it was ending too soon. She'd wanted to spend more time in France but she was never brave enough to go on her own. I don't want to have any regrets on my deathbed.'

Kevin didn't reply, staring at the crumbs on his plate. She drank some wine, glancing up as the café door opened and Nico, of all people, walked in. He looked at her and then at Kevin, and nodded. She nodded back, her heart thumping.

'OK, we'll talk about this some more tomorrow,' Kevin said at last. 'You can show me some of the places you've discovered.'

She groaned inwardly. 'But I'm getting the keys to the shop in a few days' time, and there are a million things that need to be done before then. I haven't the time to go sightseeing.'

'Not even for a day? When I've come all this way to see you?'

'It's just the worst time,' she said, hardening her heart. 'I'm sorry. Why don't you spend some time with Ben?'

'Guess I'll have to,' he muttered.

Now Pascal was bringing their food but Juliette had lost her appetite. She tried not to look at Nico, standing by the bar, but their eyes met once before she quickly dropped hers. Kevin didn't say much for the rest of the meal. It felt tactless to tell him about Paris and he didn't seem inclined to talk about his life so there were several awkward silences.

Nico walked past their table on his way out. 'Hi, Juliette. Have you picked up the shop keys yet?' he asked, taking another look at Kevin.

'Early next week,' she said (which she'd told him already), and then, because it would have seemed strange not to, 'This is my husband, Kevin.'

Nico extended his hand to shake Kevin's, nodded at Juliette again and left, the door banging behind him.

'So who was that?' Kevin asked.

'A guy who's helping me with the shop fitting.' She didn't want to go into detail.

He grunted. 'Kind of familiar for a workman. Why did he want to shake my hand?'

'I can't imagine,' Juliette said.

Kevin wouldn't hear of her going halves on the bill so she let him pay. 'I'm flying back on Sunday afternoon,' he told her. 'Can you spare the time for a coffee in the morning?'

'Sure,' she said, exhausted. 'That would be nice.'

The next day, though, he texted to say he'd changed his flight to a more convenient time and would be leaving for the States that night. Juliette felt relieved; there was no point prolonging the agony.

Ben came with her to pick up the keys to the shop a few days later, and she was glad of the moral support. She'd begun spending serious money on stock and contractors, and the full extent of what she'd undertaken was beginning to hit home. She texted Nico to say she'd be at The Forgotten Bookshop all day but there was no sign of the person who really needed to be there: Jerome the electrician. She'd been leaving him messages for a couple of days now, confirming the start date, and he still hadn't replied.

'I'm sure he'll turn up,' Ben said, wandering through the sad, echoing rooms. 'And there's plenty we could be doing in the meantime.'

'I hope so,' Juliette said. 'The engineer's coming next week to arrange internet access and we can't shelve any stock until the wiring's sorted. What do you think, though?'

'It's a bit small, isn't it?' Ben peered behind the hardboard panel. 'But these shelves are great. Do they run along the whole wall?'

'We'll have to wait and see.' Juliette took out her tape measure and clipboard; she needed to make a scale drawing of the larger room to see how many spinners could fit in and whether there was room for a display table. 'You don't have to hang around here all day,' she told Ben. 'Why don't you go off and explore?'

'I can help you this morning,' he said. 'I'm meeting Sophie for lunch later on.'

'Oh, that's nice,' Juliette said carefully. Sophie had called by her apartment a few days before to discuss bookstore business; she and Ben seemed to have hit it off straight away and Juliette had left them talking when she went to bed. It wasn't that Ben needed entertaining, but if Sophie could show him around Paris, then Juliette didn't have to feel guilty about spending all her time in the store.

Nico strolled over from the café soon after that, carrying his tool bag. He pulled a face when Juliette told him about Jerome's non-appearance.

'What is it?' she demanded. 'Does he often do this?'

'He disappears from time to time,' Nico said. 'He's been more reliable recently but maybe he's up to his old tricks. Don't worry, he'll probably turn up in a couple of weeks.'

'A couple of weeks?' she repeated. 'Are you kidding? We're meant to be opening in a month and there are a hundred things I need to do before then!'

'Well, let's wait and see. He may just have overslept.' Nico turned to Ben. 'Do you want to lend a hand in Maman's shop?'

'Let me take a few photographs first,' Juliette said. 'Before and after shots.'

When she was done she watched the pair of them working together out of the corner of her eye. Nico was tidy and methodical, precise in his movements rather than rushing at the job as she would have done, and as Ben was doing now.

Nico removed the panelling carefully, taking extra trouble when he had to tackle a particularly reckless nail that had gouged the oak underneath. By the time Ben left at lunchtime, half a wall of shelving had been revealed.

Nico stood back to admire what they'd achieved. 'Such beautiful old wood, and the joints have hardly warped at all.'

'Sure, it's lovely.' Juliette checked her watch. 'I might just try Jerome again.'

'Either he'll come or he won't,' Nico said. 'Calling him twenty times a day isn't going to achieve anything.'

'I guess you're right. Here, do you want to share my lunch? I brought a picnic in case Ben got hungry.' She smiled. 'Once a feeder, always a feeder, I guess.'

She tore the baguette stuffed with pâté and cornichons in half and they ate it sitting on the dusty floor, their backs against the wall.

'You don't look old enough to have a grown-up son,' Nico said, and she laughed, because it sounded so corny. 'No, I mean it,' he protested.

'Why, thank you, kind sir. I guess I did have the kids young. Ben has a twin sister, so we had a ready-made family in one go.'

'And what does this family feel about you deserting them to live in Paris?' he asked, wiping his fingers on his work trousers. He had strong, capable hands that she felt a sudden urge to reach out and touch.

'They probably think I'm crazy,' she said, glancing away, 'but that's OK. The kids are leading their own lives now, and my husband. . . Well, my husband is doing the same. We're separating.'

'And how long have you been married?'

'Twenty-five years.'

Nico raised his eyebrows. 'Must be a difficult time.'

'That's enough of my family history,' Juliette said quickly. 'What about yours? How come you're the one left looking after your grandmother?'

He shrugged. 'My mother died when I was young, and my father remarried and moved away from Paris. I have a brother but he lives in the States, so I'm the only one around. Anyway, I enjoy spending time with Zizi. Her younger sister who lived in Provence died last year and most of her friends have gone so she's fairly lonely. By the way,' he added, 'some more post arrived at the apartment for you. It's in my bag.'

'Thanks,' she said, a little guiltily. 'I'm sorry but I can't do anything without an address, you see, and that was the only one I could think of.'

'Yes, so you said.' He stood up. 'Well, I'd better get on.'

Jerome didn't come the next day, or the one after that. By the end of the week, Juliette was panicking. Not even the fact that Nico and Ben had revealed three walls of magnificent oak shelving in near-perfect condition could calm her nerves.

'This is going to throw the whole schedule out.' She rubbed her forehead. 'The longer we delay before opening, the more money I'll lose.'

'Do you want me to overhaul the wiring?' Nico asked.

She stared at him. 'You? After what happened with the shower?'

He laughed and held up his hands. 'OK, fair enough. But I'm a qualified electrician.'

'Then why didn't you say so in the first place?'

'I didn't want to take the work away from Jerome.' He went back to oiling one of the shelves. 'If you're anxious to get started, though. . .'

'Well, maybe you could give me a quote,' Juliette said, before going outside for some fresh air to clear her head and the chance to ring Thérèse.

'Jerome hasn't turned up,' she said, as soon as Thérèse answered her call. 'Nico says he could be away for days and he's offered to fix the wiring himself. Is he any good? He tried to fix Zizi's shower and nearly flooded the whole place.'

Thérèse laughed. 'I don't know about his plumbing skills but he's a competent electrician. He might not have Jerome's flair, but—'

'I don't care about flair,' Juliette snapped. 'I just need someone to get the job done. Sorry, I'm finding all this very stressful.'

Back at the shop, she found Ben and Nico laughing over something on Nico's phone. 'OK,' she told him. 'I'll show you the quote Jerome gave me. If you're happy with that, the job's yours – as long as you can get going right away.'

'I have some work to finish off upstairs,' he said, putting the phone back in his pocket. 'Is the day after tomorrow OK?'

She sighed. 'I suppose it'll have to be.'

'Mom?' Ben frowned at her.

'Sorry. Thanks, Nico,' she said, collecting herself. 'It's kind of you to offer and I'm very grateful.'

* * *

'You need to keep Nico on your side, Mom,' Ben told her later, when she was cooking supper for him and Sophie, who seemed to have become a permanent fixture. 'He's one of the good guys.'

'Do you think so?' she asked, brushing the hair from her forehead with the back of her hand. 'Have I told you about the way he made me clean his mother's—'

'He didn't make you do anything, though, did he?' Ben interrupted. 'I bet you offered. I know what you're like when you get an idea in your head: relentless. And it's his apartment; he's allowed to do what he wants with it.'

'I don't know. Maybe you're right.' She sighed, drained the spaghetti, and dumped it back in the pan, adding the prawns, which she'd sautéed with garlic, lemon zest and chilli and a little of the pasta cooking water to bring the sauce together. 'How's the salad coming along?'

'Nearly done.'

She glanced at the scene of devastation: lettuce leaves, carrot peelings, tomato stems and avocado skin littered the kitchen table. She'd been about to ask him to chop some parsley but it would probably be safer to do it herself with some scissors. Sophie was in charge of the dressing, since Ben was capable of creating havoc with olive oil and mustard.

'So how much longer you stay here?' Sophie asked.

'How much longer *can* you stay here,' Juliette corrected her. 'Or *will* you stay here. Don't roll your eyes at me, Ben. How else is Sophie going to learn?'

'I'm teaching her,' he said. 'She's coming on in leaps and bounds.'

Sophie smiled at him, her face lighting up. I know that look, Juliette thought, wishing for a moment she was young and besotted. She hoped Ben felt the same way about Sophie, whom she was getting to like more every day, and that even if he didn't, he'd be kind to her.

'We can stay in this apartment for another three weeks,' she told Sophie, 'and then I'll have to find somewhere else. What are your plans, Ben? I guess you'll have moved on by then?'

'Oh, I might stick around for a while,' he said. 'At least till you open the bookshop. I've become kind of invested in The Forgotten Bookshop myself.'

She put her hand to his cheek for a moment. 'Thanks for being here.'

The next couple of weeks shot by in a blur of activity. Juliette had to sign a bunch of statutes from the Chamber of Commerce, publish a notice saying she'd formed a company, agree all her loan conditions, find a wholesaler and open an account, trawl through thousands of book titles to choose her opening stock, order stationery, print flyers, hire a sign painter, design a window display . . . plus a hundred other tasks she'd no doubt forgotten. And she had a launch party to organise, too. She planned to open The Forgotten Bookshop for business on Monday, 4 July – Independence Day, which seemed appropriate – and throw a party at the end of that week, when she'd got to grips with bookselling. Elisabeth had told her that was the right way to go about things. 'Celebrate once the shop is open and you've had a few days to let the dust settle.'

At least with the rewiring under way, she could order stock in the knowledge she'd be able to shelve it. There had still been no sign of sleepy Jerome but Nico turned up every morning and worked steadily for three or four days. She brought extra food for him and they'd eat their lunch together, sitting against the wall. At first, they talked mainly about the shop but soon she felt comfortable enough to ask him anything.

'You're putting your heart and soul into this, aren't you?' he said to her one day. 'It isn't just a whim.'

'Of course not,' she replied. 'I can't afford to fail.' Her marriage was over; if her business collapsed too, she'd have nothing. 'You don't seem to have a very high opinion of Americans,' she went on, unwrapping a bar of chocolate. 'We're not all the same, you know.'

'Wait. I've brought you something for a change.' He went to his tool bag and came back with a paper bag from the *pâtisserie*, which he offered to her. It was full of *chouquettes*, delicious crispy balls of choux pastry sprinkled with rock sugar.

'Thanks. What a treat.' She took a couple. 'So come on, then, tell me about yourself. Whereabouts in the States did you live, for a start?'

'California, mostly,' he replied. 'I worked around LA as a painter and decorator, and then for a while on a ranch in Wyoming. After that I crewed for an American millionaire with a superyacht and sailed around the world for a couple of years.'

'Sounds exciting,' Juliette said.

'It was pointless.' Nico tossed a *chouquette* high in the air and caught it in his mouth. 'No reason to go anywhere, nothing to do – just eating and circling the ocean like a fat, lazy shark. I stopped off in Africa and spent a while building refugee camps for aid agencies and remote-area camps for oil workers. Then I got homesick for France and came back a few years ago.'

'Wow. My life seems tame in comparison.'

'But you've brought up your son, and what could be more exciting and important than that.' He smiled, the edges of his eyes crinkling. 'And your daughter, too. Tell me about her.'

'Emily?' Juliette wondered how to begin. 'Well, she's very different from Ben, even though they're twins. She's an adventurer, too. At the moment she's living on a research base in Antarctica.' She found a photo of Emily on her phone and showed it to him. 'She's a marine biologist.'

'You must miss her.'

Juliette gazed at Emily's determined face, her eyes narrowed against the sun and her chin lifted as though challenging the world. 'Yes,' she said. 'I really do. She won't be home until September and even then, I don't know when I'll get to see her.' Or whether she'll want to see me, she thought.

'But you are having your own adventure now. She must be proud of you.' He dusted his hands on his jeans. 'By the way, I've noticed something strange about this place. Come, I'll show you.'

It seemed perfectly natural for him to take her hand. Calm down, she told herself, loving the feel of his warm, firm grip as they headed out of the shop and around the corner. We're friends and this is what friends do – especially in France.

In the street, Nico pointed to a small window high up in the wall. 'See that? I can't work out where it opens inside.'

'In the apartment building, maybe?' Juliette said. There was a door at the back of the bookshop that led into the communal hall of the apartments above.

Nico shook his head. 'No, I've checked already. Let's go back.'

This time he didn't take her hand, and she felt ridiculously deprived. Inside the shop, he walked over to the shelves in the far corner of the larger room. 'It feels like there's some kind of cavity behind here,' he said, knocking on the wooden backing panel. 'We should investigate.'

'Well, I haven't got time to worry about that now.' She had so much to organise and messing about with her beautiful shelves was definitely bottom of the list.

'It's curious, though, don't you think?'

'A mystery for another day,' Juliette said. 'There are ten boxes of books arriving the day after tomorrow and I'll need to start shelving them asap.'

'OK. The wiring should be sorted by the end of today and I'll leave you to get on with it.'

'Really? That's great.' Yet Juliette felt a pang. 'Stay for a while,' she wanted to say. 'Who will I eat my lunch with?'

'There's one thing I was going to suggest,' he went on. 'I've hired a sander for Zizi's floors. If you like, I could do yours in here, too. It would mean the shop's out of action for a few days but better now than when the books are unpacked – there'll be dust everywhere. I'd have to charge you for the labour but it won't be very much.' He lifted up a corner of the vinyl. 'The floorboards are in good condition, considering.'

'Thank you, Nico,' she said, her heart lifting. 'That would be amazing.'

Each day Juliette ticked off the tasks on her list, added new ones, woke up in the middle of the night remembering what still had to be done, drank countless cups of coffee, ran around the Parc Monceau until the sweat poured down her back. She'd left flyers at the American Library and offices in the nearby business district of La Défense, announcing the opening of The Forgotten Bookshop on Monday, 4 July, then chewed her fingernails down to the quick when her order from the wholesaler's was delayed. The books finally arrived on the Friday before, which only gave her the weekend to shelve them, but with Ben and Sophie's help, by Sunday evening the store was taking shape. The weather had been fine all week, so Ben had been painting the outside of the store, and the sign painter she'd found had finished work on the façade, announcing The Forgotten Bookshop to the world. Ben and Sophie had just left when there was a knock on the door; Nico stood outside, with Zizi on his arm.

'I've brought you a special visitor,' he said.

'How wonderful to see you,' Juliette said. Zizi allowed herself to be kissed on both cheeks and Juliette kissed Nico, too. 'Come in and tell me what you think.'

'Looks good,' Nico said. 'Are you pleased?'

'I can't tell you how happy I am. The floor, the shelves, the windows – they're exactly how I imagined. Now all I have to do is sell some books.'

She watched Zizi anxiously as the old lady gazed around, leaning on a stick.

'This is where we had the till,' she said, pointing at Juliette's counter. 'And you must put a mirror on the wall, so you can see into the little room downstairs. People will steal anything.'

She walked slowly into the larger room, pausing on the threshold. 'Jacques put a display case there, where you have a table,' she said. 'We sold some fine first editions. Everything falls to pieces nowadays. Nothing lasts the way it used to.'

'I have some wonderful art books in hardback.' Juliette took one off the shelf and offered it to Zizi, who ignored her.

She sank into a chair in the corner, took out a handkerchief and blew her nose. 'It's difficult, coming here, and thinking about those days. Nico, will you bring me my *eau de vie*?'

He put down the book he'd been leafing through, took out a hip flask from his jacket pocket and passed it to her, patting her shoulder.

'Madame Zizi,' Juliette began, kneeling on the floor, 'I'd love to have a photograph of Jacques Duval in the shop, and maybe some of the others that your father took. I could blow them up and make copies for you, too, and have them framed. How would you feel about that?'

The old lady took another swig of brandy and replaced the cap on the flask, her fingers shaking. 'If you like,' she said. 'I was afraid to look back but it's right he should be commemorated here. This shop was his passion and it cost him his life.'

'How do you mean, Mémère?' Nico asked, taking back the flask.

'Jacques kept *La Page Cachée* open during the war, and not only for selling books. He was working for the Resistance when he was arrested.' She leaned back, gripping the arms of the chair.

'He was arrested?' Juliette repeated. 'What happened?'

Zizi shrugged. 'Somebody must have betrayed him, I don't know who.'

'But what was he selling in the shop?' Juliette asked. 'Could you explain?'

Zizi closed her eyes. 'I can't bear to remember. It's too sad. Don't ask me any more questions.'

Juliette raised her eyebrows at Nico, who shrugged. 'Maybe that's enough for one day. Let me take you home,' he said, helping his grandmother gently out of the chair.

Chapter Twenty

July 2022

Juliette was still working on her window display when Nico called back at The Forgotten Bookshop later that evening.

'Is your grandmother OK?' she asked, jumping down to the floor. 'I didn't mean to upset her.'

'I think so,' he replied. 'She didn't want to go into any detail, that's for sure, and I didn't push it. Can you stop working for a while? There's something I want to tell you that I couldn't say in front of Zizi.'

Juliette pulled a face. 'Sorry, I need to keep going or we won't be ready to open tomorrow.'

'Anything I can help you with?'

'I'm better on my own, but thanks for the offer.' She was tying up books with string and hanging them on different lengths from a pole across the window. Already the process was driving her mad and she didn't need an audience when she inevitably lost her temper, which was going to happen any minute now.

Nico put his hands in his pockets. 'I'll be quick, then. I've decided not to sell Zizi's home but keep it in the family. I'm going to put my current apartment on the market and move in there some time next year. If you want to rent the place for six months until then, you'd be welcome. In fact, I'd like you to – unless you've found somewhere else, that is.'

'Are you sure?' Juliette asked. 'I mean, we've been here before and I couldn't bear it if you changed your mind again.'

He took a deep breath. 'I owe you an apology. Several, in fact. I treated you very badly and I'd like to make it up to you. I've decorated the place so you might want another look upstairs before you decide. The rent will still be the same.'

'Thank you,' Juliette said. 'Let me think it over and I'll let you know.'

After he'd gone, she sat on the windowsill, trying to work out how she felt. Of course she wanted to live in that apartment, she always had, but her feelings for Nico were becoming too strong to ignore. A day without seeing him seemed meaningless and empty, despite all the jobs on her list; even a distant glimpse of him crossing the square with that loping, easy stride was enough to make her heart skip a beat. When they were together, she had to make a conscious effort not to gaze at his mouth or into his eyes, for fear of giving herself away. The timing was all wrong. She'd only ever had one serious relationship in her life, which was now coming to an end, while he probably moved from one woman to the next as casually as he changed jobs. It might be wiser to put some distance between them, rather than becoming closer. On the other hand. . .

She cursed as another book slipped out of its string harness and fell on the floor. Maybe she'd be able to think more clearly once the shop was finally open.

A couple of hours later, Ben and Sophie were back. 'Mom, leave it now,' Ben said. 'The place looks perfect and you need some rest before tomorrow. Here, we've brought you a takeaway pizza.'

'You're stars, both of you,' Juliette said, suddenly realising she was starving. 'And you're right, The Forgotten Bookshop is as ready as it'll ever be.'

The finishing touch would be the two sliding library ladders, which Nico had found in the shop's cellar, and which he'd taken away to polish and treat for woodworm, but for the moment they could make do with a stepladder. When people pushed open the door, they would walk into a calm and welcoming space, a sanctuary full of treasures waiting to be discovered. She'd bought a diffuser so the rooms smelt of flowers and put a vase of fresh blooms by the till. The whole place was a reflection of her taste, from the window display (which had been worth all the hassle in the end) to the greeting cards in the spinners and the books on the glorious oak shelves. She wondered for a second whether Jacques Duval would approve. When she had the time, she would try to find out what he had done in the war, and what had happened to him.

★ ★ ★

The store opened its doors for business at nine o'clock the next morning. At eleven, the first customer walked in: a guy in shorts and a backpack who asked if she had a restroom he could use without even pretending to look at the books, and stormed out when she politely refused, slamming the door. Claude and Ilse called by at midday and cheered her up by saying the shop was a triumph, and customers would soon be queuing around the square. Claude bought a collection of contemporary essays, a book about the Maquis and two novels (one in hardback); Ilse chose a volume of poetry and a lavish door-stopper on the châteaux of the Loire. Juliette could have hugged them.

Ben texted at lunchtime to ask how things were going; he was on standby to help should she be overrun by customers. She told him she was managing. Thérèse dropped in at lunchtime and bought an illustrated book about Parisian street architecture for Arnaud's birthday. In the afternoon, five customers came in that she didn't actually know: an elderly lady, who wanted Juliette's help choosing books for her grandchildren in America, spent half an hour browsing and then left to order the books on Amazon, a delightful woman from Baton Rouge who said the store was 'darling' and bought two guidebooks and a stack of cards to take home, and a mother with three-year-old twins who spent the whole time talking on her cell phone while they fought in the children's section. Going to see what all the noise was about, Juliette discovered they'd pulled down a length of bunting and torn a couple of picture books, which their mother then tried to insist had been already damaged.

'This is our first day,' Juliette told her. 'Nobody's been in that room except your kids.'

'Well, we won't be coming back,' the woman said, paying for the books with very bad grace. 'Not with this kind of customer service.'

'What a shame,' Juliette replied.

At five-thirty, she tidied up, jotted down the day's takings in a notebook by the till – 124 euros – and turned off the lights. 'Goodnight, little store,' she said under her breath. 'Tomorrow is another day.'

It would take some time for people to realise The Forgotten Bookshop existed, she thought, jogging along the paths of the Parc Monceau. She would have to distribute more flyers, contact more bloggers, maybe take out some advertising. The store had only just opened, after all. What was that quote from the baseball movie? 'If you build it, they will come.' But what if nobody does? whispered a voice in her ear. What will you do then?

Sophie cooked supper that night. 'Don't worry,' she said, dishing up the fish stew, 'business is always quiet at first. People talk to each other, and soon – boom!'

'I hope so,' Juliette replied. 'But I'm afraid it'll be a while before I can offer you any shifts.' At least she didn't have staff costs to worry about.

The next day was marginally better. Three Chinese students appeared, followed by a couple who'd picked up one of her flyers at the American Library, and then an unpleasant man with a red, sweaty face who complained she had too many books in English.

'But this is an English-language bookstore,' she said. 'There's a very good French one a few streets away. Shall I give you directions?'

'Paris is full of Americans,' he muttered, glaring at her. 'Before long we shall all be eating nothing but hamburger and drinking only Coca-Cola.'

An English au pair who was living a few streets away came in an hour later. She spent a while browsing and chatting with Juliette, who was able to recommend a novel about a nanny in France and a thriller. This lovely girl bought them both and said she would spread the word among her English-speaking friends. Two people from the apartments above appeared next, and Ben turned up at twelve to lend some moral support. Then who should walk through the door shortly afterwards but Delphine, cool as a glass of milk in a white linen shift.

'I heard you'd opened a shop,' she said. 'How is business?'

'Picking up,' Juliette replied. 'We've only been open since yesterday.'

Delphine glanced about. 'And are all these books in English? Is there nothing for your French customers?'

'We have a few of the latest releases,' Juliette replied. 'Would you like to have a look? Ben can show you.' He'd just emerged from the downstairs room and was gazing, starstruck, at the vision of beauty talking to his mother.

'And where have you found this handsome boy?' Delphine asked, tilting her head towards him with a half smile. It was a routine she must have practised so many times that it had become unconscious: chin down, knowing eyes under lowered lashes, an air of amused invitation.

'Ben is my son,' Juliette said through gritted teeth. She could tell he was flattered; what young guy of twenty-three wouldn't be?

'Come this way,' he said, slightly dazed.

Juliette had to let them go since, wonder of wonders, two customers were actually forming a queue at the till. She watched out of the corner of her eye as Delphine flirted with Ben, laying a hand on his arm and making some earnest remark. They chatted for way longer than was necessary before Delphine sauntered back to the till, swinging her hips, with the book she had deigned to choose.

'See you on Saturday,' she said, fluttering a hand goodbye.

'Who was that?' Ben asked breathlessly, once she had left.

'Nico's ex. Or she might still be his girlfriend, I'm not sure,' Juliette replied. 'Did you have to invite her to the party?'

'Why not?' he said. 'She's officially one of our customers now, and she's hot. She'll make the store look cool. Anyway, I thought you said the more the merrier.'

'I guess.' But Juliette was feeling nervous enough about the event as it was; she didn't need Delphine's particular brand of condescension.

Shortly before closing, Nico appeared, carrying the tall library ladder. 'The other one's rotten, I'm afraid,' he said, 'but there's plenty of life left in this. I've just sanded it down.'

Balancing the ladder carefully, he hooked it over the top railing and slid it along a few sections to demonstrate.

'Perfect,' Juliette said. 'Thanks.'

'Is everything OK?' he asked.

'I've been thinking about Zizi's place,' she began. 'Are you still happy for me to rent it? Because if so, I'd like to take another look.'

She'd given herself a strict talking-to over the past couple of days. How could she turn down a chance to stay in the perfect apartment overlooking her square? Lusting over its owner was not going to ruin her life. Anyway, Nico had seen her with Kevin; if he'd been at all interested in her romantically, he surely wasn't now. She would be professional and business-like, and accept his offer.

'Fine,' he replied, with a smile that almost derailed her. 'Just tell me when.'

'We could go now, if it's convenient,' she said. 'It won't take a minute to close up.'

She locked the door, wrote down the day's takings – 114 euros – and they went out through the back of the store into the main building and up the two flights of stairs.

'Apparently this is where the man who ran the book-shop lived with his wife during the war,' Nico said, opening the front door. 'It feels right you should stay for a while. Anyway, see how you feel.'

Juliette stepped inside and stood for a moment, absorbing the calm, airy atmosphere. The walls had been painted a pearly grey and the dark wooden floorboards polished so they gleamed.

'I knew it could look like this. The light is perfect, and those high ceilings. . .' She walked towards the kitchen, her footsteps echoing down the hall.

'I haven't gotten around to buying any rugs yet,' he said. 'And there isn't much furniture and it's old, as you know.'

'But it has so much character.' Juliette ran her hand over an oak dresser that took up the whole of one wall. 'Your grandparents would have used this piece every day. How could you bear to get rid of it?'

'At least I've bought a new stove,' he told her. 'Nostalgia has its limits.'

Yet the room was still delightfully old-fashioned, with its hanging pan rack and curtained cupboards. A marble-topped café table on a cast-iron pedestal stood in the corner, the perfect size for her morning coffee and croissant.

Juliette couldn't help smiling and Nico smiled back. 'Liking it so far?'

'Oh, yes,' she said, walking through to the *salon*. The chaise longue had been re-upholstered and was the only piece of furniture in the room, apart from the pot-bellied stove and a basket of logs beside it.

'I brought that stove up from the shop a few years ago,' Nico said. 'The previous owners were throwing it out.'

The bedroom was bare, too, with only a wardrobe and a chest of drawers beside the new double bed. Juliette flushed when she saw it, and he smiled.

'I'd love to take it. I can't move in straight away but I'll pay you from the beginning of July, like we agreed. Deal?'

They shook hands and she let out an inner sigh of relief, sharpened by a hint of excitement. She'd be living here for six glorious months, and who could tell what might have happened by then?

★ ★ ★

Business at The Forgotten Bookshop was quieter the next day – 57 euros – which was sobering but gave Juliette a chance to finalise preparations for the launch party. Thinking about it made her feel slightly sick. The weather forecast was good so she hoped people would spill out of the store and into the square. She'd invited her friends, of course, including the third musketeer, Baptiste, and his partner Jean-Michel, whom she hadn't seen for a while, plus some Instagrammers and bloggers based in Paris, several people she'd met through the American Library, all the inhabitants of the apartment building, and her bookstore mentor, Elisabeth. Ben and Sophie would be there and were going to serve drinks, along with a couple of Sophie's fellow students whom Juliette was paying to help. She'd hired glasses and bought wine through a contact of Robert's at the café, and a catering van serving tacos and empanadas would park up alongside the square. No doubt there were officials she should have been contacting for permission but she'd have to wing it; there simply wasn't time and, with a bit of luck, no one would complain.

Seven customers came to the store on Thursday – 112 euros – and four on Friday – a dismal 37 euros – while Saturday saw a record-breaking twelve – 145 euros – which was so exciting, she invited them all to the party. Closing on the dot of five that afternoon, she changed in the store's tiny cloakroom into the chic black frock Ilse had lent her and reapplied her make-up with shaking fingers. And then, praise the Lord, wonderful Ben arrived with Sophie, the wine was being delivered and the glasses had arrived, and the store was looking so wonderful with fairy lights glowing everywhere that she began to feel a little less apprehensive.

'Here's to you, Mom,' Ben said, pouring her a small glass of wine. 'Time to celebrate. You should be proud of yourself.'

'I don't know about that,' Juliette said, gazing anxiously around. 'Do you think anyone's going to turn up?' This party might turn out to be an extravagance she couldn't afford.

She went out into the balmy air to look for the catering van. Pascal waved at her from the café where he was laying tables for the evening service, and a game of *pétanque* was already in progress in the square. She paused to watch the intent faces of the old men playing, entirely absorbed in that moment. Life will go on, she thought; the business may fail or it may not, and all I can do is keep trying. Fretting isn't going to help.

'*Salut,* Juliette!' Arnaud and Thérèse were walking towards her. 'Sorry to be so early but we couldn't wait.'

From that moment on, the time flew. Everyone seemed to arrive at once and the store was packed with people laughing and drinking and talking about books, spilling out onto the sidewalk and sitting on benches under the lamppost. Juliette even managed to smile at Delphine, who was ridiculously overdressed in a backless evening gown and homing in on Ben like a heat-seeking missile. Her back was extraordinarily beautiful, it had to be said: smooth as polished marble, without a single crease or freckle. Juliette caught Nico watching, too, as Delphine put her arm around Ben's shoulder and whispered something in his ear.

'Do you know that woman?' Sophie asked, as she passed by with the wine bottle.

'A little,' Juliette replied. 'I know her type, let's say.'

Ilse and her friend Elisabeth were talking together. 'Ah, there you are,' Elisabeth said, taking Juliette by the arm. 'I was just saying how well you've done. Such a good selection of titles and the shop is so inviting.'

'You've taught me so much,' Juliette said. 'I couldn't have done all this without you and Ilse.' She beckoned Sophie over. 'And this is my friend, Sophie, who's been such a help, too.'

These were the women Sophie should be talking to and learning from: intelligent, supportive and kind. Yet Juliette began to feel some sympathy for Delphine as she tossed back her hair and flirted so desperately with one bemused man after another – except for Nico, whom she ignored. Why did she have to try and make all of them fall in love with her? She didn't look particularly happy. Neither did Sophie, who kept scanning the crowd to check up on Ben. Juliette sighed. There was nothing she could do; the kids would have to work things out for themselves.

Suddenly everyone was leaving as abruptly as they'd arrived, like a shoal of fish changing course in the ocean. The catering van roared away before she'd had a single taco, and if Ben hadn't pressed a couple of empanadas into her hand, she wouldn't have eaten anything. She'd lost track of Ben and Sophie, and Delphine, too, in the flurry of goodbyes; all her guests had vanished and she was alone among the smeared glasses and crumpled servi-ettes. Somebody had forgotten their jacket so she put it to one side as she tore off a garbage sack and set about tidying the place. She remembered clearing up with Kevin after all those supper parties they used to have. He'd put on some music and they'd dance around the kitchen, if they had the energy, or stand together side by side at the sink; she'd wash and he'd dry. There was nobody she could turn to now and say, 'I think it went well, don't you?' Her eyes blurred and she put down the sack for a moment, steadying herself.

'I must have left my jacket behind,' somebody said, and she looked up to see Nico walking towards her. 'Juliette? Are you OK?'

'Sure,' she said, turning away. 'There's one there over the back of the chair.'

'Leave that for a moment.' He took the bag out of her hands and set it down. 'I'll help you later.'

He put his arms around her and it was so wonderful to be held, to feel supported and safe, that gradually her tension and grief became less overwhelming.

'I'm sorry,' she said, her voice muffled and her head against his chest. 'I was wishing my mother was here.'

'I know all about that,' he said, so sadly that she raised her eyes to meet his, and then her mouth. At first it was strange to be kissing someone who wasn't Kevin, but that feeling soon disappeared as Nico's lips became insistent, releasing the passion she'd been suppressing for so long. He pushed her back against the table, scattering the debris. He wanted her too, and the knowledge gave her confidence.

'Wait,' she said, her hands around his waist, her lips moist and fire running through her belly. 'Let's go upstairs.'

Chapter Twenty-one

October 1941

The two lovers might have moved out of the storeroom but Jacques still lived in such a state of anxiety that fear became his natural condition. His senses were always on the alert; even at night, he slept restlessly, ready to wake at the slightest sound. He had no idea how badly Béatrice had been hurt, or where she'd been taken, or what she might say under the torture that would no doubt be inflicted on her. One evening he carried the crate of banned books down to the cellar, and the next night he moved them back up to the storeroom. The very existence of such a place would condemn him, empty or full, and surely the cellar was the first place the Gestapo would search. Whenever he left the shop, he felt as though he was being watched. His expeditions to collect more books from Monsieur Isaacson's storage facility became increasingly fraught; he took an ever more circuitous route to make sure he wasn't being followed and spent as little time inside the warehouse as possible. The place seemed more crowded each time he visited, with lorries offloading ever greater quantities of furniture. Walking past an open window, he glimpsed rows of workers inside, sorting through piles of belongings. The German looting was now on an industrial scale.

One day Jacques ventured out to the *Musée de l'Homme* in the hope of finding a colleague of Béatrice or Mathilde's he might recognise, but the place was full of society ladies busy doing nothing much at all. The former staff had gone, either escaped or arrested, Béatrice had told him. She'd been so careful to keep the links of her chain separate that he had no one to contact for news. Maybe she'd never completely trusted him, or maybe she thought him a weak link who would easily snap.

A few days after she'd been taken away, a young lad turned up at *La Page Cachée* with a note saying Anaïs Nin would be waiting for him by the fountain in the Parc Monceau at one. When he arrived Camille was sitting on a bench, huddled up in Béatrice's overcoat, her face as cold and grey as the stone around her.

He took off his gloves and reached for her hand. 'Do you have any news?'

'She's in hospital at Suresnes. They'll transfer her to a cell in Mont-Valérien when she's strong enough.' Camille laughed: an awful sound. 'Saving her life so they can have the pleasure of torturing her later.'

'I saw it happen,' Jacques said. 'We were meant to meet at the Tuileries Gardens but she was being followed. They shot her and pushed her into a car.'

'Someone in the cell betrayed them, though we're still not sure who. She's strong, but. . .' Camille shrugged. 'Maybe you should leave the city. Is there anywhere you could go?'

'I can't abandon Paris,' he replied. 'There's still work to be done and Mathilde might come back for me. I've heard she may be alive, hiding out in Provence. Part of me wants to go looking for her, but—'

'You can't,' Camille said. 'Things will be dangerous for a while yet and you could lead the Boche straight there. Your hiding place won't be safe until we know what's happened to Béatrice so just lie low for a while.' She stood up. 'Goodbye, and good luck. I doubt we'll meet again. If there's any news of her, I'll do my best to let you know.'

They shook hands and Jacques watched her walk away. What havoc could be inflicted on the world by one man with a lust for power!

The following winter was even harsher than the one before. Coal lorries trundled constantly down Avenue Foch to the Nazi headquarters while the rest of Paris froze. People fought over stray lumps of coal in the street and the parks were full of scavengers looking for firewood. Jacques went to the Bois de Boulogne one day and came back with a bulging haversack. The only food in plentiful supply was swede: great knobbly roots that cramped one's stomach and knotted the bowels. The queues outside shops grew longer still, and Jacques was often the only man among a long line of women. One frosty morning, he was waiting outside the *boulangerie* with his ration coupons when a German soldier pushed his way to the front, as was their habit. People jeered openly now, and one woman shouted, 'Let him pass! He's on his way to England.' She was arrested, of course, and probably fined, but the laugh she raised was worth it.

Werner Schmidt kept his distance for a few weeks after Béatrice's abduction but one day the shop bell jangled and there he was: world-weary and immaculate as ever. He walked over to the display case, which Jacques unlocked so that he could browse at his leisure.

'Such a fine selection of books,' he said, choosing one and leafing through. 'You never mentioned your supplier, Monsieur Duval.'

'Oh, I pick them up here and there,' Jacques replied.

Schmidt chuckled. 'Come now, that won't do. You should know we've taken over a furniture warehouse in the rue du Faubourg Saint Martin which, according to their records, you're in the habit of visiting. You must know the one I mean.'

'I do.' Jacques held himself very still.

'You don't have to worry about me,' Schmidt said, smiling. 'You've been profiting from a Jew, just as they have been profiting from other people for years. I won't condemn you, although others might.' He tucked the book he'd been holding into his coat pocket. 'We've both benefited from an arrangement that has now come to an end. There's no point in going back to Faubourg Saint Martin: Monsieur Isaacson's stock has been impounded. Tread carefully, Monsieur Duval. Your shop remains open for now, thanks to my protection, but that situation may change at any moment.'

He took a card from his pocket and wrote an address. 'Let's not lose touch. If you find yourself in trouble, leave a note at my hotel. And if you come across any treasures I'd like, feel free to send them my way.' Clearing his throat, he added without meeting Jacques' eye, 'We should have dinner one evening. You must be lonely on these long winter evenings.'

Jacques could only stare at him for a moment, appalled. 'Thank you,' he said at last, collecting himself and pocketing the card while resolving never, ever to make use of it.

Jacques hibernated for the rest of that winter, freezing and ravenous like most other Parisians. At Christmas he received a card signed 'Anaïs', telling him their dear friend George had died. That was a dark time; he felt more alone than he could have imagined. Six inches of snow fell on New Year's Day and stayed on the ground for several weeks.

The only consolation for such arctic weather was the damage it inflicted on the German troops, stuck in the mud around Moscow and Leningrad where flooding had followed the record snowfall. Jacques listened to the BBC every lunchtime and evening, seizing on each scrap of good news. In January, the first boatload of American troops dodged German U-boats to arrive in Britain. 'Now we're getting somewhere,' Jacques whispered to Madame Bourdain when he passed her on the stairs.

When the weather became a little warmer, he accompanied Madame Bourdain on her next trip to the country, an hour and a half south of Paris. The train was packed. Jacques spent the journey standing in the corridor outside a locked compartment with a notice on the door proclaiming, '*Für die Wehrmacht*'. No Germans boarded the train yet the ticket collector said it was more than his job was worth to open up. They got off at a small station in the middle of nowhere and Jacques left Madame Bourdain visiting her niece while he walked on to a couple of the farms she had told him about. At the first, a small girl with fiery red curls was swinging on a gate. She ran away as he approached, her chubby legs in rubber boots flashing through the grass, but not before he had recognised the Feldmans' youngest daughter, and realised just how much the grumpy concierge had helped her former tenants.

He bought six eggs, hardboiled for the journey, two pats of butter, several goat's milk cheeses, jars of preserved tomatoes, a chicken and a rabbit. He would bring the provisions back to the city and divide them between Estelle and Henri's priest; he had to do something now he was no longer hiding fugitives and this seemed the best option.

Estelle was finding life increasingly difficult. She had lost all her exuberance and was finding it hard to cope with a toddler in her tiny apartment. Jacques couldn't believe how fast Celeste was growing. Every time he saw her, she seemed to have developed some new skill, and now she was walking and getting into all sorts of mischief. Jacques would bring Alphonse when he called because the dog was surprisingly patient and Celeste adored him. She was the most enchanting little girl, always smiling and affectionate.

'Can't you take her?' Estelle had implored on Jacques' last visit. 'Surely Mathilde will be back soon? I can't bear to think of my daughter going to strangers.'

Otto had left Paris to take up a post in Vichy and broken things off for good with Estelle, so Jacques had at last dared to tell her the truth about Mathilde. 'I have no idea where she is,' he'd said, 'or even whether she's still alive. Somebody might have seen her last summer but I don't know for sure.' Estelle had buried her face in Celeste's blonde curls for some time without speaking.

Mathilde seemed very far away in every sense now; try as he might, Jacques couldn't picture the life she was leading. Maybe Antoine had been mistaken and another beautiful, dark-haired woman was working in some vineyard south of Lyon. He still yearned for her yet the same question kept whirling around his tired brain each night: why hadn't she sent him a message? She could have used a false name, surely, and left some clue only he would understand? The fear she might have fallen in love with somebody else was a constant torture.

The Feldman girls were lucky to have escaped Paris when they did; life in the city soon became even harder for Jews. At the beginning of June, Jacques passed a girl in the street wearing a yellow star sewn to her coat: Hitler had ordered that all Jews over the age of six in Occupied France should be identified in this way. The young woman blushed at his stare, lifting her chin as she looked away.

'I didn't mean—' Jacques began, but she had already passed him by. Recklessly, he broke off a spray of blossom from an overhanging tree and hurried to catch her up.

'*Courage*,' he said, pressing the flowery twig into her hands.

He watched her walk away, head held high, while people nudged each other and gazed after her as he had done. 'Shouldn't be allowed,' said an indignant woman to her husband, 'parading about in public like that. Have they no shame?'

Jacques worried about Miryam Isaacson and even called at the Conservatoire to see if anyone could tell him where she was, but nobody seemed to have heard of her. He sold about half of Monsieur Isaacson's books in his possession and went back to the country to buy more food, but when he called at Estelle's apartment in Montmartre, her door was locked.

'She's gone away,' a downstairs neighbour told him.

'What, for good?' This was a shock. 'Where?'

'No idea,' the man replied, retreating back inside.

A couple of days later, Jacques received a letter from Estelle through the post, giving him her new address in the rue des Rosiers, and asking him to call at his earliest convenience because she had an urgent matter to discuss. He cycled there as soon as he'd closed the shop, wondering along the way what Estelle was doing in the heart of the Jewish district, and why she hadn't told him she was moving when he'd seen her the month before.

The narrow cobblestoned streets of the Marais were empty, the cafés all closed as well as the shops. In the rue des Rosiers, only one elderly man with sidelocks dangling beneath his hat made his way slowly along the pavement, hugging the wall. Jacques wheeled his bicycle into the courtyard of the building where Estelle was staying. A white face looked down on him from an upper window, vanishing instantly. The outer door was unlocked so he pushed it open and cautiously mounted the stairs, which were muddy and smelt of urine. Above him, a woman leaned over the banister to watch him approach. He tipped his hat but she didn't acknowledge the gesture, merely stared as he passed. The higher he climbed, the dirtier the staircase became. Reaching the fifth floor, he tapped on Estelle's door.

She opened the door seconds later, taking him by surprise, and glanced down the corridor before hustling him quickly inside.

'Thank you for coming,' she said. 'I didn't know whether you would.'

'Of course,' he replied. 'But what are you doing in a place like this? Have you run out of money? I could have helped with the rent.'

He glanced around. They were standing in a dark, low-ceilinged room under the eaves, with a kitchenette to one side through an arch and another door opposite, which presumably led to the bedroom. Noticing a coat hanging from a hook on the back of the door, his blood ran cold.

'Estelle, is that yours?' A mustard-yellow star shone out on the lefthand side.

'I'm afraid so,' she said. 'Well, at least that saves some awkward explanations.'

'I had no idea.' He moved a newspaper from the nearest chair and sat down with a thud. 'Why didn't you say? And what on earth were you doing with—' He stopped.

'With Otto?' She sat too, shrugging her shoulders listlessly. 'I was in love and I thought he'd protect me.

Love conquers everything, or so they say. Unfortunately not in my case – it was Otto who denounced me. I made the mistake of asking him for more money so he thought he'd get rid of me for good.'

'Oh, Estelle.' He rubbed a hand over his eyes.

'You might as well call me by my real name,' she said. 'It's Esther. And I was born in Hungary, which makes everything ten times worse.'

'You should have told us,' he said, 'we could have helped you. And maybe I still can. I've been hiding people in my storeroom. It's tiny but it might keep you safe for a little while, until we can get you out of the city.'

'It's too late for me,' Estelle replied. 'I'm conspicuous and my name's on every list. People say there's to be another round-up soon, even in the next few days. I'm begging you, Jacques: do you know a family who would take my daughter? Decent people who would keep her safe until Mathilde comes back and you can adopt her yourselves?'

This wasn't the time to raise his fears for Mathilde. 'Possibly.' He rubbed his forehead. 'The concierge in our building knows people and my friend Henri has married sisters. Are you sure about this, though?'

'There's no alternative.' Estelle's face hardened. 'Her father's German and her mother's a Jew. She has no future with me. I can offer her nothing but love, and what good is that? She's asleep at the moment but I can pack a few things and wake her up.'

'I can't take her straight away,' Jacques said. 'I've come here on my bicycle, and I need to make enquiries first. You can wait a day or so, surely?'

Estelle bit her lip. 'Hurry, please – there isn't much time. You're my only hope, Jacques. Don't let us down.'

'Do you know anything about another round-up of Jews?' Jacques asked Madame Bourdain on his return that evening.

'There are rumblings,' she replied. 'People have been told to lock their doors and hide their children, even fight the police if it comes to that.'

'I need to find a home for a girl aged about one. Can you help? She's a dear little thing, if that makes any difference.'

'I'll try. Let me ask around tomorrow and see what I can do.' Madame Bourdain looked at him gravely. 'Be careful, Monsieur Duval. These are dangerous times.'

Jacques took a long time to fall asleep that night and woke every hour or so, disturbed by noises outside. He got up when it was still pitch dark and opened the shutters to see gendarmes walking down the street in pairs, capes swirling. A bus roared past, and then another, their headlamps shrouded. He got dressed, unlocked his bicycle from the landing and carried it silently downstairs, heading for the back streets. Occasionally he passed a sentry post but there wasn't a German in sight, which seemed strange, and nobody else showed much interest in a solitary cyclist. The buses became more frequent, driving along in convoy or drawing up to park by the kerb, and as he approached the Marais, he noticed more gendarmes in the grey light of dawn. There wasn't a single German about. A door slammed, dogs barked and somewhere a woman screamed.

Rounding a corner, Jacques saw a line of dark figures bursting into an apartment building, their batons drawn. The round-up had begun. He increased his speed, pedalling furiously towards the rue des Rosiers as women started to spill onto the street, their children crying as police shouted at them to hurry, they hadn't got all day. They were carrying baskets, cushion covers and sacks stuffed with their belongings, and most were clutching children by the hand. One woman had a dog on a lead, and a girl held a birdcage with a green budgerigar inside. Gendarmes shepherded them towards the waiting buses, shoving along those who took too much time. An elderly lady with crutches fell over and was dragged roughly to her feet; a little boy stumbled as he climbed the steps into a bus and was slapped on the leg by his mother. 'Quickly,' she told him, her voice high with fear.

Jacques flung his bicycle against the wall outside Estelle's apartment building and dashed into the courtyard, pushing his way through the stream of people coming the other way. Now he noticed a few men, all of them elderly.

'Out of the way,' shouted a gendarme, pushing him to one side. 'Another step and I'll arrest you.'

So Jacques waited at the foot of the staircase, looking helplessly into the face of each person who passed by. The men wouldn't meet his gaze but the women stared at him in mute desperation, their eyes wide with shock. A little girl with dark hair in plaits dropped her doll so he picked it up and handed it back to her, despite the gendarme's scowl. On and on the women came in their best coats and summer frocks, most bare-headed but others wearing hats trimmed with flowers, the yellow stars gleaming brightly on their chests.

'Are they taking us to Pitchipoi?' a boy asked his mother, tugging at her sleeve. Pitchipoi: the mythical place nobody was quite sure existed, and from which no one had certainly ever returned.

'Maybe,' she replied, putting her arm around his shoulder. 'We might see Papa there.'

At last Jacques caught sight of Estelle in the gloom, carrying a basket and helping Celeste edge her way down the stairs. She glanced outside and spotted him, her eyes locking on to his. He retreated, hanging back to one side. As soon as Estelle had passed the gendarme at the foot of the staircase and walked out into the open air, she knelt beside the little girl, kissed her, and with one swift movement, pushed her into Jacques' arms.

'Hush,' he whispered, wrapping his jacket around Celeste's body, already stiffening in outrage, and walking quickly away. 'It's all right, *chérie*, I've got you.'

He daren't look back. Celeste began to scream in earnest as he hurried across the courtyard towards the street and someone called after him but he didn't slow down. Clutching the toddler around her waist, he grabbed his bicycle, threw himself on to it and somehow managed to cycle away one-handed. Only when they were several streets away did he allow himself to stop and comfort the weeping child.

'It's all right,' he murmured, holding her close and stroking her warm, damp head. 'Maman loves you and so do I. Alphonse is waiting for us at home.'

He dismounted, sat her on the saddle, wrapped his

arm around her and set off for home, pushing the bicycle. It was getting lighter by the minute. Green-and-white buses were lined up in nearly every street; Jacques paused to watch as the doors of one closed with a bang and it pulled away. A group of children looked at him out of the rear window and a small boy waved. He couldn't wave back. Celeste sucked her thumb, the tears drying on her cheeks as they stood for a moment, gazing after the bus as it drove eastward.

Feeling someone bump into him, Jacques began to apologise, but the woman who'd been following behind paid no attention. 'Stay with this gentleman, Berthe,' she said, pushing the girl beside her more forcefully against Jacques' leg. 'He'll look after you. Be good and don't make a fuss.' Jacques caught the briefest glimpse of a paisley headscarf and a navy coat before the woman was swallowed up in the queue climbing aboard the next bus.

Berthe was about nine, Jacques estimated, with a round face and dark hair cut in a blunt fringe across her forehead. She turned to gaze after her mother and then stared warily at Jacques, clutching her bag.

'Celeste and I are going home,' he said. 'Why don't you come along, too, and we'll have some breakfast? First, though, we need to get rid of this.' He quickly took off Berthe's cardigan, folded it so the yellow star was hidden and put it in his bicycle basket.

'Will we get into trouble for doing that?' she asked.

'There'll be more trouble if we don't,' Jacques replied.

They threaded their way through the mêlée. Jacques was concentrating so hard on keeping hold of Celeste and not letting Berthe run back to find her mother that he failed to notice the exact moment someone laid a sleeping baby on top of the cardigan in his bicycle basket; Berthe had to tug at his sleeve to alert him. It was turning into quite the morning.

At last, they made it safely home without any more surprises.

'So who have we here?' Madame Bourdain said, coming out of her *loge* to intercept Jacques and his small party. 'The Pied Piper of Hamelin?'

Chapter Twenty-two

July 1942

'Where have these children come from?' asked Madame Bourdain.

'Their mothers gave them to me,' Jacques replied, jiggling the baby as it wailed. 'Have you heard? The round-up's begun.'

'And what are you going to do with them?'

'I have no idea,' he told her. 'I was hoping you might help.'

Madame Bourdain took the baby from him. 'Here, let me have her. Doesn't seem natural, seeing a man with a baby.'

Jacques' apartment was unusually crowded: Celeste and Berthe were in the *salon*, playing with Alphonse. What would Mathilde think if she could see him now, Jacques thought, missing the baby's weight against his shoulder, and what would his mother have said? She'd longed for grandchildren. He wanted to take the child back from

Madame Bourdain but the concierge had annoyingly managed to quieten her.

'There's a nursing mother in the next building,' she said. 'I'll see whether she could manage another mouth to feed while you make enquiries. As for the other two, well, I'm away for ten days next week: my niece is expecting a baby and she's asked me to stay. Maybe I could take them with me, if you can keep them here until then. I should be able to find homes for them. The little one's pretty and the girl looks sensible.'

'Oh, she is,' Jacques said. 'I'm sure she'd fit in anywhere.' Berthe had already changed the baby's nappy, using a tea towel he'd supplied at her request. She'd helped distract Celeste, who was constantly heading for the door (presumably to look for her mother), and she'd washed up the plates after they'd eaten a breakfast of stale bread and honey. He'd seen tears in her eyes but she'd blinked them away. She was a trooper.

'I hope you're not going to put the poor things in that storeroom of yours,' Madame Bourdain added.

'Of course not,' Jacques replied. 'They can stay in the apartment with me.' The storeroom had lain empty since the year before; the two young communists had been the last to use it. His association with Béatrice had clearly made his safe place not so safe after all.

'Do you know where those Jewish people have been taken, and what's going to happen to them?' he asked, watching the baby's eyelids droop as it settled on Madame Bourdain's comfortable bosom.

'The buses are going east but nobody's found out

where they're stopping,' she said. 'Maybe they'll drive them all the way to Germany.'

Jacques made up his mind. 'Would you have time to sit with the children for an hour or so? I need to talk to someone.'

It was still early in the morning, not even eight. He cycled to the sprawling apartment in the next *arrondissement* that Henri shared with his parents and a sister who wasn't yet married. He passed only one of the green-and-white buses but saw several pairs of gendarmes escorting women and children through the streets, and many of the doorways along his route were cordoned off with police tape. Arriving at the Bertillons', he found Henri finishing breakfast while his mother made him a sandwich for later.

'Have you got a minute?' he asked. 'I need your help.'

Henri shot a warning glance in his mother's direction. 'Walk to work with me and we'll talk on the way.'

'Have you heard what's happening?' Jacques asked, once they were outside. 'I've come from the Marais and they're rounding up Jews and sending them off somewhere. See?' He discreetly pointed across the street towards a gendarme escorting a woman and an elderly man with a stick, followed by two little girls holding hands and another policeman bringing up the rear. 'The Boche seem to have taken the day off but our police are everywhere.'

'So what do you suggest?' Henri said. 'We can hardly stop them.'

'I have two children and a baby at my apartment. Their mothers are desperate – they gave them to me.'

Henri sighed. 'Oh, Jacques. I never thought you were the reckless type but you seem to have lost your head since Mathilde left. Where will it end? You know what'll happen if you're caught hiding Jewish kids.'

'Listen, though. I was wondering whether Yvonne might like to take the baby. What do you think?' Henri's sister had been married for six years without any children and he'd once let slip that she was desperate for a baby.

Henri stopped. 'It's possible, I suppose. I can always ask. Is it a boy or a girl?'

'A girl, about four or five months. And she's as good as gold. No trouble at all.' Jacques was only stretching the truth a little.

'All right, then. I'll tell Yvonne and she can call around if she's interested.' Henri lowered his voice. 'I'm glad I've seen you. I'm thinking of going south. My boss is under pressure to send workers to Germany and there's a rumour that men will soon be forced to go. I've had enough. If anyone wants me, they'll have to find me first.' He glanced at Jacques. 'They might come for you before long. You should consider your options.'

'I have to stay here so Mathilde knows where to find me,' Jacques replied. He'd told Henri at the time that Mathilde had gone to stay with relatives and had eventually confided that she hadn't been in touch for a while, without going into detail.

'Still no word from her?' Henri asked, and Jacques shook his head. Henri patted him on the back. 'Don't give up.'

'I must be getting home,' Jacques said quickly. 'I'll be happy to see Yvonne whenever she wants to come, and let's have a drink as soon as we can.'

Back on the bike, he put his head down and pedalled furiously, wondering what the children might be getting up to in his absence, when a passing glimpse down a side street made him skid to a halt. A boy aged about six or seven was wandering along the pavement towards him. He wore a checked shirt and corduroy shorts, and carried a small suitcase that bumped against his knees.

'Hello, young man,' Jacques said, dismounting. 'What are you up to, out here by yourself?'

'I'm looking for Papa,' the boy replied. 'Maman said I was to hide in the cellar and he would come, but he hasn't and I've been waiting a long time. I'm hungry.'

'And what's your name?'

'Tomas.' The child reached into his pocket and brought out a pair of spectacles in two pieces. 'I've broken my glasses. Maman will be angry.'

'I don't think she'll mind,' Jacques said, kneeling down. 'Now listen, Tomas. I think your papa must have had to go away but I'm going to look after you instead. There are some other children just like you staying at my apartment and I can take you there to join them. Is that all right?'

After some consideration, Tomas nodded.

'Good,' Jacques said. 'First we have to hide this star, though. Let me turn your shirt inside out.'

Tomas looked doubtful. 'But Maman said I had to wear it whenever we went out.'

'Not anymore,' Jacques told him. 'You'll have to trust me about this. Now, hop up on my crossbar and we'll be off.'

'Really, Monsieur Duval?' Madame Bourdain said, when the pair of them arrived home. 'Another one?'

'Yes, another one.' Jacques rested his hand on Tomas' head. How many more children were in hiding across the city, waiting for help that would never come?

Over the next few days, Jacques and his small surrogate family got to know each other. He opened the shop for a few hours each day, opening late and closing early, and taking a long lunch break in between. Berthe and Tomas were in charge of Celeste when he was away, while Madame Bourdain had taken the baby around to the new mother in the next building so at least they didn't have to worry about her. Henri's sister Yvonne telephoned the shop to say she'd like to see the child, and they arranged a time for her to be inspected one evening.

'And you know nothing about her?' Yvonne asked, staring at the baby in Madame Bourdain's arms.

'We know she's healthy,' Jacques said, 'and that somebody loved her enough to give her away.'

'She's a good feeder,' Madame Bourdain added, more prosaically. 'And she sleeps through the night like a proper little angel. Do you want to hold her?'

Yvonne glanced at her husband. 'Go on,' he said. 'She looks all right to me.'

So she stretched out her arms and Madame Bourdain placed the baby inside them. They all held their breath but the baby seemed to realise she'd better behave herself and lay quietly. She nestled against Yvonne's body, then opened her tiny pink mouth and yawned.

'There,' said the concierge. 'She looks very comfortable.'

Yvonne gazed at the baby as though she'd never seen anything so extraordinary, tucking the shawl around her shoulders and then daring to rock her gently to and fro. 'What do you think?' she asked her husband, not taking her eyes off the baby's face.

'I think she'll do,' he said, and everyone smiled.

'I hope we've done the right thing,' Jacques said to Madame Bourdain after the couple had left, taking the baby with them.

'Of course we have,' she replied briskly. 'That child will be smothered in love. It's the other poor souls we should be worrying about.'

The thousands of Jews who'd been rounded up were being held at a covered cycling stadium in the east of the city, she told him. There must have been no facilities, because apparently one could smell the place for miles around. 'They have no food and no water, either. In this heat? I heard the firemen took pity on them and turned on their hoses. Who knows how long they'll be stuck there, or what's going to happen next.'

Estelle was among those people, and Berthe's mother, and probably Tomas' mother too. Tomas was full of questions, from what they would have for supper to how long they would be staying with Jacques, but Berthe never asked him anything. At night, he read to the children from a book of fairy tales while they lay in bed with Celeste in the middle. They listened silently to stories of other children making their way through a dangerous world, threatened by wolves and witches and wicked stepmothers, and he didn't know whether that made them feel braver or more afraid. Celeste was especially unsettled in the evenings and he would sometimes sit with her on his lap in the rocking chair so she didn't disturb the other two. She was afraid of the dark and hated to be left alone but Jacques could always calm her down.

Coming home to the children was an unexpected joy but it was no life for them, cooped up in the heat and having to keep quiet all the time. They'd be happier in the country, he knew that, although he wasn't looking forward to the day they'd be leaving with Madame Bourdain. At first she'd been reluctant to look for a home for Tomas, who'd be harder to place on account of being circumcised and therefore clearly Jewish, but had agreed in the end because he was, after all, such an endearing child. Jacques had mended Tomas' spectacles with tape from a bookbinding kit and he was continually pushing them up his nose as he peered at this strange new world in which he found himself.

Jacques had no way of contacting the boy's parents, or Berthe's, and he knew Madame Bourdain would find them good homes so he had no qualms about sending them away. Celeste, though, was another matter. He felt particularly close to her, partly because of knowing Estelle but also because the little girl needed him more than the other two. She would reach up her arms to be held as soon as she saw him, and at night she would cling to him so fiercely he sometimes had to fight for breath. He couldn't bear the thought of not knowing where she was, of letting her go to strangers and maybe losing touch with her forever. He owed it to Estelle to think more carefully about the right thing to do.

★   ★   ★

A couple of days before the children were due to leave, Jacques was pondering these questions in his empty shop when a man wearing blue overalls approached him at the till: short and stocky, with a tanned face and a quiet, purposeful tread.

'Don't you remember me?' he asked, fixing Jacques with a gaze that seemed somehow familiar.

'Maybe.' Jacques searched his memory. A previous customer? 'You've been here before, haven't you?'

The man smiled. 'You gave me a book by Jules Verne. It wasn't bad, actually.'

'Of course!' Jacques shook his hand, recognising the guide who had tossed and turned in his storeroom the year before. 'Good to see you again.'

The man glanced over his shoulder. 'That woman you asked me to look out for,' he said quietly. 'Well, I've seen her.'

The world turned upside down. Jacques gripped the counter to steady himself. 'Are you sure?' he whispered. 'I have to be certain.'

The guide smiled, took a crumpled envelope from his pocket and slid it across. 'I told her about you. She asked me to give you this.'

Jacques' heart, which seemed to have temporarily stopped beating, pounded in his ears as he recognised Mathilde's handwriting. He slipped the envelope into his pocket. 'Thank you.'

'You're welcome.' The man put two fingers to his temple in salute. 'One good turn deserves another. You saved my life, or so I was told.'

'And now you have saved mine,' Jacques replied. 'Will you be staying?'

'Just passing through. I'll take another story from that Verne fellow if you have one, though.'

'Of course.' Jacques hurried to take one from the shelf, his fingers shaking and the letter burning a hole in his pocket. 'No charge.'

The guide smiled. 'I'll see myself out.'

Jacques followed him to the door, locked it and turned the sign to read 'Closed' before tearing open the envelope.

My darling, Mathilde had written, *you're alive! Of course, this will come as no surprise to you but it does to me. They told me you were dead, you see, and I was stupid enough to believe them. Wait for me, dearest – one day we'll be together again. There's no time to write more but I'm so proud of you and I love you with all my heart. Stay strong!*

The pain and uncertainty of the past few months dissolved in an instant. Jacques closed his eyes, dizzy with joy. How could he have doubted her? He pressed the paper to his lips, inhaling her scent: *Je Reviens*, the perfume she always wore. *Je reviens:* I'll come back. It felt as though she were standing there, making that promise in front of him. The future seemed suddenly full of possibility and now he knew exactly what to do.

'I'm keeping Celeste with me for the time being,' he told Madame Bourdain that evening. 'Her mother might come back for her and even if she doesn't, well, I can take care of her myself for a few months, until things are clearer.'

'Can you now?' The concierge folded her arms. 'Might I ask exactly how?'

'I'll pay Sylvie to look after her while I'm in the shop for the rest of the holidays and then I'll find a mother nearby who can keep her in the daytime. My wife might be coming back at some stage, anyway.'

'And what will you say when people ask where she's suddenly sprung from?'

'She's my cousin's daughter, didn't I tell you?' Jacques widened his eyes in assumed innocence. 'My cousin who died tragically in an accident, and whose husband is a prisoner in Germany.'

'Hmm.' Madame Bourdain glanced into the *salon*, where Celeste was engaged in her new favourite activity of piling the cushions into a heap and falling face first into them. 'I suppose you might get away with it.'

'She's a child,' Jacques said. 'Is anyone really going to bother about her?'

After supper, he told the children that the concierge was going to take them to the country the next day, where there were families who could look after them and fields where they could run around, and where there would be more food than he could provide.

'But I like it here,' Tomas said. 'I don't want to go anywhere else. And if we move too far away, how will our parents find us?'

'Because I'll know where you are and I can tell them,' Jacques replied, with an air of authority that he hoped would discourage any further questions.

'Can we take Alphonse?' Tomas asked.

'I'm not sure about that,' Jacques replied. 'Maybe he'd better stay with me for the time being. I bet there are plenty of other dogs in the country, though.'

'Are we allowed to be Jewish there or must we keep it a secret?' Berthe asked.

'I'm not sure,' Jacques said. 'You might have to pretend not to be sometimes but you can always be Jewish in your heart.'

He had no idea how important their religion was to them, having no strong belief himself, but perhaps it would be a way of holding on to the parents they'd lost. He'd declined to stock a picture book featuring a character called Youpino, who'd grown from a violent baby stealing other children's toys into a sullen teenager and then a businessman who made his fortune by exploiting others – all because he was a Jew. Being Jewish meant they couldn't play in parks, couldn't ride a bicycle or go to the cinema, were constantly insulted and ostracised. Their identity was a source of suffering but it was also inextricable from the love of their families.

'What's going to happen to Celeste?' Berthe asked.

'She'll stay here,' he replied. 'I made a promise to her mother that I would take care of her myself, you see.' Berthe nodded. 'Thanks for all your help,' he added. 'You're a good girl. Your mother would be very proud of you.'

She looked at him with her dark, adult eyes and he wondered, as usual, what she was thinking, and what lay ahead for her and Tomas. He wrote about the children in his visitors' book that night, listing their names; despite the risk, it seemed more important than ever there should be some record of their existence. Maybe one day they might by some remote chance become aware of these notes and realise that someone had cared for them, and believed they were worth something.

Madame Bourdain came for the children early the next morning. If he hugged them, Jacques had an awful feeling he might cry, so he stuck out his hand instead and said with forced cheerfulness, 'Cheerio, you two. It's been lovely having you to stay. Look after yourselves, won't you?'

'Thank you for having us,' Berthe said, solemnly shaking his hand.

Tomas just looked bewildered, pushing his glasses up his nose. 'Can we come back if we don't like it there?' he asked. 'Will you—'

'I'm sure you'll love it,' Jacques interrupted heartily, hating himself. 'Now, kiss Celeste and Alphonse goodbye and don't keep Madame Bourdain waiting.'

'Will you come and see us?' Tomas asked, turning back as he was led away.

'Maybe,' Jacques promised, holding Celeste's hand. He was doing the right thing, he reminded himself; the children would forget all about him and it was silly to have got so attached. Yet he carried Celeste out onto the landing and leant over the banister to watch and listen until the children had left the building, Tomas still asking questions and Madame Bourdain becoming increasingly exasperated.

Sylvie was happy to look after Celeste for a few hours that day and seemed to accept Jacques' story about the little girl being his cousin's child. Rather than opening *La Page Cachée*, however, he cycled to the velodrome with a baguette and a bottle of water in his bicycle basket. It was a sweltering day and he couldn't stop thinking about the people who were locked inside. The rumours were true: the smell was awful.

The guards wouldn't let him in or agree to give his supplies to anyone. He hadn't been expecting to see Estelle but helping anyone was better than sitting at home, doing nothing.

'What's going to happen to these people?' he asked, but nobody seemed to know or care.

On the way back he passed a schoolyard, ringing with the shouts of those children who could still play outside with their friends and make as much noise as they wanted. Yet abruptly the noise died away as a crocodile of about twenty children walked across the playground, two by two, led by a couple of gendarmes at the front and one bringing up the rear. They were a mixture of ages, some as young as three or four up to around ten, and they all wore yellow stars on their chests. Their schoolmates stopped to watch them pass, and a couple of teachers emerged to stand silently by the main door. The Jewish children filed out of the gate and into the street, and Jacques followed them.

'What's happening here?' he asked the gendarme at the back of the line.

'Mopping-up operations,' the man replied. 'Why? What's it to you?'

'But these are children,' Jacques said, unable to help himself. He was missing his small tribe and his heart felt unusually battered.

'And children grow up,' said the gendarme. 'Stop snivelling and get a move on!'

This last remark was addressed to a small boy bringing

up the rear of the procession, hand in hand with an older child who was also urging him on.

'Hurry up!' said the policeman again, prodding them both with his baton. 'We're getting left behind, damn it.'

'Let me have them,' Jacques said.

The policeman turned to stare at him. 'What are you talking about?'

'I'll take them. Come on, what's two more or less to you? No one will know and it'll make your life easier.' The gap between the front of the line and the end was getting bigger by the second and now the smaller boy had come to a complete halt, his face screwed up in a silent howl.

'You must be mad,' the gendarme told Jacques. 'I've a good mind to—'

'Please, Dani,' begged the older child. 'We have to keep up with the others.' But now the boy was crying in earnest.

The policeman looked around. 'All right, you can have the little one, I'll be glad to get rid of him. Quick, though.'

The older boy pushed the child forward, giving Jacques a surprisingly grown-up look as he did so.

'I want them both,' Jacques told the gendarme. Stepping forward, he blocked the children with his bicycle wheel and retrieved the baguette from the basket. 'Here, you can take this in exchange.'

The gendarme sighed. 'You don't give up, do you?' Yet in a second, the bread had disappeared under his cape. 'Clear off then, the pair of you,' he said, giving the older boy a clip around the ear for good measure before turning to catch up with the tail of the procession.

Still shielding the boys with his bicycle, Jacques stripped off their jackets and stuffed them in the basket.

'Don't worry,' he said, 'I've done this before. Now, let's get you home.'

Chapter Twenty-three

July 1942

Dani was four and Georges was seven. He looked very much like the son Mathilde and Jacques might have had, with his dark curly hair and watchful, serious face, while Dani was blond and blue-eyed. No one would have thought the boys were related.

'This is a nice place, isn't it?' Georges asked his little brother when Jacques had shown them into the bedroom where they were to stay, hiding under the bed or in the wardrobe, if necessary, beneath a pile of coats. 'We'll be all right now.'

'I have to go downstairs and open my shop for a couple of hours,' Jacques said. 'Remember, don't answer the door if anyone knocks and keep as quiet as you can. Later you can meet the little girl who's staying with me.'

'Can we keep the dog?' Georges asked, stroking Alphonse.

'I'll just take him out to do his business first,' Jacques said. Alphonse seemed to have an iron bladder but even he had his limits.

He was running down the stairs with the dog when a tall, sour-faced woman emerged from the concierge's *loge*. 'I'm covering for Madame Bourdain,' she said. 'Do you live here? I didn't realise pets were allowed.'

'Jacques Duval, from the second floor,' he said. 'And this is Alphonse.'

She looked at the animal with distaste. 'He'd better not bark all day and night.'

Madame Bourdain had a spare key to his apartment, Jacques remembered as he headed outside with the dog. If this woman were the nosy type and saw him going out, she might use it. He wondered whether the boys would be safer in his secret storeroom, but it was risky taking them up and downstairs. He'd had his heart in his mouth earlier that morning, waiting till the coast was clear and then shepherding them up to his apartment. He could say they were his nephews, but Sylvie and her mother would be bound to wonder where the latest branch of his family had suddenly sprung from. Besides, the storeroom was sweltering in this heat and the children would be frightened there at night on their own. He had closed it up for the summer, tucking the visitors' book, as he thought of it, into a volume of de Gaulle's essays. He would have to write about his latest arrivals – or maybe he wouldn't. He already thought about them differently from Berthe and Tomas, though he didn't know why.

'I'll be back at lunchtime,' he said to the boys, who

were sitting up on his mother's bed when he returned with Alphonse. 'Here, I've brought you something to read.'

Dani was already falling asleep but Georges was interested in the books Jacques had brought: another Beatrix Potter story, which was probably too young for him, and *Emil and the Detectives*, perhaps a little too old.

'I can read it to you this evening,' Jacques said, and the boy nodded solemnly as he turned to leave.

A few customers still came into *La Page Cachée* so it was worth him opening, and people might talk if the shop stayed closed for too long. A woman bought a birthday card and a book about trout fishing for her nephew, and one of his regular customers bought the latest in a series of westerns. Life went on while families were torn apart and children snatched from the streets. To round off the morning, Guillaume Bruyère appeared, enquiring about copies of his novel, *It Happened in Paris*.

'I'm afraid we don't have any in stock,' Jacques said.

'Then you must order some more,' Bruyère told him. 'The book is very popular.'

'Only in some circles,' Jacques replied. 'It's no longer a work I choose to sell in this shop.' If the Nazis could ban books by Jewish authors, he could choose to ignore those written by anti-Semites.

'A decision you may come to regret.' Bruyère flushed angrily. 'I warn you, Monsieur Duval, make an enemy of me at your peril.'

He really was the most insufferable man, Jacques decided. At midday, he closed the shop and ran back upstairs. His mother's room was empty and his heart stopped momentarily, but Alphonse was nosing under the bed and he found the two boys there, huddled together.

'We didn't know who it was,' Georges explained.

They agreed on a signal. Jacques wouldn't knock on his own door, which would have seemed odd to anyone watching, but as soon as he came into the apartment, he would tap the wall three times.

'Do you live here by yourself?' Georges asked later, when they were eating bread and herrings in the kitchen.

'I do now,' he replied. 'My wife has gone away for a while.'

'Is she coming back?' Dani said. His eyes were extraordinarily blue; one would never have guessed he was Jewish to look at him.

Jacques smiled. 'Yes, although I'm not exactly sure when.'

After lunch, Georges dried the plates and cutlery that Jacques had washed while Dani wiped the table, standing on tiptoe. They were so keen to be helpful, so trusting of this stranger who'd suddenly appeared in their lives. He wished Mathilde could have been there to reassure them. Just for a moment, he let himself imagine another world in which he and his wife had children of their own and now here he was with them, waiting for her to come home so they could tell her about their morning.

Without wanting to upset the boys, he asked them about their parents. They told him that their father had died some time ago and their mother had asked a neighbour to look after them the week before because she'd had to go away, too. They didn't know where she was.

'Will we get into trouble for not following the other children?' Dani asked. 'Was that my fault?'

'No, you mustn't worry about that,' Jacques said, although of course they were worried and confused about everything. Even when he read to them from *Emil and the Detectives* after lunch, they had one eye on the door and one ear listening out for a tread on the stairs. He kept the shop open for another couple of hours in the afternoon before collecting Celeste. Sylvie could look after her for the next few days, she told him, but she was out on Saturday so he would have to make other arrangements.

'This is Celeste,' he told Dani and Georges, who contemplated her solemnly. Dani didn't show much interest and she ignored him, bringing Georges her picture book straight away and expecting to be read to. He clearly had big brother stamped all over him.

There were a couple of jars of preserved tomatoes and some beans left in the store cupboard, plus a few tins of sardines. Jacques cooked up a fish stew, calculating how long his supplies would last and pondering his options. Mathilde's letter had changed everything, setting his mind free to wander. Ever since she'd left, life had been one long series of goodbyes and he didn't know how many more he could survive. What if he was to take the children and go? They could hole up somewhere in the unoccupied zone, find a remote village somewhere in the Ardèche, perhaps, and wait out the war. Now the Russians and Americans were fighting the Germans, there was a chance Hitler might be defeated before long. News of their arrival might reach Mathilde through the underground network and anyway, he would come to Paris in September every year to wait for her. They were destined to be together, just as he was destined to look after these children who filled him with such joy and hope. They would become a family, just as Estelle had hoped. Every blow he'd suffered and every hard lesson he'd learned seemed to have been leading to this point.

Green-and-white buses were seen again at the velodrome a couple of days later, taking the people inside to some unknown destination. Without Madame Bourdain, Jacques was deprived of information. He opened the shop for a couple of hours in the morning and a couple in the afternoon, and spent the rest of his time with the children. There was plenty of paper and some coloured pencils in the apartment so they spent a lot of time drawing and writing. He'd found his mother's button box and Celeste, in particular, liked sorting the buttons into colours and sizes. Jacques read to them for hours, too: a boy nestled in the crook of his arm on either side, with Celeste on his lap. They loved being told stories just as much, so he recycled his mother's tales of daring Jean the pirate boy. Dani had a particular square of blanket that he had to hold before he could sleep and he would twist it around his fingers as he listened. Georges would gaze into the distance, looking very much as Jacques must have done all those years ago.

The idea of leaving Paris nagged at Jacques' mind until he found himself considering not whether to go about it, but how. Applying for a pass through the usual channels took months and there was no guarantee of success, while travelling on forged papers was a risk and anyway, he had no idea how to go about obtaining them. The only person he could think of who might help with an *Ausweis* – a pass – was Kriminalassistent Schmidt, whom he hadn't seen for weeks. But could the man be trusted? Jacques couldn't work out why Schmidt had offered his protection; surely he could take whatever books he liked from the warehouse without bothering to involve Jacques? Maybe Schmidt wasn't as cultured as he made out. He seemed to need guidance: the reassurance that his collection was being curated by an expert eye. And perhaps he also wanted the illusion of respectability. He couldn't bear to think Jacques might have the moral ascendancy. When Schmidt came into *La Page Cachée*, he could pretend to be an ordinary customer who just happened to be confronted by an array of goodies at bargain prices, like a child in a sweetshop with unlimited pocket money.

'I'm not stealing,' he could tell himself. 'Why, I'm even helping this poor fellow with my patronage.'

There was also the matter of Schmidt's dinner invitation, which Jacques had blotted from his memory until now and still could hardly bear to think about. Maybe it was time to find out how far he was prepared to go in return for protection. That evening, he parcelled up a couple of fine editions from Isaacson's remaining collection, cycled to Schmidt's hotel and left them there, with a note wishing him well and saying perhaps he might like to drop by *La Page Cachée* one day soon. It was worth a try; the children had been with Jacques for several days now and he felt there was no time to lose. The new concierge had called at his apartment to tell him someone had complained about a dog barking, and had craned over his shoulder to stare down the hall with her nose practically twitching – just as Madame Bourdain had done, before he got to know her. He had a feeling this woman's interest was less benign.

Herr Schmidt didn't appear at the shop but Jacques was surprised to receive a telephone call from him at *La Page Cachée*, late that Saturday morning.

'Thank you for the books,' he began. 'A kind gesture. You'll never guess where I am, Monsieur Duval – sitting in the very same café where I first met you and your lovely wife.'

'Fancy that.' Jacques wondered where the conversation was going.

'Why don't you join me?' Schmidt went on.

'But I'm in the shop,' Jacques said. 'We're not due to shut for another half hour.'

'This is important. I have something to tell you urgently. Close early and get here as soon as you can.' There was a click as Schmidt replaced the telephone receiver, followed by a buzzing line.

It was unfortunate timing. Sylvie was out for the day so Jacques had left Georges in charge of Dani and Celeste for a couple of hours: quite a responsibility for a boy of seven, but there seemed no alternative. He ran upstairs to tell the children he had to go out unexpectedly but he should be back in an hour or so, and they were to stay quietly with Alphonse and climb into the wardrobe should anyone knock on the door. A couple of his mother's dresses were still hanging there, which they could hide behind for an illusion of safety. He wondered, as he cycled to Montmartre with sweat pouring down his face, what Schmidt could possibly have to say, and how soon he could ask for an *Ausweis*.

He found the German sitting at a table near the back of the restaurant, smoking a cigar. 'Do sit down,' he said. 'What will you have to drink? Whisky? Champagne?'

Jacques asked for a beer, mopping his face with a handkerchief. They chatted for a few minutes about the books Jacques had sent over before Schmidt said genially, 'You're probably wondering why I invited you over here. Bad news, I'm afraid.'

'Not my wife?' Jacques asked, putting down his glass so sharply on the table that beer slopped over the rim.

'Not your wife,' Schmidt confirmed. 'Unfortunately, it's you.' He gave that infuriating, ironic smile as Jacques stared back at him, unable to speak.

'I beg your pardon?' he managed to say eventually.

'You've been denounced.' Schmidt tapped a cylinder of ash on to the floor. 'A man by the name of Guillaume Bruyère says you sold him a book on the Otto list. *Beware of Pity*, I believe it was called. An ironic title, all things considered. He's handed it in to us, with your till receipt. You really should have been more careful.'

Jacques swallowed hard. 'And what does that mean, exactly?'

'It's a fairly minor offence but, what with your wife's history, well—' Schmidt crossed one leg over the other. 'There's a warrant out for your arrest.'

The roaring in Jacques' ears made it hard for him to think. He focused on his hands, lying on the table as though they belonged to somebody else.

'So have you come to take me away?' His voice was that of a stranger, too.

Schmidt smiled again. 'No. In fact, I've come to save you. I feel a certain amount of pity for you myself, appropriately enough. That Bruyère fellow is the most appalling sycophant and his novel is an abomination. I've spent many happy hours browsing in your shop and I don't believe you're a bad person. Somewhat venal, perhaps, but we all have our faults. And if you were arrested, you might take it into your head to make up stories about our relationship, which as we both know has been purely professional.' Now he was looking sheepish. 'Rumours spread like wildfire these days.'

Jacques frowned, recoiling. 'I'm sorry but I don't understand what you're trying to say. Could you spell it out for me?'

'The police are on their way to your premises,' Schmidt told him. 'They'll probably search your apartment when they find the shop closed. I'm giving you advance warning – a sporting chance, you might say – for old times' sake. If you hurry, you might get to a train station before there's a general alert.' He laid a piece of card on the table. 'And I've even supplied you with a pass.'

Jacques snatched it, already on his feet. 'Yes, no time to waste,' Schmidt said, stubbing out his cigar. 'Goodbye, Monsieur Duval. I doubt we'll meet again. It's been a pleasure.'

Hurtling down narrow streets, his teeth juddering from the impact, flying down hills and straining every muscle to climb them, legs pumping, heart racing, every thought and action directed towards one end, Jacques rides headlong through the city. He cycles across a junction without stopping and a car horn blares but he pays it no attention. His wheel hits a pothole in the road, sending the bicycle skidding; he manages to regain control and carries on, the breath tearing at his chest. Nearly home. He sees a black Citröen parked at the end of his street as he flings his bicycle against the wall and dashes into the apartment building. It's quiet. Have the police been already? Is he too late? Taking the stairs two at a time, he makes it to the second floor, fumbles for his door keys and jams them in the lock with shaking fingers. No time to tap on the wall because in two seconds he's in his mother's bedroom and the children, thank God, are sitting on the floor, playing with the buttons while Alphonse sleeps beside them.

'We have to go,' he says, scooping up Celeste and taking Dani by the hand.

'Go where?' Georges asks.

'I'm not sure.' As he hurries them along the hall and opens the door, he hears men's voices below and heavy feet on the stairs.

'What about Alphonse?' Dani says.

Jacques doesn't reply. He snatches a look over the banister to see a column of round black caps advancing towards them, like the buttons in his mother's box. He and the children will have to climb upward. They stumble to the next floor, banging on doors because he doesn't know what else to do. Nobody answers. The doors are all locked. He feels Celeste's heart thump against his chest while Georges looks up at him in fear, willing this reality not to be true. The feet on the stairs are running now.

At last he finds himself outside Sylvie's apartment. She's out but maybe her mother is home: a gossip, yes, but goodhearted underneath. Her door swings open abruptly as he hammers on it and she's standing there in her apron, shock written over her face. The men are a couple of floors below, and catching up fast. Without a word, Jacques thrusts Celeste into her arms and pushes Dani and Georges towards her. Dani still clutches his hand and he has to shake him off.

'Go!' he hisses at Georges, making himself fierce and commanding while his heart breaks.

Sylvie's mother gathers up the children and her eyes meet Jacques' in an unspoken question as she holds open the door. He shakes his head and quickly, she closes it.

Jacques turns to face the men who have come for him. He has done what he can.

'Mon Père, je m'abandonne à toi, fais de moi ce qu'il te plaira. Je suis prêt à tout, j'accepte tout.'

Father, I give myself up to you, do with me what you will. I am ready for everything, I accept everything.

Chapter Twenty-four

July 2022

Lying in bed, Juliette became aware of a gentle warmth on her face and opened her eyes to a pool of sunshine, dazzling on the grey walls and golden floor. For a moment, she had no idea where she was, until she caught sight of the black dress Ilse had lent her for the party, lying on the floor, and memories came flooding back. Catching her breath, she turned to look beside her. The bed was empty. She heard running water and the sound of somebody singing before she pulled the sheet over her head, wanting the bed to swallow her up. He was singing! Did that mean he was happy? Images flashed through her mind, as though she were scrolling through a stranger's Instagram feed: the two of them running upstairs to the apartment, hand in hand, kissing in the hall because they couldn't wait another second, Nico pulling his shirt over his head to reveal a taut, muscular stomach and her – my God, what had come over her? – unbuckling his belt and unzipping his jeans. They had made love twice, once on the chaise longue because it was nearer and then in the bed, taking the time to explore each other's bodies and discover new pleasures. She had fallen asleep with his arms around her and his breath on her cheek, feeling utterly content. Now it was the morning, and she had no idea what to say or how to act. She'd never been in this situation before.

Clutching the sheet to her chest, she sat up, pushing the hair out of her eyes. The city was waking up, too; she could hear the sound of hammering from somewhere below. On a Sunday? Really? She must look a fright: panda eyes from the make-up she hadn't washed away and creases from the pillow on her cheek. Hurriedly she retrieved her bra and knickers and put them on under the bedclothes – the thought of Nico seeing her naked in the light of day was mortifying – then tiptoed across the floor to pick up Ilse's dress. When she'd had it cleaned, it would be as good as new, she told herself, struggling with the zip.

'Let me do that for you.' He untangled the zipper from her bra strap and pulled it up.

'Thank you.' She turned to face him, blushing already.

He'd wrapped a towel around his waist and drops of water beaded the dark hairs on his chest. Smiling, he kissed her on the forehead. 'Leaving so soon? I thought we could have breakfast together.'

'That would have been lovely, but I need to get home,' she said. 'Ben will be wondering where I am.'

She would take a shower and change in the minimal apartment, then come back to the bookshop and finish clearing up. That's what she would do. She made herself look at Nico and smile. 'Thanks for last night. It was . . . amazing.'

'I thought so too.' He dropped his arms, his expression changing imperceptibly. 'Well, you have my number. Call me when you want.'

'I will,' she said, looking around for her shoes and her bag. 'Um, bye for now.'

She sensed his eyes on her back as she walked away, hating herself, and then through the apartment, downstairs and out into the perfect morning. She kept her head down so she wouldn't see Robert or Pascal or anyone else in the café, and maybe they wouldn't notice her. The journey home seemed to take forever; to her horror, she'd almost made it when she caught sight of a familiar figure approaching from the other direction, also wearing the same clothes from the night before.

'Well, this is a new experience,' Ben said as he met her at the door. 'Never thought I'd be doing the walk of shame with my mother.'

She had to say it. 'Not Delphine?'

He laughed. 'God, no. She'd eat me alive. Sophie, of course.' He looked at her with his head on one side. 'No need to ask who you've been with.'

She blushed again, avoiding his gaze as she unlocked the door. 'Can you start packing today? We need to be out of the apartment by tomorrow and I want to leave it spotless.'

Standing under the shower a short time later, she closed her eyes and let the water pummel her skin. A pity fuck, that's what she'd heard the kids call it. Nico had been feeling sorry for her so they'd had sex and now he was being kind because he was a nice person, damn him. What would Ben think? Would he tell Emily? Sighing, she dressed in comfortable clothes and went out again to take Ilse's dress to the cleaners' and buy croissants. She wasn't ready to have breakfast with Nico. What on earth would they have talked about?

She was standing in the queue at the *boulangerie*, inhaling the smell of fresh bread, when her phone rang. It was him. She let the call go to voicemail, bought her croissants and a bag of *chouquettes* because, what the hell, she needed extra sustenance, then listened to his message outside in the sunshine. His voice was rushed, urgent.

'Juliette, you need to come back to your shop, right away. It's an emergency. I'm there now but I don't have the keys. Call me as soon as you get this, OK?'

'What could have caused it? You haven't been trying to fix the shower again?'

She stood, horrified, surveying the damage. Water was dripping through the ceiling in a corner of the larger room, trickling down shelves that were already saturated and collecting in pools on the floor. About a hundred books in that section of the store were ruined; she picked one off the shelf and flapped its sodden pages.

'The people in the apartment above have been renovating,' Nico said. 'The builders put a nail through one of the pipes – the hall next door is flooded too, so I saw it when I was leaving. They've turned off the water at the mains so at least the damage shouldn't get any worse. The builders' insurance should cover it, I think.'

'Thank goodness.' But she groaned inwardly at the thought of the inevitable paperwork.

He took off his jacket. 'I'll help you clear up.'

'You don't have to. I'm sure you've got better things to do with your Sunday.'

'I don't,' he said, rolling up his shirt sleeves, 'and I'd like to spend it with you.'

'Thanks,' she said awkwardly. 'I'm sorry, Nico, I'm just feeling rather shy.'

'I don't mind,' he told her. 'In fact, it's quite charming.'

Maybe it was going to be all right, Juliette thought, taking some photographs on her phone for the insurance claim. Maybe he'd recovered from the shock of waking up next to her rather than the gorgeous Delphine. Maybe they could still be friends.

She brought up some cardboard boxes from the cellar and they started packing up the damaged books. Once the shelves were cleared, she went into the cloakroom to fetch a towel. When she returned, Nico was examining the back panel, testing the wood with his fingers in a way that alarmed her.

'What are you doing?'

He turned, frowning. 'I'm not sure. Bear with me for a minute.' He pressed again and suddenly a section of the panel slid aside, revealing a gap behind.

'Have you damaged it?' Juliette started forward.

Nico was reaching his hand through, feeling around behind the shelves. 'Thought so. Here we are.'

To her astonishment, the entire wall of shelving swung open. In a few paces, she was standing beside Nico. In front of them lay a small room, not much more than a cupboard, with a mattress on the floor and a crate in the corner, covered by a cloth. It looked like a prison cell, and now she noticed the bucket.

'I knew there must have been something here.' Nico pointed to the wall. 'There's the window that opens on to the street, see?'

Juliette stepped into the space, so dark and shabby and utterly different from the world outside. She knew immediately that something important had happened here. A few dust motes floated on the still, hot air that smelt of another time and also of nothing at all. The walls were draped in black cobwebs and the floor was littered with flakes of plaster that crunched underfoot.

'I bet Zizi knew about this place,' she murmured. 'She said Jacques was working for the Resistance during the war – he must have been hiding people here. I wonder why she didn't tell us about it, and why it made her so sad. You'd have thought she'd be proud.'

Nico was swinging the door to and fro, admiring the opening mechanism. 'My grandfather fitted these shelves so he must have adapted them, too. He was a craftsman.'

Juliette suddenly longed to hug him but managed to restrain herself. 'I should have listened to you in the beginning.'

She walked to the crate and lifted a corner of the cloth. 'Oh, my goodness.' It was filled with books, stacked neatly on top of each other.

'Well, he did run a bookshop,' Nico said. 'That's not such a surprise.'

'Yes, but why keep these ones locked away?' Juliette picked up two from the top: a novel by Stefan Zweig and a volume of essays by Charles de Gaulle. 'We need to show people this room, historians who can tell us what it means.'

'But first we should speak to Zizi,' Nico said. 'She ought to know before anyone else. I usually visit her on Sunday afternoons. Why don't you come too?'

'I'd love to,' she said. 'Thanks.'

So they were spending the day together after all and actually, it was fine. At last, they walked out of the past and into the water-soaked present, closing the shelf door behind them and sliding back the wooden panel. Juliette shivered, thinking of the people who must have stayed in that confined space, fearing for their lives.

'By the way,' he added, 'I have a key to the apartment but of course I won't use it. Do you want me to give it to you, though, just to be sure?'

'Keep it,' she said. 'Might be useful to have a spare somewhere else.'

'Fine. I'm driving to Zizi's home so I'll swing by your apartment later and pick you up. *A bientôt.*' He gave her a lingering kiss and she breathed him in again, wondering how a woman her age could still be so socially awkward. It struck her then that she didn't even know how old Nico was, and would be nervous about asking. What if he was younger than her? Of course, that wouldn't really matter – and yet somehow it did.

After he'd left, she was scrolling through her phone for some light relief when she came across photos of the launch party that Sophie had posted on The Forgotten Bookshop Instagram feed. The store and the square looked wonderful and Ben was right: Delphine certainly added glamour to the occasion. There was a shot of her in a group talking to Nico and Arnaud, beside Juliette and Baptiste. Nico wasn't looking at Delphine, though; he had his eyes on Juliette, and his expression made her catch her breath.

Zizi leant her head against the back of the chair and closed her eyes. 'So you've found the hiding place. I wondered whether you would.'

'Do you want to see some photos of it?' Juliette asked, offering her phone. 'Here, you can enlarge the screen.'

The old lady stared at the picture, frowning.

'Is it how you remember?' Nico asked.

'I never saw the place.' Zizi handed the phone back to Juliette. 'Henri told me about it, after the war. He made the secret doorway, you see, and he knew Jacques was keeping people there. He met one of them once: a British pilot, I believe.'

'So Jacques Duval was a hero,' Juliette said. 'There are books in that crate that he seems to have been hiding too.'

'I know about those,' Zizi said. 'We were given a list of titles we weren't allowed to stock, mostly written by Jews. I helped Jacques take them off the shelves and pack them up. He was meant to destroy them but I always wondered whether he had.' She reached for her handbag and passed Juliette an envelope. 'I've been looking at his photograph and thinking about what you said. These pictures are for you. It's right that Jacques Duval should be somewhere in *La Page Cachée*, or whatever you're calling it now.'

'Tell us about him, Mémère,' Nico said. 'We're family. I have Papi's tools and I'm working with the same wood he did. You can trust me.'

Zizi took his hand in hers and squeezed it. 'You're a good boy,' she said, 'and perhaps, after all, you should know. His story affects other people but they're all dead now, except for me, so I suppose there's no harm in passing it on.' She smoothed her skirt over her knees and shut her eyes again for a moment, as if to bring back the past.

'Your grandfather left Paris in the summer of 1942, when things got really bad, and travelled south to hide out with the Maquis. Of course, he thought afterwards that he should have taken Jacques with him but by then it was too late. Jacques was arrested a few days after my Henri had gone, in our very building. Somebody must have found out what he was doing and betrayed him. I was out that day but I heard all about it when I got home. He had three children with him. He knocked on our door and my mother took them but she left him standing there.'

'She must have had a good reason,' Nico said.

'She said he knew it was too late for him, the police were on his tail.'

'Well, then. They'd have followed him into the apartment and then you'd all have been arrested. She did the right thing, Mémère.'

'I suppose so,' Zizi sighed. 'I still feel we let him down, though.'

'What happened to the children?' Juliette asked.

'My mother hid them in a cupboard,' Zizi said. 'Two boys and a little girl. Jewish, of course, or at least the boys were. We never found out about the girl. The boys stayed with us for a while and then our concierge helped pass them on. She knew of a children's home near the Spanish border and I believe they made it there. Who knows what happened to them after that.'

'And the girl?' Nico asked.

His grandmother smiled. 'We kept her, of course. She was your Tante Celeste.'

'What?' Nico practically fell off his chair.

'Didn't you ever wonder why she was so much younger than my brother and me?' Zizi asked. 'I used to look after her for Jacques and adored her already; she was that kind of child.' She sighed. 'And now she's dead while I carry on forever like some ancient fossil.'

'And she never knew she was adopted?' Nico said.

Zizi shrugged. 'What would have been the point? She'd only have asked all sorts of questions we couldn't answer.'

Juliette was looking at the photographs Zizi had passed her. 'So what became of Jacques?'

'He died in a concentration camp.' Tears came to Zizi's eyes. 'I think about him often: he was the best man I ever knew. I loved him and my Henri adored his wife, Mathilde. She was so beautiful, everyone fell a little in love with her. My mother made her wedding dress. They were married the day war broke out, 3 September 1939. I'll never forget it. Then Mathilde left Paris to stay with relatives before Jacques was arrested and we never saw her again. She just disappeared. Maybe she was killed or maybe she didn't want to come back. Times were still difficult after the war. People turned on each other: those who'd resisted against those who'd lived alongside the Germans and put up with them. The anger lasted for years.'

She yawned. 'Tell people about Jacques Duval and show them who he was. He deserves to be recognised. And now I'm tired. Could you leave me, please?'

'Are you OK?' Juliette asked Nico, once they were outside in the car park. He still looked stunned.

'It's a lot to take in,' he said, unlocking the car. 'I had no idea my great-aunt was adopted. Feels like something we should have known about in the family.'

He opened the door for Juliette and she slid into her seat. 'Would you like to go for a drink somewhere?' she asked.

'If you don't mind, I'd sooner be alone for a while.'

'Of course,' she replied. She wanted to comfort him but they weren't sure of each other yet. 'Come for dinner on Friday, if you're free. Around eight?'

'I'd like that.' He kissed her, although his eyes were still troubled.

Juliette kept The Forgotten Bookshop closed the next day so she could talk to the neighbours upstairs about the leak and finish mopping up, as well as moving her things into Zizi's former apartment. Ben had told her he'd be staying with Sophie for the rest of the month and then they'd be off travelling together in August through Spain and Portugal.

'Sounds lovely,' she said, hugging him.

He shrugged her off but she could tell he was pleased. 'Can you manage without us?' he asked, and she told him she'd be fine.

That morning she cleaned the white minimalist apartment for the last time, put the keys through the letterbox and wheeled her suitcase over to the Place Dorée, feeling as though she was truly coming home. Unlocking the shop, she went straight to the far corner of the larger room to reveal the hole in the wall and reassure herself she hadn't been dreaming. Running her hand over the dusty wall as though she could wipe away the years and uncover its secrets, she crouched by the crate of books and took them out, one by one. Jewish authors were banned, Zizi had said, and of course de Gaulle wouldn't have been popular with the Nazis either. She was leafing through his memoir when she suddenly came across a small notebook, slipped among the pages. *Livre d'or* was written on the front: visitors' book. Intrigued, she settled down on the floor and began to read.

The Puppy, the Mountain Eagle, the Lovers. . . the entries ran on, dozens of them, some half a page long and others only a couple of sentences. Juliette felt as though she was on the brink of discovering something important, maybe the key to a mystery she'd been trying to solve since she'd arrived in Paris. Turning the page, suddenly she found it: a paragraph she read over and over again, as the pieces of a puzzle finally clicked into place.

Chapter Twenty-five

'Slow down,' Andrew said. 'I can't understand what you're trying to say. Take it from the beginning.'

'OK, so we've found a secret chamber in the bookshop,' Juliette began, speaking at half her usual speed, 'where the guy who ran it was hiding people during the war. He kept a journal describing everyone who stayed there, and I'm sure one of the girls who passed through was Mémé.'

'Because. . .?'

'Because everything fits! I just know she's one of the Lovers − he gave them all titles, you see, rather than names. Apart from the children, that is. Listen to this: "She's very young, no more than sixteen or so, with dark hair cut in a bob and an air of fierce determination." So the age is right and Mémé used to wear her hair like that, didn't she? Plus she was certainly determined.'

'Although there must have been plenty of determined girls in Paris with bobbed hair,' Andrew said.

'There's more,' Juliette told him. 'Don't you remember Mémé telling us she was radical when she was young, and that she had a crush on a boy at her school who was a communist? Well, apparently the couple Jacques wrote about were communists, too; that's why they had to hide away, because the communist party was banned. And on top of all that—' Juliette paused for breath, 'the girl Jacques writes about has a scar over her left eyebrow, and so did Mémé!'

'Really? I don't remember.'

'I'm not sure which eyebrow it was but she told me someone pushed her into a radiator when she was a kid, and that's how she ended up with a scar.' Juliette sighed. 'Can you imagine her dodging the police with a boyfriend? I wish we'd asked her about those days when we had the chance. Isn't it amazing that I followed her painting and ended up living in this very square?'

'For sure,' Andrew said politely, though she could tell he didn't believe her. 'And how's business in The Forgotten Bookshop?'

'Getting there,' Juliette said. 'Listen, I have to go. I'll call again soon.' She felt as though her head were about to explode. Mémé had been here, in the very store she had made her own. Jacques Duval might even have saved her life. The place had been so important to her, she had carried a picture of the square to America with her, all those years ago, and hung it in her bedroom. Juliette was meant to have come to Paris: it was her destiny. The Forgotten Bookshop had been waiting for her to bring it back to life.

★ ★ ★

She spent the next few days in the store with a renewed sense of purpose, although she didn't visit the storeroom again. It seemed a sacred place. When she was sure Nico and Zizi were comfortable with the idea, they could share Jacques' story with the rest of the world.

Nico. She fell asleep at night remembering the feel of his skin, the light in his eyes when he looked at her, the curve of his mouth. She couldn't wait to tell him her theory about Mémé but he needed time to absorb what he'd learned about his own family; she'd seen how deeply he'd been affected.

Early on Friday morning she washed her hair and planned a simple but delicious menu for later: gougères made with Gruyère cheese to have with drinks, then steak and a perfect béarnaise sauce, pommes Lyonnaise with onions, fresh peas from the market and to finish, orange and Grand Marnier soufflés. Even if he didn't want to have sex with her again, she could give him a decent meal. It was such a joy to cook in her own kitchen after a long day in the bookshop that she found herself humming that evening as she chopped herbs, sliced vegetables and melted butter, savouring the perfection of the ingredients she'd chosen so carefully. But then she had to wash her hair again because it smelt of fried onions and that made her late and flustered, so she curdled her béarnaise sauce by adding the melted butter to the egg yolks too quickly, and there were no more eggs in the fridge.

Swearing under her breath, she grabbed her purse and her keys and headed out of the door. There was a deli not far away that stayed open late and sold the best eggs in the *quartier*. She had almost reached it when she saw Nico, on a café terrace. She raised her hand to wave and then dropped it again when she noticed the person he was with. Delphine was instantly recognisable, hair tumbling down her back. Nico sat opposite, looking intently at her – and he was holding her hands, clasping them in his. Juliette stared at him, unable to believe her eyes, before turning and rushing for home. The sanctuary of her apartment: she'd never needed it more.

The door buzzer sounded at eight-fifteen. She wondered briefly whether to ignore it but she was furious by then, and wanted the satisfaction of venting her feelings.

The breath caught in her throat when she opened the door because he was so painfully gorgeous and he looked a little nervous, holding a bunch of flowers. He stepped forward to kiss her, his expression changing when she drew back.

'What's the matter?'

Since it would be undignified to have a shouting match on the doorstep, she let him in, closing the door behind him. 'I saw you with Delphine just now.' The shame of having to say that sentence! Her anger subsided, leaving only an aching disappointment in its place. 'How could you, Nico? Knowing what my husband did to me?'

She saw the shock in his eyes. 'It wasn't like that,' he said. 'Please, I can explain.'

Such banal words that must have been spoken on so many occasions, all over the world; he might have been following a script.

'You were holding her hands!' she burst out.

'Because she was about to slap me,' he said. 'I know that sounds far-fetched but she's done it before. Look, can we talk? Please, hear me out.'

She wavered for a moment. Part of her wanted to hurt him as badly as he'd wounded her but she couldn't do it, not when he was standing there and all she wanted was to feel his arms around her. 'All right, then. Come through.'

She took him into the kitchen, even though it was in a mess. 'I gave up on dinner,' she said, passing him a glass of wine and topping up her own from the open bottle that was standing on the counter.

He laid down the flowers and they sat facing each other at the marble-topped table. 'Go on, then,' Juliette said. 'Explain away.'

He looked at her calmly. 'Delphine is difficult and that's an understatement. She's a damaged person and she damages other people – physically, sometimes. I've been trying to persuade her to get professional help for a while now but she refuses. She won't listen to reason and it's come to the point where there's nothing more I can do. I asked to meet so I could tell her she had to stop calling me, and that I couldn't see her again because . . . because I am falling in love with you.'

Stars exploded inside Juliette's head. She could only hear the beating of her heart, feel the blood pulsing in her veins, see his eyes meeting hers. The wave of emotion rushing through her was so strong, it threatened to sweep her away.

'You don't have to say that,' she told him, her voice unsteady.

'It's true, though. I haven't stopped thinking about you from the moment we met.'

'But you were so rude to me,' Juliette protested, smiling despite herself.

He laughed. 'Maybe I was trying to make an impression.'

Juliette shook her head. 'I'm not sure what to think. You can be honest with me: if you were only after a one-night stand, that's fine. I simply need to know what this is.'

He groaned. 'A one-night stand is the last thing I need. I want everything, Juliette, the whole deal. You're strong and funny and kind, and I'm crazy about you.' He reached for her hand across the table. 'We can take things slowly. All this is probably too much and our timing isn't great. You don't have to love me back – just say you believe me, and that you'll give me a chance.'

'Yes,' she whispered, her eyes filling with tears. 'I do, and I will.'

And then, at last, he kissed her.

They ate the gougères in bed and the steak and potatoes at the kitchen table several hours later; it turned out they were delicious, even without the béarnaise sauce. Maybe this is all a terrible mistake, Juliette thought happily, licking her fingers; right now, I don't care.

'Go and sit down,' Nico said, taking her plate. 'I'll clear up.'

She tied the belt on her robe more tightly and wandered through to the *salon*, smiling to herself. What would Ben and Emily have said if they could see her now? Miraculously, she was here in the apartment Nico had made ready for her, and that made every inch of it doubly precious. Noticing Mémé's painting propped against the wall, she sat down to examine it. What with all the rush, she still hadn't mended the frame. It came completely apart in her hands, the cardboard mount and backing falling on to the table – and with them, an envelope, and a small black-and-white photograph. She picked up the photo and stared at it for some time. Then, with shaking fingers, she took the letter out of the envelope.

'Have some more wine?' Nico said, bringing her glass through from the kitchen.

She glanced up at him. 'No, thanks.'

'Is something the matter?' he asked, laying a hand on her shoulder.

'It's so odd.' She shook her head. 'This is my grandmother's painting, the one I told you about, remember? You were pretty rude about that, too.'

'Don't remind me.' He sat beside her.

'Well, hidden in the frame I've just found a letter Jacques Duval wrote to his wife, Mathilde. Why would my grandmother have that?'

'I have no idea. Maybe somebody else put it there.'

'I haven't told you yet but I came up with a theory about Mémé,' Juliette went on. 'I'm sure she was one of the people Jacques hid in his storeroom. I found a notebook where he described them all, you see – I'll show it to you later.'

'Really?' Nico looked as doubtful as Andrew had sounded. 'Well, if you say so.'

'But there's a photo along with the letter in the picture frame.' She passed it to him. 'A couple on their wedding day. The man is Jacques Duval and the woman looks exactly like my grandmother, Mémé.'

He whistled. 'You're saying your grandmother might have been Jacques' wife?'

She shook her head. 'I haven't seen any photos of her when she was young so I could be wrong, but there's a very strong resemblance. It's impossible, though. Méme would have been only fifteen or sixteen when the war broke out and her name wasn't Mathilde. I'm wondering whether maybe she had an older sister that she never told us about. Someone who was killed in the war, perhaps?'

'Do you remember Zizi saying Jacques was married the day war broke out?' Nico said. 'We could go to the town hall and look for their wedding certificate.'

'Let's do that!' She kissed him. 'Do you realise what this means? Maybe I do have a family connection to this place. Maybe I really do belong here.'

'That was never in doubt,' Nico said, returning her kiss.

Chapter Twenty-six

3 September 1945

Mathilde sat on the steps leading down from the terrace of Sacré Coeur, looking out over the Butte Montmartre. Evening was falling and lights were coming on all over Paris. The city was almost back to its old self; the swastikas and German traffic signs had disappeared and although rationing was still in place, it wasn't nearly as strict. She had returned to Paris the year before to wait for Jacques on this day, shortly after liberation, and the atmosphere then had been fevered, verging on hysteria. Now it was the Germans' turn to surrender, and Allied airmen walked openly alongside Resistance fighters and American soldiers through the cheering crowds. De Gaulle had made another of his rousing speeches, announcing France had reclaimed Paris: 'the true France, the France that fights'.

Mathilde had felt empty. What about the France that hadn't fought? she'd wanted to ask. What about all those people who'd kept their heads down and got on with their lives? She had seen women in the streets with their hair shaved off and swastikas painted on their foreheads. Estelle wasn't among them; at the Folies Bergère, nobody seemed to have heard of *La Renarde*. Perhaps it was just as well they hadn't met again. They'd only have ended up arguing. She'd heard on the grapevine that Béatrice had died in prison and there was no sign of Camille at their apartment; no familiar faces either at the *Musée de l'Homme*.

She'd half expected Jacques to appear a year ago, walking through the blue haze of evening with that hesitant, distracted air she loved so much – hoping for the miraculous, even though she had gone straight to the Place Dorée and found the bookshop closed, and a different name beside their bell next to the front door. The concierge was new, too, and had no idea who Mathilde was. She had fled before anyone spotted her, although the past few years had changed her beyond all recognition and no doubt her former neighbours had moved away. Old Madame Duval must have died; Mathilde had known at the time they were saying their last goodbyes.

When she'd been first interrogated at the police station, the Gestapo had said Jacques would be arrested and tortured if she didn't tell them everything she knew; later, they told her he'd been killed. She didn't believe them at first, but then they'd shown her a photograph of a body: a dark-haired man with his head thrown back she assumed was Jacques. She'd escaped from police custody while being transported from one prison to another and stayed in Provence, helping the Resistance. Going back to Paris would have been far too dangerous and anyway, what was the point? And then, in 1942, a man on his way to the Pyrenees had stayed at the vineyard where she was working and told her Jacques was alive – and not only alive, but fighting against the Nazis. He'd been hiding people in his storeroom and passing them on to safety. Mathilde had practically burst with pride. Her gentle husband: she'd known he would find the fire in his belly one day. She'd sent him a message but had no idea whether he'd received it, and it had been impossible to contact him again. The Gestapo were desperate to find her and travel between the zones had become virtually impossible. So she had stayed in the south until France was liberated and then she had come to find him. When he hadn't turned up at Sacré Coeur on their wedding anniversary in 1944, she'd gone back to Provence. She'd become unused to the city, with its hysterical gaiety and recrimination, and there was still work to be done in the south.

And now here she was in Paris again, a year later, feeling just as out of place. She'd become a different person, hardened by the glaring sun and the things she had seen. The defeated Germans had retreated in an orgy of violence: burning, raping, killing. When she tried to sleep, scenes from hell flashed before her eyes. She held on to an image of Jacques to preserve her sanity: his loving kindness, the tenderness of his smile, his quiet concentration. Not knowing whether he was dead or alive, she had come back to Sacré Coeur to remember and honour him nonetheless. Even if there was no chance of him meeting her here, she would probably make this pilgrimage every year, so she could think of him and dream they were together.

It was almost dark. She was standing, shaking out her

cotton skirt, when a man called, 'Madame?' and she turned her head automatically, even though he must have meant somebody else.

An American soldier in khaki uniform came hurrying towards her, waving a photograph. 'It's you, isn't it? Madame Duval. I'm so glad I've found you.'

She stared at him, speechless, as he gave her the photograph, and she found herself looking at a picture of herself and Jacques on their wedding day.

'Who are you?' she asked.

He mentioned a name she didn't catch and said, 'Ma'am, I have news which may come as a shock. Is there some place we could go that's a little more private?'

'No,' she said. 'Tell me here. I have to know now.'

'OK, but maybe we should sit down.' He took her arm gently and guided her back down onto the step, sitting beside her. He was tall and handsome, with short blond hair and the big white teeth the Americans all seemed to have. A pleasant face, instantly forgettable. Linking his fingers, he said, 'I've come from Germany. Have you heard of Dachau concentration camp?'

She nodded. It was coming, the news she'd been dreading. She straightened her back, steeling herself.

'I met your husband there,' the Yank went on. 'He was very weak. He'd walked from Auschwitz in Poland, along with the others, but the march had been too much for him. He knew he was going to die and he gave me a letter for you, along with that picture so I'd recognise you. He said there was a chance you'd be waiting here and I happen to be on my way home to the States so I thought I'd bring it here myself.' He reached into the breast pocket of his jacket, took out an envelope and handed it to her.

'Thank you,' Mathilde said, her lips hardly moving.

'I'll give you some privacy,' the soldier said, getting to his feet and moving away.

Jacques' writing was so spidery, she wouldn't have recognised it, and it took her some time to decipher the words.

My darling Mathilde,

I don't know whether you will ever read this letter, but I am writing to you all the same. How are you, my darling? I've thought of you constantly since we parted, and memories have helped me survive these terrible years. We shan't meet again, I'm afraid, but I wanted to tell you one last time how very much I love you, and how happy you have made me. Our marriage has been the greatest joy of my life. Stay strong, my brave, beautiful girl. I should like to think of you having children and bringing them up in the freedom we have fought so hard for — if not with me, then with some other lucky man. Have no regrets. I will always be a part of you, as you are of me.

All my love, forever
Your Jacques

She folded the letter and put it back in the envelope. Later, she would cry. The American was still there, watching her.

'He died,' she said, and it was a statement rather than a question.

'Yes, Ma'am. The day after he gave me that letter. He'd written it some days before, I believe.'

'Thank you for coming here,' she said. 'I am truly grateful.'

The soldier took off his cap. 'Can I take you for a drink somewhere? You look awful pale.'

She was about to give him a dusty answer when something made her bite back the words. Looking into his eyes for the first time, she saw the misery there. 'You've come from Dachau? Then perhaps you need a drink, too.'

'To tell the truth, Madame Duval, I do. Or may I call you Mathilde?'

'No,' she said. 'It's not a name I use anymore for various reasons. I'm Marie now, Marie Garnier. What's your name again?'

'Sergeant James Talbot,' he replied. 'But you can call me Jim.'

'Well, Jim,' she said, putting the envelope and photograph in her handbag, 'we can go for a drink but there are certain things we won't talk about. Understood?'

'Yes, Ma'am,' he said, saluting her. 'That suits me just fine.'

Jim Talbot had two weeks in Paris before he flew home to America, and he spent every waking moment with her. 'I can't shake you off,' she grumbled, seeing his cheerful face that was becoming a little less forgettable every day. She'd been planning to go back south but there was nothing for her there, either, so they kept each other company in Paris. They explored the winding streets of Montmartre, the Bois de Boulogne and the

Palace of Versailles, went dancing in Pigalle and boating down the Seine. He didn't ask her about the past or tell her about the concentration camps; they kept things light and easy. He spoiled her, taking her out for dinner every night, buying her stockings and scent and flowers. On their last evening, he brought out a diamond ring and asked her to marry him.

'I know this is kind of sudden,' he said, dropping to one knee right there, on a bridge over the river with the Eiffel Tower in the distance, 'but I can't live without you, Marie.'

'So dramatic,' she sighed, looking at the ring.

'Try it on for size,' he urged.

She closed the velvet box and gave it back to him, serious for the first time. 'I loved my husband very much. Marrying you would not be fair.'

'He was a hell of a guy, I realise that,' Jim said. 'I could never replace him but I can look after you and do my best to make you happy. Maybe we can heal each other. You don't have to love me but we get along just fine, don't we? As long as you like me, that's enough.'

Mathilde sighed again. She had the rest of her life to get through. Maybe it would be easier to start again in a country with a different history, where nobody had the faintest idea who she was or what she had done. She opened the box again, put the ring on her finger and admired its sparkle in the dusk.

'All right.' She kissed Jim, whom she did like very much. 'Why not?'

Epilogue

'Tell me the whole story again.' Emily stifles a yawn. 'Sorry, Mom. The jet lag's kicking in.'

Juliette smiles. 'Sure. So, Mémé was first married to a man who died in a concentration camp at the end of the war. He'd been hiding people in his bookstore—'

'The one you're running now?'

'The Forgotten Bookshop, that's right. Anyway, Mémé must have learned he was dead before she met my grandpa in Paris and went back to the States with him.'

'And she never told anyone about her first husband? I wonder why not.'

Juliette sips her coffee. 'Maybe she wanted to keep his memory all to herself. I've read the letter he wrote her when he knew he was dying and it's so moving. He was an extraordinary man and I guess she wanted to lock him away in her heart. She might have thought Grandpa would feel jealous, too.'

She can almost hear the cogs in Emily's analytical brain whirring. 'And how did you find all this out?'

'Mémé hid a photo of their wedding day in the back of a painting she loved, so we went to the town hall and found the marriage certificate. Her maiden name was Mathilde Marie Garnier.' Juliette smiled. 'We looked up her birth certificate, too. She was actually seven years older than Grandpa, though she never admitted that, either. I guess it wasn't acceptable back then for a woman to be older than her husband, so she decided to take a few years off her age.'

'Who's "we"?' Emily asks.

'Me and Nico.' Juliette looks sideways at her daughter. 'Do you like him?'

'Come on, we've only just met. He seems OK, I guess.'

'And isn't it incredible that Nico's grandmother remembers mine, eighty years ago?' Zizi's taken some persuading to accept Juliette could possibly be Mathilde's granddaughter but she seems to be coming around to the idea. Nico says his grandfather would be delighted, and would be clapping him on the back and buying him a beer.

Emily frowns. 'But all this is so sudden. It feels like you've turned into a whole other person that I don't know. I mean: your clothes, and setting up this business, and living in Paris. What's come over you?'

Juliette laughs. 'I'm not sure. But isn't it glorious that you're safely back from Antarctica and we're here together, sitting in the sunshine in Montmartre on a Sunday afternoon, me and my grown-up daughter? Aren't we the luckiest people in the world?'

'Mom, have you been drinking? It's four in the afternoon.' Emily yawns again.

'Maybe it's time to leave.' Juliette signals for the bill and reaches for her purse as a woman waves to her from across the street.

'And you seem to be friends with so many people,' Emily says. 'Who was that?'

'One of my customers.' Juliette waves back. 'We've had a lot of publicity since Jacques' story came out.'

She felt ambivalent about that, at first; it seemed wrong to profit in any way from what had happened eighty years ago in The Forgotten Bookshop. But, talking it over with Nico, she realised people needed to know about Jacques Duval. Press and TV journalists have come to the store, as well as academics, and the idea has been mooted of taking out the storeroom and recreating it in a holocaust museum. She isn't sure how she feels about that, either. It's as though the heart would be torn out of *La Page Cachée*. Most exciting of all, a woman in Baltimore has come forward to say she was the granddaughter of Miryam Rosenberg, née Isaacson, who'd told her family about a bookseller in Paris running her father's business when he was no longer able to, and giving Miryam enough money to travel to America in 1940. Hannah Rosenberg is planning on flying to Paris next month to see The Forgotten Bookshop and receive the packet of francs Jacques set aside for her grandmother, and the press are covering that, too.

'I'm proud of you, Mom,' Emily says unexpectedly. 'It can't have been easy, staying here on your own after what happened with Dad.'

Juliette's touched. 'Thanks, sweetpea. You know, I keep thinking about Mémé. She couldn't bear to come back to Paris but maybe she'd be pleased that I have. And we can still be a family. Even if Dad and I are apart, we'll never stop loving you.'

'Sure, but what if things go wrong with this Nico guy and you're stuck out here by yourself? You only met him a few months ago.'

'Then I'll cope,' Juliette says. 'I'm stronger than I used to be. Sometimes you have to take a leap in the dark and hope for the best, like Mémé setting off for America with Grandpa. I guess we're all alone in this world, muddling through as best we can.'

They watch a couple walk up the narrow street, swinging a small child between them who squeals with laughter: such a joyful sound that she and Emily can't help smiling, too.

Juliette turns to her daughter. 'Think about it, Emily. I've lived a whole life and now I've been given the chance of another. Isn't that just extraordinary?'

Acknowledgements

Many thanks to my agent, Sallyanne Sweeney at MMB Creative, and the wonderful team at Avon Books, including my clever editor, Molly Walker-Sharp, who so patiently steered me in the right direction, copy editor Laura McCallen, proofreader Tony Russell and cover designer Caroline Young. I'm also grateful to my American advisers, Mary-Kate Serratelli, Maggie Latimer and Gillian Weiner, and to Jamie and Camille Stallibrass in Paris. Any remaining errors are all mine!

**The world is at war.
And time is running out . . .**

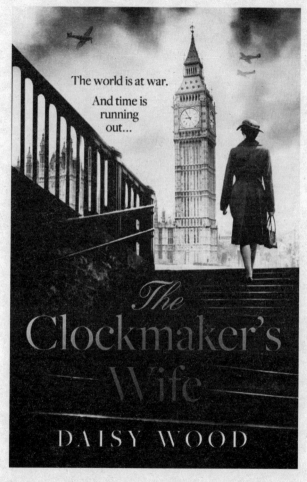

The world is at war.

And time is
running
out...

The
Clockmaker's
Wife

DAISY WOOD

A powerful and unforgettable tale of fierce love,
impossible choices and a moment that changes the
world forever.